The Return
of Mr. Hollywood

by Josh Greenfeld

The Return
of Mr. Hollywood

JOSH GREENFELD

1984
Doubleday & Company, Inc.
Garden City, New York

*The characters, situations, and events
depicted in this novel are creations of the author,
and any resemblance to actual persons,
events, or situations is purely coincidental.*

Library of Congress Cataloging in Publication Data
Greenfeld, Josh.
Return of Mr. Hollywood.
I. Title.
PS3513.R4815R4   1984   813'.52

Library of Congress Catalog Card Number 082–45202
ISBN: 0-385-18407-7

*For my wife, my mother, my father,
my sons, my sister . . . for all
my collaborators.*

The author wishes to acknowledge his debt of gratitude to the Writers Guild of America for their strike of 1981.

It's very tricky being an artist in the system. Especially if you're a personal filmmaker like me. I want to be successful. But I don't want to be successful if it means doing what they want me to do and not having any control. I'm an artist and I can't work that way. A film has to be about something I know and care about with very human people—funny and lovable and even a little crazy but still real. I deal with real reality. I don't make dumb films about cops and killers and globs in space and somebody possessed by demons. I don't make childish comic strips blown up all out of proportion. I don't care about the pictures they want to make. I care about the pictures I want to make. Because a film is a big investment on my part. It can take me a year to write. A year to get it on—to finally get a go. And still another year to actually make. And after all that maybe another year to forget.

That's why I have to have a passionate concern for what I'm doing. And a supreme confidence. I'm aware that I'm spending a lot of somebody's money. And I want my films to make money. So that I'm allowed to go through the whole agonizing process all over again. It's a wonderful art. But it's a killing business. Very tricky, as I say. But then nobody asked me to be an artist, to become a director who makes personal statements. What do the studios know or care about my personal statements anyway? To them a film is a picture. And it either makes money or goes down the tubes. They want to use my art to make their commerce and I want to use their commerce to make my art. So as long as I have a hit every once in a while the system will let me continue to function as a personal filmmaker making personal statements.

Unless all the energy in the effort of living and digesting and recording and creating do me in first. And that's always a distinct possibility. Because, as I say, the process from *Fade In:* on paper to "That's a wrap," on the set, takes a lot out of you. But who ever said it was easy to be an artist? It's not that I'm a Joyce or a Proust or a Thomas Mann or even a Fellini or a Bergman. But I am an artist. My work expresses a personal point of view. And I stand or fall on it.

Now why doesn't somebody ask me something like how come I never use Burt Reynolds or Robert Redford in my pictures so I can tell you it's because they're not Jewish and I can't afford them anyway.

From *Dialogue on Film*
The Larry Lazar Seminar
The American Film Institute
Volume IV Number 3

The question was: Would I work with Larry Lazar again? First, let me say out front I think he's a sponge with an ego bigger than the Ritz, an aesthetic hustler, a vile traitor, an evil phony, a congenital liar, and a dilettante prick. In short, a human being manqué whose only humanity is an illusion like the kind you pay to see up there on the screen. Also Larry's a pathologically cheap, vulgar, greedy, selfish, penny-pinching bastard. But would I work with Larry again? Let me put it this way: Would Goering have worked with Hitler again? Just because Larry pretends to be the best—but actually is the worst—of a bad lot is no reason to hold a grudge. Of course I'd work with him.

From *An Evening with Max Isaacs*
A Writers Guild Rap Session

He remembered Richard Conte in *A Walk in the Sun*, his fist flailing the air at a dive-bombing Stuka, shouting, "Knuckles to you!"—they couldn't say fuck in those days—"I'm indestructible. Nobody dies." . . . He remembered John Garfield in *Body and Soul*, walking through the underpassages of the arena in which he has just won the fight he was supposed to lose, arm in arm with Lilli Palmer, and approached by the gamblers he has just let down but refusing to be intimidated, chirping in New York singsong, "Everybody dies." . . . Effective endings both. But Garfield was right. Because now *he* was dying. Yes, Larry Lazar, noted film director, dead: details at eleven. He would soon find out if death was more than a rumor and if Elisabeth Kübler-Ross was full of shit. So far, he felt nothing beatific in the offering. Dying hurt; it was painful; every breath of air was a labor. Chains seemed to be scraping along the inside lining of his chest, grinding into his pectoral ribs. It was damned hard to concentrate. No wonder Dutch Schultz had come up with poetry. The mind wandered so quickly, a little bit like acid, except with the sure knowledge that death was the ultimate trip . . . And the pain, the physical pain. Not that the pain was *that* bad, he had felt worse. At the dentist's office where they called it sensitivity. "Ouch!" he'd yell through numbed lips. "Oh, you're still sensitive there," the dentist would say and then give him another hit of novocaine . . . And once when he was a kid and broke his collarbone playing touch-tackle football. Running wide around end he was suddenly bumped into the schoolyard brick wall by Fats Abromowitz. He lay there on the concrete surface in shock and pain, crying in front of his peers, wanting to tell them through his tears that what was really hurting was the sure knowledge that he'd get it from his mother for the doctor's bills she'd have to pay and the new corduroys she'd have to buy . . . Now, at least, there was no one to bawl him out. Except himself. Because it was a silly way to die. But then he hadn't spent too much time lately discovering clever ways to die either. Dying was dying and if it wasn't tragic it had to be silly. Still it wasn't as if he was checking out in the saddle. Like John Garfield. Like Nelson Rockefeller. Like countless no-names through the ages. Fucking themselves into death . . . What would Jane's reactions be if he had gone out that way? Probably nothing. Marital fidelity had its place but like all else paled in the face of death. Once, in fact, he had almost died in the saddle. Literally, in a real saddle, on a horse. It was during his first year in Hollywood when he was a young actor desperate for a job, any job in movies or television. A casting agent sent him to a director making a TV Western. The director liked his looks, pronounced him right for the part, and asked him as an afterthought if he could ride. "Of course," he said. He had never been on a horse before, not even on a pony for a baby picture. So the next day he went to Griffith Park and took a lesson, a single lesson because it was all he could afford, on a stringy old mare. And the following day he reported to the studio's Western set . . . He would never forget that day until the day he died. Which was almost that day instead of today. He had walked down the Western street: low-slung gray wooden buildings, signposts, proclaiming Bar and Hotel and Jeweler and Blacksmith and Tailor and Barber, with hitching posts before them. Nervously mounted a waiting horse, trying to remember all the pointers of the Griffith Park lesson. The director said, "And action!" He took off with the other mounted members of the posse down the Western street toward the hills of Burbank. Then the director yelled, "Cut!" All the horses stopped. Except his. She kept running, racing, as if in a stakes race at Santa Anita, while he commanded, urged, begged, beseeched, implored, coaxed, prayed for her to stop. He held the reins tightly, then loosely. He pulled in on them. He gave her slack. He tried anything; he tried everything. But the horse kept running, turning away from the hills, heading down the streets of the back lot, people getting out of the way as if the bulls were running at Pamplona. A car swerved to avoid getting hit by his horse as she ran through the Mexican village square, composed of two-dimensional flats and real California palm trees and cactus . . . over a cobblestone waterfront street, just averting a gangplank that led to a ship that never sailed . . . turning down a nineteenth-century Paris street, the spires of a cathedral pointing skyward . . . All the time bystanders and onlookers were laughing and joking while he might be dying. He remembered thinking: I got my break and now it will be a broken neck. Or another broken collarbone . . . But then the horse raced down a New York street, an East Side street of the twenties with signs in a polyglot of languages: Yiddish, Chinese, Italian. The horse slowed down and ran up a stoop and through an open door marked BILLIARD ACADEMY, and stopped, suddenly walled in between the stucco of a sound-stage wall and the superstructure of the set. And he was able to grab a support beam and swing himself off the horse, and find an exit through the window of what was labeled LEE'S CHINESE LAUNDRY . . . Catching his breath on the tenement street, he noticed he had peed in his pants. He could have died. He could have died moments before during the runaway ride, too. But now, years later, he was actually dying . . . and foolishly wasting his last thoughts on silly memories. Or was he just pissing in his pants? Anyway, he should be having better memories, more important thoughts. Wasn't the meaning of one's life supposed to flash through your head at the moment of death? Was the meaning of his life then just a runaway ride on an out-of-control horse in a lousy TV Western that ended in a fake New York street with his crotch wet? . . . No! It was just that now that he was dying he was thinking of silly ways to die and that would have been a silly way. But not much sillier than the way he was actually dying. Which wasn't fair. He didn't deserve it. Not with all the shits still living. . . . He heard thin wavering sounds, like a chorus of trained cats squealing. He had a sense of brilliant lights flashing into neon rainbows. And he thought he saw Chalky. Chalky? Did that mean he was still alive? Or already dead? Or was death something else to which he was just overreacting?

Book One

1

Larry Lazar was a chunky man with a hooked nose, puffy cheeks, and thinning brown hair combed out long, shepherd-style. Around his pink neck was a turquoise necklace; oversized tinted glasses fronted his heavy, lidded eyes; and a wide girdlelike brown belt contained the bulge of his stomach. He wore a natural suede shirt-jacket with Buffalo Bill frills over an open-necked green Adolfo shirt and full-bottomed, old-fashioned blue denim jeans that toppled down to high-topped, thick-heeled, shining beige Italian boots. With his Mao cap he looked like the Fiddler on the Roof suddenly cast in a Fellini movie. Which suited him fine. Fellini was one of his heroes and he never tried to deny his Jewishness.

He looked out the window of his office at the turn-of-the-century New York City street below: the el flying gothically over trolley-track-streaked cobblestones, gaslamp-posted sidewalks, canopies as entrances to the facades of elegant restaurants and nightclubs, and the open-spaced vista of a park garden painted onto the rear of a sound stage. All movie magic. One day soon the entire studio would be torn down for rows of condominiums or a shopping mall. Meanwhile, that set reminded him of the backdrops in those costume pictures his mother always dragged him to when he was just a sniffling kid.

Larry dipped into the plastic bag of Dorito Tortilla Chips he was holding, came up with a handful, and stuffed them into his mouth. No question about it, he mused as he chewed, he had come a long way from the kid in a Brooklyn movie theater. He had the best office of any director on the lot. Right above that of

Mike Lasher, the studio production chief. He had a terrific parking space too. Right in the middle of the first row of the traffic island in front of the administration building. And in Lois he had a super super secretary; she had been the secretary to the previous studio president. He also had a terrific wife, two sensational kids, and no problems with fuel injectors, antismog devices, or turbochargers in any of his cars. The only thing he did not have right now was a winner.

Though it was too early to consign *Herbie and Milty* completely to the tubes, the readouts from the computers over in Sales were not exactly encouraging. Still he refused to give up on it just yet and he would never be the least bit ashamed of it. After all, he was an artist, an *auteur,* a serious filmmaker. And filmmakers were like home-run hitters: You could not expect them to hit it out of the park every time up. They struck out and flew out and hit singles, too. In fact, some of the greatest artists in history were just singles hitters. Chekhov, for openers.

Larry turned away from the window and put down the bag of chips. He knew he shouldn't be eating them since he'd just had breakfast. Besides, it was junk food. But he was crazy for junk foods. Maybe it was the sodium nitrates in them? Maybe it was the street-kid Craig Claiborne in him? He was an aficionado of junk foods. He was also addicted to them. In addition, today he was nervous and when he was nervous he tended to overeat. He also tended to overeat when he was serene, sad, happy, relaxed, tense, anxious, sexually frustrated or sexually sated. He ate too much. It was as simple as that. And he would start doing something about it soon. But not just yet. Right now he had something more important to do.

He picked up the blue-vinyl-bound script on his desk and balanced it in the flattened palm of his hand as if he were a delicatessen counterman estimating the weight of freshly sliced belly lox. Then he leafed through the script, riffling its pages: The typing was professional—expert studio typing. The length was right, 119 pages; he always instructed his typists to bring in a script at around 120 pages. It looked like any other script he had ever

written. But this one was different. It was the first script he had
written all by himself. Solo.

Perhaps that was why he was nervous. He put down the script
and picked up the Doritos and emptied the bag into his mouth in
one chugalug. Crumpling the cellophane he hook-shot it over his
shoulder toward the wastebasket in the corner. Missed. A bad
sign. But he wasn't going to start being superstitious now. He
grabbed the phone and buzzed. "Lois, get me Mike Lasher,
please."

Mike was probably sitting at his own desk in his own office
directly below. Theoretically, he could have just stamped his foot
on the floor and attracted Mike's attention. And then they could
have conversed heads out the window, Brooklyn neighborhood
style. But that, of course, was not the way communications
worked in a twentieth-century film studio. Besides, Mike came
from the Bronx.

"Hi, Myrna. This is Lois," he heard on the line. "Is Mike in to
Larry?"

"I'll see." Silence. "He's in. Put Larry on."

"I'm on," Larry said.

"Good morning, Mr. Lazar. One moment please."

"Larry?" Mike greeted him with a question.

"Mike." Larry replied with an answer.

"How you doing?"

"I'm well. But say, Mike, do you have a second?"

"Yes?"

"This is something I really don't want to talk about on the
phone. Say, do you have a minute? Can I possibly come down
and see you now?"

"Sure?" Somehow Mike had managed to answer in the affirma-
tive with a question.

"I'll be right down."

Larry hung up, tucked the script under his arm, and opened
the door to his outer office. "I'm going down to see Mike," he
announced to Lois.

"Oh?" she said. As if she hadn't been listening.

"Wish me luck."

"Luck," she said, and wiped her eyes. Evidently she also had been crying.

Larry had to piss with the people. Not having a private john was the price he paid for his office's prime location. In offices, like with anything else in Los Angeles, he had gone with the location. But if he ever got *Remember, Remember* off the ground, he vowed, pushing open the door to the men's room, he would make the studio spring for the extra plumbing. As a below-the-line expense item.

Standing at a urinal, Daddy Warbucks pate shining even in the restroom's dim light, was Lionel Gold, who was in his early thirties, single, and had a violent temper. Larry always figured Lionel as the type who beat up on hookers because he didn't have the courage to be gay and face up to his own mother.

Lionel turned around. "How you doing, Larry?"

"I'm doing fabulously. What about you?"

"I just got my Evans rewrite in."

"How is it?"

"I don't know. My girl's still reading it."

They went to the sinks together, the script still tucked under Larry's arm.

"That your new script, Larry?"

"As a matter of fact it is."

"I'd like my girl to read it."

"It's only a first draft."

"I'd still like her to read it. Show her what quality is. I'm a terrific fan of yours."

"Thank you, Lionel."

Lionel crumpled his paper towel and threw it at the wastebasket near the window, missing it. Larry dried his hands, aimed his towel, and watched it sink right in. Swish. A good sign.

"Good luck with the Evans script," he said as they left the men's room.

"Good luck yourself." Lionel waved over his shoulder, and slouched down the hall.

Larry decided to take the elevator. He pushed the down button and waited. It was only one floor to Mike's office but he might as well save all his energy for the pitch. Getting any picture made these days was very tricky. People back East always thought it was a simple matter: a property, a star, a director—and *whallah* —a picture. But what property? what star? what director? and in what order? People on the coast knew that getting a picture made was more complex. Still even they tended to simplify the process by laying too much emphasis on the deal or the financial backing. You could make a great deal and still have no picture. You could make a great many deals and still never get a single picture made. You could have all the money in the world and still not wind up with something an audience could actually see up there on the screen. After all, you could not just shoot the money.

Yes, getting a picture made was a tricky business. Especially for him. Studios always wanted shtarkers and he shied away from stars. First, the use of a star could double the cost of the picture. Second, and more important, the use of a star diminished his control. With a star the picture inevitably became the star's picture. Not his picture. Not a Larry Lazar film. So he always had to talk stars to the studio, entertain all their suggestions about who was viable and who wasn't, all the while going his own way, following his own instincts. He knew he could always wait out—and fake out—the studio until they would finally accept the actor of his choice. Almost always anyway.

Because he was an acknowledged demon when it came to casting. Patiently meeting each actor he considered. Giving the actor all the time in the world. Listening to each reading carefully. And constantly changing and improving the script following each reading. So that by the time the picture was actually cast, the script was a play that had been tried out of town by some of the best actors in the business. Long scenes and speeches were shortened and short scenes were trimmed and all obvious repetitions dropped. If he knew two secrets of moviemaking, the second was that exposition was never necessary. The first: casting was the ball game. Movies were that persona up there on the screen before you. And if his policy of choosing talent not price tags had cost him some money at the box office, it had also made his reputation. Everyone knew that Larry Lazar made Larry Lazar pictures. Funny. Serious. Real. A kind of Chekhovian cinema. The serious critics like Pauline Kael and Harriet Pyle respected his work and film schools were always asking him to address them. Some day he would be ranked up there alongside Sturges and Capra and Lubitsch in the pantheon of directors. Meanwhile, as he always told interviewers, he was glad that the system—the big studios and the independent financiers—would give him the money to make the pictures he wanted and leave him alone.

The only problem was he now needed a winner. Box office. *Herbie and Milty* had been more a succès d'estime than a succès d'argent, so to speak. After opening to decent reviews, it did good business in New York and Los Angeles and Toronto. But beginning with Chicago—aside from Boston, Washington, Denver, and San Francisco—it had all been toilet time so far. Eventually the studio would recoup its money, with TV and cable sales, but the studio wasn't in business just to recoup its money. So he was more concerned with the script he was showing Mike than he liked to be. But still he felt good, confident about *Remember, Remember.* It was funny and moving and tender and it dealt with real reality. Without a doubt this was the best script he had ever written and he had written it all by himself, without a collaborator, working without a net, soloing all the way.

The elevator arrived and he pulled the door open. Saul Gelman was standing inside, playing with his floppy Fu Manchu moustache. "Hi, Larry," Saul said. "How about me?"

"How about you for what?"

"For whatever it is you have under your arm. Before I was a director and a writer I was a terrific actor."

"I didn't know that." Gelman, a former writer for Mary Tyler Moore, was threatening to become this year's Woody Allen with the success of his first picture about a sitcom writer no one takes seriously. "How's your picture doing?" Larry asked.

"Long lines around the block in both New York and Westwood."

"Terrific," said Larry. "I loved the film. And all I hear is good things about it everywhere."

As the elevator came to a stop and the door slid open Saul was still thanking Larry for both his personal reaction and the word of mouth he had reported as if Larry was personally responsible for it. Then he stopped and stared again at the script Larry was carrying. "Are you by any chance going in to see Mike?"

"As a matter of fact I am."

"Let me know if he isn't shaking."

Larry laughed. Mike was an extraordinarily nervous man, even by studio-executive standards. But Larry was also annoyed with himself for laughing. Who the hell was Saul Gelman and why had Larry sucked up to him in the first place? Except for practice. Because it was suck-up time anyway? No, that wasn't true at all. Larry knew better than that. The way to handle the Mike Lashers of the world was to come on strong, confident, as if you had all the cards. Otherwise, they shit all over you.

He waved good-bye to Saul and headed toward Mike's office.

Mussolini was dead, at least in the decor of Hollywood executives' offices. Now they all tried to offer homey, personal, idiosyncratic expressions and warm, creative environments rather than cool, imperial statements and proud peacock geographies. Gone were high ceilings and distant desks across echoing floors. Today they looked like tearooms and coffee shops, boutiques and penny arcades. As role models, foreign dictators had been supplanted by Manhattan art directors.

In Mike Lasher's office quaint machines stood about: an original Wurlitzer jukebox, an old-fashioned spinning wheel, two pinball machines, an antique one-armed bandit, a gum-ball dispenser, several crank-the-wheel movie peep-ins. Thick oily-leafed plants grew everywhere, some hanging from ceiling beams, others springing out of barrellike pots. One particular plant, huge jagged-edged leaves sprawling everywhere, looked like a banana tree, and Larry always wondered how it could grow indoors. More movie magic. Mike's desk was a rolltop which looked as if it had just been sprung from a New England county-courthouse

office, from some old Yankee lawyer, like the one who confronted
Joe McCarthy and went on to star in *Anatomy of a Murder*.
What was his name? Joseph Welch.

At first glance, Mike was nowhere in sight. But then the high-
topped barber's chair behind the desk slowly swiveled, revealing
him, perched stiffly, fingers pressed together tautly, framed like a
frozen pharaoh, a studio Tut suddenly unearthed by some on-
location archaeologist. "Larry?" he whispered.

"Mike?" Larry replied, and sat down in the college-lecture-
class-type desk chair in front of the rolltop. "How are you, old
buddy?"

"Okay. Considering . . ."

"Considering what?"

Mike leaned forward. "Considering the two pictures the studio
is counting on most are running way over budget. Considering
the fact that my daughter got busted again."

"Tina?"

Mike nodded.

"Grass?"

Mike shook his head.

"Coke?"

Mike shook his head.

Larry hesitated for a moment and then asked: "Smack?"

Once more Mike shook his head. "I don't want this to go any
further than this room," he said, lowering his already whispering
voice. "Hooking. On Santa Monica Boulevard."

Larry clicked his tongue against his teeth. No wonder Mike
had looked so gray and slight, his thin body even more cadaver-
ous than usual. Larry could certainly sympathize, understand
what he was going through. After all, Larry had a daughter of his
own. Not a hooker, but still, a daughter. So he put all the sincer-
ity and warmth he could muster into his voice, trying to sound as
supportive as possible. "How old is Tina now?"

"Fifteen," said Mike, choking back a sniffle.

"I really feel for you, Mike," Larry said. "I don't think I
should bother you now." He rose to go. "You have reality, real
reality to deal with."

Mike raised his hand like a traffic cop. "No. No. Don't go. My work is the only way I can get off these days. What's happening?"

Instead of sitting down again, Larry began his pitch, pacing in front of Mike's desk. "I know I'm supposed to have been working on *Love on the Freeway* with Sid Stein. But as I told you a few weeks ago I became obsessed with this other idea. Also an original. And I went ahead and wrote a first draft by myself. And I have to tell you, Mike, it's the most exciting script I've ever written. Even if it's the first script I've ever written all by myself. Maybe *because* it's the first script I've worked on without a collaborator. Anyway, I think it's positively brilliant. I can't wait to start shooting."

Mike pointed to the script in Larry's hand. "Is that it?"

"This is it. *Remember, Remember.* It didn't drop out of the sky exactly, but until now I always had only heard of the word "inspiration," if you know what I'm trying to say. Not that there isn't a lot of my blood and guts in this script either. But it's a whole piece and it practically wrote itself. And, as I say, I couldn't be more excited about it. It's funny and it's moving and it's tender. In other words, it's real. I think you'll love it, Mike." He placed the script on the rolltop.

Mike leaned forward and picked it up. "This is the one about the director who fucks his old girl friend's daughter?"

"That's part of it. But only part of it."

"Fucking your ex-girl friend's daughter is a nice theme," Mike mused, thumbing through the script. "I like the concept. It's a high concept. An audience can relate to it."

"It's the picture I want to do next," Larry said.

"I'll read it tonight. But then I have to ask some other people to read it too, of course."

"When can you get back to me?"

"Give us until the end of the week. The beginning of next week the latest."

"It's my next picture, Mike. Here or wherever."

Mike rose for the first time from the barber chair, patting his cheeks like a customer who had just completed a shave, and came around his desk. "I appreciate your enthusiasm." He extended his hand.

It was actually quivering.

Larry returned to his office pleased with himself. As if he had successfully pulled off a bluff in poker. Not that he was home free. Far from it. But, at least, he had acted as if the ball was in the studio's court. As if it was up to the studio to justify why it shouldn't make *Remember, Remember* instead of his having to justify why they should. And that was as it should be. Because the script felt right. And he knew that if you got the script right then the rest was a snap. Like coloring in one of those comic-book puzzles by the numbers. At least for him. He had been an actor and he knew how to handle actors. Carefully. And with a lot of bullshit. You had to nurse their shaky egos and play benevolent father, authoritarian but understanding. It was a role he could play because he knew how to temper it with humor. He would joke a lot but never about the actor personally or the character he was playing. A Larry Lazar set was fun. At least that was what the casts and crews always told him. He prided himself on the fact that there was never the charge of electric tension in the air like on the sets of so many other directors who were the critics' darlings.

Not that he didn't have a critic or two in his pocket. Harriet Pyle served as a self-appointed surrogate movie-maven mother to him. She had her favorite directors whom she always protected, giving them the benefit of every possible critical doubt by treating them as if they all were members of a single creative extended family. Her odd lot included a lush and a fag, a limey and a frog, a sensitive street Italian and a Jewish native son. That was his slot. Usually. And on his sets he did act like a borscht-belt social director. Relaxing everyone until it was his or her turn to perform. And then without a sense of great pressure. Never as if it were a life-or-death situation. After all, as Hitchcock used to say, it was only a movie. So he would allow his actors to take chances and make mistakes; he encouraged experimentation. As long as they stuck to the script. He hated the sort of impromptus which were just mumbles. He knew a good mumble had to be written. And he prided himself on having developed into a superior screenwriter. He wrote super mumbles.

But, of course, superior screenwriting was more than just setting up super mumbles. It was the key to the whole narcosis called film. He had made five films and he still didn't quite understand the writing part. Except that it was the hardest and most important: It was the base, the foundation, of a Larry Lazar film.

Yes, he had come up with a good script and he had pitched it well. Short and sweet, the mark of confidence. He deserved a reward, an old-fashioned reward; he had earned it the hard way. He reached into the bottom drawer of his desk, snatched up an Almond Joy and a Snickers, and was trying to decide which to eat, when the phone rang.

It was New York: Uncle Irving.

His mother was dead.

2

Larry's reaction was shock tempered with relief. He put down the phone, gobbled up the Almond Joy and unwrapped the Snickers, and told Lois to make a reservation for him on the noon flight to New York and ask the New York office to book him into the Plaza and to have a limo waiting at JFK.

Next, he called Jane, who was working as a volunteer at AA. His wife was one of the very few people Larry knew working for AA who did not describe herself as an alcoholic or ex-alcoholic or recovering alcoholic. Jane had never been through the program. Which didn't mean she didn't have a drinking problem. In fact, Larry often thought that she juiced too much and that the program might do her good. But she always laughed. "This shiksa is no shikker," she'd say. Still Larry felt her volunteering for AA was her way of copping out and coping at the same time.

Jane was not surprised to learn of his mother's death. "Look, we knew Sally had a heart problem," she said over the hubbub of the church kitchen in which she was preparing the coffee for the AA meeting.

"We did?"

"Of course. With all her weight Sally had to have a heart problem," Jane said, and coughed.

"Are you smoking?"

"No. But everybody else is."

Larry could picture the room. He remembered the AA meetings he had attended waiting to pick up Jane. There always seemed to be more smoke in the air at any one AA meeting than there had been in all of the hotel rooms at all of the Republican conventions ever held. It was as if the AAers had decided that if their livers weren't going to kill them, their lungs should. You could come down with black lung just hanging around there. He hoped Jane wasn't sneaking in any cigarettes at AA. They both had agreed to stop smoking.

"My mother always smoked too much," Larry said. "She did everything to excess."

"Sally was an excessive woman," Jane agreed.

"Except when it came to happiness." Larry rose from his high-backed black leather swivel and looked out the window of his office. Standing at the foot of the el were a bunch of black women costumed as slaves. Or were they studio cleaning women in their natural dress? He couldn't decide. "She wasn't a very happy woman," he said and sat down at his desk again.

"That was her fault," said Jane. "She didn't want to be."

Larry shook his head and thought that was why he had married Jane. And that was why he was still married to her after all these years—even if she sometimes drank a little too much. She was still a no-shit, no-nonsense woman. He could expect no phony sympathy from her. She had never liked his mother and she wouldn't start now.

"Anyway," she said. "I never liked Sally, so what do you expect me to say?"

"Say that you're sorry."

"For what?"

"For me."

"Why?"

"Because I'm an orphan."

"Oh, Larry," she giggled. The fact that she could laugh at his bad jokes never hurt their relationship either. "I *am* sorry for the kids. They liked Sally. She treated them well."

"Well, at least someone will miss her."

"You'll miss her," Jane reminded him. "Listen, we'll talk about this when I get home."

"I won't be home. I'm going to pick up some stuff now and leave on the twelve o'clock flight."

"So soon?"

"You forget. We Jews bury fast. You want to come with me?"

"Not on your life. How long will you stay there?"

"Just in and out. As quickly as I can manage it. You tell the kids."

"Of course."

"I'll call you from New York. The Plaza. Bye love." Larry blew her a loud phone kiss. "Bye love," he repeated and hung up. Then he dialed Dave.

A damned machine answered the phone. Dave was busy at the moment but would call back as soon as he could if you left a message at the sound of the beep. *Beep.* "Beep," said Larry. "This is Larry. I won't be able to keep our appointment for tomorrow and better cancel our tennis also. My mother died and I have to go into New York."

"Oh, I'm sorry," the machine answered.

"Is that *you,* Dave?"

"Yes, I picked up. Do you want to talk about it?"

"Now?"

"You certainly have feelings now?"

"Boy, do I have feelings!"

"What are they?"

"Guilt. Guilt. And more guilt. Plus a lot of relief. And then more guilt."

"That's to be expected."

"What's strange though is I can't seem to flash on any visual image of her. As she was or as she is—or rather was just before she died. You know what I mean?"

"Yes."

"Is that unusual?"

"It's not surprising."

"What does it mean?"

"What do you think it means, Larry?"

"It means I'm blocking in one way or another, I guess," Larry said. His secretary came back into the office sniffling. "I guess we'll have to talk about it when I get back."

"Yes," said Dave. "And that'll give me a chance to get over my shock."

"What shock?"

"The shock that our tennis is canceled. But I'm sure you'll be back for the poker game. We need you."

Larry laughed. Dave seemed to consider the fact that he was his doubles partner in tennis and poker crony more important than the fact that he was also his analyst. "Look, Dave, if I need help can I call you from New York?"

"Of course," said Dave. "As long as it isn't collect." The tone of his voice suddenly changed. "Listen, old buddy, I appreciate what you must be going through."

"Thanks, Dave."

"Beep," said Dave, and hung up.

Lois was sitting in front of his desk dabbing at her eyes with a paper tissue. "The plane is set. American. A limo will pick you up at your house. And the New York office will try to get you into the Plaza. Lloyd has to go to Paris but someone named Michael Baldwin will meet your flight personally and take care of you," she reported. "And do you want me to call Jerry Feldman?"

"What for?"

"To get a notice in the trades."

"About my going to New York?"

"About your mother."

"Oh," said Larry. "Don't bother. What does it matter? An obituary in *Variety* and the Hollywood *Reporter?* But, on second thought, she did like anything to do with show business. So why not?"

Lois leaned over his desk and picked up the phone and called Jerry Feldman. He was out. But she left word with his secretary for him to call back. Then she hung up, slumped onto the office sofa, and started picking at her eyes again with the frayed paper tissue.

Her crying bothered Larry. After all, it was *his* mother who had died and he wasn't shedding a tear. He also knew the real reason Lois was crying. Another of her affairs had just ended badly. Lois was unmarried and good-looking but past thirty and her affairs always seemed to end badly. Because she simply could not accept her age. Because she simply could not understand that she was being used. She was a sucker for younger men, forever falling for blond California beachboy types who had just laid down their surfboards in order to become writers or moviemakers but meanwhile were working as carpenters or electrician's helpers. Lois was not only a maternally supportive friend to them but also an important industry connection. Her last boy friend, for example, had been helping to remodel a kitchen in a rock star's Malibu Colony beach house while trying to finish a script. As a favor to Lois Larry had looked at part of the script and he hoped for the rock star's sake the kitchen was turning out better. The author-carpenter had also just moved out of Lois's West Hollywood apartment. Larry couldn't recall his name. Lois's boy friends all had goy California names like Brad. Or Kent. Or Roger.

Larry leaned back in his rocker. "You okay?"

"Sure," Lois nodded as she wiped her eyes. "Considering."

"What was his name again?"

"Rod."

"Are you sure Rod won't be coming back?"

"No, it's over."

Larry shrugged. "You never know."

"I know," said Lois. "He took his tapes and cassettes."

"I am sorry."

Lois rallied to her feet. "This is ridiculous. I should be commiserating you. I lost a boy friend. But I'll get another. You lost a mother. And there ain't no other." She went behind the rocker and reached over and kneaded his shoulders. "I'm really sorry, Larry."

Larry patted her right hand. Then he stood and took her in his arms, pressing her to him, and with his arm still about her waist walked her to the door and got rid of her. He didn't need Lois's problems intruding on his own. Not that he had a particular problem anymore. His mother had always been his number one problem as far back as he could remember. And now that she was gone, he really didn't have a problem. Except his next picture.

As Larry got into his silver BMW, Max Isaacs was waving to him from the sidewalk to wait. For a second, Larry was tempted to respond by gunning away. He had a good excuse: His mother was dead; he had a suitcase to pack and a plane to catch. But he saw no point in running away. After all, Max was only a writer. And, until *Herbie and Milty,* a hack writer at that. But he had known Max since their Village days together and long suspected that a real talent was lurking somewhere in him. So he had decided to give Max a shot and let him work with him on *Herbie and Milty.* The collaboration proved successful for both of them. Larry had gotten the script made and Max had raised his price. He was now working on another project for the studio for much more money than Larry had paid him.

Max banged on the car window, shouting, "I was just on my way up to see you."

Larry rolled down the window. "I'm on my way to New York."

Max leaned in. "What's up?"

"My mother died."

"Oh, I'm sorry."

"Thanks."

"Cancer?"

"No. In fact, heart attack."

Max nodded knowledgeably. "Figures."

"It took me by surprise. Why does it figure?"

"You always told me your mother was a lowlife. Nice people get cancer. Lowlifes have heart disease."

"Where the hell did you read that?"

"I didn't read it. I heard it. On the radio. Just now. 'The Michael Jackson Show.' KABC."

"Well, I'll listen on my way home. I have to get to the airport."

Max did not move; he was still leaning in the opened window. "When can we talk?"

"This isn't the time." Larry turned the ignition key. "When I get back."

"Too late. This is important."

"This isn't the time," Larry repeated above the hum of the engine. "But if you want, we can talk while I pack?"

Max nodded. "Okay."

"Then follow me home."

Larry's house was less than twenty minutes from the studio on a canyon street above UCLA in Bel Air. It was sprawling, Spanish style, with a long driveway that led to a kidney bean–shaped swimming pool with a serious algae problem because of the eucalyptus trees towering over it. Larry parked his BMW beneath the tile-topped stucco arch that framed the entrance to the driveway, and waited for Max to pull his low-slung black Mazda RX7 in behind him. Tall and thin, with pockmarked skin and bulging hyperthyroid eyes, Max scarcely fit the sportscar image as he awkwardly extracted himself, joint by joint, from his car. But then Max also scarcely fit the image of a lover. And he had gone through three marriages—each to a Hollywood sexpot—besides having innumerable affairs with others.

Max was blinking his eyes rapidly.

"Something in your eye?"

"No."

"What's wrong?"

"Nothing." Max wiped away a tear. "Just new contacts. I'm not used to them."

"I thought for a second you might be shedding a tear for my mother."

"That's your department," Max blinked again, "not mine."

Larry pushed open the unlocked front door and called out, "Dolores!" There was no answer. "That cunt can never lock a door. She still thinks she's living in some pueblo." He raised his voice again. "Anybody home?"

An Arab came out of the library carrying an opened book.

"Hi, Fati." Larry greeted him and introduced him to Max. "Fati's from Morocco. He's staying with us. In the poolhouse."

Fati dipped into his shirt pocket and handed Larry a check. "This is my rent for the month, Mr. Lazar. I'm sorry it's late. But good grief, there was a delay in the mail."

"You had me worried for a while. Thank you, Fati."

"You're very welcome." Fati bowed and disappeared out the terrace doors. Larry looked at the check, then pocketed it. "I asked UCLA to send over a minority foreign student to live with us," he explained to Max. "Figured it would be good for the kids to find out how the other half—or third—lives. Because Bel Air isn't really real. So they sent Fati. Turns out his father owns half of downtown Casablanca. Which makes him richer than Warner Brothers. So I decided to charge him rent. Let him learn what it's like to be a tenant. Except that I give him the run of the house and treat him like a member of the family. I could get a lot more for the poolhouse from an ordinary tenant, I'll tell you that." He swept by the living room and dining room entrances and started up the stairs. "Funny people, Arabs. They have a kind of Lent. Ramadan. Something like that. Where they don't eat from sunup to sundown. Did you know that?"

Max shook his head. "I don't have a single Arab in my condominium."

"Very funny," Larry said, as he rushed into the master bedroom and opened the sliding door of his closet. "What do you wear to a funeral in New York?" Then answered himself: "I guess you begin with an old New York suit. A dark New York suit." He picked out a black pinstripe and a somber black tie and put them into a suit carrier. He took an overnight bag and filled it with a pair of black shoes, several shirts, and some changes of socks and underwear. "And my toilet articles," he announced and went off to the bathroom to collect them.

Max was still standing at the entrance to the bedroom when Larry emerged from the bathroom, stuffing a kit into his overnight bag. "Look, Max." Larry stopped his packing and patted the huge TV set that sat at the foot of his bed. "Let me tell you straight off. I would rather not make a picture than lose your friendship. I value it too highly. I love you too much. We go back too far. So now tell me what's on your mind."

"You know what's on my mind."

"And it's ridiculous. It's absurd. I don't see how you can possibly imagine something like that."

"Because it happened."

Larry picked up both his suit carrier and overnight bag and swept by Max into the hallway which was lined floor to ceiling with pictures of himself and his family: Jane and the kids on vacation in Mexico. Larry on the set of *Bachelor Spouse*. Larry in "Here Comes Uncle." Larry setting up a crane shot. Larry getting into a helicopter. Larry on location in northern California. Conor in a kindergarten. Mary on a horse. Larry and James Earl Jones hugging each other.

Larry stopped in front of the still of Sally at the New York opening of *Hostile Relationships*, studied it for a second, shook his head, and then turned around. "Let's review the history," he said. "After I showed the studio a rough cut of *Herbie and Milty*, they began to pester me about what I was going to do next? I didn't know. I never know. Businessmen know their next moves, maybe. But artists don't. So you and I sat down and began to bat around ideas. Hundreds of ideas. In and out the window, you remember? But we really couldn't lock heads together on any of them. And, finally, we decided to go our separate ways. You went on to the project you've been working on for Brian Grossman. And I went into *Love on the Freeway* with Sid Stein. Am I right so far?" Larry interrupted himself. "I'm going to grab a bite. I can't stand airline food."

He turned and raced down the stairs, deposited his bags near the front door, and walked quickly through the dining room and butler's pantry into the huge Spanish-tiled kitchen where he opened the refrigerator.

"Want anything?" he called out over his shoulder.

"No thanks," said Max, who had been following.

"There's nothing to eat here anyway. Jane must think we're in Ramadan, too." He pulled out a Marie Calendar pie box and a container of milk. "But I can always OD on sweets." He opened the box and began stuffing blueberry pie into his mouth with one hand while pouring a large glass of milk with the other. "Anyway," he wiped the dripping berry slurp with his wrist, "while I was waiting for Sid Stein to finish his script, our script I should say, because I put a lot of blood into *Love on the Freeway* too, I had this other idea that had nothing to do with anything else. That came from somewhere out of my dark places."

"Wait a second." Max held up his hand.

"No. Let me finish and then you can talk all you want and correct me if I'm wrong. I wish I had a cigarette. Then I wouldn't eat so much."

Max offered him one.

"No thanks. I've stopped smoking." He tore off another hunk of pie. "Anyway, this idea just wrote itself. And that's the story of *Remember, Remember.*"

"Not quite," Max said.

"Okay, you tell me then. Let's go into the living room. So I can spot the limo in case he misses the house." Larry left the dregs of his assault on the pie at the side of the sink and led the way into the enormous front parlor.

A Baldwin baby-grand piano was in the corner of the room and a large three-part sectional sofa was shaped in a U around the fireplace. Mexican tapestries hung on one wall; on another were two paintings by Allen Gates. Near the French-doors entrance was Mira's sculpture of a cat, sitting on its haunches, surveying it all. Larry loved this room. It was bigger than both the apartment and the candy store he had been raised in back in Brooklyn.

Max sank into one of the natural suede sofas and lighted a cigarette. "You forget one thing," Max said.

"Please don't smoke."

"Since there are ashtrays," Max pointed at the coffee table before him, "I thought it was all right."

"Not today. Today is a crazy day for me."

"Anyway," Max stubbed out the cigarette. "You forget one important point. Among the ideas we tossed back and forth and finally rejected was one which was a twist on *The Turning Point.* Sort of a *Turning Point* involving the theater and movies instead of ballet with a triangle love story, and a generational thing, and a cross-generational thing. I talked about using the Village we both knew and the Hollywood we both know."

Larry smiled. "First, I don't ever recall that idea coming up between us. Second, it has nothing to do with *Remember, Remember,* believe me. It's an entirely different concept."

"I don't think so," Max said. "Because it's essentially what you've done in *Remember, Remember.*"

"How do you know? Have you read *Remember, Remember?*"

"As a matter of fact I have."

Larry was on his feet. "How the hell have you read it? Where did you get hold of a script? It's just been typed."

"I know," Max said smiling. "I had to read parts of your master copy. And you're still a sloppy typist."

"Whoever leaked it to you from the typing department, I'll have them fired. They did a very wrong thing."

"And so did you."

"I did nothing wrong. I wrote an original that has nothing to do with something you claim you brought up and that I claim I can't ever remember hearing from you."

"C'mon, Larry. You know it was my idea."

"Ideas," Larry spit out. "Ideas are a dime a dozen. World War II is an idea. The Reformation is an idea. And according to you anything with theater and movies and actors or any triangle or any love story or any cross-generational thing is your idea. And I can't buy that. Did you ever register it with the Writers Guild?"

"No," said Max.

"Well, there you are."

"I didn't think there was a need to. I trusted you."

Larry looked out the window. A black Caddy was pulling into his driveway. "There's my limo. I didn't think you were that naive. I always register everything. And mail a copy to my lawyer besides." Larry went to the door and picked up his carrier and bag. "I'm very upset today. And so are you. I think you feel rejected because I went with Sid Stein to write my next script instead of with you. And now you're trying to say that the script I wrote instead of that is your idea. Ridiculous."

He opened the door and waited for Max to follow him out.

"Harry was right," Max said behind him.

Larry turned around. "Harry who?"

"Harry Hearns. Your collaborator on *Ms. and Mr.* and *Hostile Relationships.*"

"I did not collaborate on *Hostile Relationships* with Harry Hearns."

"Exactly," said Max.

"That was an idea that Artie Fladell came to me with." Larry put his hand in the mailbox and removed the mail. He riffled through it and stuffed it all back into the box except for one colorfully stamped envelope which he tore open with his mouth. He read it as the limo driver relieved him of his bag and suit carrier. Then he handed the letter to Max. "Look at this letter from Ingmar. I really feel he's a friend of mine. A real friend."

Max frowned at the letter. "I can make out *Herbie and Milty,* but that's about all. The rest is all Swedish to me." He returned the letter to Larry. "What does he say about *Herbie and Milty?*"

"He hasn't seen it yet."

"Oh."

"But he's really looking forward to seeing it." Larry placed the letter back into the envelope and put it in his pocket. "Which really means a lot to me. And it should mean a lot to you. The man is one of the few artists in cinema today. I mean artists like myself." Larry entered the parked limo and then poked his head out of the still-open door. "Max," he said, "I told you now was not the time to talk. I still treasure your friendship. I don't want to lose it."

"What do you need my friendship for? You have Ingmar's."

"You're very confused and mistaken, Max. Believe me. But if you want to wear a Jewish hair shirt and feel abused that's your business. But I know in my heart I didn't take anything from you. I did nothing wrong. And nobody would believe you anyway. No court of law. And no motion-picture studio. Ask your agent. Ask your lawyer. It would be your word against mine."

"You shit," Max said. "You'll never have to worry about cancer."

"Save your gift for dialogue for a script."

The limo driver stood at the door. "We better be leaving, Mr. Lazar, if you have a noon flight to catch."

"Okay," said Larry. "One thing, Max. You forgot to tell me what you thought of *Remember, Remember.*"

"It's terrific," said Max. "Your best script yet. A work of art."

"Thank you. I've always valued your criticism." Larry watched Max turn away and slouch up the driveway to his own car. Max was obviously bitter and angry. But he'd get over it. Writers always did. Besides—Larry leaned back into the plush comfort of the gray velour—he himself had a far more important loss to deal with than the possible loss of a friendship, or a one-time collaborator.

3

"Pardon me," Larry Lazar asked the stewardess. "But isn't that Katharine Hepburn?" He was looking up ahead across the aisle at the Celebrity Seat, the first row of first class up against the bulkhead. He thought he had spotted her boarding the plane, walking like a queen, straight as a ruler with her royal carriage. But then he was never sure about stars. He was constantly surprised at how much older and thinner they looked in person. Also their skin always came as a shock. It was rarely cinema smooth; instead, it was just like normal skin, subject to all the splotchy ravages of three-dimensional living, making the person look common and ordinary. Yet the knowledge that the person was actually a star always made it impossible for him to avert his eyes. Hepburn made her first picture back in the early 1930s, he figured. So that meant she had to be well into her seventies. But there he was staring at her—let's face it, an old lady—even though the tall, young black girl seated beside him, thumbing through *People* magazine, was really attractive. And the stewardess hovering over him again, this time checking the overhead storage bins, was cute, too, in a redheaded, Irish sort of way.

"Miss Hepburn flies with us a lot. I think she lives back East now," the stewardess said. "But aren't you in pictures too, Mr. Lazar?"

"Yes," Larry said.

"I thought so. But you're not an actor?"

"I used to be."

"And what are you now?"

"I'm a director."

"That's right," the stewardess said, as if she had managed to extract a confession from him. "But then where have I seen you recently?"

Larry shrugged. " 'The Merv Griffin Show'? The Johnny Carson show? Flight oh oh six? Do you want me to tell you what flight oh oh six is really like?"

The stewardess laughed, revealing a bad overbite, something her family, if they had money, should have taken care of when she was a teenager. But then if they had money, she probably wouldn't have become a stewardess. It was a wash, Larry decided.

"Seriously," the stewardess said, starting up the aisle, "later on I want you to tell me the names of some of the pictures you've directed."

Credits, Larry thought; they even want your credits on an airplane. Lenny Bruce was right. The whole world was show business. Or show business was the whole world. He wasn't sure which was which and it didn't matter anyway. He turned to his seatmate and smiled. She looked down over her *People* and smiled back with pursed lips.

"We might as well introduce ourselves since we'll be together, so to speak, for most of the next five hours," he said. "I'm Larry Lazar and I snore a lot."

Her eyes opened wide.

"But it's all right. I never sleep on planes. *Qué llama Usted?*"

Now she half closed her eyes, squinting at him suspiciously.

"Qué llama Usted?" he repeated. "What's your name?"

"I'm Susan," she finally said, nodding slowly.

"Do you fly a lot, Susan?"

"Yes."

"Do you live in New York or LA?"

"LA."

"How do you like LA?"

"LA is the pits," Susan pronounced. And then she turned away and looked out the window. Across her shoulder Larry could see a food-supply truck passing under the huge wing of the 747 as it drove away from the plane. In the distance, like the smudge of an eraser, was the gray smog overhanging Inglewood. LA certainly looked like the pits and, Larry assumed, somehow their conversation was, too. But she suddenly turned back to him. "I heard you say you were a director."

"Yes," said Larry. "What do you do?"

"Guess?"

Larry wondered if she was in show business. But he decided to play it safe. "You're a computer technician at Occidental Petroleum," he said.

This time she laughed, opening her mouth wide. Her teeth weren't too bad even though a bit fangy. "I'm a stew, actually. That's why I fly a lot. But it isn't every day I'm a passenger up front." She regarded him closely as if they now shared a special first-class intimacy. "Say, you're a little crazy, aren't you? What kind of pictures do you make?"

"Pictures that are a little crazy."

"Have I seen any of them? Tell me the title of one."

"Have you seen *Gone with the Wind?*"

"Of course. But now stop pulling my leg."

Larry ogled her long legs in Groucho Marx imitation, even flicking off the ashes of an imaginary cigar. "Okay," he said, "have you heard of *Herbie and Milty?*"

Her eyes opened wide again. "You made that?"

"Yes. Have you seen it?"

"No. But I heard it was a very good picture."

"It *is* a very good picture."

"I'll see it then. I'll definitely see it. And you made it?"

"Yes. I definitely made it."

She said something in reply, but Larry could not hear her clearly above the roar of the revving engines. "Later," he mouthed, shaking his head. And as the plane taxied into takeoff position, he crossed his fingers. No matter how many times he had flown to New York and back, no matter how many times he had flown period, takeoffs always made him nervous. And it would really be ironic if he were to crash on this flight of all flights, because of the very reason he was flying there in the first place. But then irony was the one thing he still believed in.

Larry looked down at his crossed fingers—it was almost as if he were putting quotes around something he was saying to himself—and then up ahead across the aisle at Hepburn. The book she had been reading lay folded on her lap, her scarf trailing down over it, and she was sitting back with her eyes closed. Perhaps she was worrying about crashing too? But no, her clasped hands seemed to rest lightly, contentedly, on her chest. What did she have to worry about anyway at her age? And if the plane went down, it would certainly be *her* crash. She would get top billing. The only billing. KATHARINE HEPBURN AND 251 OTHERS DIE IN CRASH. And he, Larry Lazar, would just be another name in agate type among the 251 others, like in the credits that crawl at the end of a picture while the audience is walking out. After all, did anybody know who else died besides Carole Lombard in *her* crash? Someone had to be piloting that plane. And there could have been a director on board too, for all anyone remembered. Perhaps even an *auteur,* a real filmmaker, a genuine artist, like himself.

Larry closed his eyes and did not open them again until he heard the million-dollar clunk, the sound of the landing wheels retracting into the body of the plane. His seatmate, Susan, head now tucked into her shoulder and long legs curled up on her seat, nodded drowsily toward him. He turned around and the Irish-looking stewardess smiled at him. Up ahead across the aisle Hepburn had returned to the book in her lap. Larry wondered whether he should go over and introduce himself. Surely, she had heard of him. Probably was even a fan of his. You never knew: Just a few weeks ago at a Sunday night Academy screening Cary Grant had come over to him and told him how much he admired his work. *Cary Grant!* It had been eerie, standing there near the exit doors on Wilshire Boulevard, and Cary Grant introducing himself and pumping his hand. At first his only thought was: You sound even more like yourself than Rich Little. But he didn't say that. Instead, he thanked Cary Grant profusely for his generosity in offering such kind, unsolicited criticism and told him how much it meant to him because he had always respected him so much as a performer. Which was true. And when they parted—

Larry and his wife, walking toward La Peer where he had parked
—all he could think of was his mother and how impressed she
would have been to have seen him standing there with Cary
Grant. Two mature professionals, two cinema artists, saluting
each other. And, come to think of it, he was quite impressed
himself. It meant he wasn't exactly a nobody. It meant he had
come a long way.

The stewardess taking drink orders leaned across him and
asked Susan what she wanted.

"A Kahlúa, Marge."

Marge turned to Larry. "I think it was the Johnny Carson
show I saw you on. What would you like to drink?"

"I'll have a Ballantine and soda, please," said Larry. "Could
have been Johnny's show?"

"Right. And what was one of your pictures?"

"Mr. Lazar directed *Herbie and Milty,*" Susan contributed.

"That's right," said Marge. "It's a wonderful picture."

"Have you seen it?" asked Larry.

"No. But that's what I hear," Marge said, and moved down
the aisle.

Larry closed his eyes again. He was sleepy. But that was no
news. He had not been able to sleep well for years. Getting up
each morning at the crack of light. Never getting more than five
hours sleep a night. It wasn't bad when he was shooting a movie.
He could always use the extra prep time for the long day ahead.
But now when he awoke at four-thirty or five there was no problem in the day's shooting schedule to mull over. All he could do
was read a book or look at a script. They still sent mountains of
scripts to him and it was gratifying to his ego even though he had
never made a movie other than one he had actually written with
a collaborator. Now, in a few days, he would know if *Remember,
Remember* was a go, and he could be on his way again. If Mike
and the studio passed, the script would go into turnaround and
Jason, his agent, would have to begin shopping it around. To the
other studios. To independent financing. Until eventually someone would make a deal on it. On the basis of his track record.
And the fact that he was not a degenerate gambler, an incurable

alcoholic, a kinky whoremaster, or a druggie burnout. He was a hard worker who brought his pictures in on budget—or under. And they were never that expensive to begin with. A Larry Lazar film, like a Woody Allen picture, was always made for a price.

Anyway, he rubbed his eyes, he would not worry about *Remember, Remember* and Mike's reaction to it. It was unworthy of him and it was out of his hands anyway. He did have to worry about Sidney Stein though. Sidney had been developing *Love on the Freeway* for him back East. And he had promised Sidney that *Love* would definitely be his next project. But that was before he had the gestalt that resulted in *Remember, Remember*. And when he told Sidney over the phone that he was going to move ahead on it, Sidney was not exactly pleased. "These things happen all the time," he had tried to explain. "Not to me," said Sidney, "not to me." So maybe he would have to stroke Sidney while he was in the East. At least, get that accomplished. He would hate to lose a friend over a movie, but that was a price he always had to be willing to pay. One had to be ruthless if one was an artist, no two ways about it. Besides, Sidney, for all his pretensions, was still only a writer. But then who knew what would happen with *Remember, Remember?* Not only might Mike pass on it, but they might pass on it all over town. He never took anything for granted in the movie business. He might even have to reactivate *Love* some day.

Larry looked up as Marge deposited his Scotch before him. Susan already had her drink on her tray and was shaking open the bag of nuts that had come with it. Hepburn had a drink, too. It looked like a Bloody Mary. Somehow, despite her long, legendary relationship with Spencer Tracy, he did not picture Hepburn as a juicer. Larry watched as Hepburn turned a page in her book. She had made any number of pictures with Cary Grant. Offhand, he could remember *Holiday* and *The Philadelphia Story* and *Bringing Up Baby*. And there must have been another screwball comedy. He could begin a conversation with her, saying: "Miss Hepburn, I ran into an old friend of yours the other night—Cary Grant." Or: "Miss Hepburn, we share a mutual friend—Cary Grant." No, that would be going too far. And aside from not being quite truthful, it could also be a bit tricky. What if Cary Grant was not her friend? What if she hated his guts down through the years? You never knew with actors.

Probably the best thing would be for him to just go over and say, "Excuse me," and tell her how much he always admired her work, and introduce himself. Yes, that would be the best thing. Definitely. But then what if she had not heard of him? Didn't have the foggiest of who he was because she didn't keep up with the business the way Cary did—after all, he had never seen *her* at an Academy screening—and treated him as just another fan? Or worse. Maybe even put him down, curtly dismissing him in astringent, stinging Hepburnian tones with a twangy: "Fuck off, buster." That would be unbearable.

But Hepburn would never say that. That was something his mother would have said. For a Jewish mother, Sally had a *goyishe* tongue. She could curse like an unemployed longshoreman. And that wasn't the only crude quality she had. But he would not think about Sally. Not yet anyway. There would be time and place enough for that in New York. How had he gotten on that depressing train—or plane—of thought anyway? Oh yes, because of Hepburn. There she was imperturbably sipping her Bloody Mary or Virgin Mary or whatever, turning the pages of her book crisply with a tongue-moistened index finger, while the plane was, for all anyone knew, heading toward her crash. Larry tore open his bag of roasted peanuts and poured them into his mouth. Still chewing, he tasted his drink and began to think of lunch. He sorted through the in-flight magazine and the plastic-laminated oxygen-and-life-jacket instruction cards in the pouch in front of him until he found the menu card. It was the usual bill of fare and he guessed he would have the prime ribs rather than the medallion of veal or the ham. At least, the ribs didn't have to be defrosted so it must be healthier. Also probably fewer calories. He slipped his fingers under his thick belt and felt the mound of flesh that was his stomach. He was getting fat. No question about it. He would have a weight problem. Just like Sally. Well, he would go light on food once he hit New York.

Hepburn put her book and her drink down on the empty seat

beside her and slowly rose and stretched, turning around. She seemed to look as if she recognized him. He immediately dipped his head in a nod to her. But when he looked up, he could see that she had looked past him, her eyes focusing on someone further back in the plane. She turned around abruptly and sat down again.

Larry resumed the dialogue with his seatmate. Discovered she was from Chicago originally—which was the pits. Had an apartment full of plants and animals. And a boy friend who was an ex-Laker. Who was having a difficult time adjusting. He had been making six figures a year and now couldn't find a job. In or out of the NBA. He just sat around the house and sulked a lot. The only thing he was actually doing lately was feeding her pets and taking care of her plants when she was gone. She just hoped he didn't start doing drugs because that was the super pits. But that's what a lot of his friends were into. Meanwhile, she traveled. You name it and she'd been there. Took advantage of the freebies that went with being a stewardess. Although she wasn't always so lucky. In first class. And with a famous movie director. She cocked her head and looked across the aisle. "Do you know Katharine Hepburn?" she asked.

"Kate?" said Larry. "Excuse me." And resolutely stood up. Decided it was time for him to introduce himself to Hepburn and take his chances. He was a big boy now and could risk a big time rejection. He sucked in his stomach and slid into the aisle.

When he felt a light tap on his shoulder. "Mr. Lazar," the Irisher, Marge, was saying as he turned around, "there's somebody on board who's also in the movie business and would like to meet you."

"Oh," said Larry, most pleased. So she knew who he was after all. She still kept her hand in, as the saying went. He should have been secure enough to realize that. But that's what happened when you came out of a candy store. He still had a lot to learn about self-esteem. Even if the face he saw in the mirror each morning when he shaved belonged to the same half-frightened kid from the Brooklyn candy store he had known all his life, Larry Lazar was now big league. In the same league with Grant,

Hepburn. Hollywood biggies all. Skying to Gotham: To see webs. To hold confabs. To ink multi pic pacts.

"Mr. Gatto," the stewardess pointed at a handsome, dark, gray curly-haired man two rows back who was waving from his window seat, "is an Italian producer. He would like to meet you."

Larry waved and smiled. "Later, maybe," he told the stewardess. And slid back into his seat.

Larry slapped his stomach. He had eaten too much. He always ate too much on planes. But what else was there to do? Even in first class. Especially in first class. Just eat. And watch a lousy movie. Which he was doing. A tearjerker about an Olympic ice skater who had an automobile accident that left her a paraplegic. Soon she would find true love. Because once you accept yourself without legs, you accept yourself completely. Something like that. He took off the earphones. The picture wasn't *that* bad: The actress had a nice *unactressy* quality. Something real that he could relate to. But there was also something about the postage-stamp size of the screen that was a dead giveaway to the skimpiness of the story itself. Also, because of the smallness of the screen, he felt as if he were watching a KEM or moviola in public rather than in a private editing room. And there was something indecent about that. Anyway, he reminded himself, he never liked seeing movies on planes, television, at Writers Guild or Directors Guild screenings, or Norman Lear's Sunday night suppers.

The black girl beside him was sleeping and Hepburn too was wisely ignoring the movie, her overhead light focusing down on the book in her lap. Larry considered meandering back into the lounge upstairs but he was in no mood to discuss the film business with a dago producer. He knew most of the Dinos and the Albertos and they all served gourmet dinners but they were not that different from their American counterparts, the mafiosos. Continental manners, the cappuccino spiels, and all, at heart, they were still gut—and gutter—businessmen.

The captain was talking about the descent and the weather in New York. Overcast. Susan, the vacationing stewardess, was standing up, excusing herself, and Larry pulled back his legs so she could pass into the aisle. The movie screen evidently had been window-shaded back into the ceiling and Katharine Hepburn, he noticed, was no longer in her seat either. Almost simultaneously he realized that he must have been napping and that he had to take a leak. In the worst way. He quickly hurried up the aisle.

But all the toilets were occupied. People were milling about in an informal line, waiting, as if a movie house had just let out. Hepburn, he figured, was in one of those crappers. Maybe he'd get to use the same one if he didn't pee in his pants first.

Then he remembered there was always a crapper upstairs on the other side of the lounge behind the cockpit that the crew usually used. Rather than wait for Hepburn—or anyone else—he scampered up the spiral staircase. Turned right and happily found a Vacant sign showing. Locked himself into the crapper's plastic, metallic claustrophobia and pissed a long, pain-relieving stream down into the shining aluminum bowl. Flushed it into a whirling blue and washed his hands and face and patted some cold water onto his eyes and hair. Wiped himself briskly but as always couldn't figure out which of the many labeled places was the one you dumped your dirty paper towels into. Found one that looked right enough and pushed it in there.

He had left the john and started toward the staircase when a familiar face rose from a group in the rear of the lounge and came toward him, waving his hand. A good-looking kid with long wheat hair, a thick western moustache and a scar on the cheekbone that didn't go with the rest of the face. Like a Santa Monica beachboy who had been in the wrong fight.

"Hi, Mr. Lazar."

"Why hello," Larry said.

"Remember me?"

"Sure," Larry said, stalling for time. "I remember you. But where do I remember you from?"

"I read for *Bachelor Spouse,*" the kid volunteered. "Chris Tucker?"

"Of course, Chris. And you read very well, too. Only you didn't have the moustache then."

"It was a juvenile role." Chris laughed.

"How you doing?"

"I have a series." Chris mentioned a TV series Larry had vaguely heard of.

"Terrific."

"It's hiatus now so I'm going into New York to do a little PR work and see a lot of theater."

"Terrific."

"You're one of the few American directors I respect, Mr. Lazar. I mean it sincerely."

"Why thank you, Chris. That's very sweet of you. I remember your reading. You read very well. You were very good. But just a little too old for the part."

"I know. But I figured it was worth trying."

"And what night is your show on?"

"Friday."

"Friday is my poker night. But I'll make it a point to catch it."

"Don't," Chris said. "It's shit."

They both laughed knowingly, and Larry told the kid he would see him around and went down the spiral staircase trying to recall exactly why he had not cast him. There had been something that had put him off. Chris had enough experience and had given a strong reading. And the age difference actually would not have mattered that much. No, it was something else that had put him off. Something beneath the thick moustache. Then he remembered what it was. He had smelled *fagella,* which was definitely wrong for the part.

When he returned to his seat he joined Susan in looking out the window at the dotted strings of myriad lights below: New York. There was no mistaking it. The one and only. Home of his early dreams and recurrent nightmares. As usual, arriving in New York he felt a heightened sense of both dread and elation.

Dread this time because he would have to deal with his mother Sally once more. Elation because this would be the last time.

The plane pitched obliquely in its descent and his eardrums began to swell. He swallowed rapidly but they would not pop. He closed his eyes and could only think of Katharine Hepburn and Carole Lombard: Had they ever made a picture together? He crossed his fingers and hoped with all his heart they hadn't.

4

Larry was on his feet even before all the warning lights were off, overnight bag and suit carrier in hand. But other passengers were already milling at the door waiting to get off. Hepburn remained seated, her hands clasped calmly over her closed book. It would probably be the last chance he would have to introduce himself to her. On this flight anyway. He just had to walk over and say something, anything, to her. She would be civil he was sure. Especially at the end of a flight. It was silly, he knew. Ridiculous. But he just could not bring himself to do it. He would have to pass. What did he really have to talk to Hepburn about anyway? It wasn't as if he needed her for a picture.

The plane taxied to a complete stop and Marge, the stewardess, opened the door onto the gooseneck gangplank. Larry said good-bye to Susan, his stewardess seatmate, wishing her good luck with her plants, animals, and ex-Laker. In turn, she promised that she would definitely see his picture. Marge, standing beside the cabin door, hoped that he had enjoyed the flight and promised that she too would definitely see his picture. Gatto, the Italian producer, waved and he waved back. Maybe the guinea had actually seen his picture. Hepburn finally got to her feet.

When he emerged—deplaned, as they say—into the arrival area at JFK, the first sight that greeted him was a tall uniformed limousine driver holding up a small oak-tag placard: HEPBURN. He wondered for a moment, as he looked around for *his* studio people, if that placard was a sign for *him,* too, reminding him of a last chance. Another last chance. He could still wait for Hepburn and go over and introduce himself and perhaps even ride with her into the city from the airport. But then he saw his own name on a bigger placard in even bigger letters: LAZAR being held up by two girls. A pert Audrey Hepburn type in a red pantsuit, and a tall black girl in a tie-dyed dress with swirling brown African patterns. Evidently it was his day for Hepburns and tall blacks. He hurried over to them.

"Welcome to New York, Mr. Lazar," said the Audrey Hepburn. "Lloyd is awfully sorry he couldn't meet you. But he had to fly off to Paris at the last minute."

Lloyd was the studio's New York public-relations head. "I know," Larry said. He put down his bag, reached into his pocket, and found a small slip of paper. "Michael Baldwin," he read aloud. "The studio told me someone named Michael Baldwin would be meeting me instead." He looked around. "Where is he?"

Audrey Hepburn smiled. "I'm Michael Baldwin."

"What a pleasant surprise."

"And this is my friend, Inman Luk." Michael introduced the tall girl beside her.

"Look?" said Larry. "Where?"

"L-u-k," spelled Inman.

"That's more like luck. Good luck. My luck. Anyway, it was a bad joke. Sorry." Larry extended his hand. "I'm delighted to meet you."

She took his hand and smiled back. Larry gave her his serious stare, seeming to look deep into her eyes, but actually staring at an imaginary spot on her forehead. An old acting trick. Sometimes it kept him from breaking up. Sometimes it kept him from giving himself away. In any case it protected him. There was no question that Inman was a beauty, a real beauty. A statuesque African queen. Her eyes alone were an aesthetic experience. Azure, the color of a clear blue African sky. She was staring right back at him. Really staring.

"Isn't that Katharine Hepburn?" Michael asked suddenly. And, of course, it was Hepburn coming out of the gooseneck with a camel's hair coat draped over her shoulders and wearing checkered slacks.

"Yes," said Larry, still holding Inman's hand.

"You were on the same plane together," said Michael. "Isn't that exciting?"

Larry shrugged, finally releasing Inman's hand. He felt a slight parting press on his own hand as he did so. Or was he imagining things?

"Do you know her?" Michael was asking.

Hepburn was about to pass by them as she headed toward the driver to their right with her sign. Larry turned to face Michael fully. Hepburn's back was now to his as she strided purposefully toward her driver. Then he turned around and called out hoarsely, sotto voce, "So long, Katie," praying she wouldn't look back. And she didn't. He had timed it perfectly.

But when she met her driver, Larry noticed the actor kid from the plane, Chris—what was his name?—Tucker, falling into step beside her and saying something that made her laugh. Then Hepburn shook his hand manfully and they followed her driver down the long terminal corridor, their heads bent together, chatting and laughing. Son of a bitch! Larry thought, the kid had guts. But then the kid had nothing to lose. Because the kid was a nobody. A nothing. Even if he had a series. Besides, he was a fag. And you could never tell anything about fags anyway.

"If you give me your baggage checks," Michael was saying, "the driver can pick up your stuff."

Larry held up his suit carrier and overnight bag. "This is it."

"Have you had dinner?" She led the way out of the lounge.

"On the plane."

"How was the flight?" she asked over her shoulder.

"Terrific. Except for the film."

"What did they show?"

"Thin Ice."

"It could have been worse," said Michael.

"Only if the plane crashed," said Larry. "I can't watch a movie on a plane anyway." He turned to Inman who hadn't said a word, just wore her black Gioconda smile. "Is this the kind of weather you've been having?"

Inman nodded, slightly arching the stately column that was her neck, but it was Michael who answered. "Pretty much so. Just a little colder than usual for this time of year."

"Well," said Larry, "I didn't exactly come East for the weather anyway."

"I know. I'm awfully sorry."

Larry thanked her and addressed Inman again. "Are you with the studio too, Miss Luk?"

"Inman," she corrected. She had the voice of a cello.

"Inman," Larry repeated.

"Inman," said Michael, "is a friend of mine."

"I just came along for the ride," Inman smiled.

Larry immediately found himself thinking in Brooklyn street-corner cliché terms. Because smiling back at Inman he wondered about the kind of ride she could provide.

After the driver had placed his bag and suit carrier in the trunk of the black Lincoln and they settled in the back of the limousine, Larry sitting in between the two girls, Michael told him: "I tried to get you into the Plaza but they didn't have anything on such short notice. So I got the Sherry Netherland. Is that all right?"

The Sherry, Larry reassured her, was fine, as he girded himself for the part of any trip he hated most: the ride in from the airport. To him that always represented lost—or at best, limbo—time. Because you were there, at your destination in a sense, but at the same time you hadn't really arrived. It was all time out of place. Or time without a place. Driving in from the airport was certainly not part of LA time. Nor of flight time. Nor was it really part of being in New York time. It was literally lost time. If there was a purgatory, he once decided, the dimension of time there would have the quality of an endless drive in from an unfamiliar airport.

The limo pulled away from the curb in front of the terminal and braked suddenly, bouncing the two girls in a tangle across his lap. No one was hurt. The driver turned around and apologized. "Sorry. But that dumb son of a bitch." He pointed at the checkered taxi ahead cutting them off. "He just missed hitting us. That dumb son of a bitch." He opened his power window and stuck his head out. "Are you crazy or something?" he yelled at the cabbie.

The cabbie leaned across the empty seat beside him and rolled down his own window. "Who you calling crazy, buster?" he inquired. In the half-light Larry wasn't certain if the cabbie was black but there was the hint of a familiar accent in his voice. It reminded him of a boyhood friend, Chalky, who came from Jamaica. He suddenly wondered about what had happened to Chalky. He *could* have become a cabbie. He *could* have become anything. But most likely Chalky had wound up in jail or been killed in a war. Larry dismissed the thought from his mind. He had not thought of Chalky in years. Arriving in New York was tricky. It did funny things to you. Especially your memory.

"You. You're crazy," Larry heard. "You dumb son of a bitch."

The cabbie shifted back to the driver's side of his cab and then leaped out of it, carrying a crowbar. The limo driver immediately pulled out around the cab and bore down on the exposed, approaching cabbie. The cabbie somehow just managed to vault over his fender and onto his own taxi's trunk to avoid getting hit. Larry admired such life-saving dexterity. The cabbie certainly had the moves of a Chalky.

"Dumb son of a bitch!" the limo driver said, roaring away. "I should have killed him. The son of a bitch." He turned around. "Excuse me, sir."

Larry held up his hand and laughed. "No excuses. I love it. I love it. I'm a New Yorker. I love this city. The throb. The excitement. The stimulation. It's very easy to become a piece of fruit in California. I think if Kafka had written 'The Metamorphosis' in LA, the hero would have turned into an orange. Or a Mercedes. Or an orange Mercedes."

The driver turned around again and stared at Larry. Larry could tell that he was regarding him as a kook, just another West Coast movie kook. Larry stared back at him. The driver had a scar that split his right eyebrow in two. Another scar streaked down his right cheek. He looked more like a bouncer than a driver. But then New York was a violent place. "Do you drive a lot for the studio?" Larry asked him.

"Yes, sir," the driver said, his attention back on the road, his head nodding.

Larry winked at Michael. "Who was the most famous person you ever drove for?"

"You mean the biggest star?"

"That's one way to put it."

"Let's see," the driver said. They were getting onto the Van Wyck Expressway. "What's his name?"

"What's whose name?" asked Larry.

"He was in *The Sting* and all them."

"Robert Redford?" Michael suggested.

"No," said the driver. "The other one. What's his name?"

"Paul Newman?" said Larry.

"Not Paul Newman. The other one. The British one."

"Robert Shaw?" Larry and Michael said simultaneously.

"That's right," said the driver. "That's him. He was also in *Jaws.*"

"Did you like Bob?" asked Larry.

"Yeah. He's a gentleman."

Larry and Michael looked at each other. Larry shrugged and leaned forward. "He's dead."

"Too bad," the driver said. "Like I said, he was a gentleman."

Larry fell silent again, as if in memory of Robert Shaw. But after a decent interval he could not resist asking the driver the next logical question: "Ever have a star who wasn't a gentleman?"

"I could tell you a story or two."

Larry winked at Michael. This was more like what he had in mind. "Tell us," he told the driver.

"I'd rather not," said the driver. "You never know. They might be friends of yours."

"I wouldn't give you away," Larry promised.

The driver just grunted in reply.

"You're right," said Larry. "I can see you can be trusted."

"I try to mind my own business."

"That's a good policy," Larry said. "Ever drive for Katharine Hepburn?"

"No. Is the lady a friend of yours?"

"Katie and I took the same flight in together."

"I just love her work," said Michael.

"Yes. They don't make them like Katie anymore," Larry agreed. "Katie's a national treasure. Like Cary Grant. I ran into Cary the other night at the Academy. Looks marvelous. And would you believe it? He's a fan of mine."

Larry turned his head quickly, observing Inman, then Michael. Both seemed duly impressed. He leaned back and decided he just might enjoy the rest of the ride into town.

5

When the iron-grille elevator doors closed behind him, Larry found himself in a state of city shock. It happened whenever he came back to New York for the first hour or so. He would simply be shocked by the city. Shocked at how dirty it was. Or how noisy it was. Or even how lovely it was: the luminescent night lights first sighted from the plane like so many fireflies neatly bottled. Or how poor and fragile and small it was: The houses along the expressway always seemed too slight to him, as if they had been designed and constructed for some race of little people that no longer existed, had long since vanished. Most of the buildings in Queens, in fact, did not look sturdy enough to bear the weight of heavy investments. California was supposed to be ephemeral, but New York at a first glance always seemed much more frail. It was not until he crossed the bridge into Manhattan that he would feel any sense of permanence or gravity. Even then he would continue to be discomfitted by changes. Little changes, to be sure. For example, when he first had begun coming back to town the bellhops were always Italian or Irish and later occasionally even Jewish or black. But now, he realized as he stared at the bellhop holding his suit carrier, they were all inevitably Puerto Rican.

One New York truism still seemed to hold though: The more people in an elevator the less conversation took place. Both Michael and Inman were smiling down at their own feet. The bellhop was looking up at the ceiling as if in that way he was somehow controlling the direction in which the elevator was going. Everyone was silent. Including Larry himself.

And they were all still silent, as they followed the bellhop out of the elevator down a long corridor toward Larry's rooftop suite. But then no one ever talked in hotel corridors except maids, children, drunken out-of-towners, and people who had obviously misplaced their keys. Everyone always talked in motel corridors though, and he wondered why. He smiled at Inman and Michael smiled at him. The bellhop unlatched the door of the suite and went through the ritual of poking open bathroom and closet doors, turning on the lights, and pulling up the drapes in the sitting room and the venetian blinds in the bedroom. The decor was French, Louis the Expensive, and the view, of course, was Central Park. Larry went to the window and squinted out into the twilight darkness. He was unable to discern a tree or—a mugger. "Perfect," he announced, as if approving a newly edited version of a sequence.

He turned away from the window. Michael was tipping the bellhop.

"Don't," he said, fishing into his pocket.

"Don't worry. It's all right."

"Are you sure?"

"Lloyd's orders." And she handed him a card.

"A tip for me too?"

"That's my home number. In case you need anything."

Larry laughed. "Maybe I need help sleeping here." He spread his arms out wide. "All this room. All this space. All the apartments I ever had in New York in the old days could fit in here. But seriously, thank you so much. I'm so glad Lloyd's in Europe. You're much prettier. I'm sure I'll be seeing you again before I leave."

"I'm sure," Michael said.

"Nice seeing you too, Inman. By the way, what do you do?"

"I model and I teach yoga."

"I'm impressed," Larry said, and took off his jacket and proceeded to slowly puff himself into a headstand. He heard change jingling down out of his pockets and could feel the vein throbbing in his temple and knew his face must be reddening quickly. "How's that?"

"*I'm* impressed," Inman said.

With mock dizziness Larry reclaimed his feet, groping tentatively about the room like Rocky after a knockdown. He stopped before Inman. "Maybe someday you'll show me the right way?"

Inman smiled.

"Meanwhile," Larry said, "unfortunately now I have a few other things to attend to."

"We know," Michael said.

He walked the girls to the door. "Oh yes," said Michael, "the driver may change but the limo will be on duty. Always. Twenty-four hours."

"That really isn't necessary. I can always grab a cab."

"Lloyd's orders."

"Thank you," said Larry. "Ciao."

"Ciao," said Michael. Inman waved tentatively. And they left.

He closed the door after them. Went back to the window and pressing his nose against the glass and standing on his toes looked directly down at Fifth Avenue. At the lighted cars gliding by as if in slow motion. At the lighted buses moving in leisurely arcs as they pulled over to the curbs to pick up and discharge passengers and then pull away again. He remembered the old double-decker buses and the childhood thrill of riding on them up Fifth Avenue and through the park and then up Riverside Drive. He could not recall when they were phased out but it seemed to him that it was about the same time the subway fare went up from a nickel. How much was the subway fare now? Eleven dollars? He did not know. He hadn't been in a subway in years. Maybe during this trip, if he had time, he would get in the subway. Ride a Fifth Avenue bus, too. And the Staten Island ferry. Pick up some of the old New York energy. Zap it away for future use on the coast.

Suddenly he felt moisture forming in his eyes, blurring the pupils, clogging his vision. Blinking furiously he held back the tears and went into the bedroom, kicked off his shoes, lay down, and stared up at the high ceiling. So far he had been doing well, remarkably well. And he vowed to keep it up. He would not break. He would not cry. He would do what he had to do and get it over with and then leave town as soon as possible. No big deal. But first he would eat something. He picked up the phone and asked for room service.

It took six rings to connect with a female Spanish voice that answered hesitantly. "I want you to send up a chilled bottle of Pouilly-Fuissé—any good year," he told the lady, "and an order of beluga caviar. With a box of Ritz crackers—any good year." He repeated the order two more times but still wasn't sure she had it right.

Then he dialed the coast. The call went through immediately. Was answered on one ring. Again by a native female Spanish speaker. His maid Dolores.

"Buenas noches," Larry greeted her.

Dolores asked him how the flight was and told him everyone just went shopping. He asked her to tell Mrs. Lazar that he had arrived safely, that he was at the Sherry, and that he would call later. And he thanked her. All in Spanish.

He was proud of himself. Had never studied Spanish in school. But he could speak it. He'd picked it up mostly on trips to Mexico. Came in handy. Saved a lot of money in hiring help. Especially maids.

Maids were always a hassle though. They were like having another kid in the house you always had to worry about. But then you couldn't run a house without them either. It was a trade-off. A wash. And Dolores was something else again. She had a body that flaunted its sexuality: She was so round and juicy and tender-looking. When she first came to work for them he even thought of *shtuping* her. But that would have been going too far. *Shtuping* your own maid. So for a while he played around with the idea in a movie. In a script he was working on he had a character, who was one of the biggest stars in Hollywood, a male sex symbol throughout the world, women throwing themselves at his feet wherever he went, a Burt Reynolds or Paul Newman type, become obsessed with his own Mexican maid. Fall in love with her completely. But then the maid would turn him down. Repel his most fervent advances. And meanwhile fuck for the most ordinary greasers. But not for the star. Never for the star.

Because fucking her master would, in her eyes, make her a whore. And she was not that kind of girl.

Cute idea. But it never worked out in the script. In fact, nothing came of the whole project. But it had kept him from ever making even the most tentative advance toward Dolores. And so far she had lasted almost five years with them. If he had *shtuped* her, she would have been out of the house in a month. But then there would have been another maid to think of fucking. So maybe he should have fucked her after all?

Larry thought about fucking a lot. And talked about it a great deal too. To his analyst. To his friends. But he didn't cheat. Not that much, anyway. And not because of any moral qualms—he couldn't function in the movie business if he had moral qualms. Nor because he was afraid of any repercussions or retaliations from Jane. That didn't worry him. They had been married long enough to expect—and accept—almost anything from each other. No, it was simply because the right opportunities didn't often favorably present themselves. For example, he could *shtup* all the actresses he wanted. But he couldn't see *shtuping* actresses he was working with. Or worse, casting actresses that he wanted to *shtup*. Because that was the surest way of fucking up a picture. Literally. And fucking up a picture could really fuck up his life. But any actress he'd *shtup* would expect him to cast her sooner or later. Sex with an actress could only get him into Catch-22-Alice-in-Wonderland territory. So in most cases he manfully ignored the offers, turning his back on them and walking away. But, of course, there were exceptions. After all, he was only human.

He thumbed through his address book until he found the number he wanted. Dialed it. Even the tone of the rings sounded warm and familiar.

"Hello?" His Aunt Ida answered the phone with a question. Just like Mike at the studio.

"Hello, Aunt Ida. This is Larry. *Vus machst du?*"

Immediately, she told him in Yiddish how she was and asked him about himself. He replied in Yiddish, amazed at his ability to do so. After all, he had not spoken Yiddish in years. The only person he had ever really spoken Yiddish to was *Zeydah,* his grandfather, and after his death Larry had used Yiddish only sparingly. But here he was telling Aunt Ida in Yiddish that his family was fine. That the kids were healthy and happy. And that no, Jane had not come with him because somebody had to stay home and look after the kids.

There was a knock on the door.

"Excuse me, Aunt Ida," Larry said in Yiddish. "Come in," he called out in English. And then in Yiddish, "Someone at the door," he explained into the phone.

The door pushed open and a Latino waiter wheeled in a serving cart: wine in a bucket of ice, caviar in a bed of ice in a silver service, surrounded with little dishes of garnishments, chopped onions, capers, shredded egg yolks, and sour cream, and a wicker basket covered with a cloth napkin. It reminded Larry of the setting at the head of the table at a Passover seder. He motioned for the waiter to set it all down on the side table next to his bed.

Meanwhile, Aunt Ida wanted to know where he was. He told her he was at the Sherry. She said it was a nice hotel and he agreed with her.

The waiter uncorked the wine and poured a sample into a goblet. Larry tasted it and nodded his silent approval. But he frowned when he lifted up the napkin covering the wicker basket and found just saltines and some crustless toast. No Ritz crackers. The hotel was running down. Obviously. He signed the check anyway and dismissed the waiter.

All the while listening to Aunt Ida. She was giving a discourse on the hotels of the world. Or, at least, the hotels of *her* world. In English. Larry reached over and scooped up two fingerfuls of caviar and sprinkled them with onions and capers as she reached the hotels of Miami Beach and their declining states, remembering when the Fountainebleau was the Fountainebleau and no one had ever heard of a Holiday Inn. Then she must have detected something behind his monosyllabic assents to her rhetorical questions—or actually heard him chewing on his caviar—because she suggested that he come over for a bite right now.

"No," said Larry, still savoring the fishless yet sweet briny taste. "I couldn't eat a thing. But is Uncle Irving there?"

Of course, Uncle Irving was there. Sure he was there. Where should he be? In fact, he was standing next to her that very minute, waiting for her to give him the telephone. But before putting him on she wanted to wish Larry all the continued success in the world because he deserved it. And, more important, she hoped he was in good health and his children were in good health and his whole family was in good health. Because, after all, health was the most important thing in the world as he was smart enough to know without having to be told.

Larry agreed with her and thanked her for telling him that. And finally she "let him have his Uncle Irving."

If Aunt Ida's conversation was a meandering stream in autumn, Uncle Irving came on like a rushing torrent of spring. He was a little man physically, as Larry recalled, but he had a booming voice. He was also a telephone shouter, as if he could not quite trust in the instrument's ability to amplify his voice over any great distance. He was roaring. Did Larry have a pencil? Did Larry have a piece of paper? All right, then would Larry take down this address?

Larry rubbed his ear and took down the address: It was in Brooklyn. Did Larry know where it was? Larry said he knew where it was.

Then it should take, Uncle Irving estimated, forty minutes for Larry to get there, if Larry left right away. Could Larry leave right away?

Larry said he could leave right away.

There were also some legal matters to attend to, Uncle Irving told him. But that all could be taken care of later.

They would talk about it, Larry said, and hung up. He poured another glass of wine and scooped up some caviar onto a saltine. He went to the window, wine and caviar in hand, and looked out across the park. The West Side of Manhattan seemed like the fortress wall of a medieval city lit by neon. It was the kind of surrealistic effect an artistic director might strive to produce in a film.

Larry turned away from the window, swallowed the caviar, and returned to reality. It was time to go back to Brooklyn.

6

The limo turned down Third Avenue. With a different driver. This one a black, a good-looking kid who drove with a soothing authority. He neither took unnecessary chances nor gave an inch without a challenge. Which is just what Larry expected of a chauffeur in New York. But the kid's speech came as a surprise. It was too correct. Too cultured. "May I ask you a personal question, Mr. Lazar?" he was asking.

"Depends," Larry replied. "But I must warn you, if it's about masturbation I won't answer it."

The kid laughed. "I love your sense of humor. I just love it. I dig your movies a lot. I really admire them."

"Why thank you. Did you see *Herbie and Milty?*"

"No. But I mean to. I hear it's very good. But what I want to ask you, Mr. Lazar, is how come you never use blacks?"

"I use blacks," Larry protested. "I'm one of the few liberals in Hollywood who actually does use blacks. Like I can't remember a black in a Jane Fonda picture. But whenever possible I write in a black. Like the cop in *Herbie and Milty.* Which you haven't seen yet. And the hospital admitting clerk in *Hostile Relationships.* Who you should remember if you have seen it. And I'm even thinking of having a black stewardess in my next picture. Or a black yoga teacher." The last two statements weren't quite true. But they weren't quite a lie yet either. Who knew what his next picture would *really* be? Who knew if he would ever make another picture at all, in fact, the way *Herby and Milty* seemed to be dying for a lack of legs?

They stopped for a red light. "I mean," said the driver turning around, "using a black in a leading role."

"Well," said Larry, who was used to fielding the question because black students always asked him precisely the same question in film-school seminars. "I write about what I know. Not what I don't know. I'm not black. I'm white. I don't pretend to know what the black experience is. But I do know something about the white experience. Especially the white middle-class experience in America. So that's what I write about and that's who I make films about."

"But that's my point," said the driver. "You're not the typical white middle-class American. You're Jewish."

"I don't understand," said Larry.

"You don't make films about just Jews. You make films about white Americans. You could just as easily make films about black Americans."

"Not quite," said Larry. "It's not the same thing." And decided not to say anything more. To let the matter rest. Because this was ridiculous. Usually, blacks would tell him that his being Jewish didn't mean he had a clue into the black experience. That just because he was a member of one minority did not necessarily mean that he had any special insight into the problems of another minority. Especially one of a different race. But now he was getting hit ass backward.

"I hope I haven't offended you," said the driver.

"Not at all."

"But I thought I would get it off my chest."

"Of course. But do you always speak so directly to your passengers?"

"Sometimes." The driver smiled.

Larry liked the smile. Good teeth. "What's your name?" he asked.

"Douglas. Didn't I tell you?"

"No."

"Sorry. I guess I forgot. I'm supposed to introduce myself first thing."

Larry dismissed the notion of such a preliminary courtesy with a wave and then leaned forward. "Douglas, who was the most famous person you ever drove for?"

Douglas thought for a while. "You, I guess," he finally said.

"That's really flattering. But you must be kidding."

"No." Douglas flashed the toothy smile. "I just began to work for the limo service two weeks ago. Mostly it's just been taking people to funerals or driving to the airport."

"Do you like it?"

"Beats what I was doing before." He half turned around. "Parking cars. But I don't really like it."

"What do you really like?" asked Larry. And the moment he asked he was sorry, wished that he could recall that question. Second sense told him that he had fallen into a trap. But there was no way to withdraw the question because the kid was already answering it: "I really like to act. I'm an actor."

"Oh," said Larry. He should have known. By the kid's first question. Who but a black actor would have asked that question?

"I'm studying with Les," said Douglas.

"He's a fine teacher."

"He's getting on my nerves," Douglas said with a laugh.

"We all get on each other's nerves sometimes," Larry said.

Larry watched as Douglas regarded him uncertainly in the rearview mirror and then turned his attention back to the road. He didn't like cutting off the kid but he just wasn't into dealing with an aspiring actor right now either.

He settled back into his seat. It would be a long ride out to Brooklyn.

As always.

Just because they had responded to his pictures most people thought he'd automatically respond to *their* problems. As if the headaches involved in being a genuine filmmaker, a real creative artist, weren't overwhelming enough. As if he didn't have enough problems without their trying to lay their trips onto him. Especially blacks in New York. Whenever he returned to the city they always tried to make him feel guilty just because he was white. In LA he rarely had to worry about blacks. Unless there was dissension on the Dodgers or the Rams. And that he read about. Otherwise, there was only the Chicanos and La Raza and that he could handle. Because they had come into his life late. Because he had nothing to feel guilty about in his treatment of them. He had never even heard the word Chicano while growing up in Brooklyn.

It wasn't like that with the blacks whom he had known from day one in Brooklyn when they had wanted to be called Negroes and Colored persons, instead of niggers and spades. And the truth of the matter was he had nothing to feel guilty about in his treatment of blacks either. They were barking up the wrong honky when they picked on him. In fact, they were the ones who should feel guilty about the way they treated *him*. Always harassing him. Making him live in deathly fear of them as a kid growing up. If it hadn't been for Chalky, for example, he would have been cut up—and down—more than once. For sure.

He had not thought of Chalky in years. He could not even remember the last time he had thought of him. Now he was thinking of him for the second time in one day. Chalky had been his boyhood friend. In the jungle his old neighborhood rapidly became Jews and Negroes did not mix usually. Keeping to themselves. To their own kind. To their own side of the avenue. Except maybe in the gym. Or on the ball field. Even there they only played against each other. But he and Chalky had been block friends. Chalky lived in a basement down the street in the apartment house where his father, James, tended the coal-burning furnace. James tended the furnaces in most of the other buildings on the block too, hauling out the ashes and the garbage and shoveling the snow away from the sidewalks in winter. And when he wasn't emerging from a cellar or a basement he was washing windows or doing floors. James was a tall man, always in overalls, except on Sundays when he would appear in a dark brown pinstripe Bond's suit topped by a snappy brimmed gray Adam's fedora. Chalky's mother was a round woman with gold glinting teeth in a dull cotton housecoat, a drab bandana about her head, when she worked as a cleaning woman. But on Sundays she wore gay floral-patterned silks, and would look a bit uneasy in her high-heeled patent-leather pumps, her brown stockinged flesh pouring over their sides, as she walked down the street in a rolling gait, her hand clutching James's arm tightly. And behind them would come Chalky, in a blue suit and a bird's-eye checked cap and shining brown shoes. And then at the corner they would disappear onto a trolley taking them to downtown Brooklyn to see a show. To the Fox. To the Albee. To the Brooklyn Paramount. To the Loew's Metropolitan.

Sometimes Chalky and his family would even go into New York. By subway. To the Roxy or the Radio City Music Hall. Or to one of the Times Square–Broadway theater palaces: the Paramount, the Capital, the Strand, Loew's State. They would eat in restaurants that bore equally magical names: Toffenetti's and McGinnis's, Schrafft's and Childs, and Romeo's, and that most marvelous of pleasure domes, Horn and Hardart's Automat. Then on Mondays Chalky would describe to Larry with equal relish both the shows he had seen and the meals he had eaten. Baked potatoes bigger than an indoor soft ball at Toffenetti's. Pancakes thicker than a triple-decker sandwich and sweeter than a vanilla malted at Childs. The spaghetti in a portion at Romeo's had to be enough to feed the whole Italian army. And what could compare to the beef pies, baked beans, and doughnuts from the whirling compartments that devoured nickels at the Automat?

But it was the shows, on stage and screen, that Larry really liked to hear him talk about. For Chalky was a natural performer, a superb storyteller. Telling the story of a movie, he *became* the movie and everyone in it, mimicking actors, parodying bit players, dancing about on the sidewalk in front of the candy store as he went from role to role, scene to scene, offering explanations and interpretations that the movies of those days would only hint at but never dare to make. In fact, often when Larry would later see a picture that Chalky had recounted, to bend-over-the-newsstand-and-double-up-in-paroxysms-of-laughter effect, he'd be disappointed by the original. It either moved too slowly. Or was just too timid. Or simply lacked the verve and life that Chalky's inventive mind had added to it.

It was from Chalky that Larry early on learned the key to a

movie. Energy. The energy level that emanated from the screen. It didn't matter that much whether a story was logical or illogical or whether a performer was extraordinarily handsome or unusually grotesque. What mattered was the energy that exuded from him. And if a movie, for example, lacked sufficient energy, faltering and stuttering in parts, Chalky subsequently supplied his own energy—or life—in his recounting performances. In the same way he could recreate a stage performance. Adding trumpets to a band, steps to a dance, gags to a comedian's routine. Chalky always improved upon reality because he added the energy of his own life to it.

Aside from their mutual interest in movies and shows—even then Larry secretly dreamt of being an actor, a performer himself —he and Chalky had little else in common. In school their paths seldom crossed. Academically or athletically. Larry was in the Rapids, the class for the gifted in junior high who were in a hurry to get to high school and then on to college, while Chalky was in the shop class, the group which would either soon quit school to work in gas stations or the garment district, or fan out to the city's various vocational high schools where theoretically they would learn how to become textile workers and body-and-fender men.

Larry was interested in sports, as a fan and as a participant. If he could not become an actor, he would have happily accepted a job as the Yankee shortstop. Chalky, though naturally endowed with a lithe muscular body, couldn't have cared less for sports. He had no secret desire to be another Sugar Ray or Jackie Robinson. Even in a gym class he could not be coaxed into a game of any sort. He would lean back against a wood-barred wall or disappear into the green steel locker room. The teachers never challenged him either. They knew better than to confront Chalky. They could sense the energy lurking in him and were afraid of it.

After Larry graduated from junior high school he rarely saw Chalky. Except on an occasional snowy morning in winter when the boy might be helping his father shovel the snow away from the sidewalk. Or of a summer evening ducking his head into a basement as he retrieved empty garbage cans. Then they would greet each other pleasantly enough. A word or two. An observation about the weather or the season or the time of day. But no real conversation. And certainly no discussion about movies or shows either of them had seen. Yet somehow Larry felt a bond still existed between them, whether it was based on his having played appreciative audience to Chalky's most inspired performances, or a bond based on a mutual love for show business at the same time in their disparate lives, he did not know. He sensed it was there even as Chalky seemed to become increasingly remote in their random meetings.

Chalky dropped out of vocational school, disappeared from the block and the neighborhood. Larry heard vague rumors that he was working in a cleaning store and later that he was in trouble. Faced jail for stealing a car. Something like that. Meanwhile, Larry was busy with his own life. He was going to high school, acting in play productions there, dreaming of a career as an actor on the Broadway stage. Confessing these dreams to potential girl friends until he discovered that they were more interested in future optometrists and prospective gynecologists than possible actors.

One cool autumn evening Larry was walking home along the parkway from the library. He had gone there after dinner to research a paper he was doing for extra credit in U.S. History. Larry liked history, particularly the lives of the colonial fathers. Except for Washington they were all in their twenties or thirties, almost kids, closer in age to him than they were to current governors and senators. He had settled on Alexander Hamilton as the subject of his report and carried a biography under his arm. At the busy avenue intersection he stopped and bought a sweet potato from an old bearded Jew who roasted them in a white enameled wood-burning stove mounted on a baby-carriage chassis. He could never resist those potatoes on a chilly night. Although they sometimes burned his lips and tongue to the touch, they always warmed his insides all the way down.

The parkway was once one of the grandest streets in Brooklyn. Lined with elegant town houses and brownstones, the wide thoroughfare's islands of trees and benches divided it into three traffic lanes like a Parisian boulevard. When Larry was a child, it was the address of the rich and successful of the neighborhood, the doctors and teachers and businessmen. Later, like the rest of the neighborhood, it fell into a decline. Blacks with money and Jews who dressed in black, the Chasidim, began to move in. And though the homes still looked stately and proper, somehow uncollected garbage piled up before them now.

Usually when Larry walked on the parkway at night he would walk along one of the perimeter sidewalks rather than on an island. The sidewalks were not only better lit but also provided better possible escape by giving quicker access to the side streets and avenues that bisected the parkway. Not that Larry ever had had any problems personally. But sometimes he heard stories of white kids being beat up by Negroes. Of Negroes being attacked by Chasidic Jews. Or of innocents being caught up in some confusing cross fire.

But at the moment Larry wasn't too concerned. He was really enjoying his sweet potato. Besides, he had great confidence in his speed. He was a natural runner, one of the fastest white boys in his school. He could always leg it out of trouble. Nor was it very late. Just after nine. And the steady flow of traffic in both directions in the middle of the parkway was reassuring.

Still, Larry hesitated when he saw three figures, their legs sprawled out in front of them, leaning back on a bench ahead. And a fourth figure was perched on top of the bench backrest. This figure turned his head toward Larry and mumbled something to the occupants of the bench below. Then they all turned toward Larry and one of them said something that caused the others to laugh. Larry could not quite hear what was said but he did not like the sound of that laughter. It was Negro laughter.

He knew at once he had to make a choice. He could keep walking forward, munching on his sweet potato, ignoring the occupants on the bench, and assume somehow he could get past them safely. Or he could turn around, revealing his fear, advertising his weakness and cowardice in the situation, and take off in the direction he had come.

Larry chose to run. To rely more on the speed of his legs than on the kindness of the bench occupants. And as he did so he promptly heard the response he feared most: "Let's get the motherfucker!" Without thinking, still clutching the remnants of his sweet potato in one hand and his library book in the other, he pumped his legs furiously as the adrenalin of fear flowed through him.

They were on their feet now too, running after him, shouting epithets after him and encouragement to each other. He could beat them, he knew, because he had more to lose. It was the first block that really counted. If they saw that he was pulling away they would give up, easily become disheartened. But if they saw that they were gaining ground, they would keep coming, spurred on like animals by the scent of a victorious chase. He looked back over his shoulder: They were strung out behind, the last one beginning to falter. But the two closest were keeping up with him. He made a quick decision: At the corner if the lights were in his favor, he would cross the wide parkway hoping they might be stalled by getting caught in a light change.

But the lights were green. Too much traffic was racing by. He had no chance to make his dash across at the corner. He kept running, back along the parkway in the direction he had come, hoping now to reach the avenue intersection where he had bought his sweet potato. Too much activity for them to bother with him there. People buying their *News*es and *Mirror*s. A candy store still open. An all-night cafeteria where he could lose them. He was still frightened but he ran without panic. He had his wind. No breathing knives in his chest yet. He could outlast them till the intersection. He did not turn around to look over his shoulder but by the sounds of their racing footsteps and panting voices he could tell they were not gaining on him.

And then he tripped. Felt his pants tear and knees burn at the same time and his hands scraping and the potato squishing, the book flying loose as he tried to brake himself. He bounced and, turning his head, came down hard on his elbow. His face was all right: No taste of blood in his mouth. But he felt a burning pain in his elbow and in the palms of his hands.

When he looked up, they were standing over him in a blur, feigning mock concern. Someone was shaking his head, saying, "Man tried to run away."

"Shit," said someone else, retrieving Larry's library book.

A hand grabbed it away. "Let me study it."

And began to turn the pages.

"What's it say?"

"It say 'liberry book.' Maybe he stole it. That's why he's running."

"What else it say?"

"It say each day overdue two cents fine."

"What's it say if you rip it in a thousand pieces?"

"The chair. The electric chair."

"What's that there? That card there?"

"His liberry card."

"I once had one of them. Only I burned it. What's it say?"

"Larry Lazarsky."

Two of them were doing the talking. A porkpie hat. And a darker face with two front teeth missing. He was the one who had Larry's library book. The other two were their audience, laughing in appreciative snickers.

"Hey, you Larry Lazarsky?"

The book dropped on Larry's face, stinging his nose and burning his cheek.

"Next time I drop my foot. You Larry Lazarsky?"

Larry wiped his face with the book as if it were a towel and nodded. He wondered what they would do to him. He had no money. Except the change of a quarter for his sweet potato. The only valuable thing he had was the library book, *The Life and Times of Alexander Hamilton.*

"Larry Lazarsky?"

It was a different voice. One he had not heard before. From one of the blacks who had been in the background, in the audience. It sounded familiar. But he could not place it.

"You know the mother?" the voice was asked.

"I just might."

"Shit."

Larry squinted hard. A black was smiling down at him, extending a hand, and then slowly helping him to his feet.

"You all right?"

"I'm okay," Larry said, disregarding the pains in his knees and elbow and hands. "Chalky?"

"Shit," someone said.

"He a friend of yours?"

"I know him," said Chalky.

"Then what he trying to run away for?"

"Wouldn't you?" asked Chalky.

"Shit, yes."

Everyone laughed.

"This is Larry," said Chalky, as if he were making a formal introduction. "And this motherfucker is George." He pointed to the porkpie hat. "And Willie." Willie was the one with the missing teeth. "And Lester." Lester was a high yellow who looked almost light enough to be a white. Larry stared at him.

"Don't worry," said Willie as if reading his thoughts. "Lester is all-spade."

"Except for his guinea father," said George.

Lester took a swipe at George who ducked and then clinched with him.

"They're all ignorant," said Chalky. "And bad. They ruining the neighborhood. This neighborhood." Chalky indicated his companions who were still slap-fighting. "Remember when it was something?"

Chalky inspected Larry's library book. "Alexander Hamilton," he read. "We learned about him in school. You still going to school?"

"Yes," said Larry. "You?"

"Quit a long time ago."

"Are you working?"

"Quit a long time ago." This time Chalky laughed.

"Do you still like shows?"

"Shit," said Chalky. "I never watch the TV. It all shit." He handed the book to Larry. Their eyes met. The whites of Chalky's eyes were bloodshot.

"Thanks," Larry said.

"You be careful," said Chalky. He turned and walked back toward his friends. Then he called out, "If you so smart, Lucky," he said, using Larry's old block nickname, "be careful."

After that night Larry was careful. And even though the newspapers increasingly referred to the neighborhood as "racially troubled," he was never bothered by a Negro there again. He knew it wasn't simply because he was being careful. It was because of Chalky. The word had evidently gone out.

7

Some streets no longer had cobblestones; all vestiges of trolley tracks were gone. But even at night there were still familiar landmarks. A bank that looked less forbidding than he remembered it. A church that seemed to have shrunk in size. The movie house whose balcony he often frequented was now a twin theater showing pornos. But, otherwise, he could have been passing through any urban neighborhood: Not enough sky. Not enough trees. Too many anonymous gray buildings too closely crowded together. A girl from Ohio had once told him that all Brooklyn was just three Toledos laid end to end. She was right.

The limo was pulling over. "Is this the place?" Douglas asked.

Larry looked up and read the sign on the canopy. "This is the place," he said. He remembered the brown brick building, too. He had often passed it on the way to a bowling alley farther up the street. The bowling alley had been owned by an ex-Dodger pitcher. He wondered if it was still there.

"I'll park around the side and wait," said Douglas.

"I don't know how long this will take," said Larry, getting out of the limo. He walked under a green canopy awning from the curbstone to the double wooden doors at the entrance of the building, and then breathing in deeply, closed his eyes, and pushed one of the heavy doors open. The floor and the walls of the entryway were of marble and a crystal chandelier hung from a high ceiling. It all seemed proper and formal and too expensive. A different world. Not at all like the neighborhood outside. It was also much too quiet. He heard his own footsteps echoing as he walked up three marble steps into a huge parlor room with paintings in gilded frames on the walls and wooden beams in the ceiling and an oakwood floor covered with red Persian rugs. It reminded him of the board room at a studio where the executives met to approve or pass on projects. Only the oversized committee table with a water pitcher and glasses on a tray in the center of it was missing.

A plump young man came toward him. He wore a yarmulke, a brown serge suit, a pink face, and a black beard. "Excuse me," he said in a singsong. "Can I help you?"

"I'm Larry Lazar."

"Oh yes." The young man extended his hand. His fingers were short and fat and hairy; two of them bore graduation rings with rosette stones. "Sidney Rosen," he introduced himself. "Your uncle just called. He said he'd be here shortly. Won't you sit down?" He pointed to an overstuffed red brown couch and handed Larry a booklet. "And perhaps you'd like to look over our brochure."

Larry sat down, idly accepting the booklet. The cover was the front of the building on a sunny day with many green trees clustered around it, as if it stood in the middle of a park like a boathouse. The avenue even looked like a broad body of water and the sky was clear and blue. "Brochure of what?" Larry asked.

Rosen immediately sat down beside him, and leaning over began to turn the pages slowly, old friends in a living room poring over a rare book together. "As you can see we have a very fine selection." He pointed to an illustration. "Isn't that beautiful? Walnut." He wet his finger and turned another page. "Mahogany. Some people like that. It's always popular. And this," he tapped a page, "is cedar. My personal choice. There's nothing like cedar. Cedar is always outstanding."

"Cedar," said Larry. "What's a good year for cedar?"

"Excuse me."

"Never mind."

Rosen rose. "You might also begin considering how many mourners you want."

"I can decide that?"

Rosen coughed unctuously. "I mean professional mourners.

You see, according to Jewish law, the deceased should not be left alone until interment."

"Why?" Larry asked.

"Why? Because it's customary. It's just customary. You should always have at least two mourners praying all night long with the deceased."

"Is that to ward off ghosts?"

"Tradition. It's just Jewish tradition."

"I see. And what do they cost?"

Rosen stroked his beard. "Just ninety dollars each."

Almost as much as a screen extra gets, Larry thought. "Is the price Jewish tradition, too?" he asked.

"They have a union," Rosen explained. "And this is a union shop. I'm sure there are places where you could get mourners cheaper. But I assure you, you wouldn't want to use their services."

"Who wants scab mourners?"

"Exactly," said Rosen. "Now let me show you some of the testimonials we've received from satisfied relatives, appreciating the dignity and thoughtfulness of our final arrangements." He walked over to his desk across the room and picked up a black-leather-covered scrapbook, gold fleurs-de-lis flowing along its borders, and handed it to Larry. Larry remembered bargaining for a similar scrapbook at a stall in Florence. He opened it and turned the pages slowly. Beneath stiff cellophane were framed letters—some handwritten on personal stationery, others typed beneath company logos. He quickly read a few and looked up: "These are great notices."

"Thank you," said Rosen, hovering over him.

Larry read aloud: "On behalf of my three wonderful sons, their beautiful wives, my seven lovely grandchildren, and my sister-in-law, Ruth, I would like to thank you for the fine funeral you gave my dear departed husband, Max. It was just what he would have wanted." Larry closed the album. If he read more he would not be able to keep a straight face. "Terrific," he said, patting the album gently, and handed it back to Rosen. Who clutched it to his chest and carried it that way back to the desk. The way girls used to carry their books home from school. The boys always had to carry their books under their arms. Otherwise, they were considered queers. Rosen returned smiling. Larry pointed at the door behind the desk. "Is she back there?" he asked, his voice suddenly hoarse.

"Yes." Rosen nodded.

"Has anything been done to her yet?"

Rosen shook his head. "Just the preliminary preparations. We've been waiting to find out exactly what you want. Whether you want the casket open or not, for example."

Larry nodded and reached into his pocket for a cigarette. Forgetting that he couldn't possibly have any. Forgetting that he had stopped smoking a few months ago. He came up empty and asked Rosen if he had a cigarette by any chance.

"No, I'm sorry. But I can get you some."

"Never mind."

"No trouble. What do you smoke?"

"I don't," said Larry. "I stopped."

For three months he had not touched a cigarette. Gone cold turkey and stopped. But if he ever craved a cigarette it was now. And how much could it possibly hurt? Just one cigarette. Statistically, it couldn't possibly affect his heart or cancer chances one iota. And he would stop after just one cigarette. A one-cigarette-tri-monthly habit would be a lot easier to break than a twenty-year-a-pack-and-a-half-a-day habit. And he had done that. He had the will power, he knew it. And who knew how the cigarette would taste anyway? Maybe he would gag at the smoke and stamp it out immediately.

"I bet you've seen a lot of people start smoking again," said Larry.

"I've seen people do a lot worse," said Rosen.

"You mean drinking?"

"Yes."

"Maybe I better start drinking instead." Larry laughed. "That I know I can control."

"Do you want a drink?" And without waiting for a reply Rosen went to a mahogany cabinet in the corner and opened it. "We have rye, bourbon, Scotch. Brandy," he called out. "What would you like?"

"Wow," said Larry. "A full-service mortuary. I think I'll have a Scotch."

"This all right?" Rosen held up a bottle of Johnny Walker Red. "Perfect."

Rosen poured a generous shot into a water glass and brought it over.

"Thank you," said Larry. "Won't you join me?"

Rosen shook his head. Larry lifted up the glass and toasted. *"L'Chaim."* He threw back his head and was about to down the whiskey in a single swig the way actors did in Westerns. After all, he wanted the effect more than the drink. But then he heard brisk footsteps in the marble entryway. And, like an actor making an entrance on cue, his Uncle Irving was in the room, scurrying toward him. Larry repeated the word, *"L'Chaim,"* but could manage only a quick sip of his Scotch before his uncle was in his arms, hugging him warmly, saying *"boychik, boychik,"* over and over again into his shoulders.

Rosen thoughtfully relieved him of his drink while Larry looked down at his uncle's bald head and rubbed his back gently. How small Uncle Irving seemed in his arms. He could remember when Uncle Irving would scoop him up, toss him giggling into the air, catch him and pat *him* lightly on the *tush* as a signal that he could no longer play with him. His memory of Irving was always that of a busy man, scurrying here and scampering there, always coming from one place and just on his way to another. A visit would start with the warning that he could only stay a minute. He had a tenant who was complaining about the plumbing, he was on the way to the hospital to look in on a sick friend, or there was a used car in the neighborhood he wanted to look at. Larry had no memories of Uncle Irving in repose, relaxed, or pensive, simply sitting down. He was always on his feet, even at family gatherings, pouring drinks, serving food, rushing from one conversational group to another with the announcement that he had to run but was everything all right?

When Uncle Irving was younger, he bought and sold candy

stores. He would buy a store that wasn't doing well, build up its business through sheer energy and hustle, then sell it for a higher price and move on. When he noticed that the right piece of property itself could do the work for him, almost inevitably increasing in value without the drop of a single bead of perspiration from his own brow, he went into real estate. Later he moved into the stock market during a period of upswing. He was now a rich man. He owned condominiums in Miami and Israel but he still lived in Brooklyn, restlessly attending to his activities. Uncle Irving broke away from Larry and nodded toward Rosen. "Have you made a deal yet?"

Larry shook his head. Not so much in answer to the question but because he did not quite understand the question.

Uncle Irving smiled, "Good." And turned to Rosen. "Let's talk business, Mr.—"

"Rosen," supplied Rosen, extending his hand. "I was telling your nephew about our selection of burial enclosures. We have some beautiful woods. Walnut. Mahogany. Cedar."

"What about pine?" Uncle Irving ignored his hand. "Don't you have pine?"

"Yes," said Rosen slowly.

"Pine is fine then," announced Uncle Irving. "And what are you asking for it?"

Rosen handed him the brochure. "Well, as you can see, the prices are listed next to the illustrations."

Uncle Irving took the brochure and held it out at arm's length but obviously couldn't quite distinguish the numbers. He tried bringing it up close to him and squinting but was still unable to read it clearly. Finally, he shook a pair of glasses out of his breast pocket and placed them on the tip of his nose. "I see," he said, and abruptly removed the glasses and returned the brochure to Rosen in a single gesture. "Ridiculous what you're asking. Ridiculous. Now what are you taking?"

Rosen seemed confused. He was stroking his beard again. "Sir?"

"Don't sir me," snapped Uncle Irving. "I'm not Winston Churchill. I'm simply trying to talk business to you."

"But that's our price," said Rosen.

"That's *your* price. Not *my* price," said Uncle Irving. "But let's leave that for now. What I want to know is how much everything will cost us without the box. And I'll tell you what I'm talking about." He ticked the items off on his fingers: "I'm talking about no chapel here; we'll have one at the cemetery but we'll pay through you. I'm talking about a clean, well-prepared body; she should look nice. I'm talking about your wagon to take her to the cemetery. And I'm talking about the gravediggers." Then he flicked his hands over and lowered them, spreading them out like an umpire calling a runner safe. "And that's it."

Rosen coughed, went to the desk, opened a drawer, and returned with a small calculator, his fingers dancing up and down upon it. He stopped and looked up, "What about mourners? Professional mourners?"

"No professional mourners," Uncle Irving snorted. "We can all cry our own tears." And he wiped his eyes as if to offer immediate proof of his own ability to provide them.

Rosen tore off a paper tab from the calculator and handed it to Larry, saying: "I'm not recommending this." But before Larry even had a chance to read it, Uncle Irving reached over and snatched it away—as if he were grabbing a restaurant check. Then again, out of his breast pocket and onto the tip of his nose came the glasses. He studied the slip briefly with obvious distaste, removed his glasses, folded them slowly and put them back in his pocket, and turned back to Rosen. "Are you *kidding?*" he screamed. "Is this it?"

Rosen nodded.

"This is it?" he repeated incredulously.

Rosen nodded again.

"No," decided Uncle Irving. "This is not it." He slapped the slip of paper into the palm of Rosen's hand as if he had suddenly perceived the solution to a difficult problem. "Not with the discount included," he said.

"What discount?"

"The discount you're going to give us."

"Sir?"

"He's starting with the 'sir' again!" Uncle Irving roared, addressing the high-beamed ceiling and pacing across the carpet. Then he wheeled around and sailed into Rosen directly. "I can see you're just a salesman, mister. And I respect that. In my career I have been a salesman myself. But there must be a businessman around here, too. Someone I can talk business with. Where's your boss?"

Rosen, who had actually retreated until he was literally up against a side wall, was just shaking his head wordlessly. Larry flashed on the image of a bank president during a holdup refusing to divulge the combination of the vault. At the same time he thought he saw Irving wink at him in passing as he pursued Rosen.

"Where's your *boss?*" Uncle Irving was screaming. From where Larry stood it looked as if Uncle Irving's face was caught in Rosen's beard.

"My boss isn't here," said Rosen, trying to turn his head away.

Uncle Irving was relentless, his own head going with the beard. "So where is he?"

"I-I-I think he's at home," Rosen stuttered.

"He - makes - enough - here - I - imagine - his - home - has - a - telephone," Uncle Irving said as one word.

Rosen smiled weakly.

"Then call him," Uncle Irving ordered.

"Sir?" said Rosen. And his hand went up before his face. Larry couldn't tell whether the hand was up in a belated effort to hold the word back or to ward off the verbal blow that he assumed would surely be forthcoming from Uncle Irving. Larry imagined Uncle Irving positively glaring at Rosen. Because Rosen was visibly shrinking, cowering before Uncle Irving, a man who under other circumstances he would tower over.

But Uncle Irving, as Larry was beginning to realize, was no ordinary man. Now he turned away from Rosen with a sad, resigned shrug. And appealed to Larry. "Can you imagine? Every time I ask him something he sirs me back?" He winked at Larry and turned back to Rosen and spit out his words sternly, "Call your boss, sonny boy!"

Rosen quickly picked up the phone and pecked away at the push buttons. Uncle Irving looked about the room as if he at last had a chance to notice it. "Nice place," he observed to Larry. "This must be some business. Better than Hollywood, I bet."

"Mr. Liebowitz," Rosen was speaking into the phone, "I'm sorry to bother you but this is Sid Rosen and I have a gentleman here—" He stopped and started again in a louder voice. "This is Sid Rosen, Mr. Liebowitz and I have a customer here who wants to speak to you. His name is—"

The receiver jerked out of his hand. "Hello, Liebowitz," Uncle Irving shouted into it, "this is Irving Kolodny. I don't know if you remember me, but I gave you my brother Max. I gave you my brother-in-law Nat, and my brother-in-law Meyer. And I gave you my cousin Herman from the shoe store. And now my sister, Sally, is at your place. And I want to give her to you, too. So listen: We're a big family. We all intend to die. And I want to talk business. But your sonny boy here," he waved the receiver in the direction of Rosen, "is giving me prices that are ridiculous." He paused and listened, winking once more at Larry. "Okay," he leaned on the desk and said into the phone, "first, let's talk pine box."

Larry watched as his uncle listened, nodding toward him occasionally as he did so. Evidently, Liebowitz was talking pine box. "I know about inflation but I also know about markup," Uncle Irving said. "I'll give you half, fifty percent." Uncle Irving bit down on his lips in consideration. "All right. Sixty percent. It's a deal. And I just want you to prepare her nicely and drive her to the cemetery. The chapel will be there. But I'll pay through you what they charge you on your deal. And I'll pay here also for the gravediggers." Uncle Irving then took the receiver away from his ear and shook it distastefully. "No. No," he said back into it. "No professional mourners necessary, thank you. So how much is that?"

Evidently Liebowitz told him. Because Uncle Irving could not seem to believe what he heard. He removed the receiver from his ear and shook it again as if it were, in addition to being distasteful, also defective. "This can't be the price I'm hearing," he explained to both Larry and Rosen. "This can't be the price, Liebowitz," he repeated into the phone. "The cemetery isn't that far. If she was alive we could all walk there. Now please, Liebowitz: You're an intelligent man, I'm an intelligent man. Talk sense." He stopped and listened attentively. "That's more like it, Liebowitz," he said. "You're getting the idea. Now all you have to do is to come down another one hundred and fifty dollars and you can tell your boy here to wrap it up and we'll sign the papers." But suddenly Uncle Irving's face turned red and he shouted angrily, "You're not losing *any*thing, Liebowitz! I lost a sister!" Then he began nodding silently. "All right, you win," Uncle Irving said, breathing out hard in a voice of resignation. "Seventy-five dollars: We'll split the difference." He motioned with the phone for Rosen to come to it. "Wait, I'll put your man on," he said, handed the receiver to Rosen, and crossed the room quickly as if he couldn't leave enemy territory fast enough.

Larry, still sitting on the couch, moved over to make room for him. But Uncle Irving shook his head, signaling that he preferred to remain standing. Still seated, Larry could look his standing uncle right in the eyes. Until that moment he had not realized exactly how short his uncle was. Couldn't have been more than an inch or two over five feet. He also noticed that his eyes were hazel. Just like Sally's.

After receiving final instructions from his boss, Rosen hung up and came over to them, all business now. Not a drop of unction in his voice. As if two could play the game as well as one. "While I prepare the necessary papers would you like to see the deceased?" he asked coldly. The question was directed at Larry but Uncle Irving intercepted it with a quick nod, "Sure."

Rosen went to his desk and pressed an intercom buzzer. And as he sat down and reached into a drawer to assemble contract pads and papers, the oak-paneled door behind him opened and a tall black boy appeared, wearing a green apron, like a porter in an Italian hotel. "Charles," Rosen told him without looking up,

"Sally Lazarsky. We picked her up at the Jewish Hospital this morning."

Charles nodded and turned around, and Larry and Uncle Irving followed him through the doorway into a large room with a white tiled floor and stainless-steel tables in the middle of it. It reminded Larry of a hospital kitchen. Or a hotel kitchen. The one at the Ambassador Hotel in the newsreels where Bobby Kennedy was shot. Except instead of ovens and stoves along the walls there were layers of stainless-steel vaults—like trunks piled on top of each other—with handles on their sides. Charles went to one, checked the name tag hanging from it, and pulled it open.

Then it hit Larry. Not as abstract news but as personal fact. His mother was dead. He would never again have to cringe at the sound of her voice. Have to depend upon the tyranny of her praise. Have to bear the burden of her love. But there was the rub. He would never be the object of such love again either and he knew it. Maybe he should have treated her better? Let her live in LA. Sent her more money. Visited her more often. Oh God! He clenched his fists. I look at her dead and the first thing I feel is guilt. Nothing changes.

Uncle Irving next to him was covering his eyes and mumbling in Yiddish, "My sister! My little sister!" His body shook tremulously and soon he was crying, sobbing helplessly. Larry took him in his arms and held him and looked down over his slight shoulders at his mother. Across the room the black boy in the green apron was turning the pages of *Playboy*.

"You're a good boy, Larry," Uncle Irving sob-sneezed, wiping his nose with his index finger. "She was always very proud of you." And still holding Uncle Irving in his arms, Larry looked down at his dead mother again. So quiet. So still. To shoot this scene in a movie, he found himself thinking, they would have had to use a death mask. Or a freeze frame of the face and the body. You always had to fake a dead person because the heaving of the chest and the twitching of the nostrils were dead giveaways. Rather live giveaways, he corrected himself, and suddenly he was about to cry. But he blinked furiously and held his tears. He would not cry. He would not think of her. Above all he would not look at her soft upper arms and remember the warmth and comfort they had given him during his childhood. "C'mon, Uncle Irving," he said, and started to lead him away like a partner after a dance, his hand in the small of his back.

Uncle Irving shook him off and took another long look at his sister. "I would keep her closed," he said. "But it's up to you."

Larry did not understand. "What do you mean?"

"The box," Uncle Irving said. "You can keep it open or closed for the funeral."

"Then closed," said Larry. He did not want to have to look at Sally again. He knew what she looked like in life and it didn't matter what she looked like in death. And anyway, he had enough memories of her to last a lifetime. Several lifetimes.

"Closed is better," agreed Uncle Irving and signaled Charles with a wave of the hand.

Charles, still carrying his magazine, came over and began to slide the body back into the vault. "Wait," Larry said. In spite of himself he could not let her go so easily. He had to see her one more time. The hospital smock she wore looked like a nightie. Her hair was neat, each graying hair surprisingly in place. Her face was a trifle thin, as if she had just begun a diet, and a little pale. Her eyes, of course, were closed, and so too was her mouth. Almost mercifully. All Larry could think of finally was how young she looked. But he did not cry. "Okay," he told Charles and joined Uncle Irving who was waiting at the door. Uncle Irving patted him on the shoulder, then led him back into the parlor office.

No one was there.

"Rosen," Uncle Irving called out, "where are you?"

Rosen came running into the room, apologizing. "Excuse me; I had to use the lavatory."

"I could use a leak myelf," said Uncle Irving. "Where is your head?"

"The lavatory," said Rosen, "is just down the hall. Second door on the right."

Uncle Irving went off in that direction and then immediately reappeared, his finger waving in the air. "Don't sign anything," he warned, and was gone again.

Rosen tugged his beard and gave Larry a knowing smile.

"I love that man," Larry said.

"Family is everything," said Rosen. "Especially at a time like this."

Larry wondered if he was being sarcastic. But Rosen kept nodding his cherubic head so sincerely there was no doubting him.

When Uncle Irving returned, still zipping his fly, Rosen greeted him with the contract bill. Uncle Irving put on his glasses and studied it slowly. Finally, he snapped off his glasses and handed the contract to Larry. "It's all right. You can sign it." He turned to Rosen. "And can we schedule ten o'clock tomorrow morning?"

Rosen went to his desk and consulted a sheet of paper. "Fine."

Larry looked up. "So soon?"

"All right, ten-thirty," Uncle Irving said.

"I mean the day. I didn't expect it so soon as tomorrow."

"What do you want to do?" asked Uncle Irving. "Wait for the weekend and draw a bigger crowd?"

"I mean is there enough time to arrange everything?"

"What's to arrange?" asked Uncle Irving. "There's plenty of time to notify everybody. Your Aunt Ida and I will take care of everything. Why do you think they invented the telephone?"

Larry gave Rosen the signed contract. Rosen tore off a carbon copy, folded it neatly, and handed it to him.

"Come on," said Uncle Irving. "Let's go." He smiled over at Rosen. "Goodnight, young man. It's a pleasure doing business with you."

"Same here," muttered Rosen. "Goodnight, Mr. Lazar," he said to Larry. "I'm sure you'll be very pleased with the arrangements."

"Goodnight," said Larry. He followed Uncle Irving who was already briskly walking out of the room. Down the marble steps, through the entryway, out of the building to his car, a big Buick Riviera, parked in the no-parking zone directly in front of the green canopy.

Uncle Irving quickly climbed in, adjusted his seat forward, and started the motor. Then the window slid down and he leaned out of it. "Spend the night with us, Larry, why don't you? We have plenty of room."

"I have a car and driver here."

"Send him back."

"No," Larry shook his head.

"You sure?"

"I'm sure."

Uncle Irving smiled. His gold incisors glinted, reflecting his dash lights. "This way we can be sure you make it."

"I'll make it."

"So okay," said Uncle Irving. "I told you I'll take care of notifying whoever has to be notified. So you won't have that on your head."

"Thank you," Larry said.

"Don't forget. Ten-thirty. Tomorrow morning. The New Montifore. Should I tell your driver directions?"

"Don't worry," Larry said. "We'll get there." He leaned in impulsively and kissed his uncle on the cheek. "Thank you."

"For what?"

"For everything."

Uncle Irving wiped away the kiss and waved away the need for any gratitude. He blinked back some tears and said, "All right." He put the car in gear and headed south down the avenue toward Brighton and the ocean.

Larry stood at the curb, watching until the Buick stopped for a red light three blocks down. Maybe he should have gone to Brighton with his uncle. It would have been a good way to kill time, to get through the night. And spending the night in Brooklyn might have been the proper way to pay tribute to his mother. Except so far he had succeeded in keeping his mother's whining voice from whirring away in his head. So far, through an act of sheer will, he had succeeded in keeping the memory reels filed away in his brain from playing back. He didn't know how much longer he could keep them in check, but he did know a night spent with Uncle Irving and Aunt Ida couldn't possibly make things any easier.

Larry walked around to the side of the funeral parlor and found his limo. Douglas, the driver, was seated within it, smoking a cigarette, and listening to rock music. Larry got in behind him.

"Everything all right, Mr. Lazar?"

"Fine."

"Where to? Back to the hotel?"

"Yes. But first, do you by any chance have an extra cigarette?"

"Sure." Douglas held a pack of Marlboros and a lighter over his shoulder.

Larry shook a cigarette out of the pack and lit it. "Thank you." He returned the pack and the lighter and inhaled deeply.

The taste was terrific. Gold. Pure gold. Why had he ever stopped smoking in the first place? If something could give him so much pleasure it had to be good for him. Actually if not actuarially. He twirled the cigarette back and forth between his fingers, examining it and studying it, as if he had discovered some new and magical potion. But, of course, it was just an ash, glowing in the dark. He inhaled deeply again and breathed out. Now the pleasure was even dizzying and he was fascinated by the blue gray smoke emitting from his mouth. It curled upward reminding him of the balloon that came out of the mouth of a character in a comic strip. He felt a little bit like a comic-strip character himself, a cliché caught up in a traditional but still unreal situation. But then his mother could always reduce him to that.

8

Flatbush Avenue passed in a blur. It no longer contained the meccas, the Strand and the Fox, the Albee, the Paramount, the movie palaces that featured first-run films and in-person stage shows. In fact, the Paramount, Larry recalled hearing, was now a college gym. And except for A & S, the department stores were gone too: Namm's where he had once worked as a stock boy on Thursday afternoons and Saturdays, Loeser's where he had bought his first sports jacket. Larry closed his eyes and turned away from the window. Everything here brought back memories.

Even the bridge they were approaching. Larry remembered the actual aesthetic pang he used to feel at the sight of it. Once he discovered the beauty of the Brooklyn Bridge, viewing it from the Manhattan Bridge or the Williamsburg Bridge, he always felt cheated in crossing it. What a marvelous natural sweep! The suspension supports forming such perfectly fluid arcs. Both the Manhattan and the Williamsburg bridges somehow had been hastily constructed by a child prodigy with a giant erector set. Even their cables looked stringy. But the Brooklyn Bridge was the work of a poet. There was even a poem about it that they used to read in grade school. By Richard Le Gallienne. Eva's father. It was called "The Brooklyn Bridge at Dawn." Larry could not remember the poem at all. But that did not matter. The bridge was a poem itself.

How many times had he crossed over these bridges? They had been his yellow brick roads, leading him on, to Manhattan and the theater and beyond, so that all of the flickering-bulb-neon-lights dreams of his youth had come true. He recalled his first paying jobs as an assistant stage manager in a long-running off-Broadway hit and as a walk-on in a Broadway show that ran three performances. In his first role in television he was cast as a corpse, the corpse of an Italian kid, and played the part to the hilt, writing out a long character study of the life the corpse had lived, in preparation. In those days he always acted as if his life depended on it. Because it did. He knew if he failed to secure a foothold in theater and show business he would certainly fall by the wayside. Competition *was* stiff. For every part available there were thirty actors waiting at any given moment in Cromwell's Drugstore alone. And failure for him would have meant a return to Brooklyn. And the old values. Of money on the table. Of put up or shut up. Of a boy has to make a living. That he could never have endured. His dreams would have gone out the window. When television moved out to California, he picked up a used Ford, and with his furniture stashed in a rented U-Haul behind him and his wife and baby daughter beside him, drove out to the coast like a latter-day Okie.

The first years in LA were tough. He worked as a messenger, a waiter, a short-order cook, all the old temporary employments, as he hustled for acting jobs. Once he almost got himself killed on a crazy runaway horse doing a TV Western. It was desperation time. Until he landed a running part on the "Here Comes Uncle" sitcom as the Italian kid. After one season he was coming up with ideas for episodes. He sold the story for one and collaborated on writing the teleplay of two others. In the third year of the show he was given the chance to direct.

From then on he knew he had found his calling. He registered for night courses in directing at AFI and in film editing at Loyola. And when "Here Comes Uncle" after four years went the way of all sitcoms, he cowrote and directed episodes of others. Then he decided he had better move on before he became labeled a sitcom episodic director and writer as surely as he had been typed as the Italian kid.

With Harry Hearns, a comedy writer with whom he had cowritten two "Here Comes Uncle" episodes, he rented an office in the Artists and Writers Building on Little Santa Monica

Boulevard in Beverly Hills, and collaborated on his first theatrical, a comedic treatment of the Haight-Ashbury scene up in San Francisco. They sold the script but the picture was never made. They switched the locale and wrote about the hippies living in the East Village of Manhattan. They sold this script and it was made. It got some great reviews and did decent business.

On that basis their next deal was not only to write but to produce. And that was for *Ms. and Mr.* It was keyed into the burgeoning Women's Liberation Movement. The studio was anxious to do it. A star was cast, a name director lined up, a start date set. Then the director came down with mono. As producers, Harry and Larry, were involved in the desperate search for a replacement. And, at the propitious moment, Larry suggested himself. After all, he knew the script down to his fingertips, he knew how to work with actors having been an actor himself, and he had directed in television. He sweated out a nervous weekend before the studio finally okayed him.

Ms. and Mr. was a huge hit. Critically and at the box office. Sally alone must have seen it fifty times. Every night she went to a different Brooklyn movie house and reported collect the audience's reaction. Then she branched out to Manhattan and Queens. Finally, she was even venturing up to the Bronx and over to Staten Island. She would always insist it was the best picture he had ever made. But, so too, would his detractors. Because after *Ms. and Mr.*, he had enough clout to make his pictures his way, the Larry Lazar way, with his own artistic imprint and according to his own tastes. Produced, written, and directed by Larry Lazar.

When the limo pulled up in front of the Sherry Netherland Larry told the driver that he could go home. But Douglas protested. "I'm supposed to stay on duty all night. This car is booked for twenty-four hours."

"Go home," Larry repeated. "I'll cover for you."

"Another man comes on shift in the morning."

"Fine," said Larry. "And thanks." He did not wait for Douglas to run around back and open the door for him. He opened the door himself, wished the kid good luck, and told him to give his regards to Les, his acting teacher.

It had begun to rain. Slightly. But he had the protection of the canopy until he reached the revolving doors.

Upstairs, as he pulled off the messages that were wrapped around his doorknob, the phone was ringing. Messages in hand he ran to the phone on the end table and picked it up. It was Jane. He sat down on the sitting-room couch and began to twirl and untwirl the wire. "I just walked in this very minute."

"I was about to hang up."

"I tried to get you before. Did Dolores tell you?"

"Yes."

"Then that's the miracle of the week."

"Is everything all right?"

He kicked his shoes off and leaned back and told Jane all about the arrangements for the funeral tomorrow and that he would fly home as soon as he took care of whatever legal matters there were. He didn't want to stay in New York a minute longer than necessary. Had Mike Lasher called by any chance?

"No, but Sidney Stein did. I told him you were in New York. He'll call you there. Why aren't you staying at the Plaza?"

"The Plaza was full. They couldn't get me in. But you know the Sherry." He looked around the large sitting room. "It's a nice suite. How are the kids?"

"They said to tell you they miss you."

"I miss them," said Larry. "Kiss them for me."

"You can kiss them yourself when you get back. I'm not speaking to Conor."

"What's the matter?"

"Nothing. I'll tell you when you get back."

"You know something, Jane," it suddenly occurred to him; "now that my mother is gone, we could live in New York. We'll talk about that when I get back. We'll have lots to talk about."

They said goodnight to each other and he puckered up his lips and made a loud kissing sound before hanging up. Then he looked over the messages as he went to the refrigerator in the pantry. Jane had called before. And a Michael. Mike Lasher? He looked at the return number. No, that couldn't be Mike Lasher. It was a New York number. Unless Mike was so excited about the script of *Remember, Remember* that he immediately flew East to discuss it with Larry face to face. Larry looked down at the number again. No, that couldn't be Mike. It was a West Side number. But then who the hell was Michael? Oh yes. The girl from the studio's New York office. The Audrey Hepburn type with the handsome *schwartze* girl friend.

The last message was from Sidney Stein. Larry put it in his pocket, the others into the trash can, and opened the refrigerator. There were a few nibbles of caviar left. And almost the whole bottle of wine. Larry poured himself a goblet and broke off a piece of toast and scooped up the caviar. God, he loved the taste! Worth every calorie of it. The wine tasted good with it, too. But then what wouldn't? Even a Fresca.

He retrieved the message from Sidney and studied it.

Strange that he should be involved with Sidney at this time. Because Sidney had written, in his novel *Howling Horowitz*, the definitive American-Jewish mother. After Sidney's book every Jewish-mother character seemed derivative. A cliché. It was as if Sidney had broken the mold by capturing the epitome. No one could ever dare to write about such a character again. Not seriously. It would be like taking on a teenager after Salinger. The movie that had been made out of the book was a disaster. Because they had treated the book too reverentially. That was always a mistake. When it came to movies, a book had to be treated as a starting point for a blueprint. As a starting point for a blueprint to be shot. As a starting point for a blueprint to be shot and then cut and edited. And nothing more. Or as nothing more, Larry smiled to himself, than a concept. *Catcher in the Rye, War and Peace,* the Bible, *Hamlet, Oedipus Rex,* were all nothing more than concepts. *Herbie and Milty,* though, was a movie. And Sidney's calling him was neither a concept nor a movie but a coincidence. Especially tonight of all nights. The night after his own American-Jewish mother died. Larry put the message into his pocket. After the funeral, he would stroke Sidney. It was something positive he could accomplish this trip East.

But first he would eat. It was the least he could do as an American-Jewish son. According to the cliché, anyway. He would go down and have dinner in the hotel. Or better yet walk up the street to the Russian Tea Room. First he would have a little more wine.

He poured another glass and, sipping, went to the window and looked down at the park again and at its marvelous medieval aura, like that of a storybook castle. He began to feel mellow and sad at the same time, nostalgic for things he couldn't remember, for legends that had happened long before his time. It wasn't only the view and it certainly couldn't be the wine. Because it happened to him whenever he was in New York. He always fell in love with the city. And it would happen with his scarcely noticing it. In fact, hadn't he just suggested to Jane the possibility of their living in New York again? They could do it. There was nothing to hold them back. They could probably find even better schools for the kids and it certainly would be a lot different than it was when he and Jane had last lived here. Now they had money. They were out of that scramble. They could really live the life of a Gershwin tune or a Hart lyric.

He turned away from the window and poured himself another half glass of wine and decided to forget about dinner. He hated to eat alone. He didn't need the calories. And anyway, he was tired. It had been a long day. He would take a shower. Finish off the caviar and wine. And go to bed. Tomorrow was going to be difficult. It would be the last day, so to speak, he'd have to spend with his mother. And any day spent with her was always difficult. Besides, who ever heard of an easy—or pleasant—funeral?

He enjoyed the shower, the warm water was soothing, and the soap, lathering as in a commercial, left him feeling cleansed and refreshed. He dried off with a big towel. The bed was roomy; he would not have to share it with anyone. And the mattress was surprisingly firm. He was sure he would drift off to sleep in a matter of moments.

Instead, he began to toss and turn. If he lay on his right side, the moonlight piercing in from the sides and between the slats of the venetian blinds upset him. If he lay on his left side, facing the bathroom, he could hear a slight but metronomic drip from the shower which disturbed him. And when he lay on his back, he found himself staring at the swaying shadows cast on the ceiling by the venetian blinds and listening for the drip at the same time. But then he realized it was always difficult for him to fall asleep in a new bed. And he missed Jane. Not in a horny way. But just the familiar presence of her body next to his. Beside him, right there reassuringly. No, that was not true either. He missed her because if she was there he could begin making love even though he wasn't horny with the sure knowledge that soon he would be horny because it didn't matter which came first, the desire or the horniness. And after sex he could almost always fall asleep. If only to avoid having to try to have sex again at his age.

He turned onto his right side again and wondered if maybe he should jerk off. Even at his age. But no, his fingers reached down and verified, he was not at all horny; his penis was far from tumescent. Which meant hard but sounded like soft. Which he was. He could, of course, try to summon up an image, conjure up a memory of raunches past. But which one? It was always tricky. Not that it mattered so much how he started because it would always slip into montage anyway. He thought of Jane and laughed. Thinking of your own wife. That had to be the pits.

He thought of the black stewardess and now he was getting somewhere. Because immediately she became the yoga teacher, Inman, and he remembered how she had allowed him to press her hand. *Press her hand,* how Victorian! Soon he would even begin fantasizing bare ankle!

He turned over and lay on his back and gave up the idea of jerking off. All he knew was that he did not want to start thinking about his mother. But there was no way out. In death as in life she was not easy to shake off. Like a cliché. A cliché American-Jewish mother. But she was *his* cliché. And no matter how well Sidney had written the cliché it was still not *her.* Sally Lazarsky was not another banal figure. She was unique. Sui generis. The one and only mother of Larry Lazar. Maybe he would even some day do a movie about her. It might not be very commercial but it would still be a healthy thing for him to do.

But who could play his mother? Streisand? She would be box office. But Barbra was into her own thing about Jewish women. And she would be trouble. She ate up directors. Not that he was afraid of her. He could handle her. Because he wouldn't take shit from her. Still, who needed that aggravation? Besides, no matter how much he controlled Barbra, it would still end up a Streisand picture. Not a Larry Lazar film. And he wasn't about to break his balls to make a Barbra Streisand picture. Especially about *his* mother.

Who else was there? He ran down the usual list of female bankables. Goldie Hawn? Interesting. Not enough substance. Minnelli? No, she was too much the shiksa. Midler? She could be interesting but he had no desire to work with her. Because if he worked with her he might as well have worked with Barbra in the first place. Jill Clayburgh was a possibility. He liked her work. She could be desperate without being shrill. Diane Keaton? He laughed out loud. It would positively kill Woody to have her cast as an American-Jewish mother. Probably keep Woody in analysis for at least another ten years. Still, Keaton might be able to do it. Despite her Wasp edges she was a possibility. Besides, he always liked the idea of casting against type. Mia Farrow? No, that would put Woody away. Fonda? The problem with Fonda was he always thought of her father when he looked at her. Felt he was watching old Henry—or rather a young Henry—in drag. And Jane would insist on a part for a Cesar Chavez character. In a Brooklyn Jewish candy store, yet. No, Jane would be wrong. Which left Sally Field. The studio would love it. He'd tell them he was making a *Smokey and the Yenta.* Very salable.

But artistically it would be better to use an unknown. And cheaper, too. Find a good New York actress; they were all over the place, if you knew where to look for them and how to spot them, and get a performance out of her. Like Meryl Streep. Only this year's Meryl Streep, Mary Steenburgen. Or next year's Mary Steenburgen, that McGovern girl.

And then just tell his mother's story straight. Only with humor and charm and reality. Review Sally's whole frustrated life. A childhood spent in a Williamsburg ghetto dreaming of escape . . . She thinks of herself as a singer. A Sophie Tucker. An Ethel Merman . . . She meets his father, Meyer. He's good-looking and nimble on his feet in the ballroom . . . She casts him as a dancer. They'll have a Ginger Rogers–Fred Astaire life, only Jewish, she daydreams . . . Instead Meyer turns out to be one of life's losers . . . A laborer, a loader of Kirsch's sodas . . . She can never forgive him for marrying *her* . . . As if Meyer was a white slaver who kidnapped her and then proceeded to imprison her in a life of impoverishment . . . The fact is that Meyer is a decent sort in a time when decent sorts were shit upon. The Great Depression . . . Meyer loses his job . . . He goes on WPA and the family is constantly changing apartments to get rent concessions while Sally forever lives an ear-splitting life of shrieking desperation . . . Finally, they move in with Sally's parents . . . In the back of their candy store. Where his grandmother waits on customers while his grandfather reads Gogol and recites Pushkin. They are a truly talmudic couple in retrospect. And Chekhovian.

And Sally is your typical Jewish mother . . . overprotective, overbearing, overweight. Except that for a Jewish mother she has a *goyishe* tongue. She curses like a teenager. At her husband. At her son. At her father. At life in general. Her life is not a happy one. She has too much vitality and wit and imagination and energy to be cooped up in back of a candy store. In the store itself she is a performer . . . with a sharp tongue . . . a wise word for everybody. Their apartment is like a backstage dressing room where she lounges and lingers before her moments on stage, out front, in the arena as it were: the store . . . The candy store. Larry forgot he was outlining a scenario and remembered the actual place with an acute sense memory: the smell of the store, the Horlick malted commingled with the newsprint of magazines —books his parents and grandparents called them—and that of cigarettes, smoked and unsmoked, packaged and loose. For a penny a piece his parents sold "loosies," Marvels or Avalons, the cheapest brands.

The soda fountain had a marbled top and in front of it the floor was a marvelous mosaic of inlaid octagons of black and white tile. Behind the fountain was a wooden ramp and a mirrored wall. The ceiling was of corrugated steel—or tin—and the rest of the floor was covered with linoleum, buckling everywhere. In front of the fountain were three red-Leatherette-covered swirling stools, but one rendered forever useless, the boxes of candy piled high before it in tiered rows. Penny candies. Two-cent candies. Nickel candies. Hootens. Frozen Twists. Knickerbockers. Joya Halavahs. Milky Ways. Clark bars.

Toward the rear of the store was the "rent payer" . . . the pinball machine. How many nights had Larry been kept awake by the ringing of its bells and the whines of customers complaining loudly that "the machine had tilted itself," and warning each other to "quit leaning on the machine"? Larry could chart his growth in relation to the machine. He remembered the first day he could peer over it, pull back the plunger, and actually see where a ball was going. His mother had the magical key which could open the machine and give him a free game. He would try to coax it out of her with troublesome pleas. It was his big reward for being a good boy: a pinball game.

Dinner was pot roast in one of the four booths that surrounded the pinball-machine island. It was always interrupted by the need to answer phone calls, make change, wait on customers, selling everything from stamps to school supplies. No one in the history of his family ever ate a dinner straight through. To this day he gulped his food down. On summer evenings, immediately after eating, he would have to race seven blocks with a wagon to pick up *News*es and *Mirror*s so that their candy store would be the first in the immediate three-block area to have the papers. A corner booth wiped clean served as his desk, his study space, where he first pored over the mysteries of multiplication and division. Addition and subtraction he had already learned in the palm of his hand making change. In the same way that he knew how to make an egg cream before he could spell the word "milk."

In the afternoon when he came home from school he would run around the fountain counter and, standing on the ramp, lean forward and punch out of the gleaming chrome spigots an egg cream or a malted for himself. That was his first performance in public, standing on that wooden platform, literally milking every moment, before an audience of envious kids. Kids who had to cough up their own money to get an egg cream or malted never half so sweet . . .

Larry slipped his fingers beneath the stretch band of his jockey shorts and felt the mound of flesh that was his stomach. No wonder he was getting fat, had a weight problem, all the sweets he used to eat, the lousy eating habits he had developed. A snack was anything he could put his fingers on. A meal was often a series of snacks. Breakfast, for example, in winter was a pretzel, a hot chocolate, and a Charlotte Russe. He loosened his grip on his stomach, removed his fingers from beneath his shorts. It was a miracle that he did not have diabetes. Or an ulcer. Or a bad heart. Like that which killed his mother.

That, and unhappiness, he decided, and returned to the scenario: Sally is never happy . . . not even after World War II breaks out and Meyer finally gets a steady job again, going to work in the Brooklyn Navy Yard as a painter . . . Still with each passing year Sally steadily complains . . . rues her life . . . heaps both abuse and guilt upon Larry . . . yes, Larry . . . Because if it were not for Larry, she lets him know, she would have left her husband, Meyer, long ago to discover her true destiny in the West . . . She is forever singing "California, Here I Come," with the Jolson record as backing.

But when she finally comes to California . . . after Meyer dies . . . after Larry achieves some initial success . . . it is a disaster . . . She refuses to take a bus, to ride the RTD with the *schwartzes* . . . has to be driven everywhere . . . argues with Jane constantly . . . drives him crazy by putting him down every chance she gets, by destroying, with a word here, a gesture there, the self-esteem he has struggled so hard to build up . . .

Sally is just an all-around bitch . . . Larry knows that if his marriage is to last, if he himself is to survive, he has to get her out of the house . . . Moves her into a residential hotel . . . But that's even worse . . . She isn't good enough to stay in his Hollywood house, she rants. He is ashamed of her in front of the goyim, is that it? She isn't good enough for his Hollywood phony-baloney-crony friends? Because she doesn't have the champagne-and-caviar manners of her son, her sophisticated son, Mister Hollywood?

Above all, he reminded himself, he must not forget her last visit to California. *That* would make for a wonderful Larry Lazar set piece. The kind of thing he did so well. He had met Sally at LAX as usual. And, as usual, she was her overbearing self. Complaining as she came off the plane about the fact that he had not sent her money for a first-class seat so she could have spread her ass in comfort and not have had to worry about a baby sitting next to her pissing on her, complaining about the movie that was unwatchable anyway before the reel broke down and the food which was entirely inedible, complaining about the pilot who she was sure was drunk because of all the air pockets he kept hitting and the stewardesses, whores in the sky, too busy making arrangements to get laid when the plane hit LA to respond to her slightest needs. In short, she told him, as they waited for her baggage to come down the chute at the carousel, it had been a terrible trip and she felt rotten and she could tell him in all honesty that she really wasn't looking forward to spending two more fucking weeks just like it in Los Angeles which had to be the world's most boring place under the sun anyway.

"Then why did you come?" he had asked, his eyes peeled for her three ivory-colored Samsonite suitcases.

"To see you. I'm willing to go through anything just to see you. Even two weeks in LA. But, ah," she waved her hand, "you've never been able to appreciate even half the sacrifices I make for you."

"What would you be doing if you hadn't come here?" He pointed at two suitcases that came slamming down the chute. "Are those yours?"

"No. They probably lost mine. This fucking airline. With its drunken pilots and whores for stewardesses I can just imagine what its baggage smashers must be like." She took off her wide-brimmed floppy hat and fanned herself. "I'll tell you what I'd be doing. I wouldn't be sweating to death in the middle of October, I'll tell you that. And look at that air." She pointed toward the exit doors of the terminal. "It'll be a miracle I don't get an asthma attack the moment I walk out of here. Those two are mine."

Larry retrieved the suitcases and soon the third, a small one that she could have hand-carried, appeared. He handed that one to her and led her to the door where she showed her baggage-check stubs and bad temper to the security officer. Together they crossed the street and walked toward the lot where he had parked his BMW. All the while she didn't stop talking. "Where's your wife? Where are my grandchildren? Couldn't you at least have brought them to the airport to meet me? Or has your wife completely poisoned their minds against me? I remember when they were younger they would always come. They would run into my arms. They were so cute then. You were a cute child, yourself. Took after me. I was a beautiful baby. 'Oh you must have been a beautiful baby'; I used to sing that song. Cuteness runs in my family. You're very lucky in that respect. I see you don't have a new car. I told you *Hostile Relationships* wouldn't be such a big hit. I knew nobody would like that stuff about me. You got me all wrong. Nobody could rant on like that all day long, never letting up for a single moment. It wasn't really real at all. And the actress who played me. Where did you dig her up? She must have fucked for every executive in the studio, and their fathers, and maybe gave a little head to their sons, too. Is that why you used her? I hope she gave you a good fuck at least. Because she gave the worst performance I ever saw in a major American film."

Larry listened to it all, wondering how long he could take it. *If* he could take it. He put her baggage in the trunk and slammed it shut. And he was about to start the car and head out toward Century Boulevard and the San Diego Freeway when he reached into his pocket and felt something. Suddenly he was struck with a divine inspiration and knew it. The kind of idea that unfroze a blocked script or opened up a whole new approach to a character in acting or allowed scenes to be reedited in postproduction. He took the joint out of his pocket and lit it with the dashboard lighter.

"My son, the Hollywood junkie," Sally observed, as he inhaled deeply.

Larry calmly handed her the joint. "Smoke this."

"You know I don't smoke reefers." She held the joint out at arm's length as if it were a reptile or a burning worm.

"Smoke it," Larry repeated.

"Do you want me to have an asthma attack?" She pushed the joint back toward him. "What are you trying to do? Kill me."

"Smoke it. I won't leave this airport until you do."

"And if I don't?"

"Then I'm going to take your suitcases out of the trunk and put you on the next plane back to New York."

"Are you serious?"

"I've never been more serious in my life." He folded his arms and sat back and waited.

"I really believe you."

"I'm not kidding, Ma. I want you to smoke that joint. And every other joint I give you while you're here."

"How many will that be?"

"As many as it takes."

"As it takes for what?"

"For you to mellow out. To act like a reasonably happy and contented and normal human being." He took her hand and guided it toward her mouth. "Now inhale. And let the smoke stay in your lungs."

"You really mean it?"

"I really mean it. If you don't smoke this joint you'll make the Guiness World Book of Records for the shortest stay in the history of LA."

She shrugged, yawned, inhaled, and coughed, it seemed, all at the same time. "Again," he said.

"You're crazy."

"Not as crazy as you. Again."

She inhaled once more, coughing out less. "Tastes like a skimpy cigarette that somebody dipped in wine and let dry in shit," she observed mildly.

"Keep smoking."

"You want me to get cancer?"

"You smoke cigarettes anyway."

"That's not the point."

"How much does this cost?" She waved the joint.

"For you. Nothing."

"And that's all I think it's worth."

"Keep inhaling."

She settled back in the seat and held the joint casually now as if it were a cigarette. "This is no big deal." She drew in on it. "If it makes you happy I don't give a shit. I've always been willing to do anything to make you happy."

"Again." He did not want to hear a litany of her sacrifices for him. "Again," he repeated.

"I'll smoke it. I'm smoking it. You can start driving. I'm getting very hungry. You think I ate any of the crap those whores were serving on the plane? Here, do you want a puff?"

"As a matter of fact I do." Larry took a hit, passed the joint back to her, and finally turned the ignition key.

By the time they reached the freeway Sally had become comparatively quiet. Later, smiling contentedly to herself, she neither complained about the hotel he had booked her into nor the restaurant he took her to for dinner where they met Jane and the kids. In the next two weeks he taught her how to roll her own and she was a willing student. She flaunted her use of grass as she flaunted everything else and his friends thought she was a delight. His crew fell in love with her as she lit up with them, for them. She became so mellow that his kids vied for her company and even Jane seemed to enjoy her. Most important of all, *he* was able to endure her and survive her visit. It turned out to be her most enjoyable stay in LA. At least, he had given her that.

With Sally still on his mind Larry finally sensed himself drifting into sleep. Or, at least, toward sleep. Because he was not sure he was sleeping. He could still see the light leaking in through the slats in the blinds, the stolid wooden cream-colored ones, instead of the oilcloth window shades his family had had that would always suddenly shoot up at the most inopportune moments and then rip away from their staplings whenever you tried to pull them down when they got stuck. Venetian blinds always represented class to Sally. She viewed them with envy when she saw them at richer relatives' like Uncle Irving and Aunt Ida's. And now—was he sleeping and was it a dream?—he could see Sally standing in front of the blinds, one hand resting on the Louis chair he had draped his pants over, as if she were posing for a picture or about to make a speech.

Surely, if he knew Sally, it was a speech. And surely, if he knew himself, it had better be a dream.

"This is a nice place," she was saying, extending her left arm without removing her right hand from the back of the chair. "I'll bet it cost a dollar or two." She slowly looked around the room. "A lot better than where I lived, Mister Hollywood."

Larry sat up in bed and tried to remain calm. After all, it was only a dream. Obviously. Look at Sally: She was dressed for a dream. In a diaphanous white cotton see-through negligee, the outlines of her huge breasts were clearly discernible even in the half-light. But still, even though he knew it was a dream, he found himself compelled to answer her: "The studio is paying for this," he said.

"The studio," she spit out. "Too bad the studio wasn't paying for my apartment." Then she smiled and began to move toward him, swaying her hips, undulating, being as seductive as she could be considering the proportions of her elephantine body. At the same time she was still taking in the room, pausing to view her own apparition in the large vanity mirror. "Yes," she repeated, one hand behind her neck, tilting her head, "too bad the studio wasn't paying."

"Ma, lay off," he said. "It's too late."

"It's never too late." She turned away from the mirror and continued undulating toward him. "Why couldn't I live in California?"

She was near enough to the bed now so that he could reach out and touch her. That is, if she was there. Really there. But Larry was afraid to make an actual test. Instead, he argued back. "Because it didn't work out. Don't you remember? Because you and Jane couldn't get along."

"And you took the shiksa's side?"

"The shiksa is my wife."

"And I'm not your mother?" Sally was now sitting down on the bed. Larry squirmed to the other side. But she was reaching over, pulling him back toward her. "I'm the only mother you'll ever have, Mister Hollywood." She was cuddling up to him, embracing him from behind, her big tits burrowing into his back, her hand groping for his penis and then stroking it softly. "And you let me freeze to death. Not from the weather. I'm not talking about the weather. But inside. I was cold something terrible. I was alone." And she kept stroking him.

Until Larry felt himself come.

He slowly awoke, annoyed with himself for having a wet dream at his age. That was almost as bad as jerking off. Like the character in Sidney Stein's book. But almost immediately he also felt relieved—and reassured—to realize that it was definitely only a dream. That the image of Sally was gone.

Disappeared.

Larry picked up his watch from the night table. It was only 12:30. He showered again, dressed, and went downstairs.

Yes, he needed a breath of air. And a bite. He could also use a little exercise. Stretch the legs a bit. It would help him sleep after spending the whole day confined in the plane and limos.

The rain had stopped. And the lights were with him: He could cross Fifth Avenue and go for a walk in the park. The medieval vista he had seen from his sitting room window. When he was younger how often had he walked through Central Park? From Fifty-ninth Street to 110th Street? From one corner to the other? On hot summer nights, talking, planning, dreaming. With Sidney Stein. With Max Isaacs. With Mira. With Allen Gates. With any number of people. One could walk away the night, those days so to speak, in Manhattan never worrying about anything except the weather. Now entering the park would be tempting fate. And tonight of all nights he wasn't ready for a *Where's Poppa?* scene.

Larry inhaled deeply, turned left, and rounded the corner, heading down toward Lexington. There he could pick up a newspaper, get a cup of coffee. Do the sort of thing he could never do in Beverly Hills. There were people in the street, pouring out of a movie theater's last show. Larry liked that. He hurried past a Burger King, its fluorescent lighting seeping into the street through its glass doors and windows. He crossed Park Avenue and stopped in the doorway of a small grocery-delicatessen, blue and red beer signs glowing around a clock in its window.

A chubby Puerto Rican clerk was waiting on two women in out-of-style short shorts and tall high-heeled boots. One of them turned and stared at him, smiling. Larry returned the smile, shaking his head. He didn't want that. Not tonight. Certainly not the night before his mother's funeral. Especially after he had had a wet dream. Besides, at his age he never liked trying to come twice anymore for fear of failure. Or nausea. Or both. He left the doorway and walked on to the next corner.

Lexington Avenue had changed. There was still life there, to be sure, but it seemed tired, enervated. The signs on store fronts lacked luster, painted over too many times, and the plastic booths of the coffee shops were all in dull fading pastels. He picked up a *News* and *Times* at the newsstand on Fifty-first Street and then continued down to Third Avenue. That would be more his style.

And, indeed, Third Avenue seemed to have been lit by a different—and contemporary—designer. One who believed in nightlight that simulated daylight. In sharper, clearer, yet more subtle tones. And the people walking the street had perkiness and direction. On Lexington everyone had seemed to be wending their weary way homeward. But on Third everyone was going somewhere. To a bar. To a restaurant. To an apartment for a nightcap and a party. This was more like the New York he missed. The New York he liked to remember.

He walked into P. J. Clarke's and for a moment time stood still. How many times had he pushed his way to the bar and waited for a date or looked for a pickup? It wasn't crowded now because it was late and a weekday night. Larry looked over the field. The men at the bar all looked as if they sold space and the women all looked as if their space was taken. Nothing really to choose from. He checked out the back room. No one he knew. No, he decided, this was not the place for him tonight. But then what was? He bought a pack of cigarettes from the coin machine and while tearing it open thought of someone he could call in the middle of the night. Someone who might even have a party going. Lighting a sweet-tasting cigarette he went to the phone booth and dialed.

Book Two

9

Larry vividly remembered the first time he met Allen.

Wearing a snappy John Barrymore fedora with the brim down over his long, thin rubbery face, a Joel McCrea *Foreign Correspondent* double-breasted raincoat hanging from his narrow shoulders, a Bogart cigarette dangling from his curling lips, he had walked into the San Remo with a mock theatricality—or cinematicality—and a genuine girl on each arm. Oh how Larry envied him at that moment! For as Allen Gates made his entrance through the Bleecker Street corner doors he seemed the embodiment of everything Larry had ever dreamt of being.

It was Larry's first night as a Village resident. He had found a third-floor cold-water walk-up on Thompson Street: a bedroom-living room, a kitchen. The john was in the hall. It had a fireplace but also two grimy windows that looked down into a dreary areaway. The best feature was the rent: dirt cheap. The worst drawback was the fact that the previous occupant was a cat owner. Who had committed suicide.

Larry washed the apartment down, scrubbed it, and painted it before moving in. Then he cooked his first meal there, Minute Rice and sausages; afterward, without changing out of his paint-smeared jeans, he walked over to the San Remo on MacDougal Street, pushed his way up to the crowded bar, and ordered a beer. Then he stood there, an uncomfortable solitary, trying for all the world to look as if he belonged, really belonged there. A denizen of the Village at last. Someone licensed to make the scene.

Larry sipped his beer, eyeing those lucky enough to be talking to each other. Searching for a familiar face. Someone he knew from college or acting class. Someone he could latch on to. Anyone. He yearned to be part of a group like those milling about him. Having intelligent discussions about art or politics, literature and life. Even baseball. Like the two men behind him talking about Casey Stengel. Just to belong. But much as he craned his neck he could find no one he knew there. Not even vaguely. He watched the doors—the front and side doors that led into the bar and the back doors that opened into the dining room—observing each new entrant hopefully. He simply wasn't ready to go back to his own apartment. Not yet. Now that he lived in the Village he ached to be part of its Bohemian life. After all, that was why he moved there. Had fought to move there. Over his mother's strenuous objections. How could he desert her? Leave her alone with his father in Brooklyn? As if that were a fate worse than death. And besides, how could he possibly afford it? It made no financial sense. He didn't even have a job, a real job, a job fit for a college graduate. Certainly he had not graduated college just to sell shoes. Why didn't he look for a job as a teacher? As a professional? As a something? Instead, he was selling shoes and still going to school. Acting school. Did Tyrone Power ever go to acting school? Had John Garfield ever taken classes? Did Marlon Brando have a teacher?

As a matter of fact the answers were yes. But Larry knew there was no point arguing rationally with Sally. He just kept his silence and made his move. It was a move he had long dreamed of making, a dream that sustained him during his last two years of college. He was an actor, a theater artist, and he felt there was no way his art could flourish and develop in the back of a candy store in a decaying neighborhood. Not with his mother there. And as soon as he graduated, he promised himself, saving for the day, he would move to Greenwich Village.

College graduation ceremonies were on a Sunday. That Monday Larry walked the Village streets, visiting real-estate offices, roaming into random buildings and checking with supers, asking chess players in the park and waitresses in the coffeehouses for leads to cheap apartments. And by Thursday he found his pad. Amy, a blond girl in his acting class with very white skin who always wore black hose and worked as a coffeehouse waitress, told him of the suicide on Thompson Street. Larry did not hesitate. Dead was dead, especially a stranger. And an apartment was an apartment, especially a cheap one. He ran over to the building and found the Italian super at supper. Slipped him two five-dollar bills and secured the apartment. On the long subway ride back to Brooklyn he felt buoyant and triumphant. And not even Sally's subsequent harangues could diminish his elation or anticipation.

But as he nursed his beer, staring down at the tiled floor of the Remo, Larry definitely did not feel like returning to the apartment. For one thing it smelled of freshly drying paint. For another thing, to tell the truth, it already depressed him. Because after enjoying the initial exhilaration of freedom and independence he had begun to feel hemmed in. There was no phone there. He had had enough money just to cover electricity and gas deposits. But not for a phone. Even during his bleakest days in Brooklyn, in the recesses of the lower depths of the candy store, he could always be reached by phone. Soon he would discover a neighbor with one. Or scrape up enough money to get a phone of his own. But meanwhile, he would be living like a Raskolnikov in a geography that had already provided the setting for a suicide.

Two sailors walked into the bar. Then an old man with a beard hawking magazines. A waiter came out of the kitchen with an armful of pasta and veal platters and deposited them in a booth. Two pretty girls, one long, dark, and sleek, and the other chubbier and light-haired, sat there drinking wine. Across the table were two men in three-piece suits. One was holding a match a dramatically long time before lighting his cigarette. He finished what he was saying and they all laughed. But Larry noticed he licked his fingers after he finally lit the cigarette and took his first puff. Larry prided himself on noticing such little things. As an actor they were his chestnuts, to be stored away for use in future performances. The actor was an observer first, internally and externally, monitoring all his feelings and perceptions, and a performer second, as he later projected and expressed them. Reality was the base on which an actor structured his characterization.

Truth in theater was the transformation and communication of reality through the instrument of the actor. But if something was not real, did not derive from a sense memory of the experience of reality, then not all the technique in the world would help it achieve truth. Larry had learned that from his acting teachers and believed in it passionately. Up to a point. Because there was a part of reality which was not real. Not *real* reality. For example, there was that part of his own daily life which was consumed with the dream of becoming a great actor. At the same time he knew he could not live his life as if that dream were real. Yet it was that dream which gave him the courage to endure any reality. Well, almost any reality. In any event in his dream began his reality. But not *real* reality. He knew that. It was just his private reality to sustain him. But it was all very tricky stuff. And he knew that too. It was like what Scott Fitzgerald had written about the ability to have conflicting and contradictory ideas as a sign of intelligence. In other words he could have the strength of his confusion. Which he had. But still that didn't make it any less confusing.

Larry was on his way back to the crowded bar to deposit his empty glass there when the fellow in the fedora made his grand entrance. One of the girls with him was Amy, the black-legged coffeehouse waitress he knew from acting class, who had told him of the apartment on Thompson Street. She immediately came over to Larry and introduced him to Allen Gates and to the girl on his other arm who was wearing a beige cable sweater and had a pageboy hairdo which made her look like Prince Valiant. She had deep-set olive eyes and a pre-Columbian cast to her face. Her name was Mira. Larry wondered if she was Puerto Rican.

Amy asked him if he had eaten and when he lied and said he hadn't, Allen invited him to join them. Allen couldn't have been more than a year or two older than Larry but he seemed worlds away in sophistication. The maître d' standing before the funnel-like entrance into the Remo back room nodded back knowingly to Allen as he held up four fingers. "It'll only take a minute," said Allen. "Anyone want anything to drink meanwhile?"

"Gin," said Mira in a hoarse whisper, "on the rocks."

"I'll have a beer," said Amy.

"I'm sticking with beer," said Larry, as if he were playing a poker or black-jack hand. He handed Allen his empty glass. "Do you need help?"

"No thanks," Allen said. "Just keep the girls happy."

It was no problem with Amy who wanted to know about the apartment and how it was working out and if she could be of any help. But Mira seemed sullen and morose, as if unhappy to be suddenly in his company. She lit a cigarette and exhaled the smoke up past her Roman nose and El Greco eyes and looked around vacuously. When Allen returned, the drinks balanced in his hands precariously, Larry and Amy carefully relieved him of their beers, but Mira waited for Allen to hand her the gin and then cupped her hands around it and began to sip from it like a little child with a glass of milk. Allen lifted his own drink, a glass of red wine, and said: *"L'Chaim!"*

Larry could not help himself. He knew he was betraying his own lack of sophistication. But still the words escaped from him. "You're Jewish?"

"I know," Allen said. "I don't look it. But I'm also homosexual and I don't look homosexual."

Amy poked him. "C'mon, Allen. You're not homosexual. Exactly. Entirely."

"I'm bisexual then," said Allen. "But why cop a plea?"

Amy cuddled up against Allen. "Allen likes to shock people," she explained.

"Well, you've succeeded," Larry smiled.

Allen shook his head. "I don't think so. I don't think so at all. You don't look like the type who's easily shocked."

"What do I look like then?"

"You look as if you could swallow anything." He caught himself and held up his hand and laughed. "And I don't mean it *that* way either. After all, you're an actor."

"How do you know that? Did Amy tell you?"

"Amy didn't have to tell me," Allen said. "It shows."

"In what way?"

"In your eyes."

"My eyes?"

"They show you're haunted but not doomed."

Amy laughed. "This is silly."

"Maybe it isn't," said Larry, looking into Allen's own eyes directly. They were blue but gave off a dull light. "What's the difference?"

"There's a big difference," Allen said, looking straight back at him. "A painter is doomed. A writer is doomed. An actor is only haunted."

"Are you saying I'm not an artist? That acting isn't an art?"

Allen nodded slowly, his eyes never wavering, a smile forming on his lips.

"Bullshit," said Larry. "Then you've never seen Laurence Olivier. You've never seen Paul Muni. Marlon Brando. Montgomery Clift."

Allen snickered. "I've seen Monty Clift a lot, believe me." And then he smiled broadly. "But I guess you're right after all. No matter what else, Monty Clift is doomed."

The maître d' motioned that a table was free and they followed him to it, Amy nudging Larry, gesturing toward Allen, and winking at the same time. And as they sat down and reached for their menus, Larry looked up to see Allen winking at him too and somehow found himself liking him despite his pretense. Allen seemed awfully sophisticated—or at least, avant-garde. He was certainly not the kind of person Larry would run into around the store. And there were Allen's own blue eyes which Larry finally decided as he studied their dull light showed that Allen himself was definitely not doomed. Just haunted.

"Brando is a creep," Mira announced suddenly in her raspy, hoarse voice. It was as if she had just made the discovery in the menu, beside the specials of the day, scampi or osso bucco.

Larry stared at her across the table. "Excuse me."

She took her head out of the menu. "I said Marlon Brando is a creep."

"That's what I thought you said."

Allen and Amy both laughed. "Sometimes Mira seems a little strange," Allen said. "But she won't after you get to know her."

"*He* is a creep," Mira insisted.

"I'm sure he is," said Allen.

"I met him at a party. He wanted to go out with me. He kept bothering me. I told him to go away."

"Why?" asked Larry.

"I told you," said Mira; "he's a creep."

"He's still a great actor," Larry said.

"He's a creep. He wouldn't go away. He followed me home. He wouldn't leave me alone. Marlon Brando is a creep. I'll have the veal scallopini." Mira closed her menu and lay it down on the table.

"I'm disappointed to hear that about Marlon," said Larry, as if he knew him.

Allen called over the waiter and while they were all ordering Mira emptied her glass and pushed it forward. "I want another drink," she repeated, like a child insisting on more chocolate milk. But the waiter did not seem to hear her. And for good reason. She spoke in a low whisper. "And give the lady another gin on the rocks, please," Larry told the waiter. Mira rewarded him with a smile.

After dinner they walked over to Allen's loft on Wooster Street between Bleecker and Houston for a nightcap. It was three steep steel-lipped flights of stairs up above a garage. The building had a freight elevator but it wasn't running. "It's always on the fritz lately," Allen apologized. "The landlord just doesn't give a shit." On the second landing there was the odor of a dead rat entombed in a side wall. "Smell that?" said Allen. "He died waiting for the elevator."

Allen unlocked the door to his loft and opened it to a sputtering burst of light. There were fluorescent lights in the ceiling and the walls were whitewashed on three sides. The fourth wall was of natural brick—except in the corner where a black curtain hung. Against one white wall several large paintings were stacked; on another wall three paintings were hung; and in the center of the floor, surrounded by coffee cans and paintbrushes, were two giant abstract expressionist canvases of swirling colors, obviously works in progress.

Allen pulled back the curtain, revealing a kitchen alcove. From a cabinet above a refrigerator he produced a jug of red wine and Amy helped him scramble together some glasses from a cupboard near the sink. Meanwhile, Larry studied the paintings on the wall. They seemed so different from the ones Allen was now doing. The painting that interested Larry most was a representational nude of a fat woman, fat beyond Rubenesque with many folds of flesh, a Jewish Star of David dangling from her neck on a thin chain which she held seductively between her teeth. Allen, pouring the wine, spotted Larry's absorption.

"You like that?"

"Yes, I do, as a matter of fact. Where did you ever find that model?"

Allen laughed. "That's no model. That's my mother, Becky."

"You're kidding," Larry said. "You must be kidding." He looked around at the others, expecting them to share his disbelief. But Amy just slowly nodded. Mira was already lost in her drink.

"No," said Allen, sipping from his own glass. "Becky would do anything for my art. After all, she's my mother." He stood next to Larry and admired his own work as if seeing it for the first time.

Larry looked over at the works in progress. "You don't paint like that anymore."

"Becky doesn't look like that anymore."

"Is she all right?" Larry asked, suddenly concerned.

"Of course she's all right. She's a Jewish mother. Indestructible except for the gallbladder."

"My mother would do a lot for me," said Larry before finally moving away from the painting. "But I don't think she'd ever do anything like this."

"You never know," said Allen, "until you ask." He disappeared into the kitchen alcove and emerged from it with an abundance of mats and pillows which he spread along the hardwood floor. "I have to live here," he explained, "as if I'm Japanese or at the beach. Otherwise, I'll get evicted. This loft is just zoned for commercial use."

Amy put a stack of records on the turntable and joined Allen on the pillows and mats scattered on the floor. She motioned for Mira and Larry to join them there. Larry sat down tentatively, wondering what could possibly happen next. It was his first night in the Village as a resident and this could be the ultimate initiation, the definitive rite of passage: an orgy. He didn't know Amy very well and Allen claimed he was queer and Mira was, to say the very least, strange, though he could see how she was the Brando type in her Latin way. Hadn't he read in one of his mother's fan magazines that Brando always went for exotic women?

Mira slowly sat down beside him, exhaling the smoke from her cigarette into his face. He recognized the music as that of Miles Davis. He leaned back against Mira's knee, closed his eyes, and waited for the orgy to begin.

"Here," he heard. He opened his eyes and saw Allen handing a long skinny roll-your-own cigarette to Amy. She sucked in on it, holding her breath, and passed it on to Mira. Mira put down her own cigarette and inhaled in the same way. Larry recognized the pungent, incenselike smell. He suddenly realized what was happening. They were smoking Mary Jane. He had had opportunities to smoke Mary Jane, backstage after a show on a college rear-stairwell landing or in a crowded kitchen or bathroom at a cast party, but he had always demurred. Not for any moral reasons. But simply because he did not like to be out of control. Or —to put it another way—because he always wanted to be in control. That was part of the lure of what being an actor was all about. Controlling experience. Controlling your own destiny.

The first time the joint was handed to him by Mira he just passed it on to Allen. Allen inhaled again, his cheeks puffing, his eyes blinking furiously. "This is good shit," he wheezed. "Try it. Otherwise, you'll be really missing out on a treat." And Allen handed it back to him.

This time he quickly inhaled, keeping his lips closed tightly as he had observed the others do, and then coughed it all out in one blurt, the smoke getting into his own eyes.

Allen smiled benignly. "Try again. Inhale. Slowly start talking to me. And as you do so then breathe in deeply. And hold it."

He inhaled. The smoke was in his mouth. "What should I say?" he asked between clenched teeth. "Give me some lines. I don't know what to say." Breathing in deeply all the while and trying to hold it in at the same time.

"Feel anything?" Allen asked.

"Just smoke in my lungs," Larry coughed.

"Good," Allen nodded approvingly. "Now just wait."

Larry handed the joint across the mat to Amy and proceeded to wait. He felt nothing. He still wondered if the evening would develop into an orgy. Or would it just end in marijuana smoking? He hoped he was indulging in a preliminary, a curtain raiser, not in a main event.

Amy was taking another hit. She listened to the music, giggled, and passed the joint on to Mira. Mira sucked in on it casually and in almost the same languid motion gave it to him.

He inhaled again and this time avoided coughing. But he still didn't feel anything. He had felt higher on a martini. He didn't see what the big deal about marijuana was all about. And wished they'd just get on with the orgy. If that's what was going to happen. Not that he was that anxious anymore anyway. After all, Allen admitted that he was a homo. Larry had never really been sexually attracted to Amy. And he couldn't figure Mira out at all. Except that what was good enough for Marlon Brando ought to be good enough for him. Anyway, if they were going to get it on it seemed to be taking years.

Amy was emptying half a cigarette, twirling the tobacco out of it. Then she put the remnant of the joint in its place in the hollow part of the cylinder and rolled the end together and lighted it. She inhaled and passed it back to Allen who quickly handed it on to Mira. Larry got the dregs. Tasted just like an ordinary cigarette to him. Either he was inhaling incorrectly or marijuana simply had no effect on him. He took a sip of wine. Although he was drinking slowly *that* seemed to be affecting him. He could

clearly taste the wine going down. Not very good wine. Too vine-
gary. If he was enjoying anything at the moment it was the music. He found himself listening attentively. No doubt about it:
Miles was an artist.

"Miles is an artist," Larry heard himself saying.

"Yeah," said Allen.

"I'm with you," said Amy.

"I want to go home," said Mira suddenly. She sounded like
Garbo. Only with a different accent.

Larry looked back over his shoulder. "I'll take you home," he
volunteered.

"Not home here," said Mira. "Home to Cartagena."

"Where is Cartagena?" Larry asked.

No one answered. Everyone giggled. Finally Mira explained:
"Cartagena is in Colombia. Colombia is my country. I am going
back soon."

"How soon?" Allen asked.

"In two weeks," said Mira. "Unless my father dies before
that."

"Is your father sick?" asked Larry.

"No," Mira laughed. "But I wish he was."

Allen and Amy giggled again.

Larry didn't understand. But he was beginning to sense that it
wasn't going to be an orgy. And when Allen started to roll another joint he stood up. "Well, I have to be going home. To
Thompson Street. Wherever that is," he said. "I have a lot to do
tomorrow."

"Me too," said Mira, suddenly rising beside him. She finished
her glass of wine and looked about for a place to set it down. "I
forgot I have an appointment." She put the empty glass on the
rung of a ladder leaning against the wall and then crushed her
cigarette into it.

Allen didn't get up. He inhaled deeply on the new joint and
passed it over to Amy. "Don't expect me to do any honors," he
said. "I'll talk to you, Mira. Nice meeting you, Larry."

"Same here," said Larry. "See you around, Amy."

Amy blew him a kiss and he waved back at her, leaving them

passing the joint back and forth, the music now sounding more like Erroll Garner.

They descended the steep stairs, past the smell of the rat, silently, Mira leading the way. At the street level she waited for him to pull open the heavy door. Once outside in the night air she walked over to the curb and seemed to wait for him there. He joined her and looked up and down the cobblestoned street. There was not a car in sight. The only traffic sounds were distant, from over on Broadway and up on Fifth Avenue. Larry wondered if she expected him to take her home. Not to Cartagena but to wherever her pad was in the city. "Where do you live?" he asked.

"Uptown," she replied.

"How far uptown."

"Near Columbia."

"You must be kidding."

"I am," she said. "I live on Thirteenth Street. Where do you live?"

"Just over here on Thompson Street."

She hooked her arm into his. "Then let's go to your place."

He wasn't sure whether she was kidding or not but he did not ask her because he also wasn't sure what he wanted the answer to be. Mira was certainly attractive in a Latin way but she was also obviously a kook. Still Brando had seen something in her and Brando, after all, had been around more than he. Marlon Brando's experience extended far beyond college.

He led Mira to his apartment wondering what his real welcome to the Village would be like.

It turned out to be a dud.

She didn't have her diaphragm. She didn't want to screw without it. She really didn't want to screw anyway. Period. She just hadn't wanted to be alone that night. He slept on the sofa; she slept on the bed. *It Happened One Night* without anything happening.

And Larry should have left it that way. But instead he saw her again a few nights later. They went to a movie and then back to her place. And this time she had the diaphragm and was in the mood and they screwed but it wasn't that big a deal sexually. She wasn't as responsive as he expected. Yet he still saw her again and eventually they had an affair that lasted over a year. On and off. The sex improved and toward the end he even thought he was in love with her, until she tried to kill him.

Nothing personal, she said as she came toward him one night with a kitchen knife; it was just that she had decided that she hated men. They fucked her up. Like her father. Like her brother. Like her lovers and old boy friends. Like Larry. Before he was through he would leave her more fucked up than she was when they met. So she would get him first. Extract revenge on him for all the men who had fucked her up.

Of course, she was drunk and she wasn't moving in a straight line as she followed him from the kitchen of her apartment into the living room-studio. Still, he was afraid. More afraid than he would have been had she been sober. Because then he would have had a chance to talk to her, to reason with her. But she was beyond reason as she came lunging toward him, brandishing the knife like Errol Flynn in an old pirate picture except that she was stumbling over the shag carpet. It would have been funny if it weren't all so real. He quickly ducked behind the sofa.

Now she began assailing him for not liking her work. Her sculpture. Not really appreciating it. Just because she was a woman. And a foreigner. So the art world took advantage of her and American men pissed on her. Well, she'd show them. She'd show him. She was no one to piss on. She was a first rate artist and a hell of a woman. Even Marlon Brando had wanted to fuck her.

Larry pulled the floor lamp plug out of the wall socket and picked up the lamp and circled round the sofa, holding the lamp as if it were some sort of medieval jousting weapon, and came into the middle of the room, almost tripping over the shag carpet himself. "Put down that knife," he ordered.

"Humphrey Bogart."

"Mira, I'm warning you."

"I'm warning *you,*" she said and swished the knife through the air. "I'll cut your Jewish cock off."

He ordinarily would have laughed but now he backed up to the edge of the carpet, wondering if he could give it a sudden jerk the way Bogart would have done, upending her. But no, that wouldn't work. The carpet was caught under the feet of the sofa. There was just one thing to do. He held the lamp horizontally in front of him like a pole-vaulter and rushed her, the head of the lamp where the shade hung going right into her midsection. She crashed to the floor in an explosion of glass, the lamp's bulbs bursting. And then he quickly smothered her in a tackle and twisted her wrist until she released the knife.

A few moments later they made love. Right then and there on the shaggy carpet, amid the thin shards of broken glass, perhaps the best lovemaking they ever had.

But in a few weeks it was over.

She had been right about one thing. The truth was he did hate her work. He hated finding cans of clay in her refrigerator when he searched for food for a midnight snack. He hated the way her primitive statues always seemed to be staring at him catlike, accusing him of some free-floating crime.

He had other affairs in the Village days that followed that wouldn't have received the seal of approval from the American Psychiatric Association either. There was a Greek costume designer from Scarsdale who always wore green and an Italian schoolteacher from Jersey City whose family Larry had been afraid of and a Jewish actress from London who called him love and duck and had that marvelous skin, "alabaster" was the only word for it. He even once spent his entire life savings to go over to England to see her, only to discover that she had jilted him for a director they both knew. Yes, he had been around the block once or twice, so to speak, before meeting Jane. But there was no one else who remained fixed in his memory bank as vividly and clearly as Mira. Especially, the night they met, his very first night as a Village resident with his own freshly painted apartment.

10

Larry was eating a plateful of corned beef hash and drinking a German Riesling while listening to Miles Davis. He was in Allen's SoHo loft, just a few blocks south of the loft Allen had when they first met. Their friendship had lasted, down through the years. They had remained in contact, touching base, visiting each other, comparing what came to be known as life-styles. He had even bought two of Allen's earlier paintings to hang on his living-room walls. Allen, himself, went through two wives, countless boy friends, four distinctly different painting periods, and a half-dozen countries, living in Majorca, Morocco, Tangiers, France, Italy, and Greece. While Larry strayed only from Greenwich Village to Hollywood and was still on his first wife.

Times had certainly changed though. Or, at least, the laws had. The living conveniences of Allen's loft were no longer designed to instantly self-destruct and disappear, but the dining area was still furnished simply and functionally in mod international decor: Barcelona chairs and an Eames table; and the plate Larry was eating from was old Russell Wright. The walls were again all white and among the framed posters and hanging paintings and lithos Larry spotted a reproduction of Allen's nude mother teething on a Star of David. Still it all seemed somehow much more luxurious and far less Spartan than in the old days.

"I didn't know I was this hungry." Larry finished his helping of hash. "This is delicious, man."

Allen, still as thin and wiry as he was the night he had walked into the Remo in his Barrymore hat and foreign-correspondent's coat, sipped his wine and smiled: "I put garlic in it. That's the secret."

"Is that all?" Larry sopped up the plate with the heel of a loaf of French bread.

"And a little hash," said Allen. "I'm the only one I know who puts hash in his hash."

"That's either redundant. Or brilliant," Larry said. "In any case, delicious." He wiped his mouth with the back of his right hand and patted his stomach with his left hand at the same time like a sultan. Allen picked up his plate and went to the stove where a saucepan was still heating up on Warm. "Please," Larry held up his right hand, "I couldn't eat another mouthful."

"Then don't," Allen said, and swept past the stove and placed the plate in the sink across from it. "Besides," he turned around, "I have some better tastes to lay on you. C'mon."

"Where?"

Allen rubbed his hands together and giggled. "In my laboratory."

Larry followed him down to the sitting and bedroom area in the front of the loft. Allen sat down before his dresser like an actor about to make up. He reached into his jeans and extracted a glassine envelope, the kind foreign stamps used to come in when Larry was a kid collecting them. But the only foreign substance this envelope contained was an off-white powder. Larry immediately recognized it.

"I'm only into grass," he said. "I'm not a junkie like you."

Allen looked up soulfully. "This is New York. You just breathe the air and it's a high." He slowly waved the glassine envelope before Larry's nose. "You know what the street value of air is in New York?"

"No. What?"

"Inflationary," Allen said. "Just let me say in-fla-tion-ary. Highly inflationary." Then he soon became absorbed in his task. "I just made this buy before you called," he explained. "Pure stuff. Terrific stuff." He opened a dresser drawer and removed a flat mirror, a single-edged razor blade, a mortar, a pestle, a brown medicine bottle labeled Mannitol, and something that

looked vaguely like a pair of miniature opera glasses. He poured
the powdery contents of the glassine envelope into the mortar,
added a few pinches of Mannitol, and proceeded to grind the
mixture industriously with the pestle. "I'm barely stepping on
this." He smiled up at Larry. "More like tiptoeing." And then he
emptied the mortar onto the mirror, carefully sweeping out its
every granule with the razor blade, and chopped at all the powder with the blade, spading it together over and over again. It
reminded Larry of the way his grandmother used to make
chopped liver, gefilte fish. Allen next used the blade as a dustpan,
scooping up the powder and placing it in the object that looked
like miniature opera glasses.

"What is that?" he asked.

"A Victorian snuffbox," said Allen. "Like it?" The circular
snuffbox was the cerulean blue of old Korean pottery.

"Interesting," said Larry.

Allen produced a thin piece of glass tubing about three inches
long and slowly stirred the powder in the snuffbox. "This is
gold," he announced. "Pure gold." He looked up at Larry and
smiled, an alchemist pleased with the completion of his work. He
put his finger over the top of the glass straw, suction-scooped up
some coke, cocked his head back, snorted into one nostril, repeated the process with the other nostril, then tapped the side of
his nose and shook his head as he replaced the glass straw into
the snuffbox. "And now be my guest," he said, pushing the snuffbox over to Larry.

Larry hesitated.

"C'mon, this is blue chip. Hard to get. Street value: two dead
Colombians and a crippled PR maimed for life."

Larry still hesitated. God knows, he had done coke before. In
LA, after all, coke was everywhere, like jogging. In fact, coking
and jogging were the most common forms of weight control in
the West. Some directors supplied coke to their crews on location
as routinely as the catered lunch. On *Herbie and Milty,* in fact,
both his leads, his editor, his cameraman, his key grip, his sound
man, and even his production manager were always coked. Larry
was more afraid of a bust than of going over budget. He even

began to feel virtuous when he popped a val or two on a nervous day. His female lead was the biggest coker of all. Her dressing room was like a mobile headshop. She once confessed to him that she was only happy when she was on the stuff and she was happy throughout the picture. The last he heard, though, she was temporarily out of commission. Over in Switzerland or Denmark getting her nose rebuilt.

Larry looked down at the snuffbox. Hash was one thing, coke was another. For some reason he just didn't like the idea of coking before his mother's funeral.

Allen rolled his eyes benignly as if impatiently reading Larry's thoughts. "Look, babe, you are going through a very difficult experience. A very heavy experience. You called me because you couldn't sleep. In your who-knows-for-how-many-hundred-dollars-a-night suite, you couldn't sleep. Believe me, babe, I know something about what you must be going through." He looked over his shoulder to the nude of his mother on the wall. "And there's only one way to handle it. With confidence in yourself. Without guilt toward her. You've got to lighten your load."

What the hell, Larry decided. "Why not?" he said. "Tonight's my night of vice. First smoking, then coking."

"Sure." Allen quickly agreed.

And Larry took two quick snorts. Allen smiled approvingly and went into the kitchen. He returned with two opened cans of beer, placing one beside Larry, and went to the turntable and put on some new records. "Coke's a problem solver," he announced, as he cleaned the turntable needle of lint. "Lets you see through a lot of shit. Helps you make connections you wouldn't otherwise make in a million years. Have insights and understandings that you never realized you were capable of. Freud was a big coker, you know."

"I know."

"Edison, too." Allen put the needle down expertly and the music started again. Now Billie Holiday was covering the waterfront. Larry remembered film clips he had seen of her singing in a white satin dress that looked two sizes too small, a rose in her hair like a Carmen. He wondered if—like Freud, like Edison—

she was into coke when she made the record. He knew she had a drug problem, was busted several times. But that must have been for heroin. No one on coke, he was sure, could ever sing so sadly. He had never seen the movie they made about her life with Diana Ross and Billy Dee Williams. Because he knew it wasn't real. Just product. Biographical soap opera. He wasn't interested in that kind of movie. He was a serious director interested in art. And art could only be based on reality. Real reality. The rest was kitsch. The voice he was hearing tremulously phrasing, mournfully confiding, that was real. Billie Holiday was an artist. Without knowing a thing about cameras and setups she could have made a movie worth seeing. Except who would put up millions of dollars for a movie starring a junkie? And who would go to see her movie except a few pretentious art-house devotees. It would die past Bloomingdale's. No legs. Go straight to cult. It could never make it on a people break. The film clip of Billie Holiday he remembered seeing must have been in a documentary on Public Television.

Allen's voice interrupted his thoughts. For no apparent reason Allen was still standing before the turntable. "Edison invented your business, didn't he?"

Larry, still half listening to Lady's pleasure giving unexpectedly girlish squeals, shook his head. "My art."

"Whatever," said Allen.

"Lover man where can you be?" sang Billie.

11

The car horn behind them tooted.

"Fuck off," said Allen, pushing his own horn in reply as he noisily shifted into first and started up the approach to the Brooklyn Bridge. "One thing this city could lose," he said, "is its fucking drivers. They're as bad as in California."

One thing Larry did not want to get into with Allen was a discussion about drivers. In fact, he was having second thoughts about Allen's driving him out to the funeral. It had been a rotten idea. Not only was Allen's bubble-top Dodge van decorated in psychedelic rainbow waves—the imprimatur of a previous owner, Allen had hastily apologized—not quite an ideal vehicle to bear him to his mother's final rites, but Allen's driving was making him nervous. Allen was drunk and stoned and they were already running late.

When he woke up that morning in Allen's loft on the sofa, covered with a serape, Larry thought for a moment he was in Mexico. But he soon recovered his bearings because of Allen's heavy snoring. The man had passed out in a Barcelona chair, a bottle of cognac standing inches away from his dangling hand.

Larry couldn't remember exactly when Allen had switched from beer to cognac. He remembered they had talked of old times, recalling Amy and Mira, and of new times, Allen complaining how he was being driven into being more heterosexual than homosexual because these days simply everyone was gay. "It's no big deal. It's certainly not an individual statement anymore," said Allen. "Besides, I'm getting too old to have to worry about my looks. I'd rather be straight and worry about my losses." Having said that he proceeded to place his hand on Larry's knee and gently rub it. Just as gently Larry lifted it away and Allen backed off philosophically. "I have to keep trying. The obligatory pass, you understand. No hard feelings?"

"Of course not. But I better get back to the hotel. It's late and I've got to get up early."

"Relax, man." Allen pointed to the sofa. "Spend the night here. I promise I won't lay another hand on you—you're really getting too fat anyway—and I promise I'll get you to your funeral on time."

And it was then, after he had agreed to stay and lay down on the sofa, that he asked Allen about Mira again.

"She never changes," Allen reported. "She's still not married, she's still doing well with her sculptures, and she's still having affairs with good-looking young men, practically boys." And he added bitterly, "She likes to flaunt them at me."

"Why do you keep putting yourself down? You look terrific."

"Not for a faggot." Allen downed his drink. "Not for an aging Jewish faggot."

Larry wondered if Allen meant there was some special ethnic aesthetic standard Jewish homosexuals had to meet. Did they have to look ten percent better than their gay goy brothers, for example? Was there a quota against them, like medical schools? Certainly gays practiced internal discrimination—every group did—and perhaps anti-Semitism was one of the forms. But if Allen had his problems, he did not want to get involved with them. Never had. That was why their relationship endured all these years. In the dim past Allen had once even confessed to Larry that he loved him. But Larry had allowed that to pass, considering it a ploy, like the obligatory pass. Tonight Allen rubbed his knee. That night Allen professed love. It was all the same thing. Yet if Allen loved him it was flattering. It was nice to be loved by anyone. Even a faggot. Even an aging Jewish faggot.

The last thing Larry remembered before falling asleep was Allen's covering him with the serape. Had Allen leaned over and kissed him, too? Or was that part of a dream? Allen was in his dream and so was Mira. They had gone to her together to get more coke. And she turned them down at first, saying that she never sold coke to Jews. But when Allen said it was for his mother, she relented, dealt, and disappeared. Then he and Allen were on a crowded bus together drinking soda. And that was all he remembered of his dream. A strange dream. He certainly had had some strange dreams during the night. He rubbed his crotch and yawned. At least his dream involving Allen hadn't been a wet dream. That would have been too much to handle at the moment.

Larry looked at his watch: 8:47. Late. But he still had time to get back to the hotel, shave, shower, and change, and then ride out to the cemetery in the waiting limo. But first he'd piss. He got up and tiptoed silently past the reclining, still slumbering Allen to the head. He pissed quietly, emptying his bladder against the sloping side of the toilet rather than in the middle of the bowl. But then he made a mistake. Reflexively, he reached down and flushed.

The toilet exploded in a loud rasping burst and then gurgled noisily as the tank replenished itself. When he left the head, Allen was sitting up, rubbing his face.

"What time is it?"

"Ten to nine."

"What time do you have to be there?"

"Ten-thirty."

"Plenty of time. Hungry?" Allen did not even wait for an answer. For a man who had passed out the night before, Allen moved with surprising quickness. He went to the kitchen and put water up to boil. Set a frying pan on the burner. Backed up to the refrigerator and removed butter, eggs, juice, and the remnants of Allen's late-night snack. "Want some more hash? Goes good with eggs."

"No thanks. I'll pass. I better go back to the hotel."

"Nonsense. I'll get you there."

Larry stroked his chin. "But I need a shave."

"There's a razor in the john. How do you like your eggs?"

"Over."

"And your toast?"

"Dark."

The toilet tank had recovered its water level but it was still noisy in the bathroom. Not only did Larry have to listen to the drone of the electric Schick as it buzzed over his face, but also the rumble of the big trucks rolling over the street below; and from within the building came the clanging sounds of the sliding-gate doors of the freight elevator whenever it stopped. He had forgotten that he had had to take an elevator to reach Allen's loft.

"What floor are we on?" he asked, when he left the bathroom.

"Fifth," said Allen. "Breakfast's ready."

Allen was drinking a glass of wine and smoking a joint as he slid Larry's eggs off a spatula, onto a plate, and handed him the joint in the same motion. "Take a little taste. Some hair of the dog."

Larry shook his head and picked up his orange juice. "You sure you're okay, Allen?"

"Okay?" said Allen. "I'm beautiful, man." And then he embraced him. "And so are you. Now drink your juice. Orange Plus."

Larry drank his juice and ate his eggs and toast and coffee, Allen hovering over him like a Jewish mother. He showered and dressed, and Allen shepherded him out of the loft and down the street to his garage two blocks away. And now somehow Allen, drunk and stoned, was maneuvering his van across the Brooklyn Bridge. But it was getting late. "We don't have much time," Larry reminded him, as they began the downward descent toward Brooklyn.

"Relax, man."

"Are you sure you know the way, Allen?"

"Positively not. But don't panic. You told me to get on the Sunrise Highway. And I'll get on the fucking Sunrise."

Allen had obviously missed the turnoff that led onto the Belt Parkway and Sunrise Highway and now they were driving through one of those war zones of the City of New York, areas devastated by unseen air raids, unpublicized bombardments. The barnyard red brick houses still standing were boarded up, old doors in their window frames, sheaves of aluminum siding in their doorways, some even reflecting the rubble and debris in the streets before them. Areaways were full of garbage and ashes and the embers of still smoldering fires. The only other vehicles in sight were cars parked along the curb on bare wheel rims, their upholstery now sidewalk couches with springs popping through the urine-colored kapok. The street signs at the corners had been removed from their frames, the poles they hung from bent. A wild black tom, one eye closed and one ear hanging like a piece of tattered cloth, was pawing through some tin cans. Any human survivors seemed to have fled.

Allen continued driving through the metropolitan holocaust— mile after mile of urban blight—before pulling over and dropping his head onto the wheel. For a second Larry thought he was crying. But only for a second. When Allen looked up, he was laughing. "I'm lost, man," he giggled.

Larry was furious. With Allen and with himself. He had not come all the way in from California to get lost going to his mother's funeral. Not with a stoned Jewish fag drunk. He was an important director and this was an important event in his life. This sort of thing just should not happen. It was a slipup and he was responsible but it was still Allen's fault.

Larry leaned forward and rattled open the glove compartment. In it he found a flashlight that did not work, an empty brown medicine bottle, a paperback novelization of *Star Wars,* a grease-stained chamois cloth, and a pile of parking violations. "Don't you have a map?"

"Of Brooklyn?" Allen asked incredulously. And started on another peal of giggles.

"This isn't funny. It's getting late."

"Take it easy. I'll think of something."

"What?"

"How the hell do I know? But they always say that in the movies, don't they?"

"Not in my movies."

"Maybe that's the trouble with your movies lately," said Allen, and winked.

What the hell did Allen mean by that crack? Had Allen seen *Herbie and Milty* and not liked it? Or was Allen referring to *Hostile Relationships?* Not that he cared that much about Allen's critical reactions to his films anyway. Allen knew as much about film as he knew about driving through Brooklyn. Obviously not very much.

"Hey, man, where's the fucking Sunrise?" Allen was shouting out his opened window. Across the street a man in a black-leather cap, blue turtleneck sweater, and Levi's was uncertainly weaving his way down the sidewalk. In reply, the man smiled, turned his face to the sun, kicked at an old shoe that lay in his path, and fell in a heap to the ground.

Allen reached down for his wine bottle. "The poor man's stoned. Couldn't have helped us anyway." And sipping from his wine bottle he drove the van up the street.

He would *never* forgive himself, Larry decided, if he actually missed the funeral. Neither would Sally. He could already hear her chiding him: "Couldn't make it to his own mother's funeral, Mister Hollywood, the big shot; he had more important things to do." It would be just one more burden of guilt for Sally to bequeath to him for all eternity. And frankly, she would love the idea.

Larry looked at his watch. He knew they would wait five, ten —even fifteen minutes. But then they would start the service without him. Jews buried fast. They also paid for the chapel by the hour. The worst thing would be to arrive at the cemetery so late that he walked into somebody else's funeral. A complete stranger's. That would really destroy old Sally, no matter how dead she already was. "Couldn't make it to his one and only mother's funeral," Sally's voice assaulted him. "Had to go to some fucking stranger's instead. All because he fucked away the night with his Jewish fag friend snorting coke."

Larry turned off Sally's voice and looked down at his watch again. They were late, but not hopelessly late. If they found their bearings they still had a chance of getting there on time.

Allen was driving down a wide avenue, a block with broad sidewalks that once must have been the commercial center of the neighborhood. The shops were all boarded up, framed by awning rails long bereft of canvas. A lone pedestrian stood in front of what once was a barbershop. Allen spotted him and quickly pulled over. "Hey, *amigo,*" he called, cocking his head out the window, "how do we get to the Sunrise?" When the man replied in Spanish that he did not understand English, Allen immediately gunned away, calling out, "Thanks loads anyway, *amigo.*"

Larry looked back at the puzzled pedestrian then turned to Allen. "Are you crazy?"

"What do you mean?"

Larry pointed over his shoulder. "Go back."

Allen shrugged and U-turned. But when they returned to the abandoned barbershop the man had vanished.

"Just let me handle anything like this from now on," said Larry.

Allen took his hands off the wheel and mock-bowed deferentially. Then he made a right turn, running a red light.

"Didn't you see that?" Larry asked.

"See what?"

"The red light."

"Sure, I saw the red light."

"Then why did you run it?"

Allen smiled beatifically. "I wanted to show you I could drive California style," he said. "Besides, there was no traffic."

A blue Mustang was approaching and this time Larry took no chances. He leaned over the wheel and horned it down. Now his Spanish would come in handy. Help them find a way out of this jungle. Spare him some of the wrath of Sally for all eternity. The driver of the Mustang even looked civilized. He was middle-aged and wore a suit and tie. Larry called out to him in Spanish: "Excuse me, sir. But could you be so kind as to grant me the favor of telling us how to get on the highway called Sunrise?"

"No speakity Spic," replied the driver, and roared away.

Allen laughed so hard that he was soon coughing hoarsely as he tried to catch his breath. But still squeals of laughter escaped him wave after wave, until coughing and laughing and wheezing at the same time, he kept beating against the steering wheel appreciatively.

This was too much. Allen had no right to enjoy his predicament so. It was positively sadistic the way he was rasp-howling. Everyone knew that if you scratched a faggot you found a sado-masochist. But if this was heavy leather humor, Larry certainly didn't find it very funny at all.

"This isn't funny," Larry said. "I have to get to my mother's funeral. I've flown three thousand miles just for that purpose."

"I know," Allen still cough-laughed. "That's what's so funny, babe. Where's the famous Lazar sense of humor?"

"I'll laugh later," Larry said stiffly. "But first let's get there."

At the next corner stood a coffee-colored man wearing a black hat and a cream-colored jump suit. "Stop here," Larry directed. And then he took no chances; he got out of the car himself and ran over to the man. *"Buenos días."*

In reply the man turned his back and furtively started walking away. "Wait," Larry called after him in Spanish. "My mother has died and I am making an attempt to get to her funeral."

The man stopped and warily turned around, fingering a thin moustache. He had big sleepy eyes and a sad mouth. He seemed sympathetic. "I just want to ask you to please do me the favor of giving me the information regarding some traffic directions."

The man answered with a rapid flow of Spanish in an unfamiliar accent. It could have been Cuban; it could have been Colombian. Still, Larry got some of it. He expressed sincere regrets over Larry's loss. He knew what it was to lose a mother. He had himself recently lost not only a mother but also a sister-in-law in a terrible tenement fire which killed eight. Including three children. Rats had caused the fire by eating electrical wires.

He wondered if Larry had read about it in the newspaper. It had been in all the newspapers. And on television: the "Eyewitness News" at six o'clock. But not at eleven o'clock.

No, Larry politely apologized, realizing that he was at the man's mercy. But he had been out in California.

The man touched his moustache and said it might have been on the network news too, but he was not sure.

Larry said that he did not remember whether he had seen it or not on the West Coast edition of the network news but that in any case he was sincerely sorry and wanted to express his sympathy.

It was a terrible fire, the man reported. Three children died in it. Rats had caused it. He was sure that anyone who saw it would remember it.

Then he had probably not seen it on the network evening news, Larry said, trying to explain his ignorance.

They never give minorities the proper coverage, the man continued; if it had been a white fire not a Spanish fire it would have made the eleven o'clock "Eyewitness" and the network news both.

Larry agreed with him one hundred percent. The man was definitely a nut. Or a Castroite. And it was not until Larry deplored the media coverage of minority problems at length and expressed his sympathy exhaustively for the man's sister-in-law and mother that he managed to extract the proper directions for getting out of the neighborhood and onto the Sunrise Highway. Then he thanked him profusely.

"It's a thing of nothing," said the man, and walked away.

Larry returned to the van. "Please turn to the right at the next conjunction," he said to Allen. In Spanish.

Allen stared at him.

"I mean," Larry corrected himself in English, "hang a right at the next corner. And then go straight until you hit a light."

"Gotcha," said Allen, and threw the van in gear. "What took you so long?"

"I had to hear a whole megillah about a fire that killed his mother and sister-in-law. Some rats started it."

"Had to be," agreed Allen.

"I mean real rats," said Larry. "Nibbled through the wires. Eight people died altogether. Including three kids."

"I think I saw it on television," said Allen.

"Yeah, it was on the 'Eyewitness News.' The six o'clock report."

"That's right." Allen turned to him in genuine admiration.

"You caught all that in Spanish? You can really pick up that lingo, can't you? You and Carlos Castenada."

"If you live in Bel Air and you want a clean house, you have to be able to speak Spanish," Larry said.

In Yiddish.

Larry remembered his mother at his father's funeral and how Sally had monopolized the show with a monumental display of grief, as if she were an Indian princess ready to immolate herself on the burning bier. She spoke more kindly of him in sobs that afternoon than she did in sum throughout his life. She had made it seem as if she would not know how to take a single step in any direction again without her Meyer; how she would be forever unable to make the simplest decision without her Meyer's strong guiding hand. In her black dress, black stockings, black hat, and flowing widow's veil, she looked as if she had stepped out of an Italian movie. It was a hell of a performance. It made Larry sick. Poor Meyer. Sally even upstaged him at his own funeral.

Poor Meyer Lazarsky. He had died just when it seemed he had made his peace with life—or rather life had made its peace with him. He had a job as a salesman in a hardware store and he was happy at it. At home he had learned to passively ignore Sally by actively watching television. The set was always on. Tuned to a baseball game. A fight. The roller derby. A mystery, a soap, a sitcom. It did not matter. Meyer was a fan of anything that could protect him from one of Sally's tirades. He sat before the TV set, a reconditioned Admiral purchased in a Davega store, like a sentry dutifully watching whatever it showed. Even when Sally stormed into the living room and placed her massive bulk in front of the set, blocking his view completely in order to commandeer his undivided attention, he did not abandon his post. Instead, he would just gently nod, his eyes still riveted to the screen he could not see, patiently waiting her out. It was easier than arguing with Sally and certainly a lot more enjoyable than listening to her. It would even work when Sally would wheel around to see what he was still watching and be distracted into making some perceptive critical comment such as: "What shit!"

Rather than defend the program or justify watching it, Meyer would just shrug and then Sally would shake her head and saunter off, forgetting why she had come into the room in the first place, announcing to the unseen audience that seemed to follow her wherever she went—even to the bathroom: "I married some husband. He likes shit. Maybe that's because he's shit himself." And Meyer would rise from his recliner and sneak up to the Admiral and turn the volume up a notch. Those were Meyer's best days. Probably the best days of his life.

When Larry was still living in the East, he and Jane had a two-and-a-half-room garden apartment in Brooklyn Heights, bigger than anything they could have possibly afforded in the Village. They needed the larger apartment after Mary was born. To Sally, Mary's arrival served as an excuse . . . to visit them "officially." To drop in on them at odd hours "unofficially." "We were in the neighborhood." "We were just passing through." *At eleven-thirty in the evening?* They came as prototypical Jewish grandparents, toting shopping bags. Sally's was always unimaginatively stacked with delicatessen food, the same sort Larry could easily have picked up for himself a half block away on Montague Street: bagels and cream cheese, lox and chopped herring, bialys and chopped liver, chicken, salami, and a half loaf of rye. But Meyer's shopping bag was always a thing of mystery: There would be all sorts of European-made toys for Mary and little sweaters and exotic soaps and even picture books "for when she was ready." Care and thought and concern had gone into the selections. Meyer obviously loved the baby. He bounced her on his knees, he dangled his keys before her, he hid behind his muffler and peekabooed. He seemed endlessly fascinated with her and genuinely pleased by her. He enjoyed feeding her and was much more expert at changing her diapers than Sally. "They didn't have paper diapers in my day," was Sally's excuse. She ceremonially looked at the baby, held and kissed her, and then proceeded to ignore her.

But it was Sally who could eventually watch the baby grow. Not poor Meyer. Just when everything was going well—he was even finally getting his teeth fixed, his "mouth completely redone," promised the dentist—that his cancer was discovered. And too late. Usually, cancer victims die slowly. There is an early warning and a prolonged lingering. But not with Meyer. Even with cancer he had the grace to go quickly, mercifully, unobtrusively. He had severe pains on a Tuesday, went to the hospital on Wednesday, and the operation was on Friday. But it was too late; the cancer was too enlarged. They sewed him up and he died three weeks later.

And at his funeral Sally gave her virtuoso performance. It was a little eclectic, dressed like a Magnani, wailing like an Indian, but still she had herself under control, the mark of a good actress. And she could take direction, too. While the rabbi rambled on, Larry kicked her hard in the ankle and hissed, "Knock it off. You're overdoing it." Immediately, she checked a sob and nodded. He had Sally's number just as surely as she had his. It would make a wonderful scene in a movie. And if not that scene exactly, thought Larry, then something like it.

Poor Meyer. He couldn't get his due even in Larry's memory of his funeral.

They were finally on course to the cemetery, on the Sunrise Highway, a bleak stretch of road inappropriately named. Allen was blithely driving with one hand, passing every car in sight, as he sucked in from a joint clenched tightly between three fingers and drank his wine Spanish style, the jug slung over the back of his hand. Larry turned on the radio. It did not work.

"I've got to get it fixed," said Allen, wiping his mouth after slurping his wine.

"You lived in Ibiza, didn't you?" asked Larry.

"Almost a year."

"How come you can't speak Spanish then?"

"We always had maids."

"But who spoke to them?"

"I had a German lover. Kurt. He sprecht der Spanish."

"You're amazing."

Allen smiled. "I'll even get you to your funeral on time."

"I hope so."

"No sweat."

Poor Meyer had always been like a buffer between Larry and Sally. Or like a diversionary target, absorbing some of her misdirected energy. After his death Larry felt guilty. For the hard life poor Meyer had led and the little attention anyone had really paid to him. Including Larry. But what could he have done? Once he had outgrown baseball, they had no interests in common. After they had exhausted the topic of the Yankees—in the bowels of Brooklyn his father's nature or nurture had made Larry into a Yankee fan, too—they never had anything else to discuss. It was almost as if without Mel Allen present, a voiceover inquiring from the Admiral, "How about that?", no other extended conversation could take place. Otherwise, they would grunt—or grant—monosyllabic answers to each other's polite conversational questions: "How are you doing?" "Did you have a good time?" "Are you feeling all right?"

With Sally it was different. Whatever she lacked in insight and intelligence she could always make up for in energy, her forever rounding body exuding it. Not necessarily positive. In fact, most often negative. Still there was an electromagnetic quality about her which made her as attractive as she was repellent. Larry liked his weak father and could accept him at face value. Larry feared his strong mother and never knew how to handle her. If he had acceded to her wishes, she would have destroyed him, enveloping him in an emotional bind of boalike proportions, squeezing out of him the very last breath of his delicate and fragile ego. But when he rejected her wishes—and demands—as out of hand, she pursued him relentlessly, inflicting guilt at every pass and turnoff. Even last night, hadn't she come to him in a dream, driving him out of his hotel room, leaving him at a loss? Going to Allen's had salvaged the night even though it had almost savaged the day.

Larry consciously forced himself to concentrate on his father again. God knows the rest of the day would be Sally's and he thought of her often enough anyway. But he seldom thought of poor Meyer. He tried to seize on an image. But the clearest image that came to mind involved absence. He remembered a Friday afternoon in autumn when he and Jane hailed a cab in Sheridan Square and urged it to hurry down to the Beaux Arts Municipal Building on Chambers Street with the big clock and traffic flowing through its arches. They were held up because of a motorcycle accident but still managed to get to the City Clerk's office in time for their own wedding. The clerk stood at the lectern in a high-ceilinged oak-paneled room, and intoned the ceremony in an earnest chant, as if somehow by the ardor of his manner he could divest the occasion of its otherwise cold, bureaucratic taint. Which only caused Larry and the witnesses to push their lips taut in order to keep from breaking up. The witnesses were Max Isaacs and Sidney Stein, both writers, oddly enough, and Jane's kid sister Laura and her husband Robert. Jane's parents were not present because they lived in New Mexico at the time. Larry's parents were not present, even though they still lived in Brooklyn.

"How can you marry a shiksa?" Sally had ranted in the corner booth of the candy store when Larry first informed her of his intention, wiping her hands on her apron as if she had actually cooked the meal she was serving rather than ordered it takeout from the Chinese restaurant down the block.

"It doesn't matter." Larry said, searching among the containers for the spareribs. "We love each other."

"What do you know about love?" She turned to Meyer who kept sipping his egg-drop soup in level strokes and even slurps. "What does he know about love, Mike?"

"Leave the boy alone," said Meyer bravely.

Sally turned on Meyer with all her fury. "We let him go live in Greenwich Village. We left him alone enough. See what happens? He wants to marry a fucking shiksa."

Larry came to his father's aid, returning the favor. "Now you bring up this shiksa thing? Since when are you so religious all of a sudden?"

"I've always been religious when it comes to marriage. Who did I marry? Some goy or something? Your fucking father is not the pope."

"Popes don't marry," said Larry.

Sally waved away his interruption as irrelevant and out of order. "Don't give me no popes, please, Mister Greenwich Village."

"You brought up the pope."

"The pope is not Jewish. If you're Jewish," she continued, illogically, "it means you're born Jewish and you live Jewish and you die Jewish and you marry Jewish and your children are Jewish. Everything else is details and religion has nothing to do with it."

"The times are a-changing," said Larry, sucking into the gristle of his rib. "Will you come to my wedding?"

"Will you come to my funeral?" Sally replied.

He and Jane were late for their own marriage ceremony because he had waited for word from Meyer of a last-minute change of heart on the part of Sally. He had felt like a death-row occupant in an old prison picture waiting for a call from the governor's office. He had wanted that change of heart not because he cared so much about having Sally present but because he wanted his father there. But the word never came. And he should have known better than to expect his father to have the courage to show up alone. Poor Meyer, he was one of life's losers. Usually, Larry turned his back on losers. Or used them. Once you spotted a loser it was easy to add to their losses for your own benefit. The big mistake was in trying to help a loser cross over the line to the winning side. That always cost. In terms of time and energy and money. But what could you do when your own father was a loser?

So Larry made an exception. He acted as if nothing had happened. And a month after the wedding he asked his parents to dinner. Jane didn't like the idea at all. Refused to prepare the meal. Wouldn't even clean the apartment. Larry vacuumed the place and cooked dinner himself, a Hungarian goulash with noodles and a bakery cake from Sutter's for dessert. His parents arrived tentatively. Sally looked about the apartment as if she were a gunslinger entering a Western bar. Meyer embraced him and then Jane, forcing Sally to do the same. When he offered drinks, Sally asked for Canadian Club, settled for Scotch. Meyer said that Scotch was just what he wanted. They sat down on the living-room sofa that converted into a bed. He went into the kitchenette to prepare the drinks and called out for Jane to come help him. She came pouting and he hugged her but she was unresponsive in his arms. He gave her the drinks to bring to his parents and followed after her carrying their own Scotches on the rocks. Meyer and Sally were still sitting on the sofa. They might have been two strangers waiting for a train on a bench in a deserted subway station. Meyer welcomed the proffered drinks, rising to accept them. "A toast," he proposed as he handed her drink to Sally and she rose beside him. "To Jane and Larry." Meyer clicked his glass against each of theirs. "May you have a long, happy, and wonderful marriage." Everyone clicked glasses. *"L'Chaim,"* he added as he brought his drink to his lips. "To life," he translated as he sipped it. Then he slid a wheat thin into the onion dip and into his mouth and pronounced it delicious. The moment of crisis had passed.

At dinner too, everyone tried to act as if nothing untoward had ever happened. Even Sally seemed gracious. In fact, the only awkward moment came when she complimented Jane on the goulash.

"I didn't cook dinner. Larry did."

"I didn't know my son could cook."

"With the help of Jim Beard," Larry said.

"Who's Jim Beard?"

"He wrote the cookbook."

"I never use cookbooks," said Sally.

"Maybe you should," suggested an emboldened Meyer. "Delicious. Absolutely delicious. I'm proud of you, son."

Sally turned to Jane and tried again. "I must say I like the way you fixed up this apartment. And you keep it so clean. Sparkling."

"Larry cleaned it," said Jane.

"Delicious goulash," Meyer rushed in. "Copy down the recipe for me, son, and I'll try it."

The pattern was set. If Sally was ready to surrender and give grudging acceptance to Jane and their marriage, Jane could never bring herself to quite forgive Sally. It was a quality in Jane Larry loved and respected but it didn't make things any easier for him. Thank God, Jane, however, did forgive Meyer. She really did come to like him, too. Especially after Mary was born and he was so helpful. But then poor Meyer soon died. The irony of it all. Meyer, who would have so enjoyed watching Larry's kids grow, never even got to see Conor at all. Sally was around, of course, but she quickly reverted to being her insufferable self. If she had any joy in her later years, it was not watching his children blossom but rather following the development of his career. Sally must have been the only woman in Brooklyn who subscribed to both trades, the Hollywood *Reporter* and the daily *Variety.*

They were pulling into the cemetery, past the opened heavy iron gates. Larry immediately noticed a disparity in the size of the burial stones. Some were thin slabs barely bigger than a home plate. Others were like enormous marble pillboxes, structures in themselves, housing mausoleums that could contain the vaults of a Jewish pharaoh, bunkers where a Jewish Hitler could spend his last days. In death, as in life, Larry decided, there was no democracy. The size and the billing always mattered to some people. He flashed on a scene in which a hotshot director was somehow trying to negotiate for above-the-tombstone billing. And a possessory epitaph, like "John Director's Body." Or better yet: "A John Director Body."

"I told you we'd make it," said Allen.

"I still could have done without the detours."

"What the hell. I took you the scenic route." They entered a circular driveway. "This must be the place." He parked in front of a building that looked like a miniature Taj Mahal designed by a Miami Beach hotel architect. "I can wait for you," Allen said. "But I won't go inside. I don't like funerals. Especially of mothers."

"No need to wait."

"You sure you can get a ride back?"

"Positive. No problem. Thanks for the ride. Thanks for everything."

Allen extended his hand and Larry shook it. When he withdrew his hand, he found a glassine envelope in it. "No," he said, and tried to press the envelope back into Allen's hand. But Allen held his hands in the air, palms opened, shaking his head.

"You might need it," Allen insisted.

"I've got everything under control."

Allen laughed. "It takes more than a day to bury a heavy experience. Take it. You'll need it."

Larry stared at the envelope before putting it in his pocket. "Thank you. Thanks again, man. I really owe you one."

"You don't owe me anything. But there is something I want to talk to you about," Allen said. "Maybe I'll fall by your hotel tomorrow."

"Sure. Come by for lunch." He leaned over and embraced Allen and got out of the van and walked around it toward the entrance to the chapel. He turned around when he heard the van start up and waved to Allen, pulling away.

Then he sucked in his stomach and entered the chapel.

12

It was cool, clean, and comfortable. Not like the synagogues of his youth. Larry remembered the stench of fetid air on warm Yom Kippur days. Remembered old men milling around potbellied stoves on cold winter evenings. Remembered the shul where he had been bar mitzvahed, the benches made of two-by-fours nailed together that easily splintered, the floor covered with a linoleum that buckled and cracked, the windows never free of dirt or grime. Where the only riches were the jeweled Torahs behind the satin-curtained ark. In the back of that synagogue, in a corner partitioned by a removable wall of glass doors, he spent the sweatiest summer of his life learning his bar mitzvah haftorah from Rev Bookbinder, a martinet of a man who would rap against the slats of the benches with a paint-store yardstick as his metronome. The yardstick also served as a blunt instrument of discipline, beating against the upturned palm of any teenage transgressor—"Any wise guy who fooled around instead of learning"—with a painful sting.

Once the Rev Bookbinder, the victim of a summer cold, sneezed and Larry smartly said, "God bless you, Rev."

" 'God bless me,' you say." The Rev seized Larry and drew him to his feet by twisting his hand. "You dare to make fun of both God and me in one sentence. I'll show you a 'God bless you, Rev,' " and he flayed away at him with his yardstick.

Larry hated the Rev Bookbinder but still he did learn his haftorah and delivered it successfully at his bar mitzvah, even thanking the Rev for his tutelage in his speech. But after his bar mitzvah, also thanks to the Rev Bookbinder, his interest in Judaism quickly waned. He seldom ventured into a synagogue again. He knew he was a Jew and never tried to hide that fact but neither did he delight in it. He simply accepted it and let it go at that. It was no big deal—or ordeal—either. The holocaust had been in Europe and Israel was in Asia Minor. The worst blows inflicted upon him for being a Jew were those that came from the hand of Rev Bookbinder.

Still, even as a young actor, it would have hurt to change his name. Certainly he could have anglicized it to something like Lacy. Or even just picked a new name out of a hat. Like a Dane Clark or a Jeff Chandler, a Tony Curtis or a Kirk Douglas. But he had simply shortened it to Lazar. Like the Gare and the Frères. It was almost as if he had always known that he would finally make his mark in a field in which the sound and look and feel of a name usually meant little. Fred Zinnemann. Alfred Hitchcock. Paul Mazursky. What kind of names were those? Actually, Lazar, it turned out, was a great name for a director. It evoked both French and Russian connotations. It was exotic and down to earth at the same time. A Lazar could be an artist, a creative filmmaker. A Lazar could be a producer of product for a price, a practical businessman. He was both. Who could expect someone with a fanciful Waspish name to be either?

A handful of relatives greeted him in back of the chapel. His Aunt Ida, rising from a shining maple bench, announcing his arrival like a herald, "Here comes Larry!", as she came forward to greet him.

"Aunt Ida." He went to embrace her. But she averted her head and wiggled away when he tried to kiss her.

"I have a cold," she explained, holding up a handkerchief as proof. "You shouldn't catch." As Larry, instead, dutifully held her at arm's length, she inspected him. "You're looking very nice. California still agrees with you."

"You look good yourself."

"I'm not a movie star. You must know them all."

"Some."

"Do you know Joan Crawford?"

"She's dead."

"What do you know?" Ida called out as if she had suddenly extracted privileged information. "Did you hear, everybody? Joan Crawford is dead?"

A short bald man who evidently was not overwhelmed by such stale old news edged up to Larry and nudged him on the shoulder with his own shoulder. "Do you remember me, Lucky boy?"

Larry had not been called Lucky in years. He wondered for a moment if he ever had actually been called it. But, yes, some kid on the block nicknamed him that and it stuck. Probably because of the alliterative effect. Lucky Lazar. Like Lucky Lindy.

He looked down at the little bald man. He certainly seemed familiar enough but he could not place him.

"I'll give you a hint." The man smiled, revealing two gold teeth. "I'm cousin Julie from Newark."

"Of course," Larry said, grasping his hand firmly, but still not quite sure who he was. Sally had several cousins in New Jersey. He even remembered visiting them as a child, taking double-decker-London-style red buses over cobblestoned streets to get to their maroon brick houses. There were several of them, brothers he believed, all working as countermen in delicatessens. He remembered playing running bases in the back of one of the delis with his second cousin. "How are you, Cousin Julie?" Larry vigorously shook his hand. "I'm so glad you could come."

"Your mother Sally was always my favorite," Julie said, shaking his head slowly. "Oh, could she sing! Such a voice! If she was a man, she could have been a cantor. Such a voice! She belonged in show business. But those were different times. Today everything is only loud and fast. It gives me a headache. I don't understand the words. Can you understand the words?"

"Not always," Larry sympathized.

"And if you understand them," Julie lifted his shoulders and extended his arms, "who wants to hear them anyway? But I love all your pictures. I go to every picture when it comes around or I wait to see it on television later. But I tell everybody. This is my cousin Sally's boy's picture. He used to come to the deli where I worked all the time. It's some picture. They shouldn't miss it."

"Thank you."

"She would always let me know the name of your picture when it came out. Sweet Sally," Julie said, and began dabbing at his eyes with a Kleenex.

The sudden gesture touched Larry. He felt for a moment as if he would begin crying himself. "Do you still live in Newark, Julie?" he asked.

Julie abruptly threw down the Kleenex. "Are you crazy? Am I crazy?" he asked rhetorically. "I sold my store a long time ago. I live in the Oranges now. West. It's some schlepp coming here. I'll tell you."

If just going from Brooklyn to Newark in the old days had been such a schlepp, Larry could well imagine what a major excursion it had become. "Did you take the train?"

"Three trains."

"Thank you," said Larry.

"And two buses."

"Thank you."

An angular gray-haired lady in an organdy print floral dress was standing beside Julie. Larry had been assuming she was Julie's wife and he had been trying without any success to place her, too. "Mr. Lazar," she began, "excuse me, you don't know me. But Sally—your mother—and I were neighbors. She was very proud of you. She could never stop talking about you. She went to see all your pictures all the time all over town. She loved you more than anything in the world. You should always know that."

Larry did not know what to say after thanking the woman. But again, Uncle Irving, appearing at the propitious moment, came to his aid. "Excuse me," he said to the angular woman as he draped his arm over Larry's shoulder, "but the rabbi wants a word with you."

Larry bowed to the woman, excusing himself, and let his uncle lead him down a red-carpeted aisle.

"Did you sleep good, young man?"

"Yes."

"And you didn't forget to eat breakfast?"

"No."

"Breakfast is the most important meal."

"I know."

"But do you know why?"

Larry stopped. "Why?"

"Because your stomach is still a meal or two younger than the rest of your meals." Uncle Irving smiled and then shrugged. "I'm not good at jokes after any meal."

"You're terrific," said Larry.

"Here's the rabbi." They were entering an open office at the rear of the chapel. Immediately Larry sensed something familiar but he could not quite put his finger on it. The rabbi was sitting on a white Naugahyde couch talking into a white phone. He raised a ringed hand and smiled at Larry: "Okay," he said into the phone, "I'll call you as soon as I'm finished here. I have to go to work." And hung up.

Larry still stood near the doorway alongside his Uncle Irving. The rabbi rose and came toward them extending his hand. "Rabbi Greenbaum," Uncle Irving announced, "this is my nephew Larry Lazar." He winked at Larry. "I'll leave you two together." And backed out of the room. The wink had been one of assurance as if his continued presence would be an intrusion on a privacy, but instead Larry suddenly felt abandoned and very alone. Besides, he had never liked rabbis much. Not since Rev Bookbinder.

"I appreciate the terrible loss you must feel, Larry," Rabbi Greenbaum began. "And I hate to trouble you at this very moment. But I have to check some facts for my eulogy."

The rabbi went behind the desk and removed a pair of eyeglasses from one pocket and a business envelope from another. He put on the glasses and picked up a pencil as he studied the envelope. "I've made some notes already," he explained. "Your predeceased father was Meyer?"

"That's right."

"You were the only child, Larry?"

"Yes."

"Your wife's name is Jane. And your children's names are Mary and Conor?"

"That's right."

The rabbi peered out from above his glasses. "Those aren't Jewish names?"

"My wife isn't Jewish."

"Oh." The rabbi shook his head, clicking his tongue against his teeth. "I see. And is there anything special you'd like me to say?"

"I just want you to get it over with as quickly as possible, please."

"I see," the rabbi said. But it was obvious to Larry that the rabbi did not see at all, that his request for brevity had disturbed him. The rabbi kept looking over the back of the envelope, pencil in hand, as if he were checking each item on a supermarket receipt. "I understand your mother was very proud of you and your career; I'll talk about that. How you were her only child and how she sacrificed for you; I'll touch upon that. And I'll mention your children and how much she always looked forward to her visits with them in California." The rabbi paused and smiled. "You know I have many friends in California. In LA. In your business. Show business. In fact, I performed the ceremony for David Begelman's second wife's first marriage. Do you know David Begelman?"

"Yes."

"Do you know his wife?"

"We've met."

"How is she?"

"Fine."

"And how is David?"

"Fine."

"And I imagine you know his former partner, Freddie Fields."

"Yes."

"A lot of our people make it in show business. In fact, I heard your current release, *Herbie and Milty,* is very good. Though I am sorry to have to admit I haven't seen it yet. Unfortunately, I don't get a chance to get to the movies too often."

That's all right, Larry felt like saying; I don't get a chance to get to shul too much either. But he resolutely kept his mouth shut while the rabbi rambled.

"Are you working on any interesting new projects?"

"A couple," Larry answered reflexively. Projects? He could remember when all the word meant to him was a cluster of brick-slab buildings that housed poor people. And that's all the word should still have meant to the rabbi.

"By the way," the rabbi continued, "how is *Herbie and Milty* doing at the box office?"

"It's doing very well," said Larry, half closing his eyes to hide the annoyance he was sure was showing. He knew he shouldn't let the rabbi upset him, but then he hadn't come to the chapel to discuss projects and grosses. Maybe that was the familiar air about the office? It reminded him of an agent's office. Any minute now he expected a girl to come in and ask him if he wanted coffee.

"Wonderful," the rabbi was saying. "I'm glad it's doing well and I will definitely make it a point to see it. By the way, do you have a gross position?"

I'll show you a gross position, thought Larry; I'll ram my foot right up your ass. "What's the difference?" he said, this time without masking his hostility.

The rabbi got the message. But not without firing off a final salvo. "David and Freddie can tell you," he said before retreating to the back of the envelope. "All right, I think I have everything I need. Your father was just forty-six when he passed away?"

"Yes."

"Poor Meyer. Such a young age. All right." The rabbi rose, clutching the envelope as if it contained the scrawls of another Gettysburg address. "We'll begin soon. I promise you a very nice service."

"Just one thing, rabbi."

"Yes."

"I don't want anybody to cry."

"What do you mean?"

"No tears. No crying. If you make anybody cry, so help me, I'll bust you in the mouth." Larry turned and walked out, successfully fighting back his own tears.

Larry knew asking a rabbi to deliver a eulogy without tears was like the mob warning a Vegas comic that every laugh he received would cost him a broken bone. But still he had to marvel as he listened to the rabbi drone on. For, in spite of the limitations imposed upon him, the man had a captive audience that he just couldn't let go. He had begun by speaking of Sally's love for Israel—Larry had never heard her mention Israel other than as a possible place to vacation because she could always stay at Uncle Irving's condominium. And then he segued into a capsule history of the Jewish State. Which if not quite appropriate for the occasion was also not without interest. It was as if the rabbi was resolutely determined to do his complete fifteen-minute turn on the bill despite the fact that he had been summarily stripped of the effect of his closing number. Larry only seriously started to listen when he began to speak of his father, poor Meyer, and his marriage to Sally and how they had struggled together during the dark days of the depression and the bloody days of World War II—out of which, incidentally, emerged the state of Israel—and how that struggle had not been in vain because the good Lord had seen to it their union was blessed with the birth of their only son Larry, whom they nurtured and supported with love and religious guidance and the teachings of Judaism until he went on to become "a show business great." A giant. Like Eddie Cantor. George Jessel. Jack Benny. David Begelman. Only with a camera. A movie great whose pictures grossed well and delighted audiences throughout the world. Including Israel.

And now the rabbi was looking directly at Larry in his front-row seat next to Uncle Irving. "Sally loved her only son," the rabbi perorated, "the Oscar-nominated director, Larry. And she loved her two beautiful golden grandchildren." He paused to consult the envelope on the podium before him and then coughed as if he were trying to dislodge a bone suddenly stuck in his throat. "Mary and Conor," he wheezed out before continuing. "And Sally loved show business. This above all she loved: show business." Again he paused dramatically and seemed to study each member of his small audience, the handful of relatives and neighbors scattered throughout the chapel—more like a Bolting brothers crowd than a Capra one—before intoning rhetorically, the palms of his hands extended upward, "And who of us does not love show business?"

Larry cupped his hands over his face and turned around. He certainly did not want the rabbi to see him laughing. And he had visions of the Rev Bookbinder suddenly appearing and cuffing him across the face for acting like such a wise guy at his own mother's funeral.

Just as he was about to turn back, his face composed again, appropriately somber, he saw Michael, the girl from the studio office, sitting in the back row. She was wearing a black dress and seemed to be laughing at the rabbi, too. He winked at her and she nodded back. At the same time, out of the corner of his eye, he noticed someone else signaling to him. In the next-to-last row on the other side of the chapel wearing a white yarmulke and a dark suit Sidney Stein was making the fist-in-the-air fight sign.

At last came the organ music and it was over. They wheeled his mother out and he embraced his uncle and aunt and all of his relatives and shook hands with the neighbors and thanked them for coming. Hanging back from the others were Michael on one side and Sidney on the other. First, he took off his yarmulke and went to her. "How nice of you to come. How did you ever get here?"

"I have your limo."

"I'll go back with you then."

"No hurry. Take your time."

"I want to get out of here."

He went over to Sidney and embraced him with show-business warmth. "Sidney, how nice of you to come. How did you ever know?"

"Jane told me."

"But how did you know the service was here?"

"It was in the paper."

"Variety? You read *Variety?"*

"No. The New York *Times.* Under funeral notices."

"You read them?"

"When I have to."

"You look terrific," Larry marveled. Sidney's curly hair was a silvery gray, his face was richly tanned, and his stomach was flat.

"I want to talk to you."

"And I want to talk to you." Larry looked around. "But this isn't the place. Obviously." He closed his eyes as if to avert sudden tears. "But I was going to call you tonight. How did you ever get here?"

"I drove in."

"All the way from Jersey. That's some schlepp. Thank you."

"It's very important that we talk. I'll give you a ride back to town."

"I already have a ride back. I have to be with family." He turned toward Michael.

"That's nice family."

"My niece."

"Then when can we talk?"

"Tomorrow."

"Come out to Princeton tomorrow."

"That's some schlepp."

"I made it in. Come out for dinner tomorrow. My shiksa will make us good eats."

"I'll see."

"There's nothing to see. I'll expect you tomorrow night." Sidney took out a pad. "Here, let me give you directions."

Larry waved the pad away. "I'll call you tomorrow for directions."

"Don't stand me up," Sidney persisted.

"Have I ever let you down?"

"I'm not sure."

"Tomorrow night," said Larry, "I'll explain everything to you. I'm just as anxious as you to get everything straight." He spotted his cousin Julie from Jersey approaching. "And Sidney, could you do me a favor? Are you by any chance going directly home?"

Sidney nodded.

"Then could you give my cousin Julie a lift? He comes from Newark."

"Sure."

"Julie," Larry greeted him. "My friend Sidney Stein's going back your way. He'll drive you home."

"Wonderful," Julie said to Sidney. "Thank you," he said to Larry. "You're a good boy. I'll give everybody your regards."

"Newark?" Sidney asked Julie. "What part of Newark?"

"Not Newark." Julie turned to him. "I used to live in Newark. Everybody used to live in Newark. Philip Roth even used to live in Newark. But are you crazy? Am I crazy? Now it's only *schwartzes* living there. I live in West Orange by my daughter."

"That's a little out of my way," Sidney said.

"Wherever you can drop me," Cousin Julie said, "I'll appreciate."

"Terrific." Larry pressed Sidney's shoulder. "Good-bye, Cousin Julie. I'll see you tomorrow night, Sid. And we'll talk."

Larry watched Sidney and Julie leave and was stuffing the yarmulke into his pocket just as the rabbi was passing him on his way out. They nodded to each other.

13

Once more Long Island was passing in a blur, looking much like the view from an LA freeway. Except the greens seemed duller, as if the trees and shrubbery and grass were in need of a cleaning or whatever was nature's equivalent of a second coat. Larry felt dull too and found himself, not surprisingly, thinking of death. Not the death of Sally or Meyer. But his own death. And the kind of ceremony he would want, and who he'd like to have at his funeral. One thing certain: He did not want a Rabbi Greenbaum, someone he'd never met before, conducting the service. He'd rather be remembered by friends and colleagues, people he'd worked with, peers. At a place like the Directors Guild. Run film clips and have no speakers at all. Or just show his films all day at a theater on Hollywood Boulevard or in Westwood. A Larry Lazar retrospective. And they could hold one in New York at the same time on Third Avenue. Yes, that would be the memorial he would like. After all, like any true artist, hadn't he written his epitaph in his métier? In his work. And those hexagon cans of films were his work. Even if it did sound corny, he poured his life's blood into those reels of celluloid.

The Larry Lazar retrospective would take place after he was cremated, of course. He and Jane had already agreed on cremation for themselves. Because cremation was cleaner. More thorough. Better for the environment and all that. But still, it was discomfitting to think of himself burning, actually burning. His death, after all, would be merely a simple fact, period, rather than a passionate statement for a cause, exclamation point. Hell, he wasn't a Buddhist monk protesting some rank injustice. Just a dead director. Another filmmaker gone. There were no really big sins he had to burn for. Not yet anyway. Except for all the lies he usually had to tell to get his pictures made. But that was par for the course. Yes, he definitely would talk with Jane about his own final arrangements when he got back to LA. There had to be a better way of disposing of him. Like sliding him into the water off the Malibu pier. Or leaving him for the vultures in the desert outside Palm Springs, the way the Parsi did with their dead in Persia and India. That, at least, would keep the food chain going. He was biodegradable, for sure. Still, he wasn't so crazy about being a peck-at-lunch for a flock of ugly birds either. Hell, no point rushing to any quick decision. Why was he thinking such maudlin thoughts anyway? Just because he was coming from his mother's funeral. The best thing for him to do would be to get right back to work. Fly back to LA. Just as soon as he settled the few legal things that had to be done.

He leaned back and looked out the window. He doubted if he would ever make this trip again. He was not a sentimentalist. At least not when it came to matters like death. He had not thought much about his father in years. Of course, poor Meyer made guest appearances in dreams and occasional reveries. He truly missed the man he had known as a child. But with each succeeding year since Meyer's death his sense of him had diminished. And now, to tell the truth, he wasn't even sure whether he missed his father or some memory he had of him, one that had been hanging in an editing room of the mind like a strip of film. It was very tricky stuff. In the same way sometimes in memory he would confuse an actual location with the shot itself. After a while it was difficult to tell the real from the unreal, the original from the copy, the first-hand experience from the duplicated one. He had to be careful. It was all very tricky. Except dead was dead. No chance for postproduction shooting or any more cutting or editing. It was all locked in. He just hoped Sally would stop bugging him now. Would get out of his life since she was out of life anyway. Would have the grace that Meyer had. In that case he could dig up a few decent memories of her, revise and polish them, and trot them out from time to time. Give her a

Sally Lazarsky retrospective in the privacy of his own head. No that wouldn't work. She'd fuck it up anyway. No way would she give him final cut.

He laughed out loud. Michael, sitting beside him, had been quiet, as if respecting his silence. But when he laughed she turned to him and smiled. He smiled back and explained: "Just thinking about my mother. I had a funny thought."

"That's nice."

"Not what you think."

"I'm not thinking of anything."

"Do you go to many funerals?"

"Not many."

"I hate them."

"So do I."

"Then thanks again for coming. I mean I had to come. I was a principal. But you know what's really funny, though?"

"What?"

"All through the service I kept thinking where I'd put my camera if I were shooting it. You ought to see me when I'm working. I'm terrific when I'm working."

"Your work is terrific."

"Thank you. That's very sweet of you. Remind me to invite you to my funeral. And to my posthumous retrospective."

She shook her head and looked him straight in the eye. "I wouldn't have said it if I didn't mean it. I think you're a very *important* director."

"Thank you. But who else do you consider an 'important' director?"

"Bergman."

"Ah, Ingmar."

"You know him?"

"Ingmar is my best friend."

Michael wrinkled her brow slightly, like a student suddenly not quite understanding a question during an oral exam. It made her look cute in a schoolgirl way.

"I don't mean we spend *that* much time together," Larry said. "But when we are together, there's no one that I feel closer to.

No one that I can get more intimate with in terms of knowing that my feelings are understood. Down to the last nuance."

The wrinkle was still on her brow and she was licking her lips intensely. "Not even your wife?"

"That's different," Larry said. "Jane doesn't understand directing." He watched Michael closely for her reaction. If she laughed it meant she had a sense of humor and could be interesting. He knew from long experience that the most attractive quality he could find in a woman was an ability to laugh at his jokes, to share in his quirky way of looking at things. A woman who was a beat behind him in wit was as difficult for him to tolerate as a woman who was a beat ahead of him in sex.

Michael unwrinkled her brow and laughed, dimples forming in the corners of her mouth. Attractive dimples. An intelligent face. He thought of Audrey Hepburn in *Roman Holiday*. "May I ask you a personal question, Michael?"

"Depends."

"How old are you?"

"Twenty-four. Why?"

"You look much younger. I have a daughter who is seventeen and you don't look a day older than her. Say," he suddenly snapped his fingers, "maybe you can help me?"

Before she could answer him a DC-10 coming in for a landing at LaGuardia passed in a low slant overhead, its noise drowning out any possible reply. Larry followed the plane until it touched down, bouncing along the ground safely. He sighed: "Planes, landing and taking off, make me nervous. In or out of them. Especially DC-10s. The next thing you know we'll find out they have Corvair engines."

"Corvair engines?"

"Ralph Nader's first discovery. He found defects in Corvair cars. That was before your time, I guess." He dismissed the reference, discarding it with a wave of the hand, wondering why he had ever brought it up in the first place. They rode on in the smooth silence of limo comfort, some sense of connection severed, until they came to the approach to the Queensborough

Bridge where the traffic funneled in slow stops and starts. Larry shook his head: "New York traffic."

"Worse than LA?"

"Much. Even when we slow down we still make sure we're going fast enough to kill each other."

Michael laughed. "You said I might be able to help you?" she began.

"You are being very helpful."

"I think it was in terms of something specific."

"What was I talking about?" Larry put his hand to his forehead in mock senility and spoke like a doddering old man, his lips peeled back over his teeth. "You have to forgive me, dearie. My memory isn't all that it used to be. Especially today of all days."

Michael nodded and smiled. "You were talking about your daughter and how I looked her age."

He snapped his fingers. "Of course. Mary's been accepted at both Sarah Lawrence and Bard. But lately she's been talking about not going to college at all. And I'm curious. Did you go to college?"

"Yes."

"Where?"

"Brandeis."

"Brandeis University? I lectured there a few years ago."

"I know," Michael said, smiling.

"Are you glad you went to college?"

She shrugged. "Let me put it this way. I'm not particularly sorry that I did."

"What did you study?"

"Cinema."

"Were you at my lecture by any chance?"

She nodded slowly.

"How was I?"

"Terrific."

"Really?"

"Yes."

"What did I talk about?"

She smiled. "Cinema."

"Cinema." Larry looked out the window at the cabled lattice-work of the bridge. Not bad. But not the Brooklyn Bridge either. What could you expect of a bridge from Queens anyway? "Cinema," Larry repeated, "is just a form of Danish. I can't even remember what I had for breakfast. What do you say we have lunch together?"

"Okay. Fine."

"Terrific." Larry studied Michael again. Even though she looked no older than his daughter Mary, he reminded himself, she was. And that was a fact. A real fact.

Larry hated New York lunches. The food was too serious. Dinner food. And the portions were too big. Yet he always found himself compulsively cleaning his plate. Which did not do his expanding waistline any good at all. And he would drink too much. Michael had ordered Pernod as an aperitif. And he joined her. Twice. And then they had a bottle of Pouilly-Fuissé with the meal. And now in the maroon Leatherette booth of the french restaurant he was sipping cognac with his *café filtre* while Michael—she insisted—was taking care of the check. He knew it wasn't good form to let her do that. But he couldn't stand wasting money either. Just because he made more money in one year than his father ever dreamed of making in a lifetime was still no reason to waste money. Besides, having money gave him the freedom and independence to do the pictures *he* wanted to do, not the pictures *they* wanted him to do. Especially with his reputation for cost cutting, for making pictures for a price. It helped him call his shots. And any extra money he could manage he would rather spend on his family. On Jane and the kids. Why not? Just because he had to watch his money all the time for artistic and creative purposes was no reason for his wife and children to suffer. In fact, that was why he flattered the scumbags who ran the studios and why his agent and business manager had to drive such hard deals for him. He had more than just himself to think about. Besides, even if *Herbie and Milty* was down the tubes, the studio really wouldn't get hurt and he had made enough money for them in the past anyway. So he ordered a Perrier to wash down the cognac and coffee, pleased that he had let Michael convince him that she would get in trouble with her boss, Lloyd, unless he allowed her to pick up the check.

"I like the way you handled that," Michael said.

"Handled what?"

"Let me take care of the bill. You'd be surprised how many men resent letting a woman pick up a bill. It offends their macho."

"I'm an easy macho. As long as the studio picks up the tab."

"Don't worry, they will." The waiter deposited his Perrier before him and gave Michael the credit-card paperwork to sign. She tore off the cardholder copy herself, folded it into her wallet, and then placed the wallet in her purse, while the waiter bowed and thanked her.

Larry patted his stomach. "I love New York lunches," he said.

"Don't you have lunches in California?"

"Not really. I mean, not just to talk. Seriously talk. Like we've been doing. All the people out there care about is deals and points and profit positions. They're not like us." He shot her his best *I-thou* look right between the eyes, looking at an imaginary spot on her forehead. "No. They're not interested in cinema as art. Or have any respect for art itself. I can't stand those people. Especially at lunch in one of those places like Ma Maison where even before they sit down they have to do a room." Larry leaped out of his seat and went from empty table to empty booth shaking imaginary hands and kissing imaginary cheeks. He looked back to Michael for appreciation for his pantomime. "You keep looking at your watch," he observed. "Do you have to get back to the office?"

"I should check in."

Larry took her arm. "Then why didn't you say so? C'mon, I'll walk you back." He allowed his bloated stomach to expand and patted it. "I need the exercise."

"What about the limo?"

"I don't think the limo can walk."

After they left the restaurant Michael dismissed the waiting driver and then with the smile of a coconspirator slid her arm back into his. They walked down the street, crossing Fifth Avenue, toward Rockefeller Center, and stopped at the skating rink. Since it wasn't the season, there was no ice below but only an open-air restaurant. Still people leaned over the rail bars, peering down as if there was something of interest to see. All they could see, of course, were other people dining alfresco under patio umbrellas. At first impression the diners seemed to be doing their best to be oblivious to the gapers but after a while Larry noticed that many of the diners were really gapers as well as gapees themselves, watching their watchers as much as being watched. It was a comic visual ballet—everyone on stage and in the audience at the same time.

Michael, beside him, had her own thoughts. "New Yorkers will look at anything," she said.

"Anything?" He playfully mimed an ice skater, his hands locked behind his back, his knees bent, gliding down the sidewalk. A couple passing by eyed him curiously. She ran up to him laughing. "You skate marvelously."

"I wish I could." He simulated lifting a racket high over his head and coming down in a hard serve. "Tennis is my game."

"Are you any good?"

"Any good?" He retrieved the serve, maintained a difficult volley involving lobs and slices, before slamming it away. Then he leapt over the net, embraced her as his defeated opponent, and held his arms up to the gallery, slowly twirling his racket about as he basked in a deafening ovation which he supplied ventriloquistically. "Pancho Lazar," he said, catching his breath. "I'm really very good. For a slightly overweight director. I play on the Bel Air circuit and in a lot of celebrity tournaments. I can beat Chuck Heston and Burt Reynolds. But not Bill Cosby. Do you play?"

"I used to. But not much anymore. I jog though."

"I play every day out in LA. In fact, that's the best thing about LA. You can play all year round." Now, Larry decided, he would take her by surprise, see how she could react to a zinger. "Do you fool around a lot?" he asked.

"Do I what?"

"Do you fool around a lot? I don't fool around much," he continued without missing a beat. "But I masturbate. A little. Once in a while. I think that's all right. I also think that's the secret of success in marriage. Masturbation. Digital stimulation. And a variable orifice approach. Jane and I have been married almost nineteen years. That's an LA County record. Maybe a record for all of Southern California. Because California marriages are like dogs' ages. You have to multiply by seven to get a true count. Are you married?"

"No."

"Are you living with someone?"

Michael nodded.

"Have you lived with a lot of people?"

"No."

"Stop me if I'm being too personal," he pressed on. "I'm always like this after my mother's funeral. But, seriously, I'm a very honest and open person. I try to be anyway. Because I've discovered it costs me too much not to be. Like ninety dollars for a fifty-minute hour. Are you in love with the person you're living with?"

"Yes."

"How nice. What does he do?"

"Not he," Michael said quietly. "She."

"Oh," he said in a swallow, belying his attempt to show super-sophistication. "Whatever."

"You've met her."

"Inman?"

"Yes."

"She seems like a very nice person. Really. But let me ask one more question. I must warn you it's a very personal question."

"What's the question?"

"Do you ever fool around with men, too?"

Michael laughed. "Yes."

"Then there's hope for me." He swept her into his arms and embraced her with mock passion.

14

The phone.

Larry knew the phone was ringing. But he felt profoundly dislocated. He had no idea of the time of day or where he was. The gray texture of the light, the prison-bar pattern of the shadows were unfamiliar. The room was definitely not his. But as he struggled up from sleep the phone continued to ring and gradually he remembered that he was in New York, realized that he was in his hotel bedroom, and that it was still afternoon. He recalled walking Michael back to the studio's office building, kissing her good-bye at the revolving-door entrance, and then returning to the Sherry.

He picked up the phone. It was Jane. He told her that he had been napping. He told her about the funeral and how it went. He told her that he missed her and the kids and that he had no idea how much longer he would have to stay in New York because there were some legal things to clear up about his mother. But that couldn't possibly take more than a day or two and that, anyway, he was tired and wanted to get back home as soon as possible. Which was true.

By this time he was on his feet, twisting and untwisting the phone cord, checking his watch and discovering that he had slept almost three hours, emptying his pockets and coming across the pack of cigarettes and the glassine envelope. Nervously, as if there was phonevision, he quickly completed the conversation, blew Jane a good-bye kiss, and hung up.

He held the envelope in the palm of one hand, the cigarettes in the palm of the other. Put a blindfold over his eyes, he thought, and he would look like the Goddess of Justice in drag, doing her balancing act with the scales. He wondered how much the coke weighed. He could not guess. He had no idea. It was light as a feather. One thing certain: Whatever it weighed was in milligrams, not ounces, like a doctor's prescription. The cigarettes had more body, more substance. Were probably a lot more harmful for you, too. The package even carried a boxed warning from a doctor, the surgeon general. He looked at the envelope of coke: carried no warning from Allen. Impulsively, he went over to the fragile-looking antique desk, opened the drawer, and removed a crisp sheet of hotel stationery. He rolled it, and as carefully as Paul Muni playing Louis Pasteur in an MGM laboratory, jiggled out a thin line, and snorted. Then he placed the glassine envelope in a hotel stationery envelope and sealed it. Wanted to make sure he didn't overdo a good thing. Or a bad thing.

He went into the sitting room of the suite and leaned back on the couch, comfortably sprawling his legs across the end table. It had been a long day and he was glad it was almost over. But there was still the evening to get through as pleasurably as possible. And the coke would help. He could have dinner and go to a movie. But he would soon be feeling too good to be alone, to waste himself on just himself. He rubbed his fingers over his eyes and thought of Mira. She certainly had been in his thoughts last night. He would go with the flow. But where could he find her? How could he get hold of her number? He considered calling Allen and asking him for it but quickly decided against doing that. It would only complicate matters. He leaned across the table and pulled over the Manhattan telephone directory. You never knew who was listed in that book of eternal truth. After all, until just two years ago hadn't he himself been listed in the Western Area LA telephone directory? The old candy-store kid just couldn't see the point in paying an extra seventy-five cents not to be listed. Per month. Per phone. But then too many actors he barely even knew began bugging him for bit parts. And that was finally too much.

Like the Rev Bookbinder searching out the place in a prayer book, he was index-fingering his way down the small-type printing of the phone book until he found her last name. And lo and behold, she was listed there, too. Not out of any compunction about coughing up the seventy-five cents, he was sure. But just out of sheer laziness.

Larry picked up the phone and slowly dialed her number.

He had not seen Mira in ages. He recalled setting up a lunch or dinner with her some years back when he was in town for the opening of *Bachelor Spouse*. But, if he remembered correctly, she had stood him up. Which was just like her.

Her phone answered immediately. On the first ring. Which was not like her at all. "Hello," she breathed familiarly.

"Hello," Larry said.

"I'm not here right now," she continued, "but if you leave your name and number at the beep, I'll call you back later. Maybe."

Larry waited for the beep and then laughed into the phone. Mira was the last person in the world he expected to have one of these machines. But he hung up without leaving his name or number. Would be pointless. After all, he was just calling her on a whim. In fact, maybe her not being in was a sign that he shouldn't have even called her in the first place.

Still, he didn't feel like dinner alone. But who could he get on such short notice?

Larry snapped his fingers, enjoying the sound inordinately as he did so, and rose to his feet. He searched his pockets and returned to the bedroom. On the desk he found what he was looking for: Michael's card.

On the off chance that he could still catch her at the office he first tried that number. But an answering machine picked up telling him that the office was closed for the day and would not be open until nine o'clock tomorrow morning. He turned the card over and found her home number. He dialed that. Before the phone seemed to have time to even ring he heard her voice pick up: "Hello."

"Hello." He hesitated. "Are you an answering machine?"

"No," she laughed. "Are you?" Her voice sounded different

over the phone. Softer. Less metallic. More feminine. Or was that just his imagination?

"No. But I am prerecorded. You know who this is?"

"Yes. In fact, I was just about to call you. To find out how you were doing."

"I'm doing good. But I think I could be doing a lot better if you were free tonight."

"I do have a dinner engagement," she began.

"Oh—"

"But I think I may be able to get out of it."

"Oh?"

"Let me call you right back."

Larry went into the bathroom and examined his face in the mirror, rolling his skin between his fingers. He could use a shave, he decided. For some reason his hair seemed to grow faster in New York. Maybe it was the pace of the town. Reaching all the way down to his follicles. In California his hircine chemistry was much more laid back. Or maybe it was simply Allen's lousy electric shaver.

He picked up his own Norelco, with the smooth familiar burr, and started chipping away at the five o'clock shadow. When suddenly he stopped. He did not like what he was seeing. The face reflecting back at him from the mirror was his face all right. But at the same time it was also Sally's. Not the pale, young, docile face he had seen in repose yesterday. But the middle-aged harpy face, the *ponim* of the eternal *kvetch*. Would he have to live with that face-within-his-face for the rest of his life? When would that woman finally die? Yesterday he had simply instructed that the coffin be kept closed. Oh, that he could get rid of her memory so easily. But in death as in life he knew she would not let him off lightly. There would be a price to pay and he had to be ready to ante up. If some devil were to make him an offer he'd listen. Or, at least, begin negotiations. There were some things, of course, he would never give up: Jane. The kids. The house. His integrity. His next picture. But everything else was negotiable. The devil would find him a reasonable man to deal with. Far more reasonable than he himself had ever found Sally.

Was there a picture in it, he wondered, a director making some sort of deal with the devil? But it wouldn't be about the guilt trip involved in losing the memory of a mother, but rather about the picaresque adventure encountered in trying to retain one's own youth. Yes, toss in the Ponce de Leon theme. And make the director not a director but a Howard Hughes, a J. Paul Getty, a Norton—or even a Neil—Simon, the world's wealthiest man, seeking the elixir of everlasting life. And finding it, too. Or thinking he does. In drugs. No, that would be too downbeat. Wouldn't work commercially. It would make the man a loser. Movies had to be about winners. People didn't pay their hard money to watch losers. It wasn't a question of art. It was a question of fact. Reality. Real reality. It was the sole limitation of the medium. Everything else could be excused, overcome, overlooked. But you had to make pictures about winners.

The phone rang, interrupting his thought. Larry reached for the receiver, hanging from the wall, less than an arm's length away. "I love hotel johns," he announced; "they're the world's most comfortable phone booths."

"Larry Lazar?" asked Michael at the other end.

"The one and, I hope, only," he laughed. "What about dinner?"

"You're on. I can make it."

"Terrific."

"But I thought maybe you'd like to go to the theater first."

"What a wonderful idea!"

"Would you like to see a musical?"

"I'd rather see something a little more substantial. Something I couldn't see in LA."

Michael mentioned an off-Broadway hit he'd heard about.

"Terrific."

She said she would make arrangements for the tickets. He could pick her up in an hour in the limo which she would also make sure was at the hotel. The theater was in the Village and they could worry about dinner afterward. She gave him her address and hung up before he had a chance to tell her again how pleased he was.

The play was terrible. It was essentially a dumb conceit masquerading as deep symbolism. About a circus freak, a man who had the humped back of a camel, falling in love with an impotent gay. In post–World War I Weimar Berlin. In Hollywood the idea couldn't have gotten past the studio gates; in New York it was a hit. Michael even had had to use heat to extract the house seats from the production manager at the last moment, claiming that Larry was interested in casting one of the leads in his next picture.

Larry fanned himself with the skimpy off-Broadway program, wondering if he had been away too long or if the New York critics had all been out to lunch. There was no doubt that the actor playing the camel freak was good. But not good enough to make him want to sit through a show that had so little reality. Besides, he was getting hungry.

He deserved a good dinner, too. But first he'd have to get Michael out of there. He smiled over to her and yawned.

"Want to go?" she whispered.

Intelligent and perceptive. He liked that. He slowly rolled both his head and his eyes as if the play had already put him into a stupor.

She laughed and squeezed his hand. "Can you hold out until intermission?"

"If they can," he pointed up at the actors, "I can."

She took his hand and rubbed it gently, reassuringly, the way his mother did when as a child he became restless at a Joan Crawford movie.

"I'm so glad you were able to make it tonight," Larry told her as they came up the aisle at intermission. "But I'm not so happy about this show."

"Neither am I. I'm sorry."

"Oh, it's not your fault. I probably would have come here on my own before leaving town, anyway."

"Where do you want to eat?"

"Wherever."

"How about SoHo?"

"That's where I ate last night."

"So?"

"Ho," Larry said. "As in Westwood. I mean, Westward."

The attraction at the restaurant on Spring Street was not so much the food, Michael had briefed him, but the crowd: the art world. And as he picked up the menu and looked the room over he indeed had a sense of *déjà vu*. It was Max's Kansas City and the Cedar Bar a generation later, and the waitresses, though a generation taller, could also have been cast out of the old Café Rienzi which was light-years back. The diners all looked as if they were somebody in the arts: Critics. Collectors. Dealers. Even painters. The decor of the place—a preponderance of mirrors and stained woods—made it seem like the salon of a yacht that would never set sail, one forever moored at pier's end because of legal complications. A dispute over the title or the deed or unpaid docking fees.

"I'm starved," Larry said. "I haven't been so starved since the Academy Awards."

Michael wrinkled her nose and made a face. "I don't understand."

"Oh," Larry explained. "The award ceremonies begin at six o'clock. Which means your limo picks you up at four-thirty to get you to the Dorothy Chandler on time. Then from six to nine you're part of the captive TV audience. After the ceremonies it takes a good hour for you to find your limo and for your limo to find you; the place is a madhouse. Then another half hour at least to get you to the Beverly Hilton for the Governor's Ball. Which means you don't get to sit down to dinner until ten-thirty, eleven o'clock. And it's a lousy dinner—cold steak—and you haven't had a bite since lunch and it's been hard to hold that down, thinking about your acceptance speech and all the other craziness. The Academy Awards Diet Book. Think it would sell?"

Michael laughed. "In the millions."

"I'm also thinking of putting out an Academy Awards Losers' Acceptance Speech collection. Think of all those marvelously poignant and witty, carefully prepared impromptu speeches that never get made."

"How many do you have?"

"One."

"You've been nominated more than once."

"Twice. But never for directing. Only for writing. And since I never got to use my first speech I still have it ready."

"I'd love to hear that speech some time."

"So would I," Larry sighed. "So would I."

"I mean privately."

"If you play your cards right." He did his best Groucho Marx leer again and flicked the ashes off an imaginary cigar. "It's a common speech usually fooled around the house."

Michael shrugged. "I guess I'll have to wait for the book."

"That's funny," Larry said without laughing. "That is very funny." His head was into the menu now and he was concentrating on food. He deserved a big meal. But at the same time he didn't want to gorge himself either. He knew his neurosis. He could easily use Sally's death as an excuse to go off on an eating binge. Put on ten, twelve pounds in no time. Eat himself out of a little sadness into a great deal of unhappiness. No, he didn't want to do that. He would eat like a normal person. An appetizer. An entree. And he would skip dessert. He wouldn't stuff himself. "What are you going to have?" He looked up from the menu.

"I think I'll have a salad."

"A salad? What are you? A bird? That's all you had for lunch."

"And that's all I want for dinner."

"Are you a vegetarian by any chance?"

"In fact, I am."

"So is my daughter, Mary. She can't even stand the fact that my wife has a fur coat."

"I don't blame her. I wouldn't want to carry the skin of a dead animal on my back either."

"Not even as an investment?"

"You always joke, don't you?"

Larry reached over and took Michael's hand paternally, the

way he would take his own daughter's hand. "Only when I'm serious. It's a legacy from Sally."

Michael closed her menu and slowly nodded. As if he had just said something very heavy and self-revealing that she could understand. Which was exactly the effect he wanted.

He could kick himself.

The meal wasn't bad but he'd eaten too much. He shouldn't have started with the soup, for openers. But the waitress had made a big pitch about how the potato potage was the chef's specialty. And he was a sucker for potato potage. And it *was* good. Delicious. But then he should have gone lighter on the bread instead and skipped the pâté entirely. But what the hell? The company was good and the wine was fine. There was about a half glass left in the bottle and he held it out over Michael's glass. She covered the glass with her hand and shook her head. "You take it."

"I can order another bottle."

"I'm fine. Really."

He poured the wine into his own glass. "I shouldn't drink too much either."

"You don't seem to have a problem there."

"Only with the calories." He patted his stomach. "They all go here." He took a sip of the wine. "But, I guess, if I pass on dessert it'll be a wash."

Michael smiled. She smiled a lot at what he said and he liked that. She wasn't bad company at all for an a.k. like himself in New York away from home. Considering she was a dike. Or a half of a dike. Which was a bi. Anyway it was a generational thing as far as he was concerned. But what if his daughter Mary were to become a lesbian? How would he react to that? Would he take it personally because it meant she was rejecting him in an Oedipal sense? Or did that mean she was rejecting Jane more? He was not sure. It was something to discuss with Dave when he got home. He wouldn't make a professional appointment about it. Just sort of bring it up after tennis in a general sense. There was no point wasting money on it. Unless there might be a picture in it. But he doubted that. Not even a chest picture. Freddie Fields, his ex-agent, had once described a picture a fellow director made as a chest picture. "It was a picture he had to get off his chest." But now television seemed to be the place for chest pictures. In fact, if he remembered correctly, he had seen a picture with a similar theme on a "Movie of the Week." Only it had dealt with a mother's discovery of the fact that her son was gay.

"How did your parents react," he asked, "when they first discovered that you like women?"

"You mean love women."

"Whatever."

"They didn't."

"Didn't react or didn't discover?"

"Both."

"You mean you haven't told them?"

"Why should I?"

"I thought your generation was more"—he searched for the word—"liberated."

"Perhaps it is. But yours isn't."

"You never trust anyone over thirty?"

"I never trust anyone over three."

"But I thought your generation thought everything was better if it was open and above board," he persisted.

"It is," she smiled. "Generally."

"Is there any specific reason why you haven't told them?"

"Sure. It would kill them."

"But your parents aren't even Jewish."

"Of course, they are," said Michael. "I'm Jewish."

"I didn't know that," said Larry. "Now I understand why it would kill them. They couldn't stand the idea of your going with a *schwartze.*"

Michael laughed. "It certainly wouldn't help, would it?"

Over coffee and dessert—he just couldn't resist the pastry cart, and persuaded Michael to share a Napoleon and a piece of seven-layer cake with him—she told him about her background. Good Jewish family from a good Jewish neighborhood: Great Neck.

Went to Great Neck High and then Brandeis. Always interested in film, as far back as she could remember. Only child. Father in jewelry business. Mother interested in the temple and the arts. "God," she pushed the last piece of cake back to Larry, "it's all so trite, it's boring."

"If you recount any life quickly," Larry said, "it's boring."

"Not your life."

"You'd be surprised. Substitute Brooklyn for Great Neck and a candy store for the jewelry business and it's not that different."

"Plus the fact that you're an important director."

"That and five cents, as they used to say. How much is the subway now?"

"Eleven dollars. But you know what I mean? You've accomplished something with your life."

"Sometimes I wonder."

"Don't be coy. You've made some of the finest pictures of our time."

Larry was both pleased and disappointed. Pleased that she thought his movies were among the best of "our time." Disappointed that she hadn't described them as among the finest of all time. "That and eleven dollars—or whatever the subway fare really is," he said and laughed. "Do you really want to be a filmmaker?"

"Of course," she said. "That's why I majored in film. That's why I attended your lecture. That's why I took this job in publicity."

"What kind of pictures do you want to make?"

"Pictures like you make. Only about women. Real women."

"Of course," he said.

"About the relationships real women have," she continued.

"You mean like the relationship you have with Inman?"

"That would be part of it. When was the last time you saw a really honest picture about lesbian love?"

Larry shook his head. He couldn't remember. He also couldn't remember the last time he saw a really honest picture about any kind of love. Except maybe one of his own pictures. But then he was unique—sui generis. Only with occasional influences.

"That's what I mean," Michael was saying. "But I also have affairs with men. I have to make choices. Any contemporary woman does. And I never see any of that up there on the screen."

Larry agreed with her. There was a need for such movies. There was a need for any kind of movie that dealt with real reality. "But wouldn't the parents of a modern young woman have to be in a movie about such problems?" he asked.

"I guess so."

"How would you handle your parents in a movie?"

"I guess I'd have to tell them the truth."

"It would be a terrific scene," Larry said.

"I know," Michael acknowledged. "I wrote it."

In fact, she had a script that she wanted him to read. Which did not surprise him. What did surprise him was his reaction. "I really would like to see it," he volunteered. "Maybe I can pick it up later."

"That would be terrific," she said, pushing back the rest of the Napoleon.

"This Napoleon is terrific, too," said Larry as he put the last squishy piece in his mouth. "Too terrific. If I keep eating like this in New York, I'll go back to LA looking like a Jewish Alfred Hitchcock. By the way, where did you get the name Baldwin?"

"From a piano," Michael said. "My real name is Steinway."

When the waitress brought over the check Larry again had no misgivings about letting Michael pay for it. After all, she would definitely be reimbursed by the studio and he had made enough for the scumbags. They always robbed him blind anyway. Charging him twenty-five percent studio overhead for openers. Which meant when a picture was said to cost thirteen million it actually cost ten mill and change. Then the studio tacked on a twenty percent interest charge to the thirteen million figure. And when the money began coming in they deducted thirty-five percent for distribution. Distribution costs were basically just the matter of a few phone calls. Because the real distribution costs such as prints and advertising were also deducted before a picture could begin to get out of the red ink. It was all a hustle.

His last picture *Herbie and Milty,* for example, would finally recoup most of the actual dollars that had been spent on it. But you'd never know it from the bookkeeping. From the bookkeeping it would always look like a picture that was in a big hole. But, with a TV sale, it would eventually more than earn out. In fact, his business manager had told him that no big studio picture ever actually loses money. That was because the studios had a unique option in terms of tax credits: They could choose the year in which to write off a loser. In other words, they could wait until they had a big hit before declaring the turkey a loser—and in that way Uncle Sam always wound up footing the bills.

Not that any of this really concerned him. After all, he was an artist not a businessman. But theoretically he had to be aware of the business side in order to protect himself. Because it was very tricky. Because business was the downside of art. And he was constantly at a disadvantage. He wanted to use the studio to make his kind of pictures, pictures that were artistic statements. And the studio wanted to use him to make their kind of pictures, dumb pictures that they thought would make money.

Not that they knew what would make money. It was just that they remembered most clearly what had made money recently. All studio executives were agents playing Mr. Memory like the character that got shot down in that Hitchcock film, *The Thirty-nine Steps.* And he would have liked nothing better than to shoot them all down, too. Because of their edge, their advantage, in dealing with him. As an artist he could still understand business —anyone had to understand the ways of commerce in order to survive in our society. But as businessmen, in order to survive, they didn't have to understand art at all—in fact, rarely did. So communication was always down a one-way street in dealing with them. Still, he had done well in playing their game. He had gotten five pictures made. And getting up to bat was the only thing that counted in the movie business. In fact, at bats were more important than hits. You could actually build a career on at bats alone. After a while everyone forgot the rest of the box score. He certainly hoped he would be getting up a sixth time soon with *Remember, Remember.*

After paying the check with her American Express credit card,

Michael excused herself to go to the ladies' room. Larry watched her pass between the tables and the booths that lined the walls as if she were a stranger, or at least someone he did not know, wondering what he could possibly see in her. Physically she was attractive in a dark hoydenish way but no more attractive than so many of the kids he'd met on college campuses or at AFI when he lectured there. The fact that she was a film freak, in fact, should have been enough to be a turnoff. In addition, she was lesbian and had even written a script about it. Yet there he was looking forward to the next phase of the evening, wondering what shape it would take. Was it because he had lost his bearings because of his mother's death? Or had his mother's death opened up certain prospects and possibilities for him? Was it because he was deeply worried as a filmmaker about his next project? Or was he simply a lonely businessman out on the town, anxious not to return to the solitary confines of his hotel room again? Like last night. Whatever. He was still curious as to how the night would end. It was just his second night in New York and it seemed he had already spent a week here. Time always moved in slow mo away from home.

When Michael returned to the booth, she bounced her hand-bag on the table in front of her, a tricky smile on her lips, as if she had decided something in the ladies' room, too. Larry stood up and slid out of the booth. Then he noticed a couple entering the restaurant and felt himself going from slow mo into freeze frame.

"What's the matter?" asked Michael. She turned around and followed his gaze. "Oh, that's Mira, the sculptor."

Larry sank back into the booth. "You know her?"

"I know *of* her. Everybody does. She's famous."

"Oh," he said, his eyes still riveted on Mira. At first it seemed as if she had not changed at all. As if time had stood still and only now it was the Spring Street Bar instead of the San Remo and it was SoHo instead of the Village. But as she walked further into the restaurant, coming closer to his booth, he realized time had moved on and she had changed. The skin. The telltale skin was dry and splotchy, the victim of too many years of makeup abuse. For Mira had always applied her makeup in bold strokes as if she were painting on a mask to hide behind. Her eyes were framed with too much blue shadow and her face was overpowdered almost like that of a Kyoto *maiko*. But, of course, she lacked the traditional bird-walking-on-water grace of an Oriental woman. As she swung her shoulders there was the Western touch of masculine swagger to her gait.

Mira sat down in a booth on the opposite side of the restaurant, evidently still not noticing him. Perhaps, Larry ran his fingers through his thinning hair, he had changed more than she had. In addition to his lack of hair, there was his surfeit of weight. But how could she tell that while he was still seated. Unless it showed in his face, too. He put his hand on the corners of his mouth and pressed his lips together.

"Why are you making a face?" asked Michael.

"I wasn't making a face. I was just testing my face."

"For Mira?"

"Yes."

"Do you know her?"

"I used to."

"Well, the fellow with her evidently knows you. He's waving. In fact, he looks very familiar to me, too."

Larry had been studying Mira so intently that he had barely noticed the young man with her. Now the young man was not only waving but actually coming across the room, a broad smile on his face.

"I think I recognize him," Michael quickly whispered, "from television."

Larry recognized him, too. He was the actor kid who had come in on the same plane with him yesterday. The actor he had turned down for a part in *Bachelor Spouse*. For the second time in two days he tried to recall his name and couldn't. All that came up from his memory bank was the visual image of the kid walking out of the airport with Katharine Hepburn. Now the kid had walked into the restaurant with Mira and was holding out his hand for Larry to shake.

"I didn't think we'd meet again so soon, Mr. Lazar."

"My pleasure," Larry said, reaching up but not rising. Wondering, at the same time, how he could possibly introduce the kid to Michael without remembering his name. If he could stall long enough it would come to him though. It always did.

But Michael herself came to his rescue. "I know you," she said. "From television. The show with the motorcycles."

"Chris Tucker." The kid smiled politely, turning on his California ocean blues.

"Excuse me," Larry said, acting the absentminded host, "Michael Baldwin."

Chris and Michael dipped their heads toward each other. Then Chris said to him, "Do you know who was on the same plane with us?"

"Katharine Hepburn," Michael quickly answered for him.

"That's right," Chris said. "And she's a great fan of yours, Mr. Lazar. She told me she and Cary Grant think the world of you."

"Cary," Larry said. "Yes, Cary and I hit it off." And looked across the room. Mira was staring right at him. He smiled back. But she didn't acknowledge him at all. Then he remembered her bad eyes, her nearsightedness, and her vain refusal to wear eyeglasses. Thought it would destroy her idiosyncratically personal way of looking at things. So they always had had to sit up front, in the first few rows—like children, at the movies. If he had kept going with her he would have ended up blind. "How's Mira?" he asked.

"Do you know her?"

"I used to."

"Then come find out for yourself. Why don't you join us?"

"We've already eaten." Larry rose. "But I guess we can at least say hello. How do you know Mira?"

"I met her at a party the last time I was in New York." They crossed the room, Chris leading the way, and Larry impulsively put his arm about Michael's waist, wondering at the same time why he was doing so. To show off? Or to protect Michael? From what? Certainly not from Mira. Mira was weird and strange but straight. Or was it to protect himself? To have Michael ready, in body-English terms, to be interjected as a buffer with a sleight-of-hand motion between himself and Mira in case of an emergency?

But he was certainly not afraid of Mira after all these years. Her knife-wielding shtick had to be over as far as he was concerned. They were the actor kid's worries now, if anyone's. Not his.

Mira was still a marvel at underplaying. She greeted him casually, as if she had run into him yesterday and so was not surprised to see him again today. "Hi," she said.

"Hi," he said.

She turned to Chris. "I need a drink."

"This is Michael," said Chris. "I'll order you one. How about you?" he asked Larry.

"No thanks," Larry said; "we're on our way out. Just stopped by to say a quick hello."

"Make it a double," Mira told Chris, who was trying to catch the waitress's eye. Then she looked up at Larry and said, "Hello quickly."

Her skin up close looked even worse than it had from across the room. She had lost weight, her face thinning out, and now there was too much skin to be stretched over too little surface and some of it was beginning to drip down from her chin onto her neck in creased folds. Yet she was still not unattractive because of those shining olive eyes framed by her thick black hair which she wore in Gloria Steinem–Yoko Ono style. She was also wearing a smart black cocktail dress and a string of pearls hung from her neck. Which was a great departure. Larry could count the times he had seen her previously in a dress and he remembered distinctly that in the old days she never wore jewelry.

"How are you?" he asked.

"Fine," she replied. "You?"

"I'm doing good. But small world. You know who I saw last night? Allen."

"That creep."

"I hadn't seen him in several years."

"He's still a creep. And a fag. And a junkie."

Larry laughed. "You can't seem to say enough good things about him."

"How's Jane?"

That surprised him. She remembered not only that he was

married but his wife's name as well. But then Mira always had the capacity to surprise him. One of her most attractive features.

"Jane is terrific," he said. "And you look terrific." And it was true. Once he got used to her again, accepted the fact that she had aged and become older, she didn't look bad at all. For her age.

"How's Sally?" Mira asked.

Right away she was surprising him again. People like Mira just weren't supposed to remember old lovers' mothers. "You remember Sally?"

"Yes."

"Yesterday was her funeral. That's why I'm in town."

"I'm sorry."

Larry smiled. "Sally was a creep anyway."

"No." Mira shook her head. "Creeps are phony. She wasn't phony. I always wanted to do her head."

Larry shuddered to himself. Imagine having a sculpture of Sally's head in his living room, forever staring after him accusingly, in addition to Mira's cat piece.

The waitress came over and Chris ordered a double vodka on the rocks for Mira and a Jack Daniel's for himself. Once again he asked Larry and Michael to join them but Larry insisted that they had already dined and it was getting late so they really had to be going.

"Call me," Mira suddenly whispered up to him.

"Where?" As if he didn't know. As if he hadn't found her number in the phone book and called her just a few hours ago.

She wrote down her number and address on a pad that Michael quickly supplied. He tore off the sheet and made an acting point of looking at it before folding it and placing it in his pocket. "Where is that?"

"Near here."

"I'll call you," he said, doubting that he ever would because now that he had seen her again there was little need to. He bent over and kissed her on the cheek. "I'll definitely call you."

She smiled her olive eyes up at him. "Breakfast?"

"What?"

"Let's have breakfast tomorrow. Ten o'clock."

"Will you be up that early?"

"Ten-thirty." She laughed.

"Okay. Where?"

"Call me."

They were all saying goodnight and how nice it was to meet each other when the actor asked Larry when he would be going back to the coast.

"As soon as possible," Larry replied.

"Well," the actor reached across the table and took Mira's hand, turning it over as if he were a palm reader, "I'll be here a little longer than that."

And damned, if after all these years, Larry didn't feel a twinge of jealousy. "C'mon." He took Michael's arm.

15

The limo was taking them back uptown when Michael mentioned her script again and how anxious she was for Larry to read it.

"Well then, let's pick it up now. I need something to read before going to sleep."

"Are you sure it wouldn't be too much trouble?"

"I'm sure. There's no time like the present."

"I really appreciate it."

I hope so, thought Larry.

"I mean I really value your criticism. I respect you so much, you know. And please don't be afraid to tell me the truth."

"Don't be so nervous."

"Promise me you won't be anything less than candid—even if it means being brutal."

"I'm sure it won't be necessary."

"Don't be so sure," Michael said, and blew air out of her mouth. All her hard-bought worldliness and sophistication were gone now. Larry realized she was young and vulnerable, not that far removed from being a school girl. He put his arm around her gently. She reached up, squeezing his hand appreciatively. Then she bent forward and gave the driver instructions on how to get to her apartment. When she leaned back she settled comfortably against his shoulder. He looked down at her, at her straight bobbed hair and bony, if patrician face, and wondered for a moment if he was letting himself in for trouble. But how much trouble could it be? All he had to do was read the script and there was even the chance it might be good. And if it was bad, the "pits" as his seatmate had liked to describe things, so what? He could always lie. Tell her how "well crafted" or "nicely observed" it was but how it might be a stretch commercially in terms of the reality of the business. Something like that. Anyway, he would think of something.

He was always good at bullshit and never above lying when it came to the movie business. Who was he to be different? It was impossible to produce a film without lying. Constantly. Innumerable times. George Washington could never have gotten this country off the ground without lying if he had been in the movie business. America would never have been a *go* country. Just another passed project. In the movie business you always had to lie and Larry rarely had the slightest hesitation about doing so. There was even the joke about the agent described in novelistic terms: "Hello," he lied. And he could never have made *Herbie and Milty,* for example, without lying. He had looked his leading actor straight in the eye and lied to him. About how much he himself was taking out of the picture up front. About how little he could squeeze out of the budget. About how no one else was getting a penny more. And the actor believed him and settled for $100,000 less than his going market price. And that hundred thousand meant the difference to the studio between giving him the green light and passing.

It was all a big poker game and everybody lied to each other. About budgets. About conditions. About commitments. A lie to Larry was simply like a hole card he didn't have in his hand. But seldom did anyone ever call his bluff. They were all too busy covering themselves. Besides, when he lied, it was only to serve his art. Which seemed like a lie too, but was in point of fact the truth. Everything he did in life was to service his art. Most of the time anyway. Even though, he knew, ironically that the basis of all art was the lie, the bottom line being whether the lie was a means or an end. In great art lies were used to tell the truth. In kitsch and popular art, truths were used to tell a lie. Or was it the other way around? And when the great became popular did the distinctions blur? He looked down again at Michael, leaning back against his shoulder. What kind of bullshit was he feeding himself, anyway? He just wanted to lay her, that's all. Bang. Bang. It was no big deal. But to ensure fucking her he had to make her feel good about him and the best way to do that was to make her feel good about herself. By his reaction to her script. It was as simple as that. Like everything else in the movie business it would all begin with the script—and a lie.

"Turn here," Michael was telling the driver. "It's between Columbus and Amsterdam."

The limo stopped, the driver double-parking before a graystone.

"Do you want to come up with me?"

"Is there anybody else home?"

"Yes."

"Then I better not."

"I can always get the script to you tomorrow."

"No, I want to read it tonight."

"I'll bring it right down."

Larry relaxed in the comfort of the car. He stretched out and put his hands into his pants pockets. He felt the glassine envelope and rubbed it between his fingers. Maybe he did have a hole card after all.

Michael came down the stone steps, taking them two at a time, clasping her script to her breast. Flashing on the image of a mother delivering her child to a divorced spouse, Larry pushed open the limo door and waited for her to cross the sidewalk.

"Here." She poked her head in as she handed him the script. "There's still another draft I want to do."

He kept her hand. "Relax," he said. "Do you want to do coke?"

"Do you have any?"

"Back at the hotel."

"Really?"

"I'm a Hollywood guy," said Larry; "would I lie about a thing like coke?"

"I'll be right back."

He was reluctant to release her hand.

"Don't worry," she reassured him as she gently freed herself; "I'm a New York girl."

When they arrived back at the Sherry, Michael warned him, "I'll just come up for a nightcap."

"Of course. I have some bedtime reading to do." He even made it a point to tell the driver to wait and drive Michael home.

But once they were upstairs things changed utterly. After he went into his bedroom and returned to the sitting room with the coke he had been carrying all along, Michael took the glassine envelope and inspected it as if she were an assayer. She shook her head in disappointment.

"What's the matter?"

"Not enough here to base."

"Excuse me?"

"I thought you might be into smoking. Not just blowing."

He caught on at last. "You mean free basing?"

"I thought everyone in Hollywood was into smoking coke."

"I guess I'm really not that much a Hollywood guy."

"That's cute." She opened her purse and produced a small chemical measuring spoon. Then she expertly took a measure of the coke and fed it with a practiced professionalism into each nostril, her index finger wiping and covering her nostrils at the same time. It reminded him of the way his grandfather used to take his snuff. As he sat in the back of the candy store reading Gogol. In Russian.

"What are you thinking?"

"I'm thinking about you New York girls." He indicated the coke and the spoon. "Or is it a generational thing?"

"Both."

Michael handed him her spoon and he dipped into the envelope with it and did as she had done. But he was less skillful than she and felt some of the coke escaping down from his nostrils past his finger onto the tip of his upper lip, forming he was certain a moustache. Like the kind that formed on the face of a child who gulped his after-school milk down too quickly. Like that left by the froth of an egg cream or milk shake or malted on his face when he concocted his own after-school beverages in the candy store of his boyhood. He remembered with a pang the taste of Fox U-Bet, the chocolate-syrup brand used in their candy-store fountain. "I'll bet you're not familiar with Fox U-Bet," he said.

"You bet I'm not. Who deals it?"

"Never mind."

"He isn't an old Dodger by any chance?"

"Close. Except he isn't a he."

"That leaves a she or an it. I'll go with an it."

"You're very smart."

"I know what Fox U-Bet is," she said after a moment. "I bet Fox U-Bet is your Rosebud."

"More like my cup of tea."

"Oh, you want to go Proustian on me."

I'll go any way I can on you, Larry thought. He leaned forward and studied her. He liked the dimple hollow in her cheeks, the tilt of her pert nose, the way her burnished hair framed her light-skinned face. He especially liked her skin. Clean and clear as that of a model in a soap commercial. Not even a hint of a blackhead or a blemish or a mole. And her makeup was expertly applied, leaving no line or mark anywhere on her neck as if some high cosmetic tide had come and ebbed. Skin was his erotic weakness. Some men, he knew, went for feminine voices, those that had the resonance and vibrato of a string instrument. But he was a sucker for skin. Smooth skin. Translucent skin. A baby's skin. He had even flown all the way to London once because a cunty British actress's skin, up close, looked as if a thin membrane the color of pale peaches had been spread over a clear blue tropical ocean. "I love your skin." He softly touched her face. "It reminds me of Marilyn's."

"Marilyn who?"

"Monroe."

"Did you know her?"

"Just in class. We were in the same acting class together, that's all. I mean, she was a Hollywood star and I was still a skinny kid from Brooklyn."

"She married a skinny kid from Brooklyn. Arthur Miller."

"That's right." Larry snapped his fingers. "I should have put a move on her. But you know something: I was only interested in her skin. I would sit next to her in class just to worship her skin. It was the most beautiful skin I've ever seen. Innocent skin. A baby's skin. No matter how much she was supposed to have been through." He touched Michael's face again and fondled her neck, reminding himself to be exceedingly gentle, to go very softly and lightly and tenderly. After all, she was a lesbian. She certainly hadn't become a lesbian to get rough treatment, not from a man anyway.

She pressed his hand and asked suddenly. "What is Fox U-Bet?"

He told her what it was.

"My dad tells the same kind of stories about bottles of Good Health seltzer that came with spigots."

"Siphons."

"What?"

"They're called siphons. But you couldn't make a good egg cream with them. Not even with Fox U-Bet. You could only make a good egg cream with candy-store seltzer. Fox U-Bet. Milk. And a squeeze of vanilla. The real secret was to add a squeeze of vanilla." The real trick now was to get her into the bedroom. "Do you want to read to me?" he asked.

"Read what?"

"Read your script." He stood up. "I'm going to get into bed. You come read me the script. If I fall asleep you'll know what I think of it. I can't give you a more honest reaction than that."

"That's crazy."

"No, it isn't." Larry kissed her hand continentally. "I'll only be a minute."

He brushed his teeth, took a leak, washed his hands, and then looked for a place to hide his Norelco. Sure, it was an electric razor but still you could never tell about a lesbian. Maybe she'd want to shave off all his pubic hair. Something like that. He put the shaver in the desk drawer when he spotted the letter opener.

She could cut his prick off or stab him with that. He took both the shaver and the letter opener and put them into the dirty laundry sack and stuffed it into his Boston bag and threw that into the closet. Then he undressed and got into bed in his underwear and pushed the turned-back bedspread onto the floor. Michael came when he called with a bemused look on her face. She sat in the same chair across the room where, in his dream, Sally had sat the night before.

After a few pages, when the two key women characters met at a party and Larry could tell a love scene was coming, he suggested Michael come closer to the bed, sit on the edge so that he could hear her more clearly and she wouldn't have to strain her voice.

"This is silly," she said, but folding back a page of the script came over. She resumed reading, describing the two lesbian lovers' actions, becoming very explicit as she did so. "Too many stage directions?" she stopped and asked.

"No," said Larry, "but I'd go a little lighter on the camera angles. Let the director decide."

"Right." She read on. Now her lovers were in bed, caressing each other, remembering when they were little girls and how they felt the first time they had been fondled by their own mothers.

"Lovely," said Larry.

"Really?" Michael looked up pleased.

"Really." He reached up and pulled her down to him. "It turns me on. For the first time I can understand how two women together can be sexy."

"That's exactly the point I'd like to get across."

"I know." He kissed her on the lips in what he hoped was a sisterly manner. "Good," he whispered, pointing to the script. "It's very good."

"Are you sure you don't want to sleep?"

"Only with you."

She looked down at him. "You're a nice man," she considered. "I like you."

"Then come to bed," he urged. "We'll read together in bed."

Book Three

16

She was leaving his arms and getting out of bed and searching in the tangle at the bottom of the sheets.

"What are you doing?"

"I have to get to work in the morning."

"Stay the night."

"No. Besides you have to finish reading a script."

When she disappeared into the bathroom carrying her clothing he was really relieved. He had been afraid she might stay the night after all. He always hated that. After the how-do-you-do of a screw there was rarely a night's conversation left. And even if there was, who needed it? Whenever a woman lay in bed next to him for any prolonged period, he found himself thinking of his wife. Out of physical habit. The skin remembered. Then the guilt followed.

Obediently he reached back and found the script and held it up to read before him. What he really wanted to do was piss in the worst way. But somehow he still wasn't sure, no matter what they had just done in bed, whether she was up to sharing the bathroom with him for that intimacy. People were funny that way. And, of course, she was funny in a different way being a dike. Maybe now she'd want to cut it off. Good thing he'd hidden the letter opener. But maybe she carried her own knife. Like the dike that cut up Andy Warhol.

She emerged from the bathroom dressed and came over and pecked him on the forehead. "You're a nice man."

"I'll come by the office tomorrow."

"Okay. See you tomorrow."

"Goodnight."

"Goodnight."

After she was gone he took his leak and settled back and read the script. It wasn't that bad. Too many camera directions cluttered it, interrupting the reading flow. But that was usual with film-school scripts. She did have a story and knew how to stick with it. Of course, it certainly didn't have a chance in a million of getting done. Not commercially. The big studios were not exactly waiting with baited breath to produce a black and white love story between two women. Especially one set in America, in New York and Boston, with the white woman Jewish. In fact, the best scenes turned out to be the ones involving the hip Jewish parents and their inability to deal with their lesbian daughter and her black lover. Only they were a little too straight. The best way to play those scenes would have been for the real humor of the situation. Yes, there were many good things, encouraging things, he could say about Michael's script. And who knew, maybe made with independent financing on a low budget—there were mostly interiors anyway—it could wind up a festival film, one that could be shown at Deauville and San Sebastian and Texas, places like that.

He would encourage her. He would certainly encourage her. It wasn't every girl who could make him come twice. He and Jane rarely went for two in a row out of fear of failure. One fuck and it was roll over time. If they really felt good they would go at it again in the morning. But that rarely happened except on vacation.

He met Mira for breakfast in a luncheonette in SoHo around the corner from her loft studio. She was wearing slacks and a T-shirt and Japanese *zoris* and looked a lot more like herself than she had the night before. The counterman who had a pencil-thin moustache but wildly growing curly hair was busy filling containers with coffee for takeout orders and wrapping bagels and jelly doughnuts in wax paper. The place smelled of floor wax and congealed grease but also of sweet rolls and bacon. It was the kind of place he always had breakfast with Mira in in the old days. They slid into a corner booth.

"Coffee?" the counterman called out to them without even looking up.

"Yes," said Larry. "Black."

"Regular," said Mira. "And juice."

"Okay, baby," the counterman called back.

"You eat here often?" Larry asked.

"Sometimes."

The counterman brought the coffees and juice and asked Mira what else she wanted. In Spanish. She told him eggs—he knew how she liked them—with ham and a toasted corn muffin. In Spanish. He turned to Larry. Larry ordered a toasted corn muffin. In Spanish. He had not intended to order anything. He had awakened hungry and had asked room service to send up some juice, sausages, croissant, and coffee. In Spanish.

"I didn't know you could speak Spanish," Mira said. In English.

"I could not be appointed ambassador to the Organization of American States, but I have picked up sufficient knowledge of the language throughout the years so that I can manage when I am in a restaurant as formidable as this," he answered. In Spanish. "Do you think our relationship would have concluded in a different fashion if we had communicated by means of Spanish?" he then asked. Also in Spanish.

Mira laughed. "No. I hate Spanish," she said. In English.

"Why?"

"It's as creepy as English."

"What language isn't creepy?"

"French. But only in books and old movies. Not in France. Otherwise, it's creepy, too."

"Well," Larry clasped his hands, "we've exhausted the topic of language. Anyway, you are looking well, my dear."

"You're too fat," she replied.

"I don't need that. I didn't have to come downtown to a greasy spoon to be told that I'm getting fat," Larry mock reacted.

"Relax," Mira said, as the counterman brought their food. On the side of his corn muffin was a small plastic container of orange marmalade. "Do you have any grape jelly?" he asked.

"Sure." The counterman went back and reached over the counter and returned with a handful of the plastic containers which he tossed on the table as if they were dice.

"Thanks. I love corn muffins with grape jelly," Larry explained to Mira. "You never can get corn muffins in LA." He spread the jelly and tasted his first sweet buttery crumbling mouthful. "Gold. Pure gold," he pronounced. "I don't care how fat it makes me." He held up the remains of the muffin to the counterman. "I think I'll have another one." He looked over at Mira's plate. "And a slice of ham. With some eggs over." It was almost lunchtime anyway. He was going to have lunch with Allen. He would make it a light lunch. He watched Mira eat. So deliberately. Like a child who had been trained by birds. Two things never change in people, he decided: Their voices over the phone. And the way they eat.

Mira looked up. "Notice anything different about me?"

Larry shook his head.

"I talk more than I used to," she said. And fell back into silence.

Now her silence felt awkward rather than usual. "Chris Tucker is a very talented actor," he said.

Mira nodded. "You were a very talented actor, too."

"That seems so long ago. So far back. As if it was in another life."

"The same life." She sipped her coffee. "Listen, I want my sculpture back."

"What sculpture?"

"The cat. I want it back."

"Oh that piece. It's a terrific piece. I'll always be grateful that you gave it to me."

"I never gave it to you."

"Sure you gave it to me. When you were going to Europe."

"I gave it to you to hold."

"You gave it to me as a gift."

The counterman deposited his ham and eggs and second muffin before him. He bit into the muffin scarcely tasting it. The counterman returned and refilled their cups with coffee. He sipped the coffee and it tasted acidy. "Why do you suddenly want that piece back after all these years, anyway?"

"I need it for an exhibition. The gallery is giving me a retrospective."

"Wonderful. I look forward to seeing the show."

"Don't be a creep. Give me back my piece."

"I couldn't give it back to you even if I wanted to."

"You sold it?"

"No. I would never do a thing like that. I value that piece far beyond money. But my hands are tied in the matter. It's part of our collection."

"What collection?"

"Our art collection. Jane and I have an art collection. It's not like Norton Simon or Ray Stark. But it's still a collection. And it's all in the hands of my business manager and lawyer. I couldn't give it back to you even if I wanted to. Tax reasons. All kinds of complications. My hands are tied. Do you really need it for the show?"

"Yes. It's one of the best examples of my early work."

"I'll tell you what I might be able to do. Even though it would break Jane's heart—not to mention my own and the kids'—to have it out of the house for a single second. But how long will the show run?"

"Six weeks."

"Maybe we could lend it to you for six weeks."

Mira laughed. "Lend me my own piece? Lend me something you borrowed?"

"I never borrowed it. I never borrow anything. You were going to Europe and you gave it to me as a gift for old time's sake."

"And for old time's sake you won't give it back to me."

"I explained to you, Mira. I can't. It's not mine. It's Jane's. And the kids'. But we can lend it to you—or rather your gallery —for a show. Or, at least, I think I can. I'll have to talk to my lawyer. Even though it costs me a fortune to talk to him. One hundred fifty dollars an hour. Everyone I talk to costs me money.

You have no idea how everybody hits on me. But I'll see what I can do." He rubbed his face with his hand. "By the way, how much is the cat worth?"

"Fifteen, twenty thousand. I don't do that many pieces."

"It's a terrific piece. Your people would have to take care of the insurance and all the packing and freighting, of course." He sloshed up the remains of the eggs with the last bite of muffin.

Mira glared at him. "Chris was right."

"About what?"

"He said you were the Scrooge of Hollywood."

"He said that? I guess he was just bitter because I didn't cast him once. But it is true I do have to watch my budgets if I want to make my kind of pictures."

"Once a creep, always a creep," Mira said. "But I didn't know you'd wind up such a creep. Otherwise, I really would have cut your prick off." She rose. "Keep the fucking cat." And walked past him and out of the luncheonette.

Larry looked after her before calling for the check. It was so many years, who remembered the exact details? But he certainly wasn't going to give fifteen, twenty thousand dollars away just like that. Not for old time's sake. No one had the right to expect him to do that either. Not even her. Who needed her in his life anymore? She wasn't in his life anyway. It wasn't as if she was an actress or a writer he might need again.

Fuck her!

"There are some legal complications that have come up. Nothing important," he told Jane over the phone as he sat at a clean and uncluttered desk in a vacant office at the studio's New York headquarters. "Just little things. Her estate has to go into probate because she died without a will. But Uncle Irving will take care of everything. Close up her apartment, ship out anything that looks valuable or personal, and sell the rest. I don't have to worry about a thing."

"She couldn't even die graciously," Jane said.

"What do you mean?"

"Dying without a will."

Which wasn't a very gracious thing to say. Jane just wouldn't forgive—or forget. But he swallowed hard and said nothing. Instead, he promised to be home in a day or two and asked her to give the kids a hug and a kiss for him and smacked one cross-country for her, and, before finally hanging up, told her that he loved her.

Which was true. Whatever love was. Because what had happened last night with Michael certainly had nothing to do with love. Had more to do with business, the movie business, in fact.

He pushed back the swivel chair, rose from the desk, went to the window, and looked out at the midtown skyline. It seemed more angular and geometric than he had remembered it. More glass walls and fewer spires, more futuristic and less Roman, but still an interesting mix. Not like Los Angeles. Did Los Angeles even have a skyline? Not as far as the movie business was concerned. There was no studio executive building taller than three stories except for the Black Tower at Universal. The only time he ever looked out the window of a skyscraper was when he went to his lawyer's office in Century City. The only time he went downtown where there was an actual skyline hovering over the Harbor Freeway was when he went to that restaurant in the Occidental Building. Or to the Music Center. Or to Little Tokyo or Chinatown. Otherwise, in the flats of Beverly Hills he lived a quiet flat life.

He reached into his pocket and extracted the glassine envelope. There was just enough left for one or two snorts at most. He could take some now or later. Better now, he decided, since there really wasn't enough to share. He went back to the desk, opened a drawer, and found a pad of paper. He ripped off a sheet, rolled it up, and snorted the rest of the coke. Then he returned to the window, looked out at the panorama of the city below, and was suddenly pleased with his own life. He had come out of the streets, emerged from the crowd, achieved a position of stature and respect as a filmmaker and an artist. He had also made his share of money to boot. His house alone was worth more than two million and his investments were worth triple that at least. There was no question about it. He had a good life and he deserved it. His life gave him pleasure and he enjoyed it. He remembered Ernest Hemingway's moral code: If something made you feel good, then it was good. He remembered Hemingway's suicide act. Too bad, he thought, as the phone started ringing, that Hemingway hadn't been analyzed. With a good therapist, someone like David, he'd probably still be alive. Too bad Hemingway wasn't Jewish; then he certainly would have been analyzed.

Larry picked up the ringing phone. It was the studio office operator telling him that Harriet Pyle was on the line.

"Put her on," he told the operator.

Michael knocked on the door and peeked in. He motioned for her to come in. "Hello." Harriet's crackling voice sounded as if it were being transmitted through the cellophane window of an old Chiclet box. "I'm sorry about your mother."

"Thank you, Harriet. How sweet of you to call." He played with the wire and rubbed the fleshy folds of his face. "How did you find out by the way? Did you read the notice in the *Times?*"

"No," said Harriet. *"Variety."*

"Well, how are you, Harriet? How are you doing?"

And immediately she began to tell him in detail both how she was and how she did. It was as if she considered his ear the endless columns of the magazine that published her movie reviews. He circled his hand slowly around his ear to indicate to Michael how long-winded his caller was. Now Harriet was talking about getting together, complaining like a Jewish mother that she never saw him anymore.

"I'd love to see you, Harriet," he said. Which was an utter lie. Harriet had been strangely silent about *Herbie and Milty,* not having written a single word about it. True, it came out during her vacation, but usually she made it a point to cover all of his pictures. And *Herbie and Milty* could certainly have used her help. Even now it wouldn't hurt.

"Lunch," Harriet was saying. "How about lunch today?"

"Lunch today?"

"That's right."

"Lunch," he repeated. "But I'm on a diet—"

"Everyone I know is on a diet," she cut in. "Or jogging. Or both."

"You're right." He laughed too heartily. After all, lunch was her idea, not his. He did have a lunch date with Allen but he could always break that. "Why not lunch today? I'd love it. Where?"

She mentioned a restaurant, an in place, a sort of downtown daytime Elaine's. Said she would take care of the reservation and that she would meet him there at one o'clock.

"Terrific," he said.

She said that she would be on time and made him promise that he would, too. She asked if he was sure he knew where the restaurant was and he told her that he did. "Don't worry, Harriet," he said. "Good-bye, Harriet."

"Do you know who that was?" he asked Michael after he hung up.

"Let me guess," said Michael. "Harriet?"

"You're a smart girl. But Harriet who?"

She shrugged.

"Harriet Pyle," he said. "And she's smart, too. I think she's the best film critic in America. Intelligent. Consistent. Writes well. And most important of all—" He took her hand and held it up dramatically.

"What?"

"She likes my work." He released her hand. "Usually. Though she's been strangely silent about *Herbie and Milty*. Which makes me more than a little paranoid." He took her hand again. "By the way, I liked your script a lot."

"Really?"

"Really." He held up his right hand as if he were taking an oath of office. "I could never lie to a writer about a script of theirs. I know how much blood goes into it."

Michael nodded, pleased and appreciative. "What do you think I should do with it?"

"That's hard. Very hard. Because its very artistic virtues make it a difficult commercial sell. Not that I'm saying it can't be done. You never know. But you've written human beings, full three-dimensional characters, and what they seem to be making mostly these days are comic strips with cardboard characters."

"Except for people like you. Pictures like yours."

"I'm an exception and frankly I don't know if I have the strength to deal with those assholes anymore." He took her other hand. "But anything decent that gets done is an exception. So let me think about it. Let me think about what's the best way to go with it."

"Thank you."

"Thank *you.* Meanwhile, come to lunch with me and Harriet."

"Would she mind?"

"Fuck her. I'm sure she's not so crazy about *Herbie and Milty* anyway. But first I have to call my friend, Allen."

He picked up the phone and dialed Allen's number. And got an answering machine. Even Allen had one! Soon the answering machines would be running the world, leaving computerized messages for each other, dispensing with the need for people altogether. Meanwhile, he told Allen's tape to tell him that he had to break their lunch date but to fall by the hotel at three o'clock instead.

If this were a scene he was shooting, Larry thought, as he watched the waiter heading for their table, he would open with the tray bearing the drinks, pull back, and go with the waiter mincing through the tables of the crowded restaurant, and then stop when he came to their table and pan across it: HIMSELF nervously stuffing his mouth with breadsticks; MICHAEL smiling politely toward HARRIET; and HARRIET, a short, dumpy woman with gray bouffant hair, her eyeglasses pushed up high on her forehead against it, chirping away. Actually, Harriet looked more like a suburban housewife in for a theater matinee than she did an influential movie critic.

The waiter hesitated as he stood at their table. And Larry thought that would be a good touch, too. He would include that in the scene if he were shooting it. Harriet interrupted her rap and turned to the waiter a trace too expectantly, "The vodka martini is for me." Larry was surprised she had ordered a martini. He didn't think anyone drank martinis anymore except in those news stories out of Washington about how the IRS was planning to crack down on those tax-deductible-three-martini business lunches. And he didn't particularly remember Harriet as a martini drinker either.

"And the apple juice here," Larry told the waiter, indicating it was for Michael. "She's into health food. And the Campari for me. I'm into anything sounding exotic."

Harriet was already sipping her martini by the time he was toasting, "Cheers." Larry put down his Campari. "When in New York, do as the Romans do. How good to see you again, Harriet. You don't know how good it is to see you." He turned to Michael as if he had to interpret for her. "Harriet is my best friend. Though we don't get together more than once or twice a year. But when we do get together, it's always right there. I don't have many friends I can say that about. Maybe Ingmar, but that's it." He turned back to Harriet and tried to look her straight in the eye. But it was hard to catch her gaze because she kept her head bent over her martini. "I really consider you my best friend," he continued. "I mean, how many people are there like us in the world? Serious people who take films seriously. I can't tell you how much I appreciate what you did for *Bachelor Spouse*."

Harriet still eluded his efforts to establish eye contact. Instead, her head seemed to be bowing even lower into her drink. Larry shifted his attention back to Michael, explaining, "More than anyone else Harriet was responsible for getting that film launched on the right foot." He lifted his glass. "To more critics like you, Harriet. Would that there were more."

Harriet lifted her glass. But then with obvious disappointment found it empty. Larry quickly signaled a passing busboy who immediately came over. Harriet greeted him with her empty glass. "Another vodka martini. Double." The busboy looked over to Larry and Michael. They both held up their hands and covered their glasses. "Didn't I tell you?" Harriet said suddenly. "I have a new book of criticisms coming out in the fall."

"Terrific," Larry said. "Terrific. I can't tell you how much I look forward to reading it. When I get back to the coast the first thing I'll do is order it from Hunter's. What are you going to call it?" He turned to Michael. "Harriet is terrific on titles. Terrific."

"Dark Impressions," Harriet coughed.

"Dark Impressions," he repeated. "What a wonderful title! Isn't that a title?"

Harriet nodded. Not in response to his rhetorical question to Michael but to the waiter who was depositing a double martini before her. Immediately her head bent into it, reminding him of one of those mechanical birds that, once its beak is moistened, can forever bob its head up and down into a glass of water. Finally, she stopped and looked up smiling, renewed and refreshed. "I'm also working on a very interesting piece about Preston Sturges," she said.

"I love Sturges," said Larry. "In fact, when Harriet ventured to call me a 'Jewish Preston Sturges,' I can't tell you how flattered I was. It made my day. It made my week. It made my year."

"The point of my thesis," Harriet sip-lisped, "is that Sturges is so underrated compared to Capra, for example. Capra always had writers. But Sturges was his own writer."

"Exactly. And few people realize how hard it is to be your own writer," said Larry, nodding to Michael beside him in the curved booth. "Isn't Harriet insightful?" Michael nodded back respectfully, bowing her head toward Harriet. But as Michael did so he suddenly felt a hand under the table firmly gripping his thigh and then slowly moving upward toward his genitals.

"Sturges was an *auteur,*" Harriet continued, "before there were *auteurs.*"

"He certainly was," Larry said, torn between sudden pleasure and confusion. He was sure the questing, teasing fingers were Michael's. But not one hundred percent sure. "I never thought of it that way. Very astute. Don't you think so, Michael?"

A blank poker-faced expression never left Michael's eyes as he felt the hand further sliding ever so softly across his penis. "Yes," Michael smiled over to Harriet. "I would call it astute. Very astute."

Harriet bobbed her head up from her emptied glass. "I think we're ready for another round," she said.

"Preston Sturges. Yes, Preston Sturges," Larry said, beckoning the waiter. "But remember Preston Foster." He was addressing Harriet but looking Michael directly in the eye in his aim-at-the-forehead way. "When we were kids we used to have this joke: Why did Vivien Leigh? Because Preston Foster."

"A highly overrated picture, *The Informer*," said Harriet. "Just like *Herbie and Milty*." She handed her empty glass to the waiter.

At last, she was finally getting to the point of the luncheon. No wonder she had been drinking so much. Which wasn't like her. It was her way to try fueling her courage or pickling her integrity. Meanwhile, the hand—whoever's hand—was now groping his penis fiercely but exquisitely. "Oh!" he gasped. "You've seen *Herbie and Milty?*"

"Of course I've seen it. And I must tell you that frankly I was very disappointed."

"Oh!" he moaned.

"And I didn't write about it because I know how sensitive you are and I was afraid about how badly you'd take it. I mean, I didn't *have* to write about it anyway because it opened while I was on vacation. I also thought I could always tell you what I think face to face. Give you the benefit of my critical thoughts that way. Was I right?"

"Yes!" he panted. "Yes!"

"Because I don't mind telling you personally. In fact, I would think I had let you down personally if I didn't." She smiled nervously and pushed back a stray hair. "Are you sure you want to hear my honest criticism or should I stop now?"

"No. Please don't stop now." He looked hopefully at Michael. "Please, go on."

"Good. I'm glad you can react this way. Take it like a man not like a wimpy prick. But frankly the problem I had with *Herbie and Milty*—and I've given it a lot of thought—was in two areas. First, it just wasn't up to your usual energy level. It always seemed to be moving a beat too slowly. Which in lovemaking is fine but not in filmmaking. I understand what you were trying for but I think you made the wrong choice. You're not a pastoral director, you're an urban director. You shouldn't go for the pretty shots. You had a cinematographer who didn't serve you well. I think you never should have used Werner." She shook her head and clicked her teeth. "Self-defeating. I mean Werner has his lyric talents but they don't fit in with your down-to-earth virtues. Are you sure you want me to continue?" She smiled. "Can you bear it?"

"I'm trying to."

"Well, sometimes I think you really don't appreciate your own virtues. Your great gift is your ability to deliver the true cliché. Not the phony cliché which is the province of second-raters. They always force and contrive. But the true cliché is always approached head on and obliquely at the same time. Like the sitcom you did, 'Here Comes Uncle.' 'Uncle' wasn't just off the wall, he was part of the wall, if you get my point. That's what made that show so funny and real." The waiter deposited her refill before her; she paused to sip from it. "In fact, lately I've begun to think that the sitcom may be the basic art form of our time. Even the three-camera tape show. Because, no matter how much they complain, the creative people are really left alone by the networks when it comes to the important matters. A Larry Gelbart, a Norman Lear, an Alan Alda are given the parameters to deliver the true cliché. In the movie business, on the other hand, you always get some studio executive's notion of what constitutes a cliché. Which is always a phony cliché. Compare *Private Benjamin* and *Stripes* which are phony clichés to 'M.A.S.H.' which is a true cliché. Compare *9 to 5,* the phony cliché, with 'The Mary Tyler Moore Show,' a true cliché. Carroll O'Connor, Mary Tyler Moore, Alan Alda may very well turn out to have been the Chaplins and Keatons and Harold Lloyds of our time. And there's another TV show I'm excited about. 'The Hollermen.' Have you seen it? I think that actor, Chris Tucker, is exceptional. He's nothing less than a Jimmy Dean with balls and a wry sense of humor. I would love to see him in a movie."

The hand was cupping his balls, gently caressing them.

"I almost used him once," Larry said.

"I think he could be truly remarkable in the right hands. The right hands are so important for a young actor."

"For anybody," Michael suddenly contributed.

Harriet looked at her as if for the first time. "To be sure, my dear," she said. "To be sure." And returned to Larry. "Not that *Herbie and Milty* didn't have some very nice moments in it. But on the whole it just didn't work for me. Because not only did you want to have your cake and eat it, but you refused to let us in on the recipe, the true cliché basis of it all. In that way it could have been our cake as well as yours, a rich, gooey cake we could all immediately recognize and wallow in."

Michael—yes, it was definitely Michael—was caressing his penis again. If he let her continue another moment he would come up with something gooey to wallow in right then and there. "Excuse me." He stood up. "I have to go to the men's room." And raced away from the booth.

The men's room was small, cluttered, an afterthought. Obviously, the Gaels and Mimis of the world did not check out the men's rooms of the restaurants they visited. Larry felt positively claustrophobic as he stood at the solitary urinal waiting for his hard-on to go down and the piss to flow. He was also angry for having let himself in for such a jerk-off luncheon in the first place. Literally. Michael's stroking his penis had put it all into perspective. His own stroking of Harriet's ego was as absurd and profane an act—and far less pleasurable or necessary. He really didn't need Harriet anymore. In spite of his own insecurity, his critical reputation was secure. And in the real world of filmmaking Harriet could be no more influential in getting a project off the ground than his own mother.

He would give Harriet short shrift and get the hell out of there.

"You really had me going," Larry told Michael as they left the restaurant.

"What do you mean?" Michael asked innocently.

"In there."

"What 'in there'?"

"Under the table."

"What 'under the table'?" she said and smiled. "I don't know what you're talking about. Are you pulling my leg?"

The girl was playful. No doubt about it.

Or was there?

He squeezed her hand and walked her back to the studio office and arranged to meet her that night to go over her script. Who was pulling whose appendage now?

When he returned to the Sherry he found Allen sitting in the lobby, calmly smoking a joint. Which did not surprise him. What did surprise him though was the fact that Allen was wearing a three-piece blue pinstripe suit, white shirt, and striped silk tie. "You look like a banker or a network executive," Larry said.

"I like to wear costumes once in a while," Allen said. "Good for the kharma."

"Want to go upstairs to my suite?"

"I'd rather take a walk."

"Walking is terrific," Larry agreed. "I ate too much for lunch. I wish we could have had lunch together as we planned. I would have enjoyed it. But then this thing came up." He rolled his eyes helplessly.

"Something to do with your mother?"

"In a way, I guess. But why should I bore you?" Larry led Allen through the revolving doors out onto Fifth Avenue. "Where do you want to go? Uptown or downtown?"

"How about the park?"

"Terrific," Larry said. They walked to the corner and waited for the light to change. "I can't get over the way you look in a suit. Seriously, Allen. Is there any reason why you're wearing a suit?"

"I wanted to look serious," Allen said. "Seriously."

"Well, I must say you do."

Across the street, at the entrance to the park, Larry bought a bag of cashew nuts from a vendor. "I know these are loaded with cholesterol, but I can't resist nibbling on them." He held out the bag to Allen.

"No thanks."

"Did you have lunch?"

Allen nodded.

"Thanks again for the coke. It made my day yesterday."

"I can get you more."

"No thanks. Do you think I'm a junkie like you? I'm just a Sunday snorter. Anyway, I'm compulsive enough as it is. Look how I can't stop eating these things." He waved the bag of nuts. "But what the hell? I'm on vacation. When I get back home I'll go on a diet. The Malibu diet."

"What's that?"

"You throw everything that costs less than five dollars into the ocean."

They walked past two young mothers—or nannies—rocking baby carriages who eyed them suspiciously as if they might be potential kidnappers. An old man was perched on a rock, bare-chested, holding aluminum reflectors up to a nonexistent sun. Beneath him, a black man and a white girl were sprawled, their faces together in earnest conversation, their heads resting on their elbows, their hands plucking stray blades of grass. A blond Twiggy-slim roller skater, wearing leotards, a radio headset, and plastic elbow and leather knee guards, whizzed between them, almost knocking both of them over.

"Oh, the energy of New York. How I love it!" Larry said. But when he saw an empty bench ahead, he suggested they sit for a minute. He opened the bag of cashews wide and poured the chipped bits into his mouth. "Well." He licked the salt on the edges of his lips. "Well, what's up, old sport? Not that I want to rush you. But I do have some errands to do. Among other things I have to run out to New Jersey to see Sid Stein. Remember him?"

"Sure. He's a prick."

"I know. That's why I have to see him. I did him a favor and got him a movie job. And the script isn't going to get done. He can't seem to understand that. Movies aren't books. To publish a

book costs what? Twenty, forty, sixty thousand dollars. Whatever. To make a movie costs eight, ten, fifteen million dollars.
Without prints and advertising. So you've got to devour a lot of
scripts before you make a movie. It's the nature of the beast. I
tried to explain all this to him several times on the phone. But it
just doesn't sink in. He even showed up yesterday at the funeral.
But that was no time to talk. So I agreed to go out there tonight.
I guess I owe it to him for old time's sake."

"Speaking of old time's sake," Allen lit another joint and
passed it on to him, "I'd like you to do me a favor."

Larry took a quick hit and handed it back.

"I've got a little problem," Allen inhaled, looking down at the
ground. "I've left my old gallery."

"I didn't know that."

"And I haven't signed up with a new gallery yet. So I'm running a little short. I wonder if I can hit you for a small loan?"

"How small?"

"Five grand."

Larry whistled. "That's not small." Only Allen would still call
a thou a grand. But it was still a lot of money no matter what he
called it.

"I'll pay it back."

"That's not the question," Larry rubbed his jowls. "I just don't
have that kind of money lying around."

"You were just talking millions about movies."

"That's *their* millions. Not mine. All my money is tied up by
my business manager. I don't even know where. And I don't
want to know where the way the market is going. All I do know
is that I'm not very liquid at the moment. My deal on *Herbie and
Milty* was mostly deferred until break even. But the picture, for
all its fine reviews, has not been a box-office winner so far."

"Surely," Allen said, "you can lay your hands on five thousand
dollars."

"Frankly, I'm not so sure."

"What about an emergency?"

"Maybe."

"This is an emergency. I wouldn't be asking you if it wasn't an emergency."

"I'll talk to my business manager when I get back. It would be up to him and depend upon the interest rate and all that."

"What interest rate?"

"The interest rate on the loan."

Allen looked at him with seeming disbelief. "You'd charge me interest?"

"I wouldn't charge you interest. But my business manager would. Money costs money. Always has. Always will."

"Would you expect me to put up collateral, too?"

"I don't know about such things. My business manager would handle it. I'll talk to him when I get back."

"So even with collateral and interest you couldn't give me a yes or no now?"

"Of course not. All I can do is promise to talk to my manager. Otherwise, my hands are tied. It's Jane's money too, you know."

Allen stood up. "I can't believe it. I can't believe you've turned out to be such a prick."

"You don't seem to understand, Allen. Money is business. And so I have to be as businesslike as I can when it comes to money. That's why I have a business manager and a lawyer and it would make you shudder to know how much they charge me for their services. But," he pointed up at Allen's joint, "that's the real world. Real reality. And I work too hard for my money to just throw it away."

"And lending me money would be throwing it away?"

"I didn't say that. I never said that. I just said it would have to be approached on a business basis."

"What about our friendship?"

"Our friendship has nothing to do with business. I like to think our friendship has always been based on mutual love and respect and affection. And the value of that is incalculable. Immeasurable. I treasure your friendship, Allen. I wouldn't want to jeopardize it for all the money in the world."

"But you'd be willing to let it go down the toilet for a few grand."

"I wouldn't. You're the one who would. You're the one who brought the matter of money up. And, as I've said, I'll try to help you. But I can't give you a yes or no answer without consulting the people I hire to deal with such things."

"And if they said: 'Yes. Give Gates the five grand. No Interest.' Would you?"

"Certainly. But, in all honesty, I don't think they'll say that."

"Otherwise, you'd fire them," Allen spit out, and started back toward the park entrance.

Larry stood up and ran after him. "That's not called for, Allen. There's no reason for you to be sarcastic or bitter. I said I'd see what I could do."

Allen turned and faced him. "Fuck off, Lazar," he said, and then walked away.

Larry looked after him and shook his head. What an absurd figure Allen was in his pinstripe suit, his narrow shoulders hunched together, his head bent over the joint he was smoking. Mira was right. He was a creep. He was also a druggie and a degenerate fag. Why should he lend Allen his money? What right did Allen have to hit on him? *Fuck off,* he tells me. *Fuck you,* I say to him. Who needed him, anyway? Not Larry Lazar. Certainly not Larry Lazar. Larry Lazar didn't need anybody out of his past anymore. His past was gone, gone like his mother, irretrievably gone.

Larry crumpled the empty nut bag he had been holding and shot it at the trash basket beside the bench. It hit the rim and bounced in. Swish.

17

Douglas, the moonlighting actor, was back at the wheel and
Larry was back in Brooklyn again. It was the third time in three
days—once to arrange for the funeral, once for the funeral itself,
and now to try and put the lid on the whole episode so to speak.
But he and Brooklyn had altered irrevocably. He could not even
begin to reclaim a sense of the sprawling borough. They were in a
neighborhood he had never visited before, far across the borough
from the neighborhood he had grown up in; it could have been
Philadelphia for all the familiarity he felt. As Douglas slowed
down to check out addresses, Larry thought of the Thomas Wolfe
title *Only The Dead Know Brooklyn.* True: Sally knew it. Wolfe
also wrote *You Can't Go Home Again,* but he wasn't talking
about Brooklyn then. Or even New York for that matter. But he
just as easily could have been as far as Larry was concerned. This
trip East was not exactly an easy jog down memory lane. He was
discovering that not only could you not go home again, but if you
did you also had to obliterate the few traces you may have originally left behind. He was shedding mothers, Sally and Harriet,
physical and metaphysical; he was losing friends, Mira and Allen, physical and metaphysical. It was as if sentiment and nostal-
gia could not stand the test of real reality. He didn't like severing
relationships with his own past but at the same time he refused to
submit to them. If he started giving in to Mira and Allen and
Harriet whenever they put the hit on him, then the next thing he
knew Sally would begin making her own demands. Sally was
supposed to be dead; he had been to her funeral, and he wanted
her to stay that way. He was his own man at last; he had finally

even written a script all by himself, and he wanted to stay that way.

"Here we are." Douglas parked the limo before a four-story brick apartment building. On the nearby corner was a bar; across the street a dry cleaner and a Chinese restaurant. "Do you want me to go in with you?"

"No. I'm sure I can manage myself. But if I need help I'll call you."

The foyer floor was worn although scrubbed clean and the walls were freshly painted. There were nameplates in the slots next to each little black bell. Still, Larry was surprised when he pushed the super's bell and an immediate reply came over the intercom. He had not expected it to work. "Who's there?" asked a Spanish-accented voice.

"Larry Lazar. I spoke to you on the phone."

"Oh sure. Wait a minute."

An entry buzzer clicked back and Larry pushed the hall door open. A chubby woman with a child tugging at her heavy skirt was closing a door at the end of the hallway. "Just one flight up," she said, and started toward the stairway in the middle of the hall, the child still clinging to the folds of her skirt but now peering out to look at Larry.

"Hello there," Larry winked.

The child abruptly stuck his head back into his mother's skirt, almost knocking her over. "Leave go." She swatted at the kid and shook-kicked herself free. The kid scooted down the hallway past Larry.

"Alfredo," the woman called after him. "Come back here."

"How old is he?" Larry asked as he followed her up the stairs. She ignored his question or just hadn't heard it. Alfredo raced past him to the top of the stairs and waited till his mother arrived. Then he buried his head in her skirt. "Get away," she said and swatted at him again. This time he cried.

"Shut up!" she said. She was busy searching through her key ring and walking toward the front of the building. "Miss Lazarsky your mother?" she asked, as if that would help her find the right key.

"Yes."

"She was a nice lady." She found the key and reached the apartment at the same time. She opened the door and stood back. "Call me when you finished." Alfredo ran into the apartment. "Come back here, Alfredo!" Larry waited for Alfredo to run out again, patting his head as he passed. "Miss Lazarsky always give Alfredo candy, didn't she?" Alfredo shyly nodded. "Well, no more candy." She shook her head and led her son away. "Knock on my door when you finish."

Although he paid the rent through his business manager—or rather his corporation, Mary-Jane-Conor Productions, paid the rent as the tenant of record—Larry had never seen the apartment before. It was somewhat larger than he expected it to be. In addition to the step-down living room off the entryway, there was a kitchen-dinette behind a rail and there had to be a bedroom down at the end of the corridor. The apartment was also neater than he expected it to be. Either Sally had cleaned up just before she died, or, more likely, Uncle Irving had arranged to have it cleaned. He could not imagine Sally leaving everything just in place. Magazines stacked neatly on the end table, bric-a-brac resting on the bookshelf, records piled precisely near the stereo. He recognized some of the odds and ends among the bric-a-brac —for example, an old game of jacks that Sally for some reason had clung to—but none of the furniture. The samovar on the dinette table had belonged to his grandparents. He would want that. And there were some pewter wine tumblers near it that looked familiar. He would want them, too. He took out a sheet of hotel stationery and wrote that down. The television, the stereo, all the furniture, he would have Uncle Irving sell. Nothing there worth shipping out.

He went into the small kitchen and examined the cupboards. Dishes, pots, pans, they could all go, too. He opened the refrigerator: a box of chocolates, half of a six-pack of beer, eggs, sour cream, celery, Lite 'n' Lively, ketchup, mustard, mayonnaise, relish, two grapefruits, and a cucumber. In the freezer were pizzas and a frozen fish. Larry restrained himself from reaching in for a chocolate. There would be something obscene about eating the food of the dead. Even though he probably had paid for it. He closed the coppertone doors and went into the corridor.

The first door led to the bathroom where the mirror over the sink was covered with a pillow case. Which meant it was Uncle Irving who must have arranged for the apartment to be cleaned. The man didn't waste a minute. Larry looked into the medicine chest and found Sally's personal toilet articles, soaps and rinses, and pills and all that. He had no need for them. On the buff carpeted floor was a scale. Larry stood on it, leaned forward, and peered down over his stomach at his weight. He couldn't believe how heavy he was. It was a good thing he had not scavenged the chocolates. He kicked off his boots and weighed himself again. Either he had gained five pounds or the scale was off. Probably the scale, he decided, and sat down on the john and pulled his boots back on.

Nothing had prepared him for the bedroom across the hall. The mirror over the vanity dresser had a sheet draped over it, but every other inch of possible wall space was covered with pictures and clippings like the cells of inmates he had seen in prison photos. Only all the pictures were of him and the clippings were his interviews and reviews snipped from newspapers and magazines. He sat down on the bed, overwhelmed, his hand over his eyes, shaking his head. Finally, he looked up again at the vertical scrapbook, the rotogravure on the wall, of every age and stage of his life: Baby pictures. One-inch pictures taken annually in school. On the merry-go-round. At the zoo. His bar mitzvah picture. His junior high school, high school, and college graduation pictures. Playing basketball, baseball, football. College productions and professional theater and television and movie roles. Interviews from *Life* and *Time* and *Newsweek* and *People* and the New York *Times*. Reviews in English and Spanish and Italian and Yiddish. Pictures of his children, too. A single shot of Jane. Nothing of Sally alone. Only with him or with the kids. And not a single picture of his father. Poor Meyer!

Still he was moved. Oh, how he was moved. But he would *not* start crying. He was an actor and he had control. He would not cry, because he knew her. He knew Sally. She would make him pay for it if he cried. She would shrilly point out to him that he was crying out of guilt and what good was that doing her now? Which would only add to his guilt. He knew Sally well enough to know she would never let go of him if he showed the slightest weakness. In life she had used threats; in death she had already tried dreams. Guilt was her lance and tears could only ease its way in.

Larry rose and went to the dresser and peeled away the sheet from the mirror. He was not afraid of any old Jewish superstition about the image of the dead still lingering in the mirror. Hell no, he knew it was fact. Staring back at him from the mirror, leering at him from over his shoulder. It was one of those old-style mirrors whose side panels could swing out. He stuck his head between them and indeed, both he and Sally were everywhere, reflecting back together infinitely.

It would not be easy stripping himself of Sally. Not by a long shot. He picked up the sheet and was recovering the mirror when he noticed a brown paper edge sticking out of the corner of the frame, barely a sliver of it surfacing above the thick wood. For a moment he thought it was part of the mirror's backing. But then, with his fingernail, he carefully slid it out and holding it in the palm of his hands as if it were a lab specimen, examined it: one of those old coin-machine arcade pictures of poor quality, its sepia tones cracking and fading. Three faces, distant and familiar at once. A young Meyer, pushing his head into the shot, clowning as he tugged at his own ears. An even younger Sally, her mouth opened wide, exaggerated, as if she were belting out a song. And beneath Sally's head, a fat-faced Larry, a baby in a bonnet. Meyer standing, Sally sitting, Larry on her lap, their three faces in a row as if on a totem pole.

Larry put the picture in his wallet among his credit cards and redraped the mirror. He checked out the drawers of the dresser, although he knew Uncle Irving had already removed the jewelry, and looked through both the bedroom closet and the hall closet. There were a few dresses he thought Jane might want to do something with and a fur coat. He laid them on the bed and brought the samovar and the pewter tumblers and the set of jacks in and placed them on the bed, too.

Then he went downstairs, returned the key to the super, and had Douglas drive him back to the hotel. It was getting late and he had to get out to Jersey.

18

Maybe he would buy himself a 450 SL after all. They cost a fortune but they appreciated well. The car was responsive, easy to handle. It was good being behind a wheel again. Made him feel more at home. More in control. More himself. He had done a smart thing in getting rid of the limo, telling the actor-driver who was back on duty to take the rest of the day off. Because he was in no mood to have his ear chewed off again. Not after the lunch with Harriet. And the walk with Allen. Not to mention the breakfast with Mira. Not on a day when everyone was hitting on him. And there wasn't any good news out of the coast either. According to Lois, Mike's office hadn't called with a reaction to *Remember, Remember*. But it was still too early for that and Mike probably knew he was out of town anyway. Mike knew everything about the studio except how to run it right. Still Larry would be a lot happier if he knew the studio was picking up *Remember, Remember*. It would make everything much easier.

Renting the car had been easy enough. The bell captain arranged it. Larry just had to sign a lot of papers. Which he didn't mind doing. After all, it wasn't his money. It would all be on the hotel tab for the studio to pick up.

He adjusted the sun visor to cut out some of the late afternoon glare. Yes, he definitely liked the way the car handled. Especially the turning base. He always auditioned cars, so to speak, when he was on the road, renting out the models that he was considering. Way back he'd never consider buying a German car. The Nazis and the Jews and the holocaust business. But his first BMW cured him of that. He was able to sell it five years later for more than he had paid for it. He could almost do the same with his 300 sedan. That car too had practically earned out. The Germans knew how to kill Jews and make cars that were good investments.

But although he was pleased with the car, he wasn't exactly enjoying the ride. To think you had to pay to drive on the turnpike. New Jersey hadn't changed. It still looked like the back of an old radio set. And he wasn't too thrilled at the prospect of spending the evening with Sidney either. If it was any other writer but Sidney he certainly wouldn't find himself driving out to the middle of nowhere the day after his mother's funeral. But then Sidney Stein wasn't most writers. Not only was he one of America's most famous novelists with a National Book Award and a Pulitzer Prize and who knows what other awards, but more important they went back a long way together.

During Larry's first summer in the Village, Sidney had sublet an apartment in his Thompson Street building. They met one morning at the chrome mailboxes that lined the wall in the back hallway as they slid their mail keys into their respective slots. They both looked up surprised as if they had encountered each other in the same furtive act, and smiled self-consciously. They each withdrew their mail and walked toward the front entrance.

"How'd you do?" asked Larry.

Sidney held up his mail and opened it as if it were a poker hand. "Two *Please Forward*s and an *Occupant.* How about you?"

Larry revealed the envelope and postcards he was about to stuff into his back pocket. "An electric bill and two men's clothing sales."

"Where are the clothing sales?"

"Saks Fifth Avenue and Casual Aire."

"Then you win. I'll buy you a coffee at Chock Full o' Nuts."

Larry liked him immediately. Not only because they were on the same wavelength in humor. There was something else about Sidney he found even more attractive. Put simply: Sidney seemed to have everything. It wasn't until years later, of course, that Larry learned that a person who has what you want the most always seems to have everything. Even though, in fact, what you so desperately want may turn out to be the only thing that person has. What Sidney *had* in those days was the fact that he oozed with an easy non-Jewishness. His hair was blond and curly, his eyes were gray, and the line of his nose was unmarked by Semitic detours. There was neither the trace of an accent nor the hint of an intonation in his soft hoarse voice; it seemed unscarred by kitchen arguments and bathroom epithets, by wall-to-wall yelling matches, and door-slamming curses invoked Jewdo-style. There was also his height: Sidney was tall. But not in an awkward arms-dangling-loosely, shoulders-hunched-over-tightly, schoolyard-basketball-playing Jewish way. Sidney was *goyishe* tall, cool and lean and straight, Gary Cooper–Jimmy Stewart tall, slanting only into the winds of confrontation. He even walked in a non-Jewish way, on the balls of his feet, head erect, almost the paradigm of a West Pointer, with the carriage of command and control and confidence. He did not seem overwhelmed by any burden from a guilt-ridden past nor was he cringing into the face of some shameful future. Already there was the air of *goyishe* success—or success in the *goyishe* world—about him. He was a Golden Boy who knew his way, who had found his yellow brick road.

Sidney was a writer, Larry quickly learned. He had recently received his master's degree at the University of Michigan where he had won some writing award called Hopwood worth a bundle of cash. He was going on in the fall to Northwestern where he would teach, study for a Ph.D., and complete the novel he was now working on. He had already been published, too. In the *Kenyon Review.* And he had a short story coming out in the *Atlantic.* And a publisher had given him an advance on his novel. Larry who was working as a shoe salesman, taking acting classes, and making rounds looking for *anything* in television and theater, was really impressed and said so.

"And I've always been fascinated by the theater," said Sidney as they crossed Thompson Street and entered the park. "By the density of the medium; I can see what attracted Henry James so to it. And by the snatch."

"The snatch?"

"All that cunt. I would go wild just to be around some of that snatch. Maybe I'll write a play some day. Why don't you write a play?"

"I just want to act in them. Not write them."

"But wouldn't you like to be as famous as Arthur Miller?"

"If it would help me get a part I'd be as infamous as Tennessee Williams."

"I mentioned Arthur Miller because he's someone I think we can both identify with."

"Because he's straight."

"No. Because he's Jewish."

Larry stopped. They had reached the cement-lipped wading pond from which the paths of the park spoked out. "That's funny," Larry said, and smiled. "You don't look Jewish."

"We all have our small Star of Davids—or is it Stars of David —to bear. Or is it to bare?" said Sidney.

That afternoon Larry went over to the Hudson Square branch library and read Sidney's first published story, "Goldstein," in the *Kenyon Review* spring fiction issue.

"Goldstein" was about a Jew who used his own Jewish history to prey on refugees of the holocaust. For Goldstein, himself a victim, goes around soliciting funds from Auschwitz and Treblinka and Buchenwald survivors, claiming this money will be sent on to other less fortunate death-camp survivors who are still struggling. But Goldstein instead uses the money to support himself and his family with all the appurtenances and luxuries of a comfortable middle-class existence: A Forest Hills home. A baby-grand piano. A Buick Roadmaster. "Somebody's got to go on living," he rationalizes. "Those six million died so that someone else could live, some other Jew could survive. And that other Jew might as well be me. In fact, who then if not me? Because good or bad, I'm as much a Jew as anybody else. And I'm entitled to live as good a life as anybody else." And in the last scene Goldstein is seen scampering into the synagogue, putting on his *talis,* and taking his seat near the ark as he waits for the Kol Nidre prayer, symbolic embodiment of the indomitability of the Jewish idea, to begin.

It took Larry just twenty-five minutes to read the story. But as he rose from the long oak table and returned the magazine to the rack there was no question in his mind that Sidney Stein was the legitimate article, a real writer, not just another Village poseur or phony.

Sidney had been bold enough to show a man beneath his Jewish skin. Until Sidney, it seemed, each American-Jewish writer had traditionally tried to function as a one-man Anti-Defamation League, always carefully presenting the Jew in single dimension, as a cardboard character in shallow—if lovable—silhouette. But Sidney was not afraid to write about *grobber yids,* uncouth Jews, rotten kikes, who used their Jewish hair shirts as much as they were abused by them, taking immoral advantage of their disadvantages. With "Goldstein," Sidney had created his archetypal character, had already discovered precisely the right note for his talents as a writer.

As Larry left the library, blinking into the Seventh Avenue sun, he no longer considered Sidney a neighbor he had just casually met but as someone with a great future at hand. Publication in so prestigious a magazine as the *Kenyon Review,* he knew, not only marked Sidney Stein as a writer to watch but also inevitably set in motion the kind of prophecy that was rarely denied self-fulfillment.

Every morning when he passed Sidney's apartment Larry heard him typing away. Which meant Sidney was a hard worker, too. And even then Larry already suspected that the compulsion to accomplish was as much the mark of the genuine artist as of the common hack. One day, near lunchtime, Larry stopped and knocked at Sidney's door.

"Come in," Sidney called out.

Larry tried the door but it was locked.

"Who is it?"

"Larry."

"Larry?"

"From the building. From the mailbox. From coffee the other day."

"Oh, sure. Larry. Wait just one second."

Larry had to wait a lot longer than one second before the typing stopped and Sidney finally came to the door and unlatched it. "I had to get a sentence right," he apologized. "I rewrote the same sentence fourteen fucking times before I got it right. But I got it right. I guess that's what makes me a real artist. I gut it through. I always gut it through."

Larry thought: The comeback is a real artist would have gotten the sentence right the first time. But he did not say it. Instead, he asked Sidney if he wanted to feed that gut.

Sidney looked at his watch. "Why not?" he decided. But then he returned to his typewriter and studied the sheet of paper still lodged in it. On top of the fireplace mantel was a trophy. Larry went over and picked it up. It had the gold figure of a fighter in a boxing stance. Beneath it was a plaque: SIDNEY STEIN, INTERMEDIATE DIVISION CHAMPION, CAMP WAHNEE.

"I didn't know you could box."

"I can't," Sidney laughed. "It was an all-Jewish camp." He was still peering at the page in the typewriter. "I've got it right," he announced. "I really think I've got it right." Larry wondered for a moment if Sidney actually expected him to applaud. Because as he spread the cover over the typewriter he looked like an actor, the curtain falling before him.

Sidney, it turned out, had a car, an old cream-colored Chevy coupe. And on hot days after he had "gutted it through" all morning, he sometimes invited Larry to drive out to Riis Park with him, to pitch and putt on the abbreviated golf course, eat Manhattan clam chowder at the concessionaire counter, and relax on the beach. Sidney loved to lounge on a blanket, book in hand, then suddenly rise, flex his muscles, and charge into the water shouting, "Geronimo!" He would wade-dive his way past breaking whitecaps and finally come riding all the way in on the crest of a big wave. Afterward, he would towel himself down vigorously and return to his book and his blanket as if he had never left them. His talk that summer was all about his love for teaching and literature. How he was really looking forward to returning to the classroom in the fall. How he could not wait to get back to working on his novel the next morning.

One afternoon as they were returning from the beach Larry decided to ask Sidney to do him a favor.

"Depends," said Sidney. "What do you have in mind?"

Larry told him exactly what he had in mind. "Okay," Sidney shrugged. "But just for a minute or two."

"It won't take any longer than that," Larry assured him.

What had happened was this: Larry realized that they weren't that far away from the candy store. He had not been back there in weeks. And the last time he spoke with Sally she bugged him about it. Even attributing his grandfather's deteriorating health to his absence. Which wasn't true at all. His grandfather had been ailing long before he moved out. But Sally never missed a chance to throw a spitball of guilt at him. Because, no matter how absurd, it worked. She could have put the blame on him for the French Revolution, if she knew what that was, and he would have had a hard time not shouldering it. She knew her son. But he also knew his mother. And so with Sidney in tow, he figured, she would go easy, he would not have to stay too long, and still he could chalk it up as an official visit. As in "when was the last time you came out to visit us?"

Larry directed Sidney the shortest way home. Through treeless streets and cobblestoned avenues, past rows of old low-slung painted-brick attached houses and towering enclaves of new red brick city housing projects. And soon Sidney was parking before the familiar storefront, the horizontal sign proclaiming CANDY HORTON'S ICE CREAM SUNDRIES, the vertical signs advertising COCA COLA and MISSION DRINKS, the penny glass-globed nut machines that vended poly seeds and Indian nuts and pistachio nuts, standing in a row all chained together beside the splintering green newsstand where the English newspapers were laid out in flat piles and the Jewish and Italian and Spanish newspapers were furled up like flags in the racks above.

"So this is where you grew up," Sidney observed.

"Some day it'll be a national shrine," said Larry.

He got out of the car and scooped up the change that was on

the newsstand. When he was a kid he might have pocketed it. Now, after entering the store, he dutifully deposited it on the rubber pimpled circular mat on the countertop nearest the door.

Sidney, following him in, looked around. "A lot of atmosphere here."

Larry laughed. "Atmosphere is a euphemism for what?"

"No," said Sidney seriously. "I can appreciate this place a lot."

"Who can appreciate what?" They could hear her strident voice before they saw her, easing herself out of the phone booth at the rear of the store and wiping her hands on her apron at the same time. She ambled forward and smothered Larry with a wet kiss. "To what do I owe this unexpected honor?"

"We were in the neighborhood," Larry said, wiping his face. "Mom, this is Sidney Stein."

"Glad to meet you, Sidney." She cocked her head and inspected him. "Are you an actor, too?"

"Sidney's a writer."

"A writer?" She looked Sidney up and down as if she expected somehow to discover immediate evidence of that fact such as printed pages streaming out of his pocket. "What do you write? Television? Movies? Like Paddy Chayefsky? He's some writer. How much does he make?"

"I don't know," said Sidney.

"You don't know and you call yourself a writer?"

"Sidney writes short stories and books."

"Books?" Sally pointed over to the magazine racks behind the glass-enclosed cigar counter. "What kind of books?"

"Novels. He's working on a novel."

"Let him talk for himself." Sally turned and swept behind the soda fountain. She looked out the open storefront door. "Is that your car, Sidney?"

Sidney nodded.

In reply she actually sneered and kept nodding, her lip wrinkled up against her nose in obvious disgust, as if to say if that were the car Sidney was driving around in she could just imagine what kind of novel he must be writing. Her automotive literary criticism delivered, Sally expertly picked up three overturned glasses in the palm of one hand. "What do you want to drink, boys?"

"No thank you, Mrs. Lazarsky," said Sidney.

"Don't be so fucking polite," Sally scoffed. "It's a hot day. You must be thirsty."

"I'll have a Coke, I guess," Sidney relented.

"A Coke?" Sally pushed the syrup spigot. "Goyim drink Cokes. Jews drink Pepsi. What are you, a goy? You look like a goy."

"Sidney Stein, Ma. What do you think he is? I'll have an egg cream."

"You can't tell by names," Sally said. "Look at Norma Shearer."

"What about Norma Shearer?"

She was spooning away the frothy head of the egg cream. "Norma Shearer is Jewish."

"Excuse me, Mrs. Lazarsky," Sidney corrected her; "Norma Shearer is not Jewish. She just happened to be married to a Jew. Irving Thalberg."

Sally had the soda valve in reverse, adding a thin intense stream of fizz to the egg cream. It sounded like a raspberry as she laughed at the same time. "You telling me about Norma Shearer? Where do you think she got the name Shearer? Shearer is short for Shapiro."

"Ma." Larry shook his head. "Shearer is just as long as Shapiro. The same number of letters."

"Which only proves that fucking goyim can't count." She pushed their sodas in front of them. "Tell me how's your Coke, Sidney? I put a little cherry syrup in it."

Sidney sipped it like a wine taster, all but swirling it from cheek to cheek. "Excellent," he pronounced.

"Excellent?" Sally laughed. "You must be some writer. I hope you're writing in a part for Larry. He needs acting work."

Sidney smiled. "I doubt if the movies will buy my book."

"If it's any good they'll buy it. They desperately need new material. Kirk Douglas said so last month in *Photoplay*. Tell me he isn't Jewish."

"He's Jewish," agreed Larry. He took a long swallow of his egg cream. Sweet, creamy, chocolaty, and with a perfect consistency. Nobody made better egg creams than his mother. Except himself.

"Of course he's Jewish," Sally was saying triumphantly. "Just like Hervey Allen."

Larry put down his egg cream. "Who's Hervey Allen?" Sounded like some neighborhood character.

"You're a writer, Sidney. Tell my ignorant son who Hervey Allen is."

Sidney shook his head. "I'm sorry. I don't know."

Sally couldn't believe that and told the fluorescent lighting fixture above her head so. "He's a writer and he doesn't know who Hervey Allen is?" Then she leaned across the counter. "Don't tell me you never heard of *Anthony Adverse?*"

"Vaguely," said Sidney.

"Anthony Adverse was the greatest book ever written until *Gone with the Wind,"* said Sally. "And I personally believe it's a better book than *Gone with the Wind.* Hervey Allen wrote it. It was a best-seller. It was in all the rental libraries. I read it in a day and a half. And then they made a movie out of it with Fredric March. He was terrific. But they also had that actress from *Gone with the Wind* later on. She loused it up. What's her name?"

"Vivien Leigh?" offered Larry.

"No. No. Not her. The sweet one. With the apples stuck in her cheeks. The one with a sister. Olivia de Havilland. She was all wrong for the part. She must have fucked somebody. I could even have done it better." She poured the glass of seltzer she had been drinking into the sink and smiled at Sidney. "I wasn't this fat yet." She turned to Larry. "C'mon, say hello to your grandfather. He hasn't been feeling well since you moved away."

"Where's Dad?"

"He was going to go look for a suit for the holidays after work. Howard's is having a sale." She came out from behind the counter and like an usher showing a moviegoer to an empty seat led Larry toward the back of the store. Sidney hung back, hesitating.

"You too," she beckoned to Sidney. "Come meet my father, Larry's *zeydah*. And don't tell me he isn't Jewish."

As she walked past the booths in the back of the store, the tabletops piled high with assorted boxes, she pointed at them as if they were sights to be seen on a historic tour. "We're thinking of tearing these out for shelf space. Who wants the class of kids growing up now hanging around here anyway? They're all fucking scum."

"Papa," she called out as she opened the door to the apartment behind the store, "we have a surprise visitor. A special guest."

His *zeydah* was sitting in a wheelchair, rubbing his eyes. Evidently he had been napping. A folded Jewish newspaper and a graying towel lay in his lap.

Larry was shocked. The wheelchair was something new. Not that his *zeydah* had previously moved about on his own that much. "What happened?" Larry asked.

"He don't have any strength anymore."

"I didn't know that."

"You don't know a lot of things, Mister Greenwich Village. Do you live in Greenwich Village too, Sidney?"

"I'm in the same building as Larry," Sidney said. "But just for the summer."

"And in the winter Palm Springs?" asked Sally. "Or Bermuda?"

Sidney laughed. "Chicago."

"I'm sure they have slums in Chicago, too," said Sally.

Meanwhile, Larry could not take his eyes off his grandfather. How small he looked. Like an incomplete package. As if a part of him was missing, the component that gave him bulk and size. His *zeydah* had obviously aged a great deal in the few weeks since Larry had last seen him. Before he was old, now he seemed senile. He was studying Sidney suspiciously.

"This is my friend, Sidney, *zeydah*, " Larry shouted in Yiddish.

His grandfather politely nodded and asked Larry how he was. Larry told him he was fine. His grandfather said that he missed him and that he himself wasn't feeling too well. Larry said it was probably because of the summer. His grandfather said the winter would be worse. Then his grandfather reached into his pocket and took Larry's hand and placed a quarter in it. He closed Larry's hand into a fist and rubbed it gently. He reached up for Sidney's hand and deposited a dime and a nickel in it.

Larry opened his hand and examined the money. "What's this for, *zeydah?*" he asked in Yiddish.

"Take it," Sally counseled. "It makes him feel good. See the resemblance, Sidney. Shave his beard and you've got my Larry. Okay, papa. Go back to sleep."

Larry bent over and kissed his grandfather on the forehead. His grandfather suddenly smiled up at him. "It's a tip," he said in English.

Three days later his grandfather fell out of the wheelchair, breaking his hip. And a week and a half later he died in the hospital of pneumonia. Sally never called Larry during that period. "Why should I have told you?" she argued at the funeral. "He was on so many drugs he didn't know who he was anyway. And I figured if you didn't care enough to come to see me except when you went to the beach, how much could you care about him? Besides, this way you could enjoy yourself bumming around Greenwich Village with your friend Sidney looking to get laid."

Sally, like all Jewish parents, had always tried to protect him from death but not from guilt. Never from guilt. There was no logic to her statement. Immediately he felt guilty. Any involvement with Sally always ended up with the verdict: guilty. Even her death. Especially her death. But so far he had been handling it well, not shedding a single tear. For that would have been an admission of guilt. Dead was dead and he was accepting the fact. He was just eating too much. As if he were trying to eat for two people. He had to watch himself there. He had Sally's genes anyway when it came to eating. Even now, in spite of himself, he was wondering what kind of dinner he would be having at Sidney's.

19

The barn-red farmhouse, framed by a cluster of maples and dog-woods, stood just a few feet from the blacktopped highway, but surveyed a vista of Currier & Ives rolling hills. Larry parked the Mercedes in the gravel driveway and walked past an open garage containing a beige Cadillac El Dorado onto a brick terrace that led to a surprisingly large swimming pool. A tan Yorkshire terrier, darting in circles, toward and away from him, yapping loudly, announced his arrival. Patio glass doors slid open and Sidney came out wearing a bright blue sweat suit and red Adidas. He looked more *goyishe* than ever to Larry and a lot younger than he had in a funeral suit.

"Welcome to the country, old sport. Now it wasn't that bad a schlepp was it?" Sidney greeted him in a hoarse rasp, sounding like an Irwin Shaw and Scott Fitzgerald character at the same time. Larry pulled back and marveled as if he had not seen Sidney just yesterday. "You look terrific. And this view." He held up an imaginary viewfinder, framing it. "I'd love to shoot it. Breathtaking." He paused and looked around again. "No wonder you still live in the East. No wonder you can keep your sanity and perspective. This is real. All this marvelous space. The rest is bullshit."

"I like it," Sidney said. "It's a good place to work. When I can work. Sit down." He led Larry to an arrangement of wrought-iron patio chairs around a glass-topped table. "Let me get you something to drink."

Larry held up his hand. "Please. I'm fine. Besides, I'm getting too fat."

"I wasn't going to notice it. But I do remember how lean and hungry you were when we first met. Again, I'm sorry about your mother. Don't let it get you too down. I wrote the book on Jewish mothers and I know what alchemists they are. Even dead they still can turn anything into guilt. Are you sure you don't want something to drink? I'm getting a beer."

"All right. I'll have one then, too."

The moment Sidney entered the house the Yorkshire terrier reappeared, coming around the corner to bark at Larry again, approaching him and then retreating. Larry kicked out his foot. "Get away, you mutt. Or I'll string you up. Which is what Sidney, I know, would like to do to me." But he also knew they would have to go through all the charades and amenities of friendship before getting to the point. Over the phone the openers usually took just a few minutes. At dinner you never got down to business until after the meal itself was served. It would be a long evening.

Sidney returned with two bottles of beer, topped with glasses, and a bowl of nuts on a tray. "Is Henry bothering you?"

"Henry?"

"Go away, Henry," Sidney said, sitting down. The dog delivered a farewell salvo of barks at Larry before running off toward the garage. "I named him Henry because he's so high-strung. Like the James boy. But he can be a nice warm presence on a cold wintry day. It does get cold here."

"I'm sure."

"I hope you like this beer. It's Norwegian," Sidney said as he poured a glass for himself.

"Fine," Larry said, recalling for some reason that when he had lived back East there was a Norwegian beer that was the cheapest of all the imported brands sold in the supermarket. He picked up the bottle and twirled it, inspecting the label. But couldn't remember if that was the beer or not. "Looks fine," he said, and poured a glass. "Skoal."

They clinked glasses. "Yes, it does get cold here," Sidney continued. "Five, ten below in the winter is not uncommon. Not like your climate." He leaned back in his chair and studied Larry.

"So here we are: Two middle-aged Jews. Or two aging Russians. Or two young Americans."

The dog came around the corner of the house barking again. "Hush, Henry. Hang fire, Henry," Sidney called out. A car had pulled into the driveway and now a tall Asiatic girl wearing oversized sunglasses was walking up the patio, her hair in long pigtails, American-Indian-princess style, clutching a paperback book in her hand. Sidney went to her and kissed her warmly, his hand loitering on her back. "You know, Terry," he said to Larry who had also risen, "don't you?"

"No," Larry shook his head.

"My daughter Terry. I was sure you'd met. I asked her to drive out for dinner because she's interested in cinema."

"How nice," said Larry.

"I admire your work," she said softly.

"Which is more than you can say about my work, isn't it?" Sidney said, his arm still about her. "Do you think it's right for a daughter not to like her father's work?"

"I don't know if it's right," said Larry. "But it's normal. My kids would rather see *E.T.* again than any of my pictures."

Terry freed herself from Sidney. "Where's Molly?"

"Out shopping. There was something she forgot to get. In fact, I thought you were her until I heard Henry barking."

At the sound of his name the terrier started yapping again at Larry's feet. "Shut up, Henry." Sidney picked him up and handed him to Terry. "Why don't you put him in the house and get yourself something to drink? But first let me see what you're reading." Reluctantly she surrendered the paperback she had been clasping. "What crap!" Sidney examined it. "Why do you read such crap?" He tossed it over to Larry as if he were a fellow storm trooper at a book burning. The book cover was of a red costumed brunette with a low bodice, her tits flopping out of it, being passionately embraced by a gentleman in evening dress while a house on a hill behind them blazed ominously in the background.

"I read it," said Terry, "to relax."

"While driving?" Sidney asked incredulously.

"No, before sleeping," she said. "I might stay the night." She retrieved the book from Larry and, still cradling the dog, retreated toward the house.

"We didn't read trash like that, did we?" Sidney asked after her.

"You forget. We read worse," said Larry. "How old is Terry?"

"Eighteen."

"She's beautiful."

"Isn't she? I'm tempted to go after her myself except I wouldn't be sure which tabu I was violating. Incest or rape."

"Well, it wouldn't be incest exactly."

"Said Byron to his sister. Maybe it wouldn't be incest technically, but certainly legally. Terry's my legal daughter now. Isn't that a joke? Chicky's last *goojah*"—he rammed his fist in the air —"from the grave. The bitch!"

Larry girded himself to hear in life as in his literature—it even turned up in his *Love on the Freeway* draft—another Sidney Stein diatribe against his dead wife. Larry's own memories of Chieko were pleasant enough. In their meetings she had always struck him as strong and purposeful but never as the fire-eating Dragon Lady Sidney now insisted she actually was. True, Larry could never quite understand Chieko's original appeal to Sidney. But then he could rarely fathom what most of his friends actually saw in their wives. It seemed to him they usually put more care into the selection of a car or a house or a project—or even a mistress or lover—than in a marriage partner. And perhaps rightly so. There was always an almost tragic inevitability in the choice of a mate that not all the analysis in the world could ever satisfactorily explain. How could you ever explain unavoidable accidents? And that's what most marriages were—as inexplicable as unavoidable accidents. Perhaps there was a picture in that? Unavoidable Marriages. An Unavoidable Marriage. He liked the title. It sounded comedic. In fact, come to think of it, the story of Sidney's marriage was basically comedic, not tragic. Even though it did end with violent death. But even death could be funny if both its manner and repercussions were funny.

What had happened was this: At the end of that summer in the

Village, Sidney went off to Chicago. And in the next few years his stories appeared in the *New Yorker,* the *Paris Review,* the *Atlantic Monthly, Esquire,* and the annual O. Henry collections. His first novel was published, then a collection of his own stories. He wrote front-page reviews for the New York *Times* "Book Review." He made all the right stops on the ascendant spiral of literary success. When he came into New York he'd often call Larry, who was still struggling as an actor, and over a drink or dinner, Larry would hear all the latest news of Sidney's career and grand pronouncements as to Sidney's future: Sidney would never go to Hollywood; he would never appear on television; he would never do anything, he once told Larry in all seriousness, that Tolstoy would not have done. And then he would name-drop: Bellow. Roth. Malamud. Writers with whom he was being compared. Writers he considered his equals. But still Sidney would insist that he'd go on teaching. A writer had no home but his desk, so a writer needed a place of belonging, a community of interest. And a classroom in academia was the best place. There he could read books, have a captive audience for an intelligent discussion, and find ready snatch. In fact, Sidney often made it seem, as he detailed his sexual adventures in Evanston and Old Town and the Near North, that Chicago was as appropriate a home for him as it was for *Playboy* magazine.

Then Sidney met Chieko, a divorcée with a young daughter. Her family came from the state of Washington but she had been born in a Japanese relocation camp in California and grew up in Chicago where she married a Chinese accountant. After she became caught up in Women's Liberation, she returned to school and took a writing course with Sidney. Their affair followed, she left her husband, and the rest was matrimony to Sidney. When her ex-husband left America for a job in Singapore, she and Sidney became the sole legal guardians of her daughter. But then, after a few years, the marriage soured. He and Chieko were separated but still not yet divorced when she died in the crash of a DC-8. Two weeks later her ex-husband was killed when his Datsun Bluebird ran into a British Petroleum truck in Singapore.

"If it's a joke," Larry was saying, "you have to admit it's funny."

"Sure, it's funny," Sidney agreed. "How else could I have become the Jewish father of a Sino-Japanese child? Who could believe it? It's as if I'm living my life in the middle of a sitcom. And that's what I call a *goojah* for a serious writer. Did Tolstoy—let alone Pushkin—have any black grandchildren? Did Proust have a sex-change operation? Was Henry James ever involved in a palimony suit? No. But Sidney Stein who has a sperm count lower than his lifetime schoolyard batting average—too low to have his own kid—has an Oriental daughter instead. Chicky's revenge."

"I didn't know you couldn't have children."

"Neither did I," said Sidney. "But Molly wanted a kid. And we really tried. So finally we both had tests. And I came up a few million spermatozoa short."

"I'm sorry."

"I'm not. I never wanted kids anyway. I'll tell you the one thing that disturbed me though with my Jewish Freudian background is this. I couldn't help but wonder if all the jerking off when I was a kid had anything to do with it. But my doctor assured me it wasn't that. He said if that was the case we'd be a sterile nation. Do you think Tolstoy ever jerked off?"

"Only," Larry sipped his beer, "into his beard."

"Really," said Sidney. "What a disgusting picture!" But he laughed too appreciatively.

The dog came around the corner of the house, yapping again. Sidney picked him up: "How'd you get out, Henry?"

"I let him," said a full-bodied blonde following after him, wearing a blue wraparound skirt and a tight-fitting white sweater. Her voice had a thin quality considering the amplitude of her physical presence. She sounded to Larry like a Liv Ullman badly dubbed and he had the feeling that he had met her before.

"I didn't hear you come back," said Sidney.

"I parked in front. The driveway was full."

"Well, this is the reason. Molly, I'd like you to meet Larry Lazar."

"Don't get up," she said. "My condolences."

"Thank you."

"I've heard a lot about you." She smiled.

"Don't believe a word Sidney says unless it's fiction to begin with."

"Not only from Sidney. I read newspapers and magazines. I go to films. I especially liked *Hostile Relationships.*"

"Thank you."

"And I hear good things about *Herbie and Milty.*"

"Have you seen it yet?"

"No."

"Better catch it fast then," Larry suggested.

"I guess that's one good thing about books," Sidney said, lowering the dog. "They're always around. I mean you can pick up a book and read it any time you want. It's always available. It's always there. At least, theoretically."

"So are video cassettes and video discs for that matter," said Larry.

"A cassette to Sidney is the Yiddish word for something untranslatable," said Molly. "And the only discs he would know about are the ones that slip in your back."

Larry laughed. "That makes us even. We haven't quite discovered books—as differentiated from properties—yet in California. At least, theoretically."

"Well, I better go get dinner started," Molly said. "Excuse me."

Sidney stood up and kissed her, as if she were departing on some long journey. "How do you like my shiksa?" he asked while she was still well within hearing range.

Larry watched as her broad back disappeared into the house. Now he realized why she had seemed so familiar to him. She was like all the other girl friends of Sidney—except for Chieko—he had met down through the years. Because just as Sidney always featured an archetypal Jewish mother in his fiction, he always boasted a real live shiksa mistress in his life, blond, Aryan, and milk-clean, pink-cheeks-healthy-looking, a sort of zaftig and athletic Grace Kelly. She usually had a glamour profession, too:

Museum curator. City planner. Public-interest lawyer. She also usually had a secret vice which Sidney would later reveal after he had parted from her. The museum curator was a dipso, the city planner was a druggie, the public-interest lawyer was a nymphomaniac.

"Isn't Molly something?" Sidney was saying. "What do you think she does for a living?"

"She's a nuclear scientist."

"Guess again."

"She's a dog trainer?"

"Close. Molly teaches Greek at Princeton. Very bright girl. This semester she's on sabbatical working on a translation of the *Odyssey* that is going to knock everything else right out of the box."

"Do you think there's a picture in it?"

"Maybe. But strictly X. Because I've got to tell you that when it comes to sex she's a little kinky."

"Aren't we all?"

"I'm not talking Jewish kink. Jewish kink is swallowing a blow job. I'm talking *goyishe* kink."

"What's that?"

"Gargling it." Sidney exploded into laughter at his own locker-room humor. Recovering, he leaned forward and slapped Larry on the knee. "Gee, but it's good to see you, old sport. Beats talking to you over the phone."

"I'm sure we can get our differences straightened out," said Larry.

"I hope so. I'm awfully proud of you, Larry. I can't tell you how thrilled I was that year you won an Academy Award."

"I never won an Academy Award. I was just nominated. Twice. For writing."

"Same thing. Listen, I won the National Book Award and they never even put my face on television. All they did was fly me in from Chicago and hand me a check and a few drinks. Books are a pissant business. But a great art. The only trouble is," he sighed, "I don't seem to be going anywhere with my new book and according to the critics I didn't go anywhere new with my last book. Did you read it?"

"No," Larry lied. "I've been waiting until I had the time to give it the attention it deserves."

"It isn't as bad as some of the reviews. I think a lot of latent anti-Semitism was being directed against me. And anti-Semitism is on the rise. The whole turn to the right in Washington is something I don't like. Do you know him?"

"Know who?"

"Reagan?"

"Not really."

"Who do you know?"

"Cary Grant," Larry smiled. "And Katharine Hepburn. We flew in from the coast together."

"I'm impressed, Mister Hollywood," said Sidney. "I am impressed. The summer we first met I was sometimes afraid you'd never get out of the Village. End up one of those people who hangs around there for years just fucking Negresses. Or waiting to fuck Negresses. Have you fucked a Negress yet?" He stopped and laughed. "But I'll say this: Chieko always had faith in you. She didn't like most of my friends, old buddy, but she did like you."

"I liked her. In fact, I never can understand why you continually have to bad-rap her. But that's your trip and I don't want to get into it."

"I bad-mouth her because she was a bitch. Worse than a bitch. She was a cunt. A slant cunt. You don't know the half of it."

Larry put up his hand. "And I don't want to know it either. But before you completely rewrite your own past history let me ask you this: Why is it that whenever I met you with her, I remember, you could never keep your hands off of her?"

"That was only in front of you, old sport," said Sidney. "Only in front of you."

From where Larry sat at the heavy walnut dining-room table he could see pots and pans hanging from every available rafter in the large farm-style New England kitchen, but the main dish was

Japanese. Beef teriyaki, strips of beef barbecued in a marinated soy sauce and served with plops of rice. Larry wondered if Molly prepared it because Sidney had become accustomed to Japanese food during his marriage. Or just to give him another *goojah.* You never knew what went on between two people. Even if you were one of them. And, especially, if one of them was Sidney. He could never quite figure out Sidney, a Golden Boychik in every respect, except—or including—his Jewish need to suffer. It was as if Sidney, who had first achieved fame by exposing the use of Jewish suffering for selfish gain, needed the history of Jewish suffering to justify his own personal unhappiness. And it was especially funny, because like the punch line, Sidney didn't even look Jewish. Except watching Sidney wave his chopsticks in the air as he spoke, Larry did flash on Bernstein conducting the Philharmonic. "Beats Chock Full o' Nuts," Sidney was saying, "doesn't it, Larry?"

"Terrific food. Delicious, Molly."

"Thank you."

"Perfect." Larry laid down his chopsticks. "Just perfect. Really perfect." He had eaten too much but it was good food. Otherwise, dinner had actually been a bore. Sidney's daughter, Terry, it turned out, was like most teenagers, more interesting at first glance than when subject to any further scrutiny. At odd moments she seemed adult but the more general impression she gave was one of childish shyness. Not only did she seldom contribute to the conversation, but her presence seemed to inhibit it. That was also because of Sidney's clumsy attempts to involve her. Sidney did not seem to know that the best way to father teenagers in public was to leave them alone. Larry felt sorry for the poor kid. But after she had expressed an interest in film schools because she thought she "might want to do something in the movies," and he told her to call Michael who was closer to her generation for advice, he really didn't have anything to say to her. Nor did he have much to say to Molly. She laughed at Sidney's jokes and smiled a lot but what was going on in her head was all Greek to him: The more he looked at her the more she began to look like FDR in drag and he wondered if the secret vice she had that

Sidney would confide to him one day after their inevitable breakup was bisexuality. Or was bisexuality just something on his mind lately?

After a dessert of fruit compote he and Sidney retired to a booklined parlor for coffee and cognac and little Schimmel Penninck cigars which Sidney produced while Molly and Terry took care of the kitchen details. Then Sidney, playing with the thin cigar in his mouth, smiled. "Well?"

Larry leaned over and lit his own cigar with the lighter on the end table. He had forgotten that he had stopped smoking cigars even before he had stopped smoking cigarettes. But what the hell? One cigar. And such a tiny one, not much bigger than a cigarette anyway. How much could it hurt? Besides, it fit the scene. After all, now that the preliminaries were over they would finally get down to business. The movie business. "Well what?" He snapped out the flame.

"You said you'd explain the situation to me and then I'd understand it."

"I said I hoped you could understand it. Because, look Sidney," he aimed a look at the imaginary spot on Sidney's forehead, "let me tell you out front I would rather not make a picture than lose your friendship. I treasure it too highly. I value and esteem you too much as a person. The last thing I want to do is hurt you in any way. You know that." He put the cigar on an ashtray but kept staring at Sidney. "So that there's no confusion let's review the history, put everything out front. Now, in order to get *Herbie and Milty* made I had to give the studio an option on my next project. And when they saw how well *Herbie and Milty* was coming along, they began to bother me about what I was going to do next. Now, I never know what I'm going to do next. I'm an artist, not a businessman, and I can't be programmed—or program myself. But I thought I wanted to work with Max again, give him first crack, since our collaboration on *Herbie and Milty* turned out so well. But then Max and I couldn't get together on a project. And, at that moment, you happened to call me. You were up in Berkeley giving a lecture and wondered if we could get together down in LA. You said you had an idea for a movie you wanted to try out on me. I said, 'I would love to see you.' I always love to see you. Am I right so far?"

"So far," Sidney acknowledged, flicking off the ash of his cigar.

"And we had lunch in the studio commissary. You ordered veal, I remember, and were impressed when you saw Fred Astaire and O. J. Simpson and that guy from 'M.A.S.H.' sitting there. I also remember that since this was the first time in all the years I'd known you that you expressed any kind of interest in writing a movie, I thought I had to warn you. So I told you then and there that you *really* didn't want to write a movie. Because writers were the Jews of the movie business. They got all the heat but none of the real power. I said: 'They just pick the grapes but they don't get to drink the wine.' And I remember very clearly your pointing to yourself and asking, 'How much could this Jewish grape picker get?' Which was not a bad line. But I still couldn't believe you were really serious and said so. And you said that you were as serious as Cesar Chavez. Stop me if I'm wrong."

"No. So far you're right."

"Then you asked me if I thought we could work together? And I told you that nobody knew about collaborations of any sort, about the real chemistry of them, until you tried them.

"And then you brought up the question of money. And since I knew the East always has a highly inflated idea of what writers get in movies, I explained to you that even though you had stature as a novelist you were still a writer without credits as far as the movie business was concerned. But you weren't exactly just off the streets either. So I really couldn't answer you. I told you it was something you should talk over with your agent. I explained to you that the business part of the movie business is always business anyway." Larry leaned forward and poured a healthy dose of cognac into a snifter. "Anyway I never have anything to do with those things really. I make it a point. I always let my agent and my lawyer handle all that and the less I know about it the better. I'm like you when you sit down to write a novel. I'm just interested in creating a work of art. The rest is all so much nonsense I have to put up with as far as I'm concerned. You know what I'm saying?"

"But you had your own company," Sidney said.

"I always have my own company. But I don't even know my own company's name some times. It changes from picture to picture, deal to deal. I have to have my own company because it lends out all my producing and directing and writing services. Anyway, as I say, that's something that's all in the hands of my business manager and lawyer. And the less I know about it the better even though they charge me an arm and a leg for their services."

"But my contract was with your company, Mary-Jane-Conor Productions," Sidney said.

Larry put down the snifter. "You're running ahead of the story. I want to retrace everything, step by step, in order to clear up any misconceptions you may have picked up or assumed along the way. Now, you had said you had an idea for a movie you wanted to try out on me. Everybody I know always wants to try out a movie idea on me. But the trouble with most people's idea of an idea is that it isn't an idea at all. Not for a movie anyway. Not for a Larry Lazar movie definitely. So I wouldn't listen to just anybody who came to me with an idea. I don't listen to ideas just off the street. It's for my own protection also." He rubbed the tops of his eyelids, suddenly tired. "You have no idea of the people—writers included, writers especially—who later accuse me of lifting their ideas. But you, of course, weren't coming to me just off the street. You were a writer of stature and besides, we have our personal relationship going way back. So I let you tell me your movie idea.

"It was about a Ukrainian taxi driver in New York who was a religious nut and a refugee from a gulag and couldn't speak much English who somehow winds up a home-run hitter on the Yankees. And you wanted to make a whole megillah about the symbolism of the fact that life on the Yankees was not that much different from life in an authoritarian Stalinist state except that the pay was better. Something like that. Now, I'm a Yankee fan and I hate Steinbrenner and I still thought it was a terrible idea. Its only virtue was that it was a one-sentence idea. And I leveled with you and told you that.

"But as long as we were talking ideas and you were telling me that you wanted to work on a movie, I tried out an idea on you. I'd always wanted to do an episodic film like the ones the Italians still make and Hollywood used to make, like *Tales of Manhattan*. So I told you about *Love on the Freeway,* a *La Ronde* in LA, where you'd introduce the characters in each new episode by having their car pass the car of the characters in the previous episode. Which was an original idea I'd been toying around with for a long time."

Sidney laughed. "You and Schnitzler."

"And who knows who Schnitzler lifted it from? I wasn't around Vienna in those days and neither were you. That's why I never listen to ideas. They're all in the air. And then when you make a picture somebody's always ready to sue you for breathing. Anyway, am I right so far?"

Sidney shrugged.

"And I asked you if you'd be interested in working on developing *Love on the Freeway* with me. We took a long walk through Century City discussing possible episodes and different means of possible collaboration. We both agreed only one person should go to the typewriter at a time. And we agreed you'd be the first one. But that we'd develop the storylines for the episodes together. And on that basis I went to the studio and made the deal. Right?"

Sidney nodded.

"And I must say your cunt agent back East drove a very hard bargain for you. Really. You can ask around and see what other writers of your category without credits are getting. Never mind what they say they're getting in Elaine's, but what they're *actually* getting. But that isn't the point. You deserve whatever your agent got for you. Because you're a very talented guy. You write terrific books and you're a very funny man. But, as I warned you, you should never have gone near a movie script. But that was your decision. *You* said you really wanted to work on a movie with me and frankly I was flattered. A writer of your stature. And we did work on the story together. You stayed over an extra two days and we did a lot of walking and talking. I went into

New York for a weekend and we got together again and did some more work. And then I can show you what my phone bills were like because we were on the phone a lot. I put a lot of my blood into that script. There's a lot of my heart in there. You can't say I didn't contribute—"

"But you didn't write a word."

"Where does writing begin and end? I don't know. And I don't think, for all your novels, you know either. You have no right to tell me how the writing process works. Not in the movie business. We're not talking literature. We're talking script and how a script gets written."

Sidney slowly rose, stubbing out his cigar. "Let's go outside. Get a breath of air as long as you're in the country."

Larry took another sip of his cognac. "I'm perfectly comfortable. This is fine."

"No," Sidney insisted. "Let's take a walk."

"What about Molly and Terry?"

"We'll be right back. But I better tell them we're taking a walk anyway." He left the parlor and went into the kitchen. Larry put down his drink and his cigar and inspected the books that filled every available shelf. There were row on row of Sidney's books in foreign language editions: Japanese and Hebrew, Swedish and Dutch and Portuguese as well as German, French, Italian, and Spanish. There were British editions and South African paper imprints and German magazine condensations and Polish and Russian translations. Larry had forgotten that publishing was as international as film. And, for the most part, on a much higher level. The movies that had legs around the world were usually the spectacles that featured violence and sex, or children's stories without subtleties of any sort. But with stars, of course. Sidney was his own star in publishing. Also his own director. When it came to a movie, he had had to take a back seat to Larry. A seat pretty far back. As just a writer. Movie making was never a democratic process. Especially for a writer. He wondered how he could ever possibly make Sidney understand this. He would hate to lose another friend in order to make another film. But didn't Thomas Mann say that you couldn't expect to pluck a single leaf from the laurel tree of art without paying for it with your life. Then why not pay for it with a friend? Even a few friends? A lot cheaper.

Sidney returned, blinking a flashlight on and off. "We don't really need this. But it makes Molly feel better." Larry followed him out the front door and down a winding path to a white-gated picket fence. It was pitch dark. But the sky was not clear. He could not have spotted a constellation of stars even if he had known how to identify one.

"I love to walk," Sidney said, as they crossed the blacktop and headed into the darkness. "But no one told me walking at night in the country was even more dangerous than in the city. In the city the spaced-out junkies can get you. Here it's the local shiksas you have to look out for. They're hell on wheels."

They were walking on the right side of the highway in the direction of oncoming traffic. As if on cue a single headlight, looming in the distance, began weaving toward them.

"Is that a motorcycle?" Larry asked.

"Doubt it." Sidney shined his flashlight in front of them. "He probably lost the other headlight in an accident. Hitting a fat Jewish pedestrian from out-of-state."

There was no need for such a hostile remark but Larry let it pass as they both moved over onto the shoulder. Soon a pickup truck, with a mashed in fender and a dangling, inoperative headlight, veering dangerously close to them, roared past. The driver obviously had not even seen them. Larry had second thoughts about continuing the walk.

"Isn't this beautiful?" said Sidney. "So quiet. And you can really fill your lungs here." He lit another cigar. "I'm no Squire Allworthy, but the country has a lot to say for itself. The foliage out here is fantastic. Breathtaking." He pointed with his cigar as if it were still visible there in the darkness out of season. "Should never have given up my apartment in the city, though. They just went co-op and I could have made a bundle on it. A fortune. Listen!"

Larry heard a sad and eerie sound, like that of an animal in pain.

"Know what that is?" said Sidney. "An owl. They usually travel in pairs. Male and female. That's a male owl calling for his mate. She must be lost."

"How do you know that?"

"I don't," Sidney laughed. "But I figured you weren't any great maven about owls either."

They walked in silence until they came to a turn in the road. For the first time that night Larry could see a sliver of the moon. "Let's go back," he said.

Sidney smiled. "First let's finish our business."

"Here?" Larry indicated the sandy shoulder of the two-lane blacktop in the middle of New Jersey that they were standing on in complete darkness.

"Here," Sidney insisted.

"Ooooh," the owl hooted.

Okay, if Sidney wanted to play Halloween he could play the game, too. "The point is we agreed," Larry said, "that you'd take a whack at the first draft of *Love on the Freeway* and then I'd take a whack at it. I didn't rush you. I didn't bug you. And I didn't have any intention of working on anything else. But then I had this other idea that had nothing to do with us or what you were doing. That came to me from somewhere out of my dark places. Where it was obviously just waiting around, dying to be written. Because it just wrote itself. And that is how *Remember, Remember* came about. Born full grown. Ready to go. Consciously, I had very little to do with it. It was just all there. And I didn't try to hide anything from you. I even sent you a rough draft of the script for your opinion which I respect and value. Anyway, it's a script I can start prepping and casting as soon as the studio gives me a go."

"They'll give you a go, as you call it, I'm sure."

"I'm not so sure. I'm not sure of anything in the movie business. I don't assume anything is going to happen until I see it happen." Larry started walking again. Back toward Sidney's house. He had lanced the wound. It was time to dress it and go. "Now tell me what's bothering you, Sid? Aside from the fact that you feel rejected. I can understand that. I can relate to that."

"Well, try relating to this." Sidney grabbed his arm. "All of the things you've left out. First, there's the fact that the script I've written is not *Love on the Freeway.* Because when I told you I wanted to concentrate on one episode, or rather on one of the episodes we had discussed, and develop it full length, you said: 'Okay, go with the flow.' And I did. So the script I wrote is not *Love on the Freeway.* It's *The Merry Widower.*"

"It's the same thing whatever you want to call it." Larry tried to free his arm but Sidney only tightened his grip. "The studio put up the money for you to write something and you took the money. And who knows? It might wind up an episode in *Love on the Freeway,* after all. I haven't dismissed the script. I haven't dismissed the project. Far from it. As I said, I poured a lot of blood, a lot of heart, into the project."

"Not into the script. Not into the writing. You didn't sit down at the typewriter for a single minute on it. That's one of the reasons I'm so pissed off. We were supposed to be collaborators, cowriters, but you've never written one word. You haven't given the script a *shot* or a *whack* or whatever you call it at all."

"Oh, that's not fair," Larry protested as he managed to shake himself free from Sidney's grip. "That's not fair at all. Don't you think I haven't thought about it a lot. A lot I'll tell you. And nobody wishes more than me to lick it. But I haven't been able to lick it."

"That's because there's nothing to *lick.* That's because it's all there."

"That's your opinion and you're entitled to it. But, as I say, I have thought about it a lot. Critically and creatively. And, in fact, I am annoyed that you're limiting the creative process to moments actually spent at the typewriter. I resent that. You're insulting me. I've never been one of those pages-pages-give-me-the-pages producers with you. Asking you for so many pages per day. So many pages per week. That's how most producers are in the movie business. That's how they do things. But I happen to know something about writing. I may not be able to write books or novels like some of my friends. Because that isn't my trip. But when it comes to writing movies I know a lot about writing. I didn't get two Academy Award nominations in writing for nothing. I have great understanding and empathy for the writing process. I know all the pain that goes into it."

"Then why haven't you given *The Merry Widower* the benefit of some of your writing process?"

"And I'm telling you I have. If I knew what else to do with it I'd be at the typewriter tomorrow on it. But I don't know what to do with it. Maybe it's because my head is into *Remember, Remember* right now. I don't think so. But I don't know. And I don't know when I'll be able to think about it again. But if you know how to lick it, please go ahead. Nothing could make me happier."

"There isn't anything to *lick. The Merry Widower* has far more real substance and content, narrative drive and genuine style than *Remember, Remember.*"

"I disagree with you one hundred percent," said Larry, moving down the road again. "Anyway, look: I don't want to put my script in competition with your script. Because I feel close to both scripts. It just so happens that *Remember, Remember* is the script that I think is ready and that I want to do next."

"Larry, you promised me. You gave me your solemn word of honor *Love on the Freeway* would be your next movie."

"Never. I would never make such a promise."

"You did. Several times. Once in the parking lot of the studio. Once in that Mexican restaurant. And once over the phone before I signed the contract."

"You must have misunderstood me. Out of wishful thinking. It happens all the time."

"Not to me. I teach English and I'm a professional cynic. But I had no reason to mistrust you personally. So I believed you."

"You're wrong, Sidney. What else can I say? Who am I to promise a script will be made? I'm not a studio. I'm not a bank. I have to sweat out each picture I get made. I have to be grateful each time I get a chance to get to bat." Larry rubbed his hands over his eyes again. He was weary, he didn't like the road, he didn't like the walk, and he didn't like the discussion. He should never have left Sidney's parlor; he should get back to New York as soon as possible. "Anyway, what do you want me to do now, Sidney?"

"I want you to sit down and do your cowriting on *The Merry Widower.*"

"I have been coworking—"

"But not cowriting—"

"I have been," Larry rushed on, *"involved*—let me use the word 'involved.' Deeply involved in *The Merry Widower.* But I'm telling you now I don't see a picture there yet. Not a full-length feature. Maybe it could be an episode in *Love on the Freeway* someday."

"I don't see it as an episode. I see it as a whole movie."

"Well, I'm the director. And it's not a whole movie I want to direct. Not just yet."

Sidney breathed in hard. "That doesn't leave me much, does it?"

Larry shrugged. "There's not much that can be done."

"Except to give the studio the script," Sidney said.

"Your script?" Larry asked incredulously. *"The Merry Widower?"*

"Why not?"

"I told you it's not ready. I don't think it's ready. You want me to hand it in and say, 'Here's something I don't want to direct.' I could do that. But I think that would be the worst thing to do. Totally destructive. You should never let them see a piece of work until you think it's ready."

"It's better than abandoning the script."

"No one's abandoning the script. Between you and me we're abandoning the script. But not between us and the studio. As far as the studio knows we're putting it on the back burner for a while. It happens all the time. And, as I say, I may get back to it some day. Who knows the creative process?"

"Meanwhile then," Sidney said slowly, "I'd like to have my agent show it around."

"You can't," Larry replied. "They own it. The studio owns it."

"And you say I can't show it to them?"

"That's right. How can you show it to them? Who are you?

You're not the producer. I'm the producer. You're not the director. I'm the director. You're only the writer."

"Cowriter," Sidney said sarcastically.

"That's the deal. You have a very smart agent. And you're smart yourself. You made the deal. You have to live with it. Besides, the best way to kill any chance of ever getting it done is to show it around now. Believe me, I've been around Hollywood long enough to know what happens to material labeled damaged goods."

"Suppose," Sidney said, "I just give back the money I've been paid. Couldn't I buy the script back and then do whatever I want with it?"

"No."

"Why not?"

"Because that means somebody would have to give back the money I've been paid. And I'm not about to do that."

"It can't be that much."

"It's a lot."

"For just supervising the development of a script?"

"I'm a cowriter, too. I had to get my writer's fee."

"How much did you get?"

"What's the difference?"

"I'd like to know."

"All right, I have nothing to hide," Larry said. "First, I made a producing and directing deal through my company. Then the studio was financing the development of the script we were writing through my company. So all together it came to quite a bit. I don't know the exact figure. But I can give you a ball park."

"What's the ball park?"

"Over two hundred fifty thousand."

Sidney whistled. "That's some ball park. That's Yankee Stadium compared to Ebbets Field. That's three times more than what I'll wind up with. And you haven't put a word on paper."

"That's how they do things out there. I don't think it's fair either. But I can't change things. Look, Sidney, all I can do is promise you again that I'm not finished with *The Merry Widower* by a long shot. Who knows if I'll ever get *Remember, Remember* done anyway? And I have nothing else on my agenda. Look, Sidney, Max and I had to wait two years to get *Herbie and Milty* done; did you know that?"

"I'm not Max Isaacs and I don't write for the wastebasket. I write out of real experience. I write out of my gut until I get something right. *The Merry Widower* is about something very personal in my life."

"And who suggested that you use the personal aspect? That you use whatever you knew? I did. It was my idea. And I won't walk away from it. But I can't respond to your deadlines. Anyone's deadlines. That's not what art is all about. And I am an artist. You have to admit I'm an artist. If nothing else I am an artist."

Sidney was silent.

"Try to understand things from my point of view. I'm a filmmaker. I have to find a film I want to make. Which is very difficult. And I've found one. It just so happens I've found one that I happened to write—or rather happened to write itself. I'd just as soon it had been one we wrote together or you wrote alone. But that's how it worked out. What more can I say? Except that I did warn you about the movies; I told you not to get involved with them. It's a business with its own conventions." Larry slapped his hands against his sides helplessly. "Now it's getting late. I have to be starting back to New York."

Sidney was smiling and shaking his head. "And that's it?" he said. "That's supposed to be it. I'm supposed to walk away and let you walk away and we both live happily ever after. Fade out. Just another convention of the business?"

"There isn't anything else you can do."

"Wrong, Lazar. Dead wrong." Sidney was still smiling.

"Look," Larry said, "if you want to start talking about lawyers I can tell you right now you'll be in over your head and you'll only wind up spending a lot of money. Talk to your agent; she's smart. Talk to your lawyer. They'll both tell you, you have no case."

"I wasn't thinking of lawyers."

"Good. I thought you were too smart for that."

"I'll tell you what I was thinking about though: Busting your balls. Beating the shit out of you." Sidney took a step toward him. "Right here and now."

"You must be joking?"

"I'm not joking. The lesson of the holocaust. Jews have to strike back. Not take *goyishe* shit. Even from Jews. And you're a shit, Lazar. Remember my story 'Goldstein.' You're a Goldstein of the movies. And I'm not going to let you get away with it."

Larry looked about into the night. He had no idea where they were, how far they had walked, how great the distance was back to the house. Sidney was obviously serious. He was also obviously stronger and in better physical condition. Had the height and the reach on him, too. Also knew the terrain. It looked like he would have to talk his way out of this one. "Sidney," he began, "after all, *you* came to *me*—"

"My mistake." Sidney shoved him hard, making him almost lose his balance.

"This is ridiculous, Sidney. We're two writers. We're both artists. Certainly we can resolve our differences in a more civilized way. No need for the Hemingway macho. We're not goyim. We're not barbarians."

"As far as I'm concerned," said Sidney, "morally, you're a total barbarian. You're a goy." He cocked his fist.

"You lay one hand on me and you'll be in big trouble," Larry warned. "There are lawyers. There are courts of law."

"Look who's talking lawyers now." Sidney shoved him again. This time Larry fell. Onto the seat of his pants. Into a tangle of weeds and thorns.

Larry sat there.

"Get up!" Sidney stood over him.

"I will not get up until you stop this John Wayne nonsense. This is ridiculous, Sidney. Two Jews fighting out in the middle of New Jersey. With owls hooting. I'll tell you what I'll do: I'll do as you suggest. As soon as I get back to California I'll go to the typewriter on *The Merry Widower.*"

Sidney laughed and shook his head. "Too late, Lazar. I have to teach you a lesson. I'm going to beat the shit out of you."

"It's not fair," Larry protested. "You were a boxing champion."

"Sure," Sidney looked down at his fists. "And these are lethal weapons."

"I remember that trophy in your apartment."

"What trophy?"

"From some camp."

Sidney laughed. "Some camp is right. Camp Wahnee. I *was* the Intermediate Boxing Champ."

"Exactly," Larry said. "See what I mean? It's not fair."

"I'm also a .428 lifetime schoolyard hitter. But they'll never vote me into Cooperstown. Get on your feet!"

"Stop it, Sidney. You have no excuse. You're not even drunk."

"I'll get drunk after I break your balls. Then I'll have something to get drunk about."

"I'm not getting up, Sidney."

Sidney kicked him. Hard. In the shins. He had not expected it and sprang to his feet. "That wasn't called for."

Sidney did not answer him. Instead, Sidney was hopping around, holding onto his foot, and moaning. "I forgot," he finally oohed and ahed, "I was wearing Adidas." He put down his foot and limped back toward Larry. "Put up your hands. We'll settle this with fists."

"I will not box with you, Sidney."

"Too bad. Because I'll box with you." Sidney flicked a jab into his face. It stung him just beneath the eye. Larry saw another jab coming and was able to step away from it in time. But this was ridiculous. He was no Sugar Larry Lazar. Eventually, Sidney would start getting through to him. His only escape was in his legs. He just might be able to out run the limping Sidney. Get back to the house and away from the madman. Sidney flicked out another jab, grazing his chin. Back at the house Sidney would have to stop this nonsense. Molly looked like she could beat him up if necessary.

"Come on, Sidney," he pleaded.

"You're evil, Lazar. Evil as the devil."

"That's banal," Larry replied. "Beneath you."

Sidney lunged with his right and missed him. Larry put out a short, soft defensive jab. Sidney missed him again with another long jab. But Larry was getting tired. Just ducking and trying to fend Sidney off. This was no way to use up his energy.

"I'll teach you to fuck around with Sidney Stein. It's one thing to fuck with Hollywood hacks like Max Isaacs. But nobody fucks with Sidney Stein."

"You're as crazy as Norman Mailer is supposed to be," Larry panted.

"He doesn't fuck around with me either." Sidney landed another jab on the side of his face. Larry felt a burning sensation in his cheek and wondered if a tooth had been chipped. He'd read somewhere street fights usually lasted only a few minutes and resulted in broken teeth or busted hands. But this was not a city street fight but a country fight. A two-lane-blacktop-highway fight. And Sidney was boxing like a Gentleman Jim Corbett with a gimpy leg. But Larry still was no match for him.

"What are you trying to prove?" he breathed out. "That you have more *cojones* than me? Granted then. Let's stop this nonsense."

"You lied to me. This is my way of getting even."

Larry had no choice. Sidney was coming at him again with the long jab. He hated to do it but it was the only way out. He did not want to get hurt by the half-crazed Sidney. He turned and ran. Back toward the house.

"Fucking coward!" Sidney called out.

"Discretion," Larry shouted back, "is the better part of—"

"Bullshit," Sidney completed.

As Larry ran along the sandy shoulder on the side of the road he could hear the crunching sounds he was making. But no sounds of Sidney. Then he turned, looking over his shoulder. There was Sidney coming after him, limp-running down the white line in the middle of the highway, with surprising speed, silently. Sidney's Adidas gave him the advantage in footwear. Larry's own boots weren't exactly made for distance racing. Except on a horse maybe. But not on foot. He wondered how much further he had to go when he felt a breathing knife in his gut. He didn't like the way his heart was beating either. Could almost hear it thumping. He was used to running in stops and starts with rest between. Like in tennis. Lobbing and retreating but then stopping to serve. But not just running flat out. Which was supposed to be better exercise. But wasn't his exercise.

"You can't outrun me, you fat fuck," Sidney was rasping. "Even with one leg I'll catch you."

Larry half turned. And it was true. Sidney was gaining on him. There couldn't have been more than a half-dozen yards between them. He pumped his legs harder and felt the pain more keenly. Runners always had pains like this. He'd read about it. But then the pains would pass. Hitting the wall they called it. He would just have to hold out until he hit the wall. Then the pain would pass. Meanwhile, he would save his breath. He wouldn't dignify Sidney's threat with a reply.

He saw headlights in the distance, two of them. A car heading toward them. Now, Sidney was behind him on the shoulder, his crunches echoing his own. Maybe he should flag down the car. But what good would that do? What would the driver think? Two middle-aged Jews running down a two-lane country highway in pitch-black New Jersey. The car came closer, the lights, he was sure, catching them. But just to play it safe he turned off the edge of the shoulder away from the road. No point getting hit by a drunken goy while being chased by a crazed Jew.

When he ran into a bush and tripped over it.

The earth came up, hitting him. He lay there sprawled, tasting blood in his mouth. Reflexively, he reached for his knees. Somehow, he was relieved to find his pants weren't torn.

Sidney was immediately over him, pulling him to his feet. Larry held his hands before his face as a shield. "Don't hit me."

"I won't hit you," Sidney said, as if that were the most absurd notion in the world. "Are you all right?"

"I guess so. Except for my heart attack." He still felt a pain in his gut. Now there was one in his chest, too. He had not hit the wall yet. "Go away." He shook off Sidney's hands. "You're crazy. You're a *meshugenah*."

"And you're a *mumser*. I had to teach you a lesson."

"You've been teaching for too many years. If this is the literary scene in the East, I'm glad I live in the West."

They walked silently, side by side. Less than fifty yards from where Larry had tripped, around a bend, was Sidney's house. If he had not run into that bush he would have made it. "Seriously, Sidney," he said, "I will be talking to my attorney."

"You're a shit," Sidney said with a laugh. "But you don't have to be a prick, too."

"And you're a hooligan. A Nazi hooligan."

Sidney laughed again. "You don't understand. Throwing a few punches at you has saved me a lot of trouble."

"You'll be in big trouble after I talk to my lawyers. Believe me. You hooligan. You Nazi hooligan."

"Not as big trouble as I'd be in if I didn't try to beat up on you," Sidney shuddered. "Imagine, having to talk to my analyst about you. Or even worse. Having to spend six months in my study dealing with a character like yours. It would drive me crazy. This way, it's all out of my system. It would have been better if I landed one good shot. But this will have to do. I feel expiated. You're out of my system." But then he laughed and suddenly grabbed Larry and shook him viciously. "But the script isn't. You better figure out a way how to make moral redress to me on *The Merry Widower*. Otherwise, I'll come out to the coast and really beat the shit out of you. Or out of your kids."

"I'll have you arrested," Larry said. "You are worse than a mafioso."

"Of course," said Sidney, "I'm a Nazi hooligan."

They walked up the winding brick path into Sidney's house. The girls looked at him as he hurried into the bathroom to wash up. "He fell down," he heard Sidney explain. Later, Larry did not try to explain anything. After he washed up he got into his car, and with the dog yapping again, backed out of the driveway, hoping to hit the mutt.

20

Larry couldn't retrace his steps—or wheels—fast enough. He quickly found his way out of Princeton and was glad to get back on the Jersey Turnpike. With truck drivers. Normal citizens. Ordinary people. Sidney Stein was crazy. A kook. National Book Award winner, Pulitzer Prize recipient, .428 lifetime schoolyard hitter, and 99.44 percent deranged. No question, there was definitely something wrong with the man's head. He needed help. Psychiatric help. No wonder Sidney had been in analysis for eleven years. His psychiatrists needed help. Which proved how crazy he was. *Moral redress?* It sounded like the Moral Majority's answer to stripping. Sidney was a nut case, no doubt about it. And he lived in that temple of culture, Princeton. Which proved how full of shit New York and the East were. Always pissing down on Hollywood and LA as if from some intellectually superior level. It was true most movies were piss poor and most people did live shallow lives in LA. But no one he had seen recently was living a life of such great depth in the East either. He flashed on Sidney's El Dorado, sitting in his Princeton garage. The only people he knew driving El Dorados in LA were middle-aged real estate agent ladies who wore dinner gowns at open houses on Sunday afternoons. The very sort of people Sidney liked to poke fun at in his books. Crazy Sidney. Larry rubbed his face. His jaw still hurt. If there was a doctor or dentist's bill he would send it to him.

The turnpike was dull driving. Even in the Mercedes 450 SL. Everyone was crawling at 60 but he was afraid to open up. He wasn't looking for any more trouble tonight. He pushed on the radio and found a station playing lively Spanish music. That would help keep him awake. And a cigarette. He reached into his pocket and found one and lighted it. The pain in his cheek had gone away but his throat was beginning to feel a little funny. As if he had eaten too much acidy food. Or drunk too much coffee. It was a funny sensation, just in the corner of his throat. The meal at Sidney's hadn't struck him as so acidy but then he never did get a chance to digest it properly. That crazy Sidney. It would be the last time he would work with him. Let him try to survive in *goyishe* splendor on his jerk-off Jewish books.

The taste in his throat wouldn't go away. And the air in the car began to feel close. Talk about smog in California: The air in New Jersey wasn't even breathable. He was certainly starting to miss California. LA. Hollywood. Beverly Hills. His house. Even his swimming pool with the algae problem that was such a pain in the ass. He opened the window all the way down and flicked out his cigarette. No more smoking. No more coking. He would get back home as soon as possible. Maybe even catch a morning flight out. He looked at the dashboard clock: Just a little past ten. Still early. And Michael would be meeting him at the Russian Tea Room at eleven. For a little script discussion and a . . . It suddenly occurred to him that he might have been plugging the wrong dike in the tandem. Still it would be a sayonara screw. And it had been a screwed-up trip anyway. He had come to bury his mother but he seemed to have spent more time with her in the past two days than he had in the past ten years. In memories and reveries, in undertaking parlors and funeral chapels, in cameos in Brooklyn and guest shots in Manhattan, and even surprise appearances in sundry dreams and hotel latrines. She just wouldn't let go and die, *really die,* stay dead and buried, the chapter over, the film finished, the final credits crawling as the lights go up.

It was the same with the rest of his past: Allen. Mira. Sidney. All hitting on him. All wanting something from him. While he did not need them anymore. He was his own man, his own artist, free, independent, unencumbered. An *auteur,* a single, he could work alone without collaborators—past or present. So he had

had to shuck them off as surely as he had shucked his own mother. Good riddance!

Only he wasn't so sure he was rid of Sally. She was tricky, she was tough, she was like that character in that Hitchcock picture who just wouldn't die.

He touched his throat. It still felt funny. Now he was having pins and needles in his arm above the elbow. Must have kept the arm lodged in the same position too long while driving. He tried twirling it over his head but that didn't help any.

As he reached the approaches to New York City, Larry felt pain in his leg, too. His right leg. Not the leg Sidney had kicked him in. He was also running short of breath. As if the nearer he got to the city the worse the air became. He took the exit that led to the Holland Tunnel. The Lincoln Tunnel would have been more convenient. But now he just wanted to get back to the city. To Brooklyn. *What* Brooklyn? To Manhattan. New York City. Jersey was bad luck for him.

But, once in the tunnel, a wave of nausea hit him. He felt brackish. Everything smelled oily, too. Even the lights of the tunnel looked oily to him. And he was sweating profusely. Then suddenly an otherworldly pain rumbled across his chest, jolting him. It was as if an earthquake was taking place beneath his ribs. He stopped the car and held on to the wheel. A Port Authority traffic cop, walking the ramp, was energetically waving him on. Drivers of the cars behind him blew their horns, the sounds echoing off the tiled walls. The cop was leaning over the railing, shouting to him. He could not hear what he was saying. The cop looked black. Reminded him of Chalky. Chalky?

The world was black.

Was he actually dying? . . . But why? . . . Just because he would not lend Allen money? . . . or give Mira her sculpture back? . . . or had broken his word to Sidney? . . . or had lifted one of Max's ideas? . . . Certainly not . . . He had done far worse before and lived . . . thrived . . . endured . . . enjoyed . . . survived . . . No, it was his lousy diet and his rotten genes . . . But what a stupid place to die . . . in the mid-

dle of the Holland Tunnel . . . he hoped it was the middle . . .
past the middle . . . on the New York side . . . He would hate
to die in Jersey . . . Especially in the Jersey side of a tunnel
. . . a tunnel was no place to die anyway . . . with everyone
leaning on their horns . . . And it was a terrible place to shoot
. . . no crane shots . . . no tracking shots . . . Besides, Fellini
had already used the idea in the opening scene of *8½* . . . the
George Washington Bridge a much better place . . . More original . . . the lights of Manhattan as picture postcard backdrop
. . . Or, if he was going to die on a bridge, then the Brooklyn
Bridge . . . Shooting that at night would be sheer poetry . . .
prizewinning . . . Fucking Sidney! . . . he could have at least
lived in Brooklyn . . . Norman Mailer lived in Brooklyn, why
couldn't Sidney? . . . He should have gone to see Norman
Mailer, instead . . . not that he knew him . . . but he probably wouldn't have gotten into a fight with him either . . . he
had never broken his word to Mailer . . . and even if he had,
Mailer, for all his hot temper, would have understood . . .
Mailer knew a thing or two about hustling . . . Didn't have that
holier-than-thou attitude of Sidney's . . . that's what came from
teaching college . . . moral redress while undressing coeds . . .
and a dog named after Henry James . . . Henry James ruined
more writers than Hollywood, whiskey, drugs, sex, and poverty
combined . . . But Sidney Stein may have ruined him . . .
May have killed him . . . Because it looked like he was dying
. . . Felt like he was dying, too . . . In the middle of a tunnel
. . . If not the George Washington Bridge he could have taken
the Verrazano . . . Stupid name but it would have been a good
place to shoot, too . . . A death in an automobile at night on a
bridge . . . always a wonderful scene . . . A crash would be
even a better way to go . . . more cinematic . . . The Tribor-
ough was another possibility . . . He could have visited somebody on Long Island . . . But there was nobody on Long Island
he would have visited except all the way out in the Hamptons
past the Jericho Turnpike . . . Still he didn't have to take his
own death so literally . . . He could take a little license . . .
shoot wherever it was easiest and cheapest to get the permit . . .

The Queensboro Bridge? The Bronx-Whitestone? The Throgs Neck . . . there were many candidates . . . After all, it was *his* life . . . It was *his* picture . . . A Larry Lazar film . . . Produced, written, and directed by Larry Lazar.

The paramedics came and again he thought he saw Chalky, the black savior of his boyhood, and he felt cold goo on his chest and a needle in his arm and he was lifted onto a stretcher and carried into an ambulance that immediately sped away, sirens wailing. If he was dying, *actually* dying, it wasn't that bad. He must remember that if he pulled through. He was also glad, at least, about one thing: money. He had made enough money to cover this eventuality. He hated the whole concept of life insurance, the idea of having to bet on oneself on the go line, so to speak, but he had allowed his business manager to talk him into carrying a bundle. More important was the real estate: The warehouse in the City of Industry. The singles apartment complex in Sherman Oaks. The new office building in Santa Monica. Not to mention his portfolio with all the cable stock. And the residuals that would keep coming in from his pictures. Plus the house, of course. Even after inheritance taxes, Jane and the kids would be in good shape. They would not have to go hustling on the streets. There was enough so that the kids could have good educations, go to decent colleges. Funny, though: He had always considered himself an artist but here he was embracing middle-class values, completely, dying a burgher, a businessman, no different really than his hustling Uncle Irving or his grandfather who, for all his reading of Gogol in the back of the candy store, actually called the shots when it came to running the store up front. "Only my candy store," he carefully framed the concept as if he was being interviewed, "was always up there on the screen." And then, gasping for breath, he dismissed the imaginary interviewer and, sensing the reality, the real reality of the situation, lost consciousness again, thinking he heard Chalky's name once more, reverberating as if in an echo chamber.

O Lord!

21

Larry Lazar, for all his disbelief, was in heaven.

He saw the cotton-white, blurry rippling mountains of clouds. Heard soft stringy music. Smelled the rich fragrance of roses and mums and lilies and the scent of fine French perfumes and eaus de cologne.

But heaven and all eternity could be blinked away by his eyelashes. First, the white mountains of clouds came into focus: billowing sheets covering him. Next, he recognized the music. Muzak. And then the sources of the rich fragrances and marvelous scents as the earthly flowers crowding his hospital room and Michael and her girl friend, Inman, hovering over him. He rubbed his eyes and smiled: "I thought I was dead."

"So did everyone else," said Michael.

He was in a hospital room, elaborate machines built into the walls with spaghetti wires coiling in every direction. Intensive Care from the looks of all that apparatus. "What hit me?"

"They're not sure yet," said Michael. "At first they thought it might be a heart attack. But now—" she hesitated.

"But now what?"

"But now they think you might have just suffered an acute case of food poisoning. Toxic food poisoning. From something you ate."

"From something I ate?"

"That's right."

"Of course." Larry feebly tried to snap his fingers.

"Of course what?"

"Wasp teriyaki. I'll bet it was that Wasp teriyaki I had at Sid Stein's. I'll bet the fucker was trying to poison me."

"Whatever," Michael said. "They want to keep you over another day. Till they know the results of all the tests. Just to make sure."

Later that morning the cardiologist reported to Larry that the enzyme and blood gas tests revealed that he definitely had not suffered a heart attack. In the afternoon the internist told him that he was strongly convinced that Larry was not the victim of any toxic food poisoning. That night Larry lay awake, unable to sleep, wondering if he might not actually be coming down with cancer.

Finally, he decided to call Dave. After all, Dave was not only a poker crony and tennis partner but also his analyst. The phone was picked up on the first ring. But it wasn't Dave. Did he have a wrong number? Usually, he was good at remembering numbers with the tips of his fingers. "Who's this?" Larry asked.

"Who's this?" the voice replied.

"Is this Dave Lehman's residence?"

"Yeah. Who's this?"

"A friend."

"Which friend?"

"Larry Lazar."

"Hi, Larry. How are you? Paul."

"Paul?"

"Paul Hirschberg."

Paul Hirschberg was a line producer with a thick black beard who sometimes joined their poker sessions. He was an old friend of Dave's. "How many Pauls do you know? Where are you Larry? Why aren't you here?"

"I'm in New York."

"That's right. I heard you were in New York. I'm sorry about your mother. I read about it in the trades."

"Thanks. What are you doing at Dave's now?"

"It's poker night. Remember? Tonight's his place. I was in the crapper, figuring it might change my luck, when the phone rang so I answered. He's such a Hollywood guy now, Dave. Phones in the crapper. With holdbuttons even. When I first knew him in the old neighborhood in the Bronx, his toilet wasn't even in the apartment. It was out in the hallway. They had to share it with the other tenants. And the phone. The only phone was down the block in the candy store. But what would you know about such things, Larry? You were always a rich kid from Brooklyn, right?"

"Wrong. I've always been a small-chocolate-and-two-cents plain guy."

"Stop. You're making me homesick. How is New York?"

"Terrific."

"You want to talk to Dave?" said Paul, as if he were the person who was suddenly cutting through all the shit. "I'll get him."

Dave soon came on the line. "Larry, the boys all send their best and want you to just send money. Seriously, *bubi*, I've been worried about you. How are you?"

"The truth?"

"The *emess*. What else is there?"

"Do you have a minute?"

"I can make a minute. Wait, just let me close the door to my study here."

Larry heard a familiar sound. It wasn't that of a study door closing. It was that of a piss trickling down. "Hey, where are you, Dave?"

"The truth?"

"What else is there?"

"I'm in the crapper. When Paul told me you were on the phone I thought I'd take it here and take a leak at the same time. Nothing personal. But what's happening, *bubi?* Couldn't it wait until you got back?"

"Do you know where I'm calling from?"

"I have no idea."

"I'm calling from the hospital."

"What's the matter?" Dave's voice seemed to assume its native Bronx tones. "Are you sick? Are you in treatment?"

"Treatment? I'm into script."

"Tell me what happened?" His voice was laid back, California again, a whisper under control.

"They thought I had a heart attack. I seemed to have all the symptoms."

"And?"

"According to the tests I didn't have a heart attack."

"Mazel tov!"

"So they thought it might be acute food poisoning."

"That's right," said Dave. "Similar symptoms. Especially if the esophagus goes into spasm. Then it really feels like a heart attack."

"How do you know?"

"You forget. I went to medical school. Anyway, was it toxic food poisoning?"

"No."

"Terrific."

"I'm not sure. Call me a hypochondriac but not knowing what it was bothers me a lot. I can't sleep."

"But you do know what it was that caused the distress," Dave corrected.

"I do?"

"Of course you do. Think for a moment. Why are you in New York?"

"Because of my mother's death."

"Exactly."

"I don't understand."

"All right," Dave said, slowly, patiently, as if he were addressing a child. "What did your mother die of?"

"A heart attack."

"That's right. Now can you put it all together?"

"Not quite."

"Then let me do it for you because it's late and you've caught me in the middle of a game. And you know my feelings about poker. Poker and tennis, they're my passions, they're my life. I live for them."

"And," Larry couldn't resist adding, "corned beef."

"But only lean. Anyway," Dave said, "it's not uncommon to suffer symptomatically the same kind of death as that of a loved one or someone close to you who has just died. It's part of the mourning experience. The literature is filled with examples."

"Are you saying my whole heart-attack, food-poisoning, whatever syndrome, was completely psychosomatic?"

"In all probability, *bubi*. Now, ask the night nurse to give you a valium or a dalmine and go to sleep. What time is it in New York now anyway?"

Larry checked his watch. "A little after two."

"Good night, *bubi*. Call me in the morning if you still feel like talking."

"Will you be taking calls?"

"No. But my machine is a good listener. Seriously, I hear your pain. I hear your concern. We'll schedule a few sessions when you get back. Now go to sleep."

Larry heard the click at the other end. Almost simultaneously there was a knock at his door. Had the night nurse been listening in to his phone conversation the way some secretaries always do? And was she now bringing him a val? "Come in," he said.

A smiling black dressed in hospital whites sidled in. He didn't seem as tall as Larry remembered and there was some gray at the edge of his sideburns but there was no mistaking him. His smile broadened as if Larry had just said something very funny. But Larry had not said a word. Finally, Chalky nodded. "I heard you were still here. I knew it was you."

"I knew it was you, too. They still call you Chalky. I heard your name. But then I passed out. Or thought I passed out. How you doing?"

"Good."

"Thanks for last night."

"My job. I'm a paramedic," said Chalky. "I hear you're okay now."

"It was probably just nerves. False alarm."

Chalky smiled. "Happens all the time."

"How you doing?" Larry repeated. He didn't know what else to say.

"Good. Real good."

"It's funny, Chalky, I've been thinking about you a lot. Ever since I landed in New York."

"Bullshit."

"No, I have. I really have. I was wondering what ever happened to you. And now," he laughed, "I guess I found out. But how did you ever become a paramedic?"

Chalky shrugged. "One thing led to another. I fixed cars. I stole cars. I drove cars. Then taxis, trucks, ambulances. Like I say: One thing led to another."

"You married, Chalky?"

Chalky grinned. "A couple of times."

"Got any kids?"

"Two sons and a daughter."

"They live with you?"

"They live with their mothers."

"And you? Who do you live with?"

"I live with my girl friend. She works here."

"Is she black or white?"

Chalky smiled. "Puerto Rican. She's a nurse."

"Terrific."

"Yeah."

"Chalky, remember the time you once saved my ass on the parkway?"

Chalky laughed. "I don't remember much about the old neighborhood. I'm surprised I even remembered you."

"Do you remember my mother?"

"Yeah. She was a funny lady."

"She just died. How's your mother?"

"Fine. She's back in Jamaica."

"And your dad?"

"Passed on a long time ago."

"So did mine. Chalky, do you remember the old stage shows at the Paramount and the Roxy and the Capital and the Strand and the Fox and the Albee and the Brooklyn Paramount?"

"Yeah."

"And how you used to imitate all the performers and performances?"

"I don't remember anything like that."

"You were a wonderful, wonderful performer. You were marvelous. You had such talent. You could have been a professional." Larry sat up in bed. "You know I make movies now?"

"Yeah. I heard you made *Herbie and Milty.*"

"Yes. Have you seen it?"

"No. But somebody was talking good about it."

"See it," Larry urged. "It *is* good."

"A lot of action in it?"

"Not really."

Chalky considered: "I'll see it anyway. I have to get back on duty. Just thought I'd say hello."

"Thank you, Chalky. And thanks again for last night."

"My job. So long, Lucky."

Larry watched him go and reached for a Kleenex. If he was ever going to cry now was the time. He could cry for his entire past, for his lost Brooklyn boyhood, for his own personal history. But that would mean crying for Sally, too. No, he put down the Kleenex and with an act of will held back his tears. He would not cry. He could not cry. Even at the cost of another phony heart attack. He'd pay that price if he had to.

Larry had one more visitor before leaving the hospital. He heard him in the hallway before he saw him. "I'm not a visitor. I'm family," Uncle Irving was shouting over his shoulder as he pushed open his door. "Can you believe it?" he greeted Larry. "They didn't want to let me see you, these sisters. What are you doing with these goyim, anyway? If you're not really sick, why are you here?"

"Sh!" Larry put his finger to his lips as if to shush him. "I'm doing an exposé of hospitals."

"Hospitals." Uncle Irving surveyed the room with obvious distaste. "I have no use for them. Like doctors."

"What's wrong with doctors?"

"Do you mind if I sit here?" Uncle Irving sat down beside the bed sinking almost below eye level. "I'll tell you about doctors.

Do you realize fifty percent of them graduate in the bottom half of their class at medical school?"

"That's funny," Larry said and smiled.

"That's also true," Uncle Irving insisted. "I read it in Ann Landers. Or Myron Cohen said it. Anyway, what happened exactly?"

"I passed out in the Holland Tunnel."

"New Jersey," Uncle Irving spit out. "What were you doing in New Jersey?"

"I was visiting Sidney Stein."

"That's no reason to pass out. Did you drink too much?"

"No. It was just a nervous reaction to Sally's death."

"Thank God it was just nerves. You had us worried, *boychik.*" Uncle Irving looked around the room again. "What are they charging you for this?"

"I don't know yet. Couple of thou at least."

"A couple of thousand dollars? Ridiculous!" Uncle Irving shot to his feet.

"Where are you going?"

"Downstairs. I'll talk business to them."

"Don't worry, Uncle Irving. My insurance will take care of it."

"All of it?"

Larry nodded.

"Are you sure?"

"I'm sure."

"A couple of thousand dollars," Uncle Irving repeated. "This is some business the nuns have here. I wonder how they got into it."

Larry shrugged. "I think they started with just one bleeding man and worked their way up."

Uncle Irving shook his head and then kissed Larry quickly on the cheek. "So I'm off. Call me if you need anything. When will you be leaving?"

"After breakfast."

"Take my advice, *boychik,*" said Uncle Irving, heading for the door, "don't fly out of Newark."

The plan was for Larry to go directly from the hospital to JFK. Michael wanted to accompany him to the airport but he saw no point to it. But she came to the hospital to see him off. Along with Inman. Together they pushed his wheelchair—it was hospital regulations that he leave that way—down the tile-walled corridor to the exit, his suit carrier draped across his lap and his feet resting on his overnight bag.

On the sidewalk in front of the hospital a Hare Krishna group was tambourining away, its bald, sheet-clad members chanting mantras as they clapped beatifically toward heaven. Larry smiled up into the sun as he rose out of the wheelchair. "Maybe I ought to get reborn, too."

Douglas took his bag and opened the limo door. "How you doing Douglas?" Larry asked.

"Fine, Mr. Lazar. I'm glad to see you're all right."

"Just a scare," Larry said. "Nothing to worry about."

While Douglas was putting his bags in the trunk, Inman returned the empty wheelchair to the foot of the ramp, abandoning it there like a supermarket shopping cart. Michael leaned in and kissed him. There was not much he could say to her. Perhaps they would meet again? Or this would be it? You never knew.

"Ciao," he said.

"Ciao."

Inman, smiling without her teeth showing, reached in and shook his hand. He held her hand an extra moment before releasing it.

When Douglas pulled out Michael and Inman were still on the sidewalk, waving. Larry waved back through the rear window until the limo stopped at the next corner for a light and a produce truck cut in behind it, obscuring them completely.

Douglas turned around. "By the way, Mr. Lazar, I'm up for a part in the new Woody Allen."

"Terrific," Larry said. "Say hello to Woody for me. Tell him I'm sorry I didn't get a chance to touch base with him this time East."

As the light was changing, Larry looked out the rear window again. The produce truck was pulling into another lane. He could see the sidewalk in front of the hospital. The Hare Krishna were still there. But the girls were gone.

Book Four

22

Every cobblestone and gaslamp was in place. The turn-of-the-century New York set outside his window had not aged a day. It was good to be back. It had been good yesterday afternoon when Jane welcomed him with open arms and soft lips. It had been good last night even though the kids had greeted him less joyously than he anticipated, disappointed because he wasn't bearing gifts for them. He didn't bother to explain that funeral homes and cemeteries and hospitals weren't shopping malls. Just kissed and hugged them until they ran off, Mary to a rock concert in Pasadena and Conor to a sleepover down the block. He and Jane had a sushi dinner delivered, polished off a bottle and a half of white wine, and went to bed early. They even had sex for the first time that month. But after Jane turned over on her back and started to snore, he got out of bed, went downstairs, made popcorn, and watched television in the den, an old Western with Burt Lancaster, until he finally fell asleep. In the morning, before going into the studio, he played two sets of tennis with Dave at Plummer Park, finding himself in surprisingly good form. Especially his back hand. He won both sets. No question about it: it was good to be home again.

Larry turned away from the window when Lois came in with a cup of soup for him. She point-blank refused to serve him coffee ever since attending a Women in Film meeting and discovering that was a sexist act. But soup was all right. So he had developed a midmorning soup habit instead. She hovered over him solicitously as she served it to him. "Are you sure you're okay?"

"Of course, I'm okay. I've already played two sets of tennis and I'm going to swim later this afternoon."

"Well, you certainly gave us a scare."

"Us?"

"Keith and I. You haven't met him yet. But he's very anxious to meet you."

"Who's Keith?"

"Keith," Lois twirled away from his desk as if she had suddenly been cast as Doris Day in a fifties movie, "is my new feller."

"How nice." Larry stirred his soup. "What does he do?"

"He's an animator."

"An animal?" Larry purposely misheard.

"He's also that." Lois gave a deep-throated laugh. "But he works as an animator. Over at Hanna-Barbera. He's also a very talented writer. He showed me one of his scripts."

"Speaking of scripts," Larry said and put down his soup. "Get me Mike Lasher, please."

Lois picked up the sofa phone and told Myrna that Larry wanted to talk to Mike. Then she covered the mouthpiece. "I really like Keith a lot. You'll like him, too."

"Has he moved in with you yet?"

"You're terrible, Larry," she blushed. "Actually, he wants to discuss it with his therapist first. Pick up on two."

Larry picked up his phone and asked Mike if he had a minute. Mike said he did and Larry told him he would be right down. Then he hung up and announced to Lois as if she hadn't overheard the conversation: "I have to go down and see Mike. Wish me luck."

"Luck," Lois said, and reached up and squeezed his hand as he quickly walked past her and out the office door.

To tell the truth he was nervous about seeing Mike. The son of a bitch had not gotten back to him sooner. Which was a bad sign. But Mike was ready to see him now. Which was a good sign. The fate of *Remember, Remember* hung in the balance. It would be good to get *Remember, Remember* positioned and on track. That was the key. Getting a picture on track. Because once on track a project developed a life and momentum of its own and almost nothing could stop it. It was as if it had to go simply because it was on track in the first place. The right nod from Mike and *Remember, Remember* was on track. The wrong nod and it was on its way to the glue factory. At least as far as this studio was concerned. And he didn't want to even think about other studios yet.

He stopped off at the men's room to give himself a final grooming. Also to piss. Lionel Gold was standing at a urinal, a pained expression on his face, as if he had just developed a prostate problem. Larry purposely chose a place two spots removed from him. Lionel looked over his shoulder across the vacant urinals between them.

"How you doing, Larry?"

"I'm doing well."

"Sorry about your father."

"Thank you. But it was my mother."

"Same thing. You know what I mean. And I heard you were sick, too."

"Not really. How are you doing, Lionel?"

"Fine, I guess. Everyone tells me my Evans rewrite is terrific."

"Have you shown it downstairs yet?"

"No, I'm waiting for an element: A star. A director. I don't want Mike and them reading it cold."

"That's wise." Larry zipped up his fly with one hand and pushed the flusher button with the other.

Saul Gelman strutted into the men's room, sniffing. "I smell shit," he announced.

"I can't even piss," said Lionel.

"It must be some of the studio's recent product then," decided Saul. "How are you Larry?"

"I'm well," said Larry, going to the sinks.

"I'm sorry about your mother."

"Thank you."

"And I heard you were ill."

"A false rumor. Some critic must have started it," Larry said.

He leaned as far forward as possible and tried to comb some of the longer strands of his thinning hair over his emerging bald spot. "How's your picture doing, Saul?"

"Gangbusters." Saul rolled his eyes. "Unbelievably well. This week was even bigger than last."

"You'll get rich," said Lionel.

"That's not why I make pictures," said Saul.

"That's the only reason I make pictures," said Lionel, moving back from the urinal like a defeated fighter at the end of a losing round.

"Saul wants to be a filmmaker," Larry explained. "He wants to be an artist."

"You and him are no different from the rest of us, Larry," Lionel said. "If your pictures don't make money with all your artist bullshit, you're still out on the street."

Saul laughed. "You have a point there." But he winked at Larry. "That's why I hope you haven't forgotten about me for your new project. I'm sure there's a part written just for me."

"I'm available, too," said Lionel. "If both you pricks can act then so can I. I'm specially good as one of Santa's reindeers. That was my last part."

"Seriously," Saul said. "I would be honored to act any role in any picture of yours. I would be honored to have anything to do with any of your pictures in any capacity, Larry. I really mean it. You're one of my idols."

"Thank you."

Lionel leaned over Saul's shoulder, making it a three shot in the mirror over the sinks. "You're one of my idols too, Larry. Good luck on your new project." He turned to Saul. "Good luck on all your projects," he said and walked out.

"He's a schmuck," Saul mouthed after him.

"Lionel's not so bad," said Larry. "He's just been striking out a lot lately. Been having a hard time getting anything off the ground."

"I know," said Saul. "But he's not one of us. He has nothing to do with us."

Larry wasn't so sure he liked the way Saul was lumping them

together. Saul hadn't earned that right. He'd only made one picture. That might be the only picture he'd ever make. Still one was more than none.

"Isn't it a miracle," Saul was saying, "how any of our pictures ever get made?"

The chutzpah of the kid. He even wanted in on Larry's miracles.

Larry shrugged. He glanced at himself once more in the mirror and left the men's room, intent on his own miracle.

"I'm glad you're all right. I'm sorry about your mother. Did you get my flowers?" Mike Lasher greeted him as if he were reading off a page of notes.

Larry slipped into the college-lecture-class-type desk chair before Mike's desk. "At both the funeral and the hospital, Mike. Thank you. In fact, when I saw all those roses I thought for a second I must have won the Kentucky Derby. Thank you. It was very sweet of you, Mike. I really appreciate it."

"I'm just glad you're all right," Mike repeated. "The industry needs you. The studio needs you. I need you."

"Thank you, Mike." Larry noticed a picture of Mike's daughter was now perched on the corner of his desk. "How's your daughter?" he asked, tilting his head toward the portrait. "How's Tina?"

"Tina?"

"Tina."

Mike picked up the picture and clasped it to his chest. "Tina is terrific," he said, patting the picture. "Why do you ask?"

"I thought—" Larry hesitated. "I thought there was a . . . a problem . . ."

"A problem? With Tina? Never!" Mike put the picture back on his desk and gazed at it fondly before looking up again. "I meant to get back to you sooner on *Remember, Remember.*" Mike cleared his throat. "But then knowing what you were going through I figured I wouldn't bother you."

"Thank you, Mike. I appreciate that," Larry said, still staring at Tina's portrait. She wore a print dress and had neatly curled hair and smiled with bright bulging eyes. She certainly didn't look like a hooker. Not in that picture anyway.

Mike held up a copy of *Remember, Remember.* "I want you to know, Larry, I read this script three times. I don't think I even read my own studio contract three times, if you know what I mean."

Larry did not know what he meant but did not say anything.

"I always love your work, Larry. You know that. You're one of my idols. I'm probably your biggest fan in town," he continued. "I'm proud of *Herbie and Milty* no matter what it finally does at the box office. I'm proud that this studio made *Herbie and Milty* while I was in charge. If they just put, 'He made *Herbie and Milty*' on my tombstone I will die happy. It's a quality picture not comic-book dreck." He rose out of his barber chair and came around the desk, still brandishing the script. "And I want to congratulate you on this script. Quality." He riffled through it. "This script has the mark of quality on every page. It's one of the finest scripts I've ever read and it will make a wonderful picture some day. A picture I would be proud to do and one that could make a lot of money besides. Because the concept of someone fucking his old girl friend's daughter is very marketable and quality at the same time. I mean it will grab the public by the balls and the critics by the brains. And I would give you a go on it this very minute except—" He turned his back on Larry and paced across the room. "Except—"

"Except what?" Larry asked his back.

Mike turned around, rubbing his face. "Except, frankly, Larry, I have a problem with it," he whispered.

"Problem? What problem? Creative problems are my business," Larry said. "In fact, something is a problem only until someone comes up with the solution."

"Perhaps I shouldn't have said 'problem.' It's not really a problem. It's more a reservation."

"What's the reservation? Maybe I can help you."

"It's not really even a reservation. It's merely, I guess, a suggestion."

"I'm always open to suggestion. What's the suggestion?"

Mike returned behind his desk and sat down in his barber chair again. "The suggestion is this. Not that it isn't a wonderful script with a terrific high concept as it now stands. But frankly, for me, it lacked humor. It lacked the humor of *Herbie and Milty,* for example. And I know you're a very funny guy and it would play a lot funnier than it reads—"

"And it will read a lot funnier after I put it through my typewriter for a polish," interjected Larry.

"I'm sure," nodded Mike. "But I have an idea. A suggestion like I say. And I hope you'll give it some serious thought."

"What's the suggestion?"

"Saul Gelman."

"What about Saul Gelman?"

Mike cleared his throat again. "Saul is a terrific talent. We're all very high on him here at the studio. I think you ought to give him a whack at *Remember, Remember.* Or both of you take a whack at it together. However you want to work."

"You mean for Saul to collaborate as a writer?"

"Exactly."

"As just a writer?"

"Exactly."

"*Remember, Remember* is very tricky," Larry said. "I agree with you that Saul is very brilliant. But I'm not so sure this material is up his alley."

Mike smiled: "I have a hunch. Go with my hunch."

Larry shook his head. "I really have it up for this project now. I'm anxious to go with it as it is."

"I can understand that," said Mike. "It's a terrific script even as it is. But can you blame me if I want it better? Whose side do you think I'm on anyway? And I'm talking play-or-pay for you as the director by the way. So please think over what I'm saying, Larry, before you or your agents go running off to some other studio."

"I will," said Larry. "I will definitely think it over."

Mike got out of his barber chair and walked Larry to the door, holding out his hand to him. Larry took it and felt no tremor but his own.

No one could quite do a room like Jason Cooper. With a carnation in his lapel and a pencil moustache across his lip, he looked more like a duke from Devonshire than an agent from William Morris. Actually, Jason was a Jew from Golders Green whose chief claim to local fame was that he was one of the few Jews in the industry with a drinking problem. He even once had complained to Larry: "In Hollywood you can fuck a snake, stick coke or Ajax or Massengill up your nose and no one cares. But God forbid you should get drunk at lunch at high noon in the MGM commissary and drop your head into your matzo-ball soup." Which, unfortunately, Jason had done, winding up in the LAPD drunk tank. Now he was making a comeback. Larry watched him kiss the hand of an actress who was always fucking for important producers only to come up with unimportant roles. Next Jason was slapping the back of a Broadway actor, passing through town in a musical, and pausing to chat with the new production chief at Paramount. Larry himself had made the same stops on the way in but not with quite the same aplomb. Maybe he lacked the British accent? Or maybe it was just an alchie's natural way in a saloon or bistro? In front of a fellow agent's ex-wife Jason was removing his boutonniere and placing it in her hair as if it were a rose and he had just run across Carmen. Finally, he arrived at their table, breathless from completing his grand circuit.

Larry stood and they embraced each other. "Well, my *landsman,*" Jason said, making the Yiddish word sound really foreign and exotic. "I must say you're looking well. In spite of what you've been through."

"I am well," said Larry. "It was all just a false alarm."

"Not your mother's death?"

"No. That was real enough."

"I liked your mother. I remember her well; I scored some very good grass for her. She was a funny lady when she was high." Jason picked up the menu and put it down again, as if it were too heavy a burden for him to handle just yet. "Have I had a day! And it's just lunchtime. If I were still a drinking man . . ." His voice trailed off. "Anyway there was your phone call and I'll get to that. But the agency also lost a client this morning. Or I lost the agency a client."

"Which client?"

"Rule number one of agenting," Jason leaned forward, "is to never talk about one client to another. But it was Sir Richard."

"That must be a blow," sympathized Larry.

"A blow?" laughed Jason. "More a full-fledged storm. I could always get one hundred thou per for him for three weeks work just by answering the phone."

Larry asked the obvious question. "Why'd he leave you?"

"Rule number two of agenting is never tell a client the truth. After nine years of representing Sir Richard and getting along with him famously, I told him the truth."

"Which was?" Larry cued him.

"That he was not really a star anymore."

"That was a mistake," Larry agreed. "You never should have told him that."

"I didn't tell him that in so many words. I'm not that stupid. But that's how he correctly interpreted me. He's not that stupid. So he fired me. Or rather the agency. And then you called."

The waiter came over to take their drink orders. "I'll have a Perrier with a twist of lime and bring him a double Scotch for me."

"No," said Larry. "I'll have a Perrier, too."

"C'mon," insisted Jason. "One of my chief pleasures these days is watching other people drink. Don't deny me that."

Larry patted his stomach. "I'm trying to watch my weight. And, instead of bread," he told the waiter, "bring me some rye script. I mean Ry-Krisp. You can see what I have on my mind, Jason?"

Jason, who was busy blowing a kiss to a passing redhead, did not miss a beat in responding to him. "As you know I think *Remember, Remember* is a brilliant script as it is. Positively brilliant. After you called I immediately took some soundings around town. Of a few people I can trust a lot. And there was interest. But not what I could call terrific enthusiasm. Which wasn't surprising. Considering the state the industry is in at the moment. I mean there's very little action anywhere. Even for bullshit projects."

"What are you trying to say, Jason?"

"I'm saying that eventually I promise we can get *Remember, Remember* set up someplace else. But it will take time. Given the climate and the fact—let me be honest with you—that audiences aren't really breaking down doors to see *Herbie and Milty.*"

"Herbie and Milty," Larry defended, "is a good picture."

"Herbie and Milty is a fine picture. *Herbie and Milty* is a great picture. I'm its biggest fan. I'm proud of the role I played in getting it made. I would like to be able to drink to it right now. But you, Larry, I can be honest with. *Herbie and Milty* is not exactly a big plus going in with a new project at this time. Except with Mike possibly. So I have a suggestion."

"I've heard one suggestion today already."

Jason spread his arms wide. "How much can it hurt having Saul Gelman take a whack at *Remember, Remember?* You always have what you already have and if he comes up with anything you've got that too. But more important the project is on track with you tied in play-or-pay as director. And the more money locked in behind the project, the more likely it is to go further forward."

Larry considered. "So that's your advice."

"Professionally."

"And personally?"

Jason laughed. "The same thing."

The busboy deposited their Perriers and a basket of Ry-Krisps and breadsticks. Jason seemed more interested in stirring his drink than sipping it. Larry, on the other hand, was thirsty. He downed his Perrier in one long gulp. And belched.

"Jason, I don't want to collaborate with Saul Gelman. I can't do it. It's demeaning."

"What's demeaning? Was it demeaning to collaborate with Harry Hearns on *Ms. and Mr.?"*

"That was a long time ago."

"What about collaborating with Max Isaacs on *Herbie and Milty?* Was that demeaning?"

"That's a different story, too."

The waiter came over and asked if they were ready to order. They both nodded and he pointed to the menu. "In addition to what's listed," he said, "today's specials are an excellent turbot in a fresh butter sauce. A bouillabaisse which I can highly recommend. And also, specially for today, we have a superb ragout and a rack of lamb."

"Do you have cottage cheese?" asked Larry.

The waiter nodded stiffly.

"I'll have a cottage cheese salad with some fruit."

"And I'll have my usual Western omelette," ordered Jason. "Bertrand knows how I like it with lox instead of Canadian bacon."

"Very good," said the waiter, and bowing backed away.

"I have an idea," said Jason, playing with the lime in his Perrier. "Would you be willing to let Max take a whack instead of Saul Gelman?"

"I'm not sure Max would be willing to."

"Nonsense. Of course he'd be willing to." Jason dismissed such a notion as absurd. "Suppose I talk with Mike and try to switch him. I know he's very high on Max Isaacs because of the work he did on the Brian Grossman project. In fact, the more I think about it the more confident I am that I can convince Mike that Max Isaacs is better casting as your collaborator. What do you say?"

Larry rubbed the bridge of his nose. "Suppose I agreed to work with Max and Max agreed to collaborate with me; meanwhile would it be possible to set up *Remember, Remember,* the script I've written as it now stands, someplace else? In a very confidential way, of course."

"While Max and you were working on it for Mike?"

"That's right."

"It wouldn't be very ethical," Jason smiled.

"I didn't ask you if it was ethical. I asked you if it was possible."

Jason speared the lime in his Perrier and inspected it with surprise, as if he had expected to find something else. Then dropped it back into the glass. "I'm reduced to noticing the fruit in a drink," he said sadly and looked up. "Certainly, it's possible. This is a small town. But everything is possible. You're protected contractually from having to accept any rewrites anyway."

"In that case," Larry picked up a breadstick, "I really don't have anything to lose."

"You ought to be an agent," Jason said. Agents always said that when they wanted to pay you the supreme compliment.

"No," Larry said. "I would never know how to handle Sir Richard."

"You'd know enough not to tell him the truth." Jason took a sip of his Perrier and closed his eyes distastefully. "By the way, Larry, I can't recollect if there's a part for him in *Remember, Remember,* but if there is, do me a favor and write it out."

Back from lunch Larry pulled into his spot in the middle of the first row of the traffic island in front of the administration building. If the traffic island could speak, then the language would be German. Forget the model year, it was downtown Stuttgart during the Third Reich: Mercedes after Mercedes with an occasional BMW and Porsche thrown in. But no Jewish cars. Not a Buick or a Plymouth or a Dodge in sight. White paint stenciled onto the asphalt before each car proclaimed the names of executives, producers, directors, and stars. But not writers. Writers did not fit into the Hollywood hierarchy. A lot Sid Stein knew about reality. Real reality.

Larry walked back through the traffic island, his hand on his forehead as if saluting some unseen officer—actually, he was shielding his eyes from the midday sun—and then down a narrow studio street. The lot was literally shrinking all around him. A Mexican village square was giving way to a high-rise glass condominium; the confluence of buildings that had once housed props and wardrobe and carpentry shops had been flattened and an office building was taking its place. These developments—or destructions—did not faze Larry much. Because they had little to do with him. He never really considered himself part of the industry or its lore. In his heart he knew he was as transient as any set, as expendable as any setup. At best, he was an artist, a serious filmmaker, just passing through the industry on his way to cinematic immortality. At worst, he was a hired hand, waiting to be brokered by a studio bazaar to the consortium of banks that supplied its credit line. Nothing to get sentimental about.

But he was glad that the Western street still stood even if it was unattended; the barber pole tilted, paint peeling on the sign above the jewelry store, and the window of the saloon broken. But then when was the last time the studio had made a Western? He kicked the red dirt at his feet like a Gary Cooper and it rose in a swirl and settled on his boots.

When he first came to the studio, a walk down that street took him back to the Saturdays of his Brooklyn boyhood: In the morning his mother would give him a bagful of bagel and bologna sandwiches and he would rush off to the neighborhood movie house to lose himself in a dark dream, watching the serial and the newsreel and the coming attractions and each of the double features twice. He'd sit far back in his seat, nibbling on his all-day lunch, while stagecoaches were robbed and posses were formed and riderless horses cantered by, dragging bodies behind them. And then he would race up the aisle, past the admonishing glance of the white-uniformed matron, waving her flashlight at him, and run out through the lobby into a crisp Brooklyn evening and hurry home to help assemble the early Sunday editions of the *News* and the *Mirror,* the *Times* and the *Trib.* Everyone pitched in. Sally held her tongue. Meyer did not mope. Even *zeydah,* planted in a booth, applied himself to the stack of sections before him. They all worked with a necessary camaraderie; Saturday night was the store's most important night. Because when people came to buy their Sunday papers they also picked up cigars and cigarettes and treated their kids to ice-cream sodas and sundaes and sometimes even bought boxes of candy for their wives, especially before a holiday. Larry loved Saturdays. The dreams throughout the long afternoons at the movies. The reality of the busy evenings in the candy store. It was the only time the Lazarskys ever really functioned as a family.

Now they were all gone—even the indestructible Sally—and only he was left. It was a heavy responsibility. He had not quite absorbed it yet. He did not have the time. It was like a childhood Saturday again. He was still occupied with dreams and business. He was trying to get a movie made.

At the end of the Western street was the old Writers Building as differentiated from the new Writers Building rather than the young Writers Building. There was no young Writers Building Larry knew of unless over at some Montessori school. The old Writers Building had been designed back in the 1920s to resemble some eastern campus academic hall and crawled with ivy and had a corner arch for its entryway. As Larry climbed the two flights of stairs to Max Isaac's office, he felt as if he were on his way to see a don.

Max's office door was closed. But Larry knocked on it sharply, as if he indeed had a conference appointment. Then he tried the door and it pushed open. Max's long body was stretched out on his office couch, an opened book lying on the floor beside it. Larry coughed loudly. Max stirred, sat up, and yawned: "Siesta."

"I'm sorry," Larry apologized. "I should have called you first."

"It's okay," Max rubbed his eyes. "I hear you're back."

"That's funny," Larry said. "But I'll tell you what wasn't very funny. It wasn't a very pleasant trip."

"I'm sure," Max yawned again, his head in his hands.

"Are you sure I'm not disturbing you? Because I do want to talk to you. I think there's a misunderstanding between us and I'm partly—perhaps wholly—responsible for it and I don't like leaving things that way. We've known each other too long. We go too far back together."

Max went to his desk, sat down, and rubbed his hands across the keys of his typewriter.

"By the way, how are you doing with the script you're working on for Brian Grossman?"

"I just have a polish to do and I'm home free."

"Good. And what are you doing next?"

"There are a couple of offers on the table that my agent is talking about."

"Terrific. I'm glad for you. But before you accept any of them I want you to think about our project."

Max looked up. "Our project?"

"Remember, Remember. Have you forgotten it? Because let me tell you something by way of apology. I had in a sense forgotten about it. And not until I was away from all this nonsense here," Larry pointed past the ivy tangle on the window ledge, the palm trees and cactus flowers below, "and I could recollect in tranquility so to speak, did I realize that you were right and I was wrong. That we had discussed *Remember, Remember* together. It had just slipped my mind, I'm sorry. I want you to work on it with me now. I owe it to you. I owe it to myself." He went over and placed his hands on Max's shoulders. "Because if my mother's death taught me one thing, it's this: There are very few people in this world who are really important to me. Not *Hollywood* important. But *New York* important. And you're one of them, Max."

Max blinked his eyes and Larry wondered if the new contacts were still giving him trouble. But then Max rose and embraced him, slapping his back, and he saw that Max was actually tearing, big wet ones. Sentimental Max. Like all writers. No wonder he'd been married three times.

Max stepped back. "I'm very touched."

"Never mind touched." Larry made believe he was wiping away a tear of his own. "But are you ready to work on *Remember, Remember?* I read it again carefully while I was in the East. It definitely needs another go through on the typewriter. It needs to be funnier. It needs you, Max. With your help I can make it into an important movie, a real work of art."

"Like *Herbie and Milty?*" Max said and smiled.

"Herbie and Milty is a real work of art. It's a terrific picture no matter what it's doing at the box office. As artists we both should be very proud of it."

Max shook his head. "I don't consider myself an artist."

"You are when you work with me. We're both artists," Larry insisted. "Let's face it. I know I'm not a Balzac or a Rodin or a Victor Hugo but this isn't exactly nineteenth-century Paris either. And I'm not just talking literature and sculpture. In cinema, filmmaking, movie directing—whatever it is you want to call what I do—I am an artist as long as I am faithful to my own personal vision, cockeyed as it may be."

Max nodded slowly and smiled. "In the land of the bland and all that. If Mel Brooks is a genius and John Cassavettes has talent, then I guess Larry Lazar can be called an artist."

"And so can Max Isaacs. I'm not joking. You put yourself down too easily. Just because you've done some hack work. Everyone's done hack work. Even Balzac and Victor Hugo, I'm sure. I didn't know them. But I did know you, Max, when you were young and still unashamed of your dreams. And I also know those dreams are still alive in you now. They never die, Max. That's why I want to be able to tell Mike you're available."

"I'd have to talk to my agent first."

"Of course."

"But Phyllis will go along with whatever I want."

"Wonderful woman, Phyllis. Smart. And talented, too. If Jason starts drinking again, she'd be my number-one choice to represent me. And you can tell her that." Larry started toward the door. The sale was closed; it was time to go. "Don't let me keep you from your beauty rest. Ciao."

"Ciao."

"To be continued." Larry smiled and closed the door behind him.

23

When Larry stopped for the red light on Santa Monica Boulevard and Beverly Glen he pinched the bridge of his nose. The smog was getting to him; his sinuses were clogged and his eyes were smarting. It had been a long day. First days back always were. But he had also accomplished a lot. *Remember, Remember* was on track. Max was in his pocket for the rewrite and Jason would deliver Mike on the switch. Mike would settle for another writer on board and later he would even feel a proprietary interest, as if he were the writer himself. Mike would refer to *Remember, Remember* as *my* picture to other executives and really believe he was shaping the final result.

Larry couldn't care less what Mike believed. What was important were Mike's actions. And from this point on they would be positive. Which was all to the good. Especially for Larry. Because now he could finally let go of *Herbie and Milty* and all the emotional energy that bound him to it. There was nothing like your next picture to make you forget your last picture. Not forget exactly. A filmmaker could no more forget his last picture than a mother forget a previous child. But now he could relegate *Herbie and Milty* to its proper place in the scheme of things, perceive it with a little more perspective and a great deal more objectivity. And, to tell the truth, already he could see there was a lot more wrong with *Herbie and Milty* than he would have liked to admit. Starting with the casting. He had really fucked up using a cokehead as the female lead. She turned out to be too frantic and fenzied. There was no flow and balance in her performance. And the picture could have been funnier, too. He always underestimated his own comic talents. Or rather sacrificed them for the sake of reality. He might have to reexamine his perception of reality. Real reality might be even funnier than he had assumed. And funny was what the great *they* out there all seemed to want these days. Even at the sake of true. Especially at the sake of real.

Anyway, success or failure, *Herbie and Milty* was at last off his back. No longer did *Herbie and Milty* have to carry his ego weight and no longer did his ego have to carry the weight of *Herbie and Milty*. All his living energies could now be directed into his next film. His existence would have a meaning again without *Herbie and Milty*. Oh, how he loved seeping himself into a new vision! Oh, how he thrived on the concentration demanded by the very process of filmmaking itself! It was his opiate, his high, his way of getting off. When he was shooting a film, there was nothing that mattered except the camera and the actors he was directing. It was the only time he was truly happy. It was the only time he was completely selfless. His heavy ego trips came before, during prepping, and after, during postproduction, but never during shooting. Then he was no more than a filter, a gel, a lens. Time and its measurements disappeared. World events did not take place. Personal emotions were sidetracked. The forty-five days of a shooting schedule were such an intense experience that it would all blur together in memory into a single fuzzy freeze frame, like a snapshot taken by a psychic. It was as if freed of time, freed of ego, he was thus freed of death and the fear of it. Only a filmmaker knew directing's irresistible lure. Only a director himself knew the extravagant cost. Because all else paled beside the experience. But then that was the price any artist had to pay. It came with the territory.

Yes, now he felt like a junkie who knew where his next fix was coming from. So what did it matter what his last fix had been.

A white convertible VW Rabbit pulled up alongside of him. Its driver looked like she might float away at any moment. She was wearing one of those pirate-peasant outfits, a high-necked full-sleeved beige blouse with ballooning white pantaloons. She had California blond hair and California tanned skin and when she caught Larry staring at her, smiled back showing fine white California teeth. With exaggerated lip motions Larry whispered toward her: "I love you." In response, she threw back her California head, laughed and gunned away. Larry followed after her until she turned right on Wilshire. Then he blew a wistful kiss in her direction and continued on toward home.

Yes, it was certainly good to be back home. Never mind the fact that he was suffocating and going blind in the smog. At least he wasn't dying, consumed by the *schmutz* like in New York. If California was lotus land then the day of the locusts was in New York. How could anyone survive there? Allen? Mira? Sidney? None of them had a normal family life. Not like him. True, his relationship with Jane was more often a habit than a passion but still they were together under the same terra-cotta-tiled roof with their two kids who were his soul's delight despite the fact that Conor had greeted him last night as an "asshole" and he wasn't too happy about Mary's going to so many rock concerts either because that meant she was smoking grass already. But it was all part of normal family life. Real reality. All grist for his artistic mill. And no one back East, not among his old friends anyway, was a better artist than he was, either. He was more important in his medium than they were in theirs. If they had not failed, he at least had achieved greater success. Because the kid from the candy store was a tough competitor who always played to win. In punchball. In stickball. In touch-tackle. And in art, too. If Larry Lazar films had a hallmark, a unifying leitmotif, it was the fact that his heroes were all winners. Like Larry Lazar himself.

Oh, he knew all the jokes about southern California and LA: LA was sixty oranges in search of a navel. The center of LA was the car you happened to be driving in. Living in LA added ten years to your life which you hoped to spend in New York. But the real reality was simple. You just had to look around you at the verdant greens, at the sprawling homes, at the dynamite cars. LA was obviously the city of winners.

Larry turned left off Beverly Glen onto Sunset Boulevard and headed west toward the ocean and his Bel Air home.

As he parked in his driveway he heard splashing from the pool and went back to check it out. There, Conor, Rachel from across the street, and a black girl he had never seen before were—there was only one word for it—frolicking. Gracefully diving in and out of the water, they were a study in youthful insouciance. Larry admired Conor, his long legs, his ribbed stomach, his bony shoulders, his sandy hair glistening in its flat wetness. But Rachel, who was the same age as his son, was already a woman as far as her figure was concerned. She even seemed to move like a woman, flat-footed yet daintily at the same time. He had never seen the black girl before. Maybe the neighborhood had completely deteriorated while he was in New York. He was only joking, of course, folks. The famous Lazar humor which his next picture could use more of. But he would ask Conor who the girl was when he had the chance. An attractive kid, though. Reminded him of Inman, tall and native-African-looking. But since this was Bel Air her father was probably a brain surgeon. Or a rock singer. Or an athlete who had just gone into free agentry.

Larry shouted a greeting to Conor and the boy came over and not only said hello, but graciously extended his hand. He could never figure him out. Usually when Conor saw him alone he called him "asshole," like last night, and when he was with friends he tried to ignore him as if he were a complete embarrassment or some utter stranger. But now when he came over he warmly shook his hand, fell into an embrace, and got his shirt all soaked besides. "Where's Mom?" Larry asked him.

"At a meeting, I think."

"And your sister?"

In reply Conor shrugged and took a running dive back into the pool. At the same moment, as if the pool could hold only one of them at a time, Rachel came out of the water looking like some starlet at Cannes. He wouldn't have been surprised if she had flicked off her top.

"Hello, Mr. Lazar," she said. Water dribbled down her bikini, forming puddles at her feet. He stepped back and studied her.

"Hey, Rachel." There was no question she was sexy. Soon his own son would be thinking of *shtuping* her. Maybe even more than thinking? Maybe he was even more than thinking already? Who knew what was really going on with kids these days anyway? Especially in southern California where sex came with the very air they breathed. He looked over at the black girl who was now tugging at Conor's boogieboard, her prepubescent shape emphasized by her bikini. He personally wouldn't mind *shtuping* her either in a year or two. Meanwhile they were both all Conor's and he wasn't the least bit jealous. Or was he? Because, if he was, maybe there was a picture in it? The best pictures grew out of confusion and ambivalence. Not conviction or absolute certitude. Better to begin with a question mark than an exclamation point. The black girl smiled at him with wonderful teeth and he smiled back. It could be a very personal film.

Kids or no kids he would take his dip now. Larry went into the house to change and passing through the kitchen saw a bag of Famous Amos chocolate chip cookies on the counter. Reflexively his hand reached in. But then like a Dr. Strangelove, he seized the hand and pulled it back. It had been an up day—why bring himself down? So far, over breakfast and lunch, he had manfully watched his diet and there was no point in falling off the wagon now. Proud of keeping his resolve, he scampered up the stairs, two at a time, to his bedroom. He found the trunks he wanted, baggy ones that wouldn't make him look too fat, and kicked off his boots and took off his shirt. As he wiggled out of his slacks, his wallet popped out of his pocket and onto the floor. He kneeled down to pick it up. The wallet had opened. In the same plastic fold as his American Express card was the Coney Island penny-arcade shot of Sally and Meyer and the fat-faced baby in a wide-stitched bonnet who was trying to look away.

He was staring at the picture when suddenly his knees gave way and he fell flat on his back as if he had been knocked down by a blow from a real fighter, not like some Sidney in the middle of the New Jersey woods. His fall was cushioned by the soft pile of the nylon carpeting and he sat up still holding on to the picture, its sepia tones slowly blurring before him. One leg out of his pants, in his jockey shorts, on the floor of the bedroom in his

Spanish house in Beverly Hills he was suddenly crying. At first he tried to sniffle back the tears but soon they were coming in torrents, cascades of them streaming down his face. Because he was crying uncontrollably, unabashedly, completely, his body rocking tremulously. The tears kept flowing and he delighted in them. They were palliative tears, they were joyous tears. He felt emancipated and liberated, he wanted to dance, he wished he could sing. Because at last he was crying, crying for Sally, and not crying out of guilt but out of love. And now that he was crying for her he knew she would finally be willing to die. That bitch! But oh how he loved that bitch!

Yes, call her Jocasta, call him Oedipus. Call her Mammy, call him Sonny boy. Call her Sally, call him Lucky. *He loved his mother.*

Or was it all just jet lag?

He stood up, rubbing his eyes, and went into the bathroom and threw cold water on them. But still he continued crying and he still felt marvelous, as if his very soul were being cleansed.

Clinging to the picture, he pulled off his jockey shorts and naked as a baby, crying like a baby, returned to the bedroom and lay down on the king-sized bed and rubbed the picture gently, lovingly. Yes, he loved his mother. Yes, he loved his father. Yes, he was a part of them. They were all part of the same picture. Larry Lazar was the result of a collaboration. Larry Lazar was a Sally and Meyer Lazarsky creation and he loved them both for it.

Mary and Conor were a part of him and he was part of them, too. Jane was a part of him and he was part of her because marriage was both a biological and an environmental state. Between nature and nurture life was a collaboration. Real reality was a collaboration. Love was a collaboration. And guilt was simply the refusal to acknowledge that fact. What an insight! He would tell that to Dave. He would tell a lot more to Dave. Socially, not professionally.

When he returned to the pool Conor and the girls were gone. He put down his towel and lay back on the recliner. He thought again of Chalky. In the hospital he had promised himself he would do something nice for Chalky. Like give him a vacation in California. All expenses paid. Yes, he could certainly do that. And while he was at it he would speak to Jane about Mira's sculpture. They really didn't need it. And he would talk with Frank, his business manager, about setting up a no-interest loan to Allen. He could afford it. And he would send Sid Stein a letter saying he was planning to do some rewriting on *Love on the Freeway* soon. He could find the time. And when Harriet's piece on Preston Sturges came out he'd drop her a line saying how much he liked it. Simple enough to do. Getting the past in order was no big deal. He might even send for Michael. He still had her script. He could always come up with a reason for having her come out here.

Larry dived into the soothing warmth of the heated pool. Nothing like it. He wouldn't trade it for all the Fox U-Bet in the world. And the afternoon sun breaking through the smog and the screen of the eucalyptus trees didn't hurt any, either. This was the life. Effortlessly he swam laps, gliding back and forth, pleasurably shedding calories. Still he could not help but think of dinner and where he and Jane and the kids might go. He had a craving for Mexican food. He always had a craving for Mexican food whenever he returned home to LA. Even when he returned home from Mexico. But now he was determined to watch his weight. Where could he find a place that served diet tacos?

He came out of the pool refreshed and was briskly toweling himself down when Fati, leaving the poolhouse, waved to him. Larry waved back and suddenly had a terrific idea: Fati would be returning home to Morocco soon and so he could put Chalky up in the poolhouse. Chalky could even bring his Puerto Rican nurse girl friend with him. Plenty of room. Of course, they could always also stay in a hotel. But hotels in Beverly Hills were not cheap. Then he had another idea. A dynamite idea. He would speak to Max about it. They could write in a bit part for Chalky in *Remember, Remember.* In fact, they didn't have to do that. He knew just the place in the script where the character could be black. The drunken dancer in the party scene. It would even add a value. And then when the picture was shooting he could send for Chalky and the studio would not only pick up the tab for Chalky's visit but also pay him for coming. It would be a nice thing to do for Chalky. It would be a nice thing to do for himself.

He wished he could send for Sally that simply. But that wasn't possible anymore and had never really been necessary anyway. Because she was with him wherever he went. Because she was part of him whatever he did. Because, though she was dead at last she would also live within him forever. Because life was a collaboration, whether you wanted it to be or not—just like a movie. We all needed collaborators. We needed them to get into this world. We needed them to get through this world. We all needed driving mothers and defeated fathers and unfathomable children and unflappable wives and ephemeral affairs and outrageous friends and ridiculous agents and even high-concept play-or-pay projects. It was all part of the looney tune of living that would end inevitably with a "That's all, folks."

Sure, it was always nice to see your name all alone up there on the screen. Produced, written, and directed by Larry Lazar. But did it really matter? What difference could it possibly ever make in Kansas City—or eternity—if there was one Jewish name more or less up there on the big screen? Not a whit that he could think of. He would make that part of the theme of *Remember, Remember.* It would be a personal statement that was also very universal.

Larry wrapped the towel around his protruding stomach and padded back into the house on bare feet looking forward to a Mexican dinner with his family. Somewhere on Fairfax there had to be a place that even featured kosher diet tacos.

JOSH GREENFELD was born in Malden, Massachusetts, grew up in Brooklyn, New York, and now lives in Pacific Palisades, California. In addition to the prizewinning *A Child Called Noah* and *A Place for Noah,* he has written the novels *O for a Master of Magic* and *Harry and Tonto,* the plays *Clandestine on the Morning Line* and *I Have a Dream,* the television special *Lovey,* and was nominated for an Academy Award for the screenplay of *Harry and Tonto.*